Book One
The Souls Of Aredyrah Series

THE FIRE
AND THE LIGHT

Tracy A. Akers

© 2006 Tracy A. Akers

Publisher's Cataloging-In-Publication Data
(Prepared by The Donohue Group, Inc.)

Akers, Tracy A.
  The fire and the light / Tracy A. Akers.

      p. ; cm. -- (The souls of Aredyrah series ; bk. One)

  ISBN-13: 978-0-9778875-0-7
  ISBN-10: 0-9778875-0-2
  ISBN-13: 978-0-9778875-1-4 (series)
  ISBN-10: 0-9778875-1-0 (series)

  1. Prophecies--Fiction. 2. Cousins--Fiction. 3. Fantasy fiction. 4. Bildungsromans.   I. Title.

PS3601.K47 F57 2006
813./6   2006925419

Ruadora Publishing
P.O. Box 1887
Zephyrhills, FL. 33539
ruadorapublishing@msn.com

Cover Design: Annah Hutchings
Interior Design and Typesetting: Publishing Professionals
Publishing Shepherd: Sylvia Hemmerly
Editors: Julie Gabell and Leslie McCutchin

Printed in Canada

For Marv

Table of Contents

Acknowledgments

First and foremost I would like to thank my husband and soul mate, Marv, who gave me the green light to "quit my day job" and pursue writing full time. Without his emotional and financial support, I would never have fulfilled my dream of seeing this series of books published. He is my champion.

I would also like to thank my friend Alina Kolluri. Her knowledge of ancient history provided me with many of the visuals I used to enhance the cultures of Aredyrah, and our brainstorming sessions led to several story ideas that are contained within. Alina may not have written the book, but her support is woven within the pages.

In addition I would like to say "thank you" to the following people for their encouragement and guidance: David and Ellie Williams, Lili Kolluri, and Dick Akers, readers of my early draft who offered sound feedback; author Judy Candis, my teacher at the University of South Florida who taught me so much; Jessi Dickinson, Belea Keeney, Audrey Jacobs, and Elvira Weaver, members of my critique group who gave me nothing but sound advice; editors Julie Gabell and Leslie McCutchin for their professional expertise; Sylvia Hemmerly, the book shepherd who guided me through the complicated process of publication; artist Annah Hutchings who agreed to illustrate my book cover; my brother, Grady Orr, who designed my web site; my son Dylan who believes his mom can do anything; my mother, Shirley Orr, and my sister, Lucy Orr, who embraced the story of Aredyrah and supported my goal to share it with the world; Florida Writers Association which gave me the opportunity to learn from and network with like-minded people; Director Peter Jackson whose Lord of the Rings movies changed my life in a very weird way; and composer David Arkenstone whose wonderful music inspired so many of the scenes contained within the chapters.

Dayn

Dayn barreled down the rain-drenched street, mud caking his boots and splashing his trousers. Shouts rose and fell as pedestrians scrambled from his path. Eyes darted in his direction as warding charms were traced into the air. But Dayn spared them little notice. Even whispers of "demon spawn" would give him no pause.

He leapt across the boardwalk and swung around the nearest corner. He slid to a halt when he realized his mistake. The alley was a labyrinth of dark corners and teetering debris. Rats scampered in the shadows, screeching their alarm. Dayn glanced over his shoulder and gulped down the spit that had lodged in his throat. He had already met the pack once today and had no desire to meet it again. As bad as running from his enemies was, being caught by them was worse.

Dayn worked his way in, stepping through garbage that shifted beneath his feet. There were maggoty bits of carcass mixed with roach infested produce, and bloated scraps of bread floating on green slimy puddles. Strange, he thought, how food could be discarded so easily, especially when clans such as his barely scraped a living from the rockier terrains. But there was no time to dwell on social ills, not when there were ills of his own to dwell on.

Dayn quickened his pace, realizing he was losing precious time, but a sound from the rear stopped him in his tracks. He spun around, expecting to find danger fast approaching. But he saw no sign of clenched fists or sneering faces, only a tabby glaring from beneath a heap of debris. *Looking back on life will do you no good, boy,* his father's voice sounded in his head. *Best keep your eyes ahead of you.* "Easy for you to say, Father," Dayn murmured. "You never had a pack swarming over you." But he followed his father's instruction. He knew better than to dispute the man. He moved his eyes and feet toward the passage ahead, but it was hard to ignore the subtle flurry of activity that had begun to accompany his every step.

The end of the tunnel seemed miles away, but when Dayn reached it he felt no relief. The pack was probably just biding its time, waiting for him on the other side. He pressed his back against the wall and peeked around the corner. No one of consequence could be seen, just a few late-afternoon shoppers who had braved the day's earlier rains. Dayn pulled in a steadying breath and eased himself around, then made a lumbering attempt down the boardwalk.

He bolted through the double-doors of the smithy and stopped to grab the stitch in his side. His eyes swept over the room. The usually busy shop seemed strangely deserted. There were no customers; even the blacksmith was nowhere in sight. Dayn glanced at the street behind him, then moved from the gray light of the portal. Inside the smithy or not, safety was never assured.

A jumble of barrels caught Dayn's eye, and he quickly sidestepped between them. With arms raised high, he navigated a narrow path to the far side of the room. He shrank into the darkness of the corner, where he watched and waited. But nothing shadowed the doorway. He closed his eyes and released a sigh of relief. The pack was gone—for now.

"Sheireadan's gang after ye again, boy?" the smith asked from across the room.

The sooty forgeman now stood before the furnace, holding a blade grasped in a pair of long tongs. By his bland expression, it was clear the old man was not surprised by Dayn's sudden and dramatic entrance. He had, after all, been hiding him in times of trouble for the past several years now, ever since Dayn's differences made him a target for the local bullies.

The smith raised an eyebrow. "Got ye good this time, did 'e?" But he did not wait for a response and instead turned, tongs in hand, to the anvil at his back.

Dayn lifted a hand to his swelling eye, then looked down at his fingertips and grinned. "Not so bad, Jorge. See . . . hardly any blood."

Jorge paused and glared in Dayn's direction. "When are ye gonna take a stand against those troublemakers? You're fifteen now and certainly bigger'n they are."

Dayn looked down at his gangly limbs still pressed against the wall and frowned. Yes, he was bigger than the other boys, by several inches or more, but that wasn't the only difference between them. There were other things, all of which resulted in his being labeled an outcast. And being an outcast was miserable indeed.

He flicked a shock of white-blonde hair out of his face and inched his way around the barrels. A pail of water sat atop a nearby bench and he worked his way to it. Scowling down at his watery reflection, he winced and fingered his tender eye. "I told you a hundred times, Jorge, I do try to fight them, but I'm not very good at it. Besides, I'm always outnumbered." He dipped his hands into the water and splashed the cool comfort onto his face.

Dayn wiped his wet hands down the front of his wool tunic, one of the few parts of him not splattered with mud, and limped over to a stool near the warmth of the furnace. He plopped down, his long legs sprawled on either side of it, and watched Jorge hammer the blade.

The smith shook his head. "Maybe ye just need some trainin'."

"I don't want any training. You know I don't like to fight. Besides . . ."

Jorge slammed the hammer and tongs down across the anvil. He stormed over and inspected the battered, half-closed eye. "Humpf," he said, grabbing Dayn's jaw in his grimy hand. "And *this* is what ye get fer it!"

Dayn jerked his face away and rubbed his now filthy jaw. "I'm sorry, Jorge."

"Don't say you're sorry to me, boy. It's your skin, not mine." Jorge turned away and beat on the blade once more. "So what were ye doing this time—breathin'?"

"No, talking to Falyn." Dayn's one fully opened eye twinkled, the blueness of it brightening at the thought of the girl.

"Sheireadan's sister? God, so ye are brave after all. Well, I hope it was worth the lickin' ye took."

"She talked to me today, Jorge. And she actually laughed at something I said."

"Laughed with ye or at ye?"

"With me, Jorge, and she smiled, you know, like she really liked me or something." Dayn rested his chin on his fist and stared across the room. "Do you think she really could like me? I mean, I know I'm not like the others, but that doesn't mean she couldn't like me, does it?" He studied Jorge's face, hoping for a positive reply, but Jorge remained silent.

"Jorge? That doesn't mean she couldn't like me . . . does it?"

"Course not." Jorge plunged the red-hot blade into a vat of water. A rush of steam coiled from it with a loud hiss. "It's gettin' late, Dayn," he said, glancing toward the door. "Best be gettin' yourself home now. Ye got a long walk back. Don't wanna be caught out near the woods after dark. Demons do their huntin' then, ye know."

Dayn jumped from the stool, knocking it to the floor. It would take at least two hours to get to his family's farm and it would be dark well before that. He raced out of the smithy, hurriedly waving farewell. There was no time for courtesies.

Dayn paused in the darkening street, glancing from side to side, worried that Sheireadan's pack might have decided to linger about. But he saw no sign of it and continued on, his shoulders hunched against the chill. He slanted his eyes toward the buildings towering on either side of him. They would have appeared deserted had it not been for the slivers of light peeking out like cat-eyes through the shutters. Dayn turned his attention back to the muddy ruts at his feet, but he could not shake the fear of what lurked in the woods between here and home.

He passed the last house quickly and followed the road up the hill toward the gate leading from the city. As he approached he could not help but notice the fortress surrounding Kiradyn was more like a huge sloping bank than a wall. Although he had seen it hundreds of times, it never failed to leave him curious. No one could recall why the thing had been built in the first place—it was there long before the demons pushed their way from the fiery bowels of the earth—and as far as anyone knew, the clans of Kirador had never been at war with one another. Since there were no other human inhabitants on the island of Aredyrah, it was assumed the wall was meant to keep out the beasts of the forest. But regardless of its original purpose, the residents of the city were grateful to have it. One could never tell when the demons might decide to make Kiradyn their own.

As Dayn drew near the gate, he kept his eyes cautiously averted. He always feared the gatekeeper would stop him, but the old man never did, not since Dayn's father had put a stop to the harassment. He seemed to recall an incident when he was little, something about 'keeping the demon out', but that was long ago. He could not help but feel the familiar nausea, however, as the gatekeeper's mutterings followed him out.

Dayn hurried on, working to keep his focus on the ruts ahead of him instead of the encroaching darkness around him. But he soon found his eyes drawn to the mountain range that rose like jagged teeth to the south. He cringed at the sight of it. The mountains were beautiful, with their pastel colors of blue, green, and pink. But their beauty was deceiving, for that was where the demons lived. He had heard the fantastic stories about them his whole life, how long ago some people tried to go into the mountains, only to be devoured by the evil creatures. And that was why no one went there now—ever.

Dayn's foggy breath quickened. Darkness was upon him and it was getting colder. His clothes were still damp and he doubted even his long-sleeved tunic would keep him warm in the rapidly dropping temperatures. Nights in the high altitudes of Kirador could be strikingly cold, even during the warmest of months. It was easy to be tricked into complacency by a tepid afternoon. Dayn shivered. In his haste to deliver a bottle of his mother's remedy to a family in town, he had rushed out of the house without his coat. He clutched the collar of his tunic close to his neck, cursing his own stupidity.

The path stretched unevenly up and down the hillsides still wet from the afternoon showers, but the clouds had moved on to the south, leaving a bright full moon to light the path home. As Dayn's eyes darted between the cloudless night sky and the creeping shadows of the forest, he began to whistle nervously. He stopped mid-tune when he realized it might invite unwanted attention, but he could not stop his teeth from chattering. "Don't be such a baby," he whispered. "You've been this way a hundred times." But he had never been this way after dark, at least not without his father.

Dayn glanced toward the trees. They creaked and groaned, and for a moment seemed to stretch their skeletal arms toward him. He shot his attention back to the path, determined to stay focused on what was real—a slippery trail that would tumble him into the mud if he didn't watch his footing. But keeping his eyes on the ground would not help him if a demon decided to make a meal out of him. Dayn's mind raced. What would his parents think when he didn't return home? Would they search a long time for his body? Or would they content themselves with the fact that they had borne a stupid son who couldn't even run an errand without getting himself killed. Guilt gnawed at his already churning insides. He hated the thought of causing his parents any more grief. He was such a disappointment to them already.

It occurred to him that Falyn might cry for him, and he felt almost hopeful at the thought of it. He could see the girl in his mind: her dark hair piled up under her mourning shawl, her almond-shaped eyes filled with tears, her trembling hands clutched to her heart as she proclaimed her undying love for him. For one foolish moment the thought of being attacked by demons seemed desirable. But a sudden snap of a twig brought Dayn's fantasies to a halt. He froze, his eyes darting toward the woods. No other sound could be heard, only the drumming of his heart and the breeze whispering through the trees. He released a ragged sigh and continued on.

Dayn had not gone far when another noise caught his attention, but this time it did not sound like a snapping twig. It was something else, strange, like the clacking of sticks against one another. He paused and listened, wrapping his arms around himself in an effort to stop the feel of icy fingers racing down his spine. The tapping stopped and he became conscious of a strange and heavy silence.

Then Dayn heard it again. He turned and scanned his surroundings, rotating in a slow circle. The noise, now coming from different directions, was intensifying in both volume and rhythm. What had at first sounded like two sticks being beaten together, now sounded like hundreds—maybe thousands— echoing through the woods.

Then he saw it—movement—behind the trees—a dark shape racing in and out—running noisily through the underbrush —running his way. Dayn turned and forced his legs into a sprint. The ruts at his feet seemed to test every step. He willed himself to run faster, but his limbs felt as though they were weighted by stones. The clacking increased and he doubled his efforts, his speed finally matching his panic. But as fast as he was running, he could not shake the creature that was darting between the maze of trees.

Dayn ran blindly up the winding path, dodging unknown objects that appeared out of nowhere. He tripped and threw out a protective arm, then caught his balance and staggered forward. Glancing back, he realized that more than one creature was pursuing him. Shapes were all about him now, and they would soon be upon him.

"Daaayn," he heard an eerie voice howl. "Daaayn."

Demons! Dayn's throat constricted with fear, forcing his lungs to labor even harder. He could see little in the blur of the trees as he ran past, but in the silvery light he knew he must be shining like a beacon. Should he hide or should he stand and fight? He had no weapon and he had never won a fight, not with anyone or anything. How could he possibly expect to defeat a pack of demons? But before he could consider his options further, something pelted him on the side of the head, knocking him off balance.

He tripped over his own feet and fell hard to his knees. Another object hit him on the back of the head and threw him forward. He moved to scramble up, but was pushed down as a nameless weight leapt upon his back. He struggled, but could not release himself from the crushing pressure to his spine.

"Daaayn," the voice above him said. But it no longer sounded like that of a demon. And this time it was followed by laughter.

Dayn felt himself rolled over roughly as Sheireadan removed his boot from his back. Staring up at the pack of black-haired boys that surrounded him, Dayn could see they all carried sticks, except for one, and he carried a sack. The others reached into it, laughing and hooting, and grabbed up handfuls of the dark stuff it contained. Dayn threw his arms across his face as his body was pelted once more.

Sheireadan knelt down and grabbed Dayn by the front of his tunic, digging a knee into his gut. With a free hand he reached into the sack being held out to him and smeared the foul smelling stuff across Dayn's face.

Dayn gagged, realizing in an instant it was manure. He wrestled to free himself, but a hand shoved him down, slamming his head to the ground with a painful *thunk*.

"Will you never learn, spawn-boy? Stay . . . away . . . from . . . my . . . sister . . ." Sheireadan said, striking a blow to Dayn's face with every word he spat.

"We—were just—talking." Dayn sputtered the words, but he knew the minute he said them he had made a mistake. No one disputed Sheireadan, not even his friends.

Sheireadan rose and planted his boot on Dayn's chest. "Just talking? What right does an abomination like you have to even breathe the same air as her?"

Dayn spat blood and manure from his mouth and clawed at the boot that was crushing his chest like a boulder. He could barely breathe, much less answer Sheireadan's question, but his efforts for relief were greeted only by increased, grinding pressure to his ribs.

Sheireadan glared down with dark, narrow eyes, then twisted his scowl to a sinister grin. He winked at the other boys who laughed and nodded their approval. Reaching his hands down to the front of his own trousers, Sheireadan fumbled for a moment. Then he spread his legs and relieved himself upon Dayn in one long, pelting stream.

Dayn gasped as warm urine ran down his face, neck, and chest. The boys' laughter echoed in his ears. He went sick with humiliation. Sheireadan had done many cruel things to him in his lifetime, but this was by far the worst.

"There, demon spawn," Sheireadan said, tucking himself back into his pants. "Now the rest of you matches your hair."

The pack tossed their sticks onto the huddled form at their feet and turned away, chortling as they strutted back to town. Dayn curled himself up, clutching his ribs as he listened to the boys' voices fade into the distance. He rolled onto his back and lay motionless on the cold, damp ground. The only warmth he could feel was that of the blood and urine running down his face.

Staring up at the canopy of stars that blanketed the night sky, Dayn wished more than anything he had wings to fly. He recalled all the times he had been abused by Sheireadan and the others. It was more than the issue of Falyn, Sheireadan's younger sister, he knew. He was fifteen now, and the harassment had been going on for as long as he could remember. Many of the residents avoided him when he went to town, whispering and crossing the street as though he would contaminate them in some way. He looked so different. His eyes and hair were pale while everyone else's were dark. And he was tall, taller than even the tallest man in Kirador. The details of his birth were a great source of gossip; few believed his birth had been a natural one.

"Why am I so different?" he asked the stars as though they could answer.

Then he saw it, blazing across the night sky, a great stream of light, its dazzling colors of red and gold coursing through the heavens. He stared as it streaked past, its brilliance reflected like sparkling stars before his eyes. But just as quickly as it had appeared, it vanished into the blackness.

"Are you my answer?" he asked, wondering if Daghadar, the Maker, had finally seen fit to acknowledge his pain in some mysterious way. "Well, your answer is going to have to be better than that."

He lay there for a long while, staring up at the stars, searching for another sign of the magnificent light. But he saw nothing more of it and realized, message from the Maker or not, he had to be getting home. He pulled himself up and staggered toward the path.

It seemed to take hours to reach the last crest, but when he did he paused to gaze at the timber house nestled in the mist below. Its windows shone with a golden glow from the firelight within, and a stream of smoke spiraled from the chimney and dissipated into the cool night air. Dayn smiled, the warmth of the house matching the relief he felt at the sight of it.

As he drew nearer, he heard the familiar chimes tinkling their tunes on the porch that wrapped around the house. His mother had placed them along the beams to ward off demons. Too bad something as simple as a chime could not ward off his own. He limped across the yard, his stomach heavy with dread. Father, he knew, would be furious; Mother would cry, of course; and Alicine, his sister, would threaten revenge against his attackers, and probably get it. In their childhood, Alicine had frequently kicked Sheireadan's tail on his behalf. But Alicine was fourteen years old now and spending more and more time with herbal lessons and friends. Dayn didn't want his sister defending him anyway. That was almost as humiliating as the beatings.

The door of the house swung open and slammed against the wall at its back. Alicine bolted through and ran across the noisy planks of the porch, her wool skirt lifted almost to her knees. She jumped across the steps at the porch's end and sprinted across the yard toward him. Her long, black braids bounced wildly at her back.

"Dayn, what happened?" she cried. She eyed him up and down, then frowned and wrinkled her nose at the stench of him. "Never mind . . . as if I don't know."

She looped her arm through his, but he shrugged it away. The way she constantly mothered him made him feel like a baby. "I'm fine, Alicine," he said.

"Fine? You call this fine?" She grabbed his arm and hooked it back through hers. "We were worried. It was getting so late."

Dayn glanced up and felt his throat constrict. His mother was standing in the doorway, her silhouette outlined by the light of the fireplace burning in the room behind her. Though he could not see her face clearly, he was certain it was etched with worry. Then his father moved to stand behind her, his huge shape swallowing the light at his back. Dayn felt fear mixed with shame. His father would not be proud of him, he knew.

"Oh, my poor boy," his mother cried, her dark eyes scanning his battered body up and down. "My poor, poor boy." She moved toward him, her arms extended, but Dayn's father placed a firm hand on her shoulder.

"Leave him be, Morna," he said. "He's not a baby."

"But Gorman, he's hurt!"

"It's not the first time and it won't be the last. The boy refuses to fight so this is what he gets for it."

"Well he doesn't deserve this." Morna shrugged her shoulder from her husband's grasp and moved to usher her boy inside. "I'm fine, Mother. Really," Dayn said. But he wasn't so sure. From the expressions on their faces, he knew his injuries, and the filth that covered him, looked bad. He hobbled to the kitchen table across the room and eased down onto the bench, leaning on the tabletop for support. His attention was suddenly directed to a visitor sitting in the corner and he jumped up, his shame returned tenfold.

"Spirit Keeper," he said, bowing his head and clenching his hands to keep them from shaking. It was bad enough facing his parents, but to have Eileis, the Spirit Keeper, see him like this was beyond humiliation. The tiny, aged woman just looked at him and smiled.

"I—I didn't know you would be here," Dayn stammered.

The old woman raised herself from the chair and walked toward him, pulling her patched and faded shawl about her thin shoulders. "It was time I came," she said.

Dayn looked down at his feet, then back up at Eileis whose stare felt like heat on his face. But the kindness of her expression eased his fears. She was always good to him and would surely understand what he was feeling. The Spirit Keeper had a way of knowing things others could not. She was, after all, Healer and Advisor of the Kiradyn people and possessed a wisdom beyond that of any ordinary person.

"Please, Dayn," she said, waving him back to the bench, "don't stand on my account. You need tending to and I see your mother's anxious to treat those wounds."

Dayn glanced at his mother who now stood beside him holding a bowl of water and a handful of cloths. Alicine was at her side, clutching a bottle of herbal remedy. Dayn lowered himself back down onto the bench and sighed. Now would begin the ritual of his healing, traditionally performed with great drama by his doting mother and younger sister.

After treatment was complete, Dayn's mother stepped back and surveyed him with concern. Dayn looked at her reluctantly. Her braided hair was somewhat disheveled and her face more lined with worry than usual. He felt a pang of guilt. His mother had always been frail, having lost many infants to premature births. It was a wonder she had managed to conceive him and his sister at all. What kind of son was he to cause her such grief? He slanted his eyes in his father's direction and knew from the man's expression he was thinking the same thing.

"Now go upstairs and change into some clean clothes," his mother said. "And for goodness sakes, clean the rest of that filth off you. There's water in the basin in your room. I'll fetch you something to eat."

Dayn nodded and moved toward the stairs that led to the sleeping quarters above. The ascent was difficult, as steady pain had set in, but he protested when Alicine tried to help him, and limped alone up the planks to the bedroom they shared.

He headed for his bed, longing for the comforts of a feathery mattress, but then he thought better of it. His mother would have his head if he soiled the sheets. He stopped alongside it and stripped off his grimy tunic, then tossed it to the floor. Balancing his weight against the bedpost, he pulled at his boots, cursing them under his breath. They were soaked through and the long laces that snaked up his legs were twisted into knots. After struggling for several minutes, he managed to kick the things off and went to work on his equally soggy trousers.

Undressed at last, Dayn stood before the reflective plate on the wall and stared at himself in the lamplight. Turning this way and that, he inspected his face and body. His normally pale complexion was spotted with bruises, and his blond hair was darkened by the filth that still clung to it. He wiped the dirt from his neck, then fingered the flower-shaped birthmark that remained there. *That is where Daghadar the Maker kissed you*, he recalled his mother telling him when he was little. "Kissed indeed," he groused. "Who would want to kiss me?" Even without the filth and bruises he would have still looked ugly. The fact that his mother and sister told him time after time he was beautiful had done little to change his opinion of himself.

Dayn finished wiping himself off and pulled on fresh clothes, then made his way down to the kitchen where everyone was gathered at the table. No one said a word as he trudged to the bench and sat. A plate of meat, cheese, and bread had been prepared for him, but he could only stare at it.

"Eat, son," his mother said.

"I'm not hungry," Dayn grumbled. He frowned at the plate, then pushed it away.

"You heard your mother," Gorman ordered.

Dayn scowled and shoved a piece of bread into his mouth, chewing slowly and deliberately. He could feel the eyes of everyone upon him, analyzing every chew. The bread scraped down his throat, but he did not reach for a second piece. "Why am I so different?" he asked.

His question was met by stony silence and awkward expressions. He had asked his parents this question many times before, but they always managed to give him some evasive explanation. Maybe this time they had finally run out of them.

"Dayn, not tonight," his mother said. "It's getting late and—"

"Please, Mother. I need to know." He looked at her with pleading eyes, but she turned her face away.

"You heard your mother, it can wai—" his father started to say.

"No, it can't wait!" Dayn shouted. He sprang from the bench that would have toppled if Eileis, who sat next to him, had not quickly steadied it. "Now! I want to know now!"

Gorman pushed up from the other side of the table and splayed his hands across the tabletop. He leaned in threateningly. "You will not speak in such a tone in this house."

Dayn glared at his father, noting the redness of the man's face and the purple bulges in his neck. Dayn stood his ground for a determined moment longer, then sank back down. "I have a right to know, Father, and I've waited long enough."

Gorman stiffened, his tan face blanching at his son's response. A stern man, his children always showed him the utmost respect. But now his son was challenging him and it was obvious Gorman had not been expecting it.

Morna rose and placed a hand on her husband's arm, then glanced at her son with anxious eyes. "Dayn," she said, "we've told you before. The fact that you look different is simply because that is the way Daghadar made you. There is no other answer to your question. You are who you are."

"Well, then, who am I—exactly?"

"You are our son, nothing more, nothing less," Gorman said firmly.

"Am I your son? I mean your real son?" The words almost lodged in Dayn's throat. He had finally asked the question he'd never had the courage to ask before.

For a moment Gorman seemed to struggle for words, then he responded with indignation. "Of course! Who else's son could you possibly be?"

"Could something have happened that . . . could I be from someplace else?"

"Where else could you be from?" Gorman said. "You know there's no place else but Kirador. You know the rest of the world was long ago destroyed, burned into the sea during the Purge of Aredyrah."

"But maybe there could be other people somewhere. People like me."

Gorman banged his fist on the table, causing the dishes to rattle and the people seated around it to jump. "There are no other people, Dayn," he shouted. "Have you learned nothing during your religious training? Have you learned none of the Written Word? By the Maker, boy, you know the people of Kirador are the chosen ones, the only ones deemed worth saving by Daghadar. You *know* there are no others!"

"But what of the demons? They're others . . . aren't they?"

"What are you saying?" Gorman said. "Are you implying your mother—?"

"No! No, Father, I only meant—"

"Now you listen to me, boy." Gorman leaned across the table and stared Dayn hard in the eye. "You're our son, do you understand? Our son, no one else's. The demons are all that is left of the minions that cracked through the earth during the Purge. They are twisted creatures, abominations, nothing like us. They survive only to serve as reminders of what can happen if we do not heed the Maker's message. There are no others, Dayn."

Dayn lowered his eyes. "Well, I don't believe it," he said. The round of gasps that reverberated around the table left Dayn cringing. No one had ever uttered such blasphemous words, certainly not in this household.

Eileis rose from the bench and walked around it. She had remained silent throughout the entire conversation, but all eyes turned to her now. "Gorman . . . Morna. Do not be overly concerned by your son's budding independence. He's at the age to be questioning. It's a natural thing." She turned to Dayn and placed a hand on his shoulder. "You're a gift of the Maker, Dayn, as we all are. Daghadar is wise and has a purpose for us all. It's late, child. You're tired. Take yourself to bed. Things will look different in the morning."

"No," Gorman said. "The boy will not take himself to bed. He will sit at this table until I am satisfied he knows the Written Word and understands it."

Gorman stormed over to a wooden cupboard across the room, removed the peg from its latch, and opened its creaking door. He pulled out a large, leather-bound book and dropped it onto the table.

Dayn winced. "Father, please . . . no."

"Gorman, the boy is tired and—" Morna said.

"He will stay," Gorman said. He straightened his back and crossed his arms. "Morna, escort Eileis to her bed. Alicine, you'd best take yourself to your room."

Alicine rose from the bench and made her way along it. She looked over in Dayn's direction, but said not a word. Dayn could not imagine what she must think of him. His sister was so committed to the Written Word and was never one to question their parents or the teachings they had been raised on. She must surely hate him.

"Now, we will begin," his father said. "Open the book."

Dayn opened the book slowly and frowned down at the worn parchment pages. He knew what each one contained; his father would be teaching him nothing new. Time and time again he had read the sacred words as he had been expected to since he was old enough to read. To the Kiradyns, religious training was part of their everyday life; there was little separation between the sacred and the secular. No one had ever questioned it. There was no need. Everyone was perfectly content to believe and live by the tenants they had been taught.

Dayn made sure his distaste was apparent as his father directed him to a passage and ordered him to read aloud. He complied grudgingly, determined not to appear interested. When he finished, his father questioned him about the meaning of the text, expecting a detailed account. After replying to his father's satisfaction, Dayn was directed to another passage, and another, and so it went, passage after passage, question after question. At first Dayn debated the issues, but after being put sternly in his place, he resolved to just agree with everything the man said. It would be much easier that way.

"Yes, Father, we are Daghadar's chosen people. The world wept in darkness until Daghadar made the world of Kirador for . . ." Dayn yawned and felt his eyelids grow heavy. He jerked his head up and widened his eyes. "For us, the chosen people! All others perished!"

It occurred to Dayn that there would be chores to do in the morning. He eased his gaze over to the kitchen window. It was still dark, but it seemed like the sun would be up any minute now. Would his father allow him any sleep at all? *Just say what he wants to hear. Just say what he wants to hear.* "Yes, I'm your son! Thank you for helping me understand."

Gorman nodded and closed the book. "Get yourself to bed," he said, "and in the future there'll be no more foolish questions. Understand?"

"Yes, Father, I promise. I won't question you again." Dayn rose and moved toward the stairs, then paused. "Goodnight, Father," he said over his shoulder.

"Goodnight, son. Now off with you."

Dayn trudged up to his bed and threw himself upon it. The blanket, he noticed, had been folded back neatly for him. He looked in the direction of his sister's bed on the other side of the room. She had not closed the curtain separating her side from his.

"Alicine," he whispered. He rolled onto his side and stared at her shadowy form through the darkness. There was no response. "Alicine?" he repeated. Again no reply.

Dayn lowered himself onto his back and rested his hands behind his head. He stared at the blackness, then squeezed his eyes shut, willing himself to sleep. But it was no use. He could not stop the events of the evening from churning in his head.

He rose from the warmth of his bed and reached for the blanket he had kicked into a wad. Pulling it around his shoulders, he crept toward the window centered on the wall between his and Alicine's beds. He glanced in her direction. More than anything he would have welcomed his sister's company, but her steady breathing told him she was sound asleep.

The floorboards felt smooth and cool against his bare feet, and he prayed as he crept across them that they would not creak beneath his weight like they usually did. The house seemed eerily quiet as he lifted the window's latch and pushed the grating hinges open. A breeze drifted in and played at the hair on his neck. Even the blanket around his shoulders could not prevent the tiny goose bumps rising on his arms. He leaned against the window frame and gazed out at the sky. A spattering of stars dotted the fading darkness. "Are there any more messages for me tonight?" he whispered.

The unexpected sound of hushed voices diverted his attention to the porch below. It was his father and the Spirit Keeper, and their discussion seemed to be a heated one. Dayn cocked his head and leaned out. At first he could not understand their words, they were obviously trying to keep their voices down, but their tones were clear enough. He leaned out further and held his breath. He thought he heard his name and something about a cave, but the rest made little sense.

Then came the words that were all too clear, words that penetrated him with a cold far deeper than his skin. Dayn staggered back from the window. The blanket dropped from his shoulders to the floor. His mind raced to replay the questions he had asked that night and the answers he had been given: *you are our son, no one else's . . . there are no others . . . the demons are nothing like us . . .*

He stepped toward the window hesitantly and leaned out again, longing to know more, yet terrified of what else he might hear. But the only sound he heard was that of the front door opening and closing, then silence.

Dayn gazed out the window as though in a daze. The first rays of dawn played across the forests and hillsides. The stars were nothing more than tiny faded pinpricks now. Somehow the sky and surrounding landscape looked different, although he couldn't quite put his finger on it. Then he realized that nothing would ever look the same again, at least not to him.

He made his way back to the bed and sank down upon it, his shaking legs no longer able to support him. His eyes turned to the sleeping form of his sister. "Did you know all this time, too, Alicine?" he whispered.

Then his thoughts turned to his father, and an unfamiliar hatred filled his heart. "You lied to me, Father. All this time . . . you lied to me.

2
Ruairi

The young prince of Tearia stood poised and ready, a long, etched sword clutched in his hand. The lion was crouched within feet of him, its body half hidden by tall, dull-colored grasses. The prince stared into its primitive eyes and raised his weapon high. The blade sparkled momentarily in the reflection of the light, then sang as it arced though the air.

"Challenge me if you dare, foul creature!" the prince shouted.

The lion did not move. Its cold stare never wavered.

The prince cried out and lunged at the beast, thrusting the blade to the fore. He yanked it back and repositioned his hands on the hilt, then wheeled around in a circle to face his opponent once more. He leapt back, then forward a second time, plunging the tip toward the creature's heart. With a loud shout of victory he pushed it to the mark. Then there was silence.

The prince sighed and stepped back, then lowered the weapon to his side. His mouth hooked with disappointment. The lifeless creature had not even shuddered.

"You never were much of an opponent," he said to the image on the wall.

The fresco on the plaster was barely visible anymore, but it did not matter. The prince knew it well enough by heart. He had often stared at that picture as a child, pretending to be one of the Tearian warriors depicted with swords drawn against ferocious lions. But there were no more lions in Tearia, and no real warriors. The Tearian Guard was mostly for show these days and there wasn't anyone to be enemies with anyway; the Jecta peasants that lived outside the city walls had long since been beaten into complacency. The prince shook his head and turned away. Perhaps the time had come to put aside childish dreams.

He was fifteen years old now, a man, not a child, and this was to be the night of his betrothal to his future bride. He knew he would never truly be a warrior. His future was already laid out for him. He was a prince, but would one day be husband, then father, then king. That was all he would ever be, nothing more, nothing less.

He crossed over to the dressing table, laid the sword upon it, and traced his finger along the span of the magnificent weapon. The rune-etched blade had slain many an ancient enemy, and the leather-wrapped handle had been held by generations of kings. But what truly set the sword apart was the golden lion molded at the hilt, its image reflective of the history and power embedded within it.

The weapon was called, quite simply, The Lion, but it gave its bearer a sense of power that was anything but simple. It had been in the prince's family for generations and had recently been given to him by his father for his coming-of-age birthday. It was the only possession he owned that really mattered to him. But he would have been much happier about owning the thing if he'd actually had cause to use it.

He moved toward the window of the second-story bedchamber and gazed out at the evening sky. The sun had settled behind the sloping landscape of Tearia, leaving the only light in the room that of a lone oil lamp. He glanced up at the spattering of stars peeking out of the blue-black sky and leaned his elbows against the sill. From where he stood he could see the range of mountains to the north, its purple peaks marching like an army along the horizon. He had never been to that sacred place. That was where the gods dwelt and it was forbidden for anyone to go there, even a prince. He closed his eyes and said a silent prayer. If just one of the numerous gods that resided there would grant him wings to fly, he would be happy. But he knew it wasn't likely.

"Ruairi?" a muffled voice said, followed by a tap on the other side of the door.

"Enter," he said.

The door swung open and a woman entered, a look of annoyance clouding her blazing blue eyes. "It is as dark as a cave in here," she said. She swept past him in a swirl of yellow and marched toward a table near the window.

Ruairi glanced up at her, then over to his bed. He scowled at the golden tunic draped across the ivory coverlet, and the silver braided belt and amethyst clasps nestled at its side. "Brina, why do I have to wear that thing?" he said. "It is so uncomfortable. The clasps, the belt, the—"

"Stop your complaining, nephew. What would you go down wearing? Only the undercloth wrapped around your hips?" She flitted about the room, lighting a second lamp, then a third. The room lightened to a sunny glow. "There, that should brighten your spirits," she said, glancing in his direction. "Well, at least the *room* will be brighter."

"Yes, thank you, my spirits are indeed brightened," Ruairi said dully.

Brina faced him, her arms crossed, and looked him up and down. Her face was screwed up with displeasure, making the creases around her eyes look deeper than usual. Although she was his mother's younger sister, to Ruairi Brina seemed older. She was not one to sit before the mirror all day applying potions to her face as his mother did. Even her white-blonde hair was piled up less meticulously than his mother would have dared worn it.

"Why the face?" Brina asked. "This is the evening of your betrothal for goodness sake. You should be jubilant." She crossed over and gathered up the day-clothes he had discarded onto the floor in a heap.

"Let the servants take care of that," Ruairi said.

"Do not be ridiculous. Servants have more important things to do than this. You should be picking them up yourself, lazy child."

"I am a man now, Brina. Do not forget I have just turned fifteen."

"Very well, *man* then." She dumped the bundle of dirty clothes into his arms. He tossed them back down to the floor.

"You never answered my question," Brina said. "You are happy about the betrothal, are you not?"

Ruairi strolled over to the bed and plopped down on the edge of it, barely missing the neatly laid out tunic. "Of course I am. You know I love Cinnia more than anything."

And he did, too. He had known Cinnia his entire life and had loved her almost as long. She was beyond beautiful and his body betrayed him every time he thought of her, especially when his thoughts turned to their wedding night. It was the one thing he actually looked forward to. But the marriage would not take place for a year yet, as Cinnia was only fourteen and not yet of age. Ruairi rested his chin on his fist and raised a brow as a scheme worked in his mind. If things went as planned, he would not have to wait that long. Tonight was their official betrothal, was it not? He and Cinnia could slip away after the reception, perhaps to this very room where—

"What are you daydreaming about?" Brina asked, noticing the unusually happy expression on Ruairi's face.

"What? Oh, nothing, Brina. I just have things on my mind, that is all."

Brina slitted her eyes. "Well, those things had best not be any of your usual antics, dear nephew. You cannot afford to enrage your father tonight. He is still fuming from your last escapade and if you were to do anything here in Labhras's home . . . well, I cannot even form the words to describe the anguish you will suffer." She gathered up the day clothes from the floor once more. "You had best be getting yourself dressed, Ruairi. Your father will be expecting you soon and—"

"Humph! Father!" Ruairi stood up and grabbed the tunic, intentionally crumpling it in his hand as he did so. But he pulled it over his head anyway, wrinkles and all, and reached for the belt that would bind his waist in misery all evening. He wrapped it around himself haphazardly and stood facing Brina, his arms extended at his side. "There, I am dressed!"

"Well, you do not have to snap at me about it. I am only here to offer you some support. I knew the state you would be in tonight."

"I hate all these formalities."

"What do you expect? You are a prince. That is what princes do."

"Well, it makes me feel like a pony doing tricks. I have no say in anything whatsoever."

"I see," Brina said as she crossed over to adjust his clothing. "And I suppose you had no say at all in this betrothal?" She tugged at the tunic that bunched at the belt and hung crookedly.

Ruairi rolled his eyes. "Dear, sweet Brina; you are so naïve. It is luck alone that allows me to marry the girl I love. If Cinnia were not the daughter of Father's closest friend, I feel quite certain I would be getting betrothed to someone entirely different tonight."

"Oh, you do not give your father credit. Close friend or not, if Labhras's daughter was not to your liking I doubt he would force her on you." She smoothed the fabric, adjusted the belt, and pinned the clasps at his shoulders, pinching the material where it draped over them. "There, now you are at least presentable."

Ruairi walked over to the dressing table, grabbed up the comb, and raked its teeth through his long, red hair. Then he pulled his hair away from his face and bound it at his back.

"Your father will not want your hair tied back like that," Brina said.

"It is too hot to wear it down," Ruairi said. "Besides, everyone always stares at it. It makes me feel self-conscious."

Brina shook her head. "Are you not satisfied with anything? It is not every day a child is born with hair the color of
yours. You should appreciate your special gift."

"Well, I despise it," Ruairi grumbled. "Why could I not
have been born with blond hair like everyone else?"

"Because you were born to be the Red King, that is why."

"Regardless, if I had been born one minute later I would
not have to put up with all this."

The door burst open and King Sedric stormed into the
room. "What is taking you so long, boy? The guests are waiting!" he bellowed.

Ruairi wheeled around to face him. His father was a large
man, tall and broad shouldered with flashing green eyes that were
further emphasized by dark arching brows. But he could have
been half his size and still demanded attention.

Sedric eyed his son's hair with disapproval. "Unbind your
hair," he said, motioning to it.

"But Father, it is too hot."

Sedric stormed over and reached a hand behind Ruairi's
head, yanking the binding from his hair. "You will wear it down,
do you understand?"

Ruairi's violet eyes flashed in his father's direction, then he
shook his head furiously, his long hair flying into a tangled
explosion of red. "There, it is down!" he shouted.

Sedric threw his arms up in exasperation. "Brina, do something with him."

Brina walked over to her scowling nephew. Spinning him
around by the shoulders, she pressed him down onto the dressing
table bench to face the mirror. She picked up the comb and began to smooth the mess he had made of his hair, then glanced in
Sedric's direction. "Do not concern yourself, Sire," she said,
nodding toward the door. "I will see to it he comes down looking
like a prince."

Sedric moved to the doorway, then turned to face his son
whose back was still to him. "I expect you to be on your best behavior
tonight, Ruairi. None of your foolish pranks. Understand?"

"Of course, Father," Ruairi said, but the slight grin playing at the corners of his mouth indicated he had other ideas.

"Of course, Father," a mocking voice said from the doorway. Ruairi turned in response and grinned. It was Whyn, his brother, come no doubt to add his fuel to the already raging fire. But Whyn he could handle. They were twins and Ruairi had, after all, been handling him ever since they had shared their mother's womb.

"Go see the mess your brother has made of himself, Whyn," Sedric said crossly. "Perhaps you can talk some sense into him." And with that the king exited the room, his loose blond hair flying at his back.

Whyn entered the room and stood behind his brother. "Why do you torture Father?" he said. "He only wants what is best for you."

"Who is torturing whom?" Ruairi said.

Ruairi watched his brother's reflection in the mirror. To look at them one would never know they were twins. Whyn was blond and blue-eyed, his features soft. Ruairi was the opposite, his hair bright red, his eyes violet, and his features chiseled. But their differences were more than physical ones. Whyn was much more prince-like: always saying the right things, always paying rapt attention to their father, always involving himself in the business of the great city-state. Whyn would make a much better king, but as fate would have it, the fiery prince was born one minute before the golden one.

"Why the attitude tonight, brother?" Whyn asked. "So what if Father wants your hair down. Is that such a price to pay for becoming betrothed to the most beautiful girl in Tearia?"

Ruairi laughed. "Well, you could have had your chance with her, but you were too slow."

"One minute too slow," Whyn said, but by the expression on his face, he regretted it the instant he said it.

"What do you mean by that remark?" Ruairi asked. "Do you think she only wants me because I am first?"

"No, of course not. I only meant—" Whyn lowered his eyes.

"I know exactly what you meant!" Ruairi slapped Brina's hand aside, then rose and stormed to the window.

"I—I am sorry," Whyn said. "I did not mean it that way."

Ruairi glanced back at Whyn's downcast face and felt a twinge of guilt. It was not his brother's fault his twin had pushed his way out into the world before him. "I am sorry, Whyn," Ruairi said stiffly. "I just want these formalities over with, that is all."

Whyn strolled over and placed a hand on his brother's shoulder. "Just relax and try to enjoy it. It will be over before you know it."

"Let us get on with it then," Ruairi said, shrugging his shoulder away and heading for the door. He jerked it open and stepped into the hallway, then marched toward the steps that led to the torch-lit corridor below. Brina and Whyn followed silently at his back.

Ruairi arrived at the double doors leading into the reception room and paused. The voices of hundreds of guests could be heard on the other side of it. "I feel like I am going to an execution," he said between clenched teeth.

"Oh, go on," Whyn said. "It will be all right."

Ruairi stiffened his spine and walked into the cavernous room, then made his way to the dais and the food-laden table that sat stretched across it. He seated himself in a great armed chair centered behind the table and stared at the sea of blond heads and pale faces bowed before him. To his way of thinking they all looked alike. The only thing that set them apart was the color of their tunics, and that was determined solely by their status within society, not by any choice of their own. Regardless, it must be a pleasant thing to blend in like that. He forced a smile in their direction and motioned them to rise.

A place was reserved on his immediate left for his father who could be seen consulting with two temple priests in the back of the crowded room. Ruairi watched their moving mouths, trying to decipher their words, but then his attention was diverted to his mother who was making her usual grand entrance. Isola lifted her beautiful chin, demanding the attention of all in attendance, and strolled to the ornately carved chair to the left of the king's. Whyn and Brina, who had waited for the queen to be seated, entered to take their places on the other side of her. Further on, a place was reserved for Mahon, Brina's husband, no doubt delayed by his duties as Commander of the Guard. Ruairi leaned around and looked down the table at Whyn who winked in his direction, and Brina who offered an encouraging smile. But his mother did not look at him at all.

He felt a movement to his right and glanced up to see Cinnia taking her place in the chair next to him. He took her hand in his, squeezing it tight.

"You are so tense," she whispered.

He smiled and nodded, feeling the source of his uneasiness pleasantly redirected. His eyes scanned Cinnia's flawless face, then trailed down her neck to the golden ringlets that spilled across her shoulders. Her silky, mint-green gown was cinched at the waist and barely concealed her fully developed figure. Gazing at her, he felt his heart soften, even while the rest of him could not.

His thoughts turned back to the room. The rest of the families had taken their places at the table and the crowd was now staring at him, silent and ready. The tedious business of ceremony was about to begin.

Ruairi and Cinnia rose and made their way over to the priests who now stood before the room. Cinnia's hand was draped across Ruairi's outstretched one, and she walked with all the grace and splendor of a future queen. Ruairi's heart could not help but swell. He stole a glimpse at the audience and was proud to note they were equally mesmerized by her beauty. It was one of the few times attentions were focused on something other than the color of his hair.

The ceremony was a long one, fraught with chanting, proclamations, and incantations to the gods. Ruairi thought it all terribly outdated. As soon as he was king, he determined, rituals far less painful would replace the antiquities. For now, though, he would just have to endure.

The priests droned on and on, and Ruairi found it difficult to stay focused on what they were saying. The righteousness of their tones sounded monotonous, and their words seemed all but meaningless. Ruairi's mind wandered, but he managed to respond as expected, though usually following an awkward pause. Finally he and Cinnia were allowed to return to their seats, and Sedric took his place before the guests. The king's speech was particularly long-winded as he took the opportunity to interject politics, business, and various affairs of the state.

While the guests listened to Sedric with rapt attention, Ruairi stifled yawn after yawn. He counted the torches on the walls, squinted at the details of the frescoes across the room, and analyzed the intricate mosaics beneath the hundreds of sandaled feet. Then he felt hopeful. It was now Labhras's turn to address the hall, and Cinnia's father, he knew, would be the last to speak. To his utter disappointment the man's speech made all the others seem short in comparison.

Ruairi squirmed in his chair. It was hot and he had been sitting there for what seemed like hours. When was the agony going to end? He looked down the sprawling table toward Whyn who was being his usual self: watching Labhras with great interest, laughing at the boring jokes, applauding in all the right places. It was most annoying. Ruairi intensified his gaze, hoping to capture his brother's attention. Whyn glanced his way and mouthed a silent "what?" Ruairi grinned and popped a grape into his mouth. Whyn's eyes widened with horror.

Ruairi sucked in his cheeks and winked. If he aimed the grape just right he could probably pelt the back of Labhras's head with it. The man was standing before the crowd, his back to the table, extolling the virtues of the royal family and his future son-in-law who would one day lead Tearia to further greatness as the Red King. Ruairi was tired of it all and knew that the grape, now primed for battle in his mouth, could add a bit of interest to the otherwise boring speech. But an icy stare of disapproval from his mother brought his plans to an abrupt halt. He scowled and spit the grape onto his plate.

The reaction from the crowd brought his attention back to Labhras who was now holding a wine goblet in the air. The long-winded toast was over at last. Ruairi straightened his aching back and smiled, nodding to the crowd that had turned their eyes to him and Cinnia rather than her father. He stood and took Cinnia's hand in his and kissed it. The guests clapped wildly and cheered their approval.

But relief was short lived and hope for a private moment with Cinnia on hold. The reception line had formed to their right. Ruairi surveyed the room, contemplating a quick escape, but one look in his father's direction quickly doused the notion. The man was watching him intently, his brows raised in warning. Clearly he had no intention of letting his unpredictable son spoil the otherwise lovely affair.

Ruairi groaned for the thousandth time that evening and walked down the steps of the dais to the eternal line of well-wishers. An hour of handshaking, small talk, and forced smiles left him with the overwhelming desire for fight or flight. While fight was not possible, flight certainly was. The instant the last guest departed from the line, Ruairi turned, grabbed Cinnia's hand, and pulled her from the stifling room to the fresh air of the gardens outside.

The yard was bathed in silvery moonlight and the scent of the botanicals that enveloped the garden filled Ruairi's senses. But it was the essence of Cinnia that made his head spin. "Gods, I thought we would never get out of there," he said. He took her face in his hands, pulling it toward his eager mouth, and kissed her deeply. The concerns of the day evaporated.

Ruairi had kissed Cinnia many times before, and though she always left him wanting more, he had never taken it much further. It wasn't that he didn't want to. He was a healthy young man, after all, and was more than ready for the intimate touch of a woman. But he was patient with the desires of his body, believing it best to wait until the time was right. That time, he knew, could only be with Cinnia, and that time would hopefully be tonight.

Cinnia pulled back and glanced over her shoulder. "Someone might see us," she whispered.

"But Cin . . . we are betrothed now," Ruairi said, leaning in for more.

"You know I want you, but it is too risky. What if we were found out? My father would be furious. And your father—"

"Oh, who cares about them. They are nothing more than a couple of old men who have long forgotten what it is like to be kissed by a beautiful woman."

Cinnia laughed. "Oh, I doubt they have forgotten. They do have beautiful wives after all."

"None so beautiful as you," Ruairi said. He traced a finger down her breastbone and felt her shiver at his touch.

Cinnia glanced around, then turned back to him and smiled. "Very well, meet me in my room later. I will leave a candle in the window to let you know when it is safe."

Ruairi glanced up toward the window that arched above them. Cinnia's room. He would have no trouble finding his way there. He was well acquainted with Labhras's great estate; his family had spent much time there in his childhood. It was in this very maze of a garden that Ruairi, his brother, and Cinnia had played hiding games and planned fantastic adventures together. But the adventure planned with Cinnia tonight would be his greatest yet.

"There are still many courtesies to attend to with the guests," Cinnia continued, "and mother will be twittering about me of course. But I will try to slip away and then—"

"Yes, then," Ruairi said, and he kissed her once more.

They strolled back into the great reception hall together, their faces masks of innocence. Before long they found themselves separated by the crowd of well-wishers, but their knowing eyes continued to communicate with one another across the room.

Ruairi excused himself from a talkative guest and worked his way over to a nearby refreshment table. His mouth was parched from too much talk, and a mind-altering drink sounded particularly good. He reached his hand out toward a wine vessel, but a sudden grip on his arm kept him from his goal. His first thought was that it was his father, angry about something he had done, but he was surprised to discover it was Whyn.

"What are you doing?" Ruairi asked indignantly.

Whyn did not reply, but instead dragged him into the corridor beyond. "I thought your dalliance with Cinnia would never end," he said.

"Who says it has?" Ruairi replied, grinning.

Whyn frowned. "Wipe that foolish grin off of your face. There is trouble brewing."

"Oh gods, what now?" Ruairi jerked his arm away.

A few guests who lingered in the corridor looked up, then bowed and excused themselves. Whyn's eyes darted back and forth as he opened a nearby door and pushed his brother through it into the room beyond.

The room was small, but elegantly furnished. A tall, carved rack towered against a whitewashed wall, its numerous compartments filled to overflowing with rolled up parchments. An ornate chair backed the gray and pink marble table at the room's center, and a couch inlaid with gold rested along one wall. A great tapestry was displayed behind it, and thick drapes of the finest material separated the room from the atrium beyond. Oil lamps lit the space in a soft golden hue.

Ruairi glanced around the room. It was Labhras's office, and he didn't like the idea of being there. He rubbed his arm and scowled at his brother. "Whyn, I have no interest in hearing about any troubles tonight. I have just started to actually enjoy myself."

"Well you had best show some interest, dear brother. Father found out about your latest adventure and he is not happy about it." Whyn narrowed his eyes and stared hard into Ruairi's apathetic face.

"Which adventure?" Ruairi said. "The one where I urinated in the wine vessel in the temple or the one where I switched out the—"

"No, the one where you sneaked into the holding cell and almost got yourself killed by a Jecta."

"Oh, that," Ruairi said with an indifferent wave of his hand.

"Oh that? Oh *that*?" Whyn said, struggling to keep his voice down. "Do you not understand what could have happened to you? Do you not realize you could have been injured, or worse?"

"Nothing happened, Whyn. The foul creature grabbed my tunic, nothing more. I told you . . ."

"Crymm reported you and he was demoted because of it."

"Crymm? Demoted?" Ruairi crossed his arms and stared down at his feet in momentary contemplation. "Well that is what he gets for opening his mouth."

"He has been your bodyguard for thirteen years, Ruairi. You could show a little sympathy."

"Why should I? The man hates me."

"Who can blame him? You have led him on one merry chase after another all these years, and his job has been on the line more times than not. You should at least be grateful he saved your neck."

"Humph! I was not in any real danger. Crymm was just trying to make himself look good. That is probably why he said something to Father about it, so he would come out looking like some kind of hero. If he had been doing his job like he was supposed to, it would never have happened. He got what he deserved."

"It is not just the issue of Crymm, Ruairi. It is the fact that you allowed yourself to be touched by a Jecta, and the wretch is to have his hand cut off for it."

Ruairi rolled his eyes. "What concern is that of mine?"

"You should be at least concerned for the fact that your precious skin could have been damaged."

"But it was not."

"But it could have been. And you know a damaged prince cannot be prince at all."

"What are you implying, Whyn? That if I was marked I could no longer be prince? Father would never allow that to happen."

"Father would have little say in it, brother. It would be the decision of the Priestess. You know the law requires Tearians to keep their bodies as perfect as possible. It is the will of the Goddess and is written as commandment. You know what the consequences are for one who blatantly disregards it."

"Well, what do you expect me to do about it now? What is done is done." Ruairi turned away from Whyn's icy stare, then strolled over to the desk and ran his fingers along its surface.

"I heard Father talking," Whyn continued. "It seems the Priestess is most unhappy about your behavior. One of the priests said she does not think you are suited as a prince, much less a king. I fear the Temple will work against you if you do not change your ways. Father has been listening, Ruairi, and I think he is beginning to agree."

Ruairi scoffed and eyed the wall of scrolls and parchments. His brother was surely overreacting and Whyn's paranoia had begun to bore him. Perhaps a distraction was needed. He pulled out a large scroll and unrolled it, then scanned its contents with pretended interest.

"What are you doing?" Whyn cried.

"These scrolls must be really important," Ruairi said. "Probably some invaluable record of Labhras's business dealings."

"Put that back!" Whyn demanded, taking a threatening step in his brother's direction. He glanced over his shoulder at the door they had closed behind them. "You know Father's temper. If he catches you . . ."

Ruairi ignored him, caught up in the adventure of the moment. He stepped toward the desk and lifted the oil lamp. "You know, these lamps are a hazard. I cannot believe that Labhras would keep this thing lit unattended in a room full of documents like this." He squinted his eyes at the parchment. "I can barely make out these words. Perhaps if I were to bring the flame a bit closer . . ." He glanced up at Whyn whose face had turned a ghostly white, and grinned, delighted by the sudden horror he saw there.

Whyn took a step forward and reached out a hand. "I said put that down," he said between gritted teeth. "This is not the least bit amusing."

"Oh, you worry too much."

Whyn took an unexpected leap in Ruairi's direction and grabbed for the scroll. Ruairi jerked it just out of his reach and laughed. "Do you want it?" he said. He circled the table, keeping it between him and Whyn, who was still struggling to reach him.

Whyn leapt again and threw himself across the table, knocking inkwells, quills, and documents to the floor. Ruairi jumped back and his thigh rammed into the arm of the chair, sending his feet out from under him. He flipped back and rolled off the chair toward the floor, his arms flailing as he fought his descent. The lamp flew from his grasp and into the drape, and oil and flame spilled down the beautiful fabric.

Ruairi gaped at the burning drape as flames raced toward the ceiling and the cubby of scrolls nearby. He pushed himself up and reached for the drape, intent on pulling it down, but Whyn grabbed him and yanked him back.

"Do not touch it, fool!" Whyn screamed, shoving him aside. "You could get hurt!" Whyn rushed toward the door. "I will get help," he called back as he ran from the room. "Do not do anything stupid!"

Ruairi nodded in silence, unable to form a single syllable. As he watched his brother disappear into the hallway, he felt his limbs begin to shake. He hadn't meant for this to happen, he was only joking around, but for the first time he genuinely regretted his foolishness. He twisted his body around and scanned the room for something to douse the flames, but there was nothing. The fire swept along the ceiling toward the parchments.

The rack of parchments ignited and roared into a billowing explosion of flame. The smell of smoke filled Ruairi's senses; the crack of flames echoed in his ears. He backed toward the door, coughing and wiping at smoky tears. He felt himself suddenly yanked through the doorway and shoved against the opposite wall, the breath knocked nearly out of him.

"By the gods, what have you done this time?" his father shouted.

The redness and fury in the man's face left Ruairi weak.

"Father, I—"

"No excuses, boy!" Sedric clutched the front of Ruairi's tunic and pulled him forward then slammed him back against the wall.

"It was an accident!" Ruairi cried. His eyes darted toward the room at his father's back. It was completely engulfed in flames now and clouds of smoke were rolling into the hallway. Servants attempted to make their way in with buckets of water, but were driven back by the heat and smoke.

Ruairi's father jerked him away from the wall and pushed him down the smoke-filled corridor. It was difficult to see through the haze, but clearly the fire and pandemonium had spread. The shapes of the guests were all around them now: pushing and shoving, tripping and falling, screaming and shouting. Ruairi stumbled, but was yanked back up by his father who steered him to the right and into the garden beyond.

He staggered out, choking and fighting for breath. Sedric still clutched the back of his tunic, and Ruairi quickly found himself face down on the grass. His father knelt beside him and rolled him over, then pulled him up by the shoulders and shook him violently. "Do you realize what you have done? Do you realize you have destroyed a man's home and endangered every guest in it?" Sedric threw him back to the ground in disgust.

Ruairi felt a great lump in his throat. "Is everyone out?" he asked, his voice cracking.

"We can only pray."

Ruairi sat up and scanned the gathering crowd. Many faces were covered with soot, and he searched them for any sign of familiarity. Whyn was nearby . . . and Brina . . . Mother . . . but, Cinnia?

He jumped to his feet and leaned his body around, craning his neck to see through the sea of dismal faces. But he did not see Cinnia. He directed his eyes to her bedroom window. A candle could be seen on the sill, its delicate flame flickering against a pallet of orange. Terror seized him. What if she was still up in her room? What if no one knew?

"Where is Cinnia?" Ruairi cried to his father. "Have you seen her? Is she out?" He moved in the direction of the house, but his father grabbed hold of his arm and held it tight.

"You are not going anywhere!" Sedric shouted. "You have caused enough trouble."

"But, Father, Cinnia, she is not out here!" He looked back into the crowd. "Where is Labhras? Did he get her out?"

"Of course he got her out. I got you out did I not? And you did not even deserve it."

Ruairi was stung by the words, but he knew his father was right. He had risked everyone's lives with his foolishness here tonight. But a sudden scream turned his attention from his own self-loathing to the open window above. It was Cinnia—still in her room—the room where she had been waiting for him.

He jerked away from his father's grasp, but Sedric regained his hold. "You will not go back in there," Sedric ordered. "Let the servants take care of what must be done. There can be no risk to you, understood?"

Ruairi shoved his father away and staggered back. "It is my choice, Father!" Before Sedric could say another word, Ruairi spun around, ran toward the corridor, and disappeared into a sea of smoke.

The hallway was a poisonous tunnel of fumes that stung Ruairi's eyes and forced him to breath in slow shallow breaths. He pulled his tunic up over his nose and held it, then squeezed his eyes shut and reached a hand to the wall at his side. The wall was all he had to guide him; if he just followed it, he knew he would eventually reach the stairwell. Timbers popped over his head, leaving him with the uneasy feeling that the ceiling would soon collapse upon him. He risked a glance at the hazy corridor behind. The screams of the guests seemed a thousand miles away.

He forced his feet forward, but tripped over an unknown object and fell hard to his knees. The feel of the wall disappeared, and he felt around desperately. Hope was rekindled when his hand finally came to rest upon the rough stone surface of a step. Ruairi clambered on all fours up the stairwell, praying for a pocket of fresh air. His head was spinning and his lungs felt as though they were about to ignite in his chest. He reached the end and fell, sprawled upon the tiles of the upstairs hallway.

He peeked open an eye, then rose and dragged in a lungful of air. It was fresher than what he had left below, but it still left him doubled up with painful spasms exploding from his chest. Clutching his gut with one hand, he pulled the tunic back over his nose with the other. He staggered in the direction of Cinnia's room, keeping below the perilous cloud that roiled above his head. Then he froze. Parts of the hall ceiling were raining down in chunks before him, and fire had completely engulfed Cinnia's door. Ruairi glanced around for something to use as a battering ram, but there was nothing. His eyes shot upward; flames raced along the ceiling toward him. Time had run out.

He sprinted toward the burning door and shoved it open with both hands, using every ounce of strength he could muster. It slammed against the wall at its back, sending sparks spinning into the air. The momentary but intense pain of Ruairi's hands at first surprised him, but he forced it from his mind and ducked through the doorframe. He could barely see Cinnia through the smoke. She was lying, face down and unmoving on the bed across the way.

"Cinnia! Cinnia!" He ran to her and rolled her over, but she made no response. Gathering her into his arms, he clutched her body close to his, then headed for the window. A timber crashed in front of him, pulling part of the ceiling down with it. Billows of smoke and bright orange embers roared and funneled around them. Ruairi staggered back, then turned toward the doorway. Sucking in one last breath of air, he raced through it and disappeared into the raging inferno beyond.

Ruairi didn't remember getting Cinnia out of the burning house. The next thing he knew he was kneeling over her on the cool, damp grass of the garden. A crowd of onlookers surrounded them, their mouths either covered by their hands or hanging open in disbelief.

"Why is no one helping?" Ruairi shouted, turning his eyes angrily in their direction. Then he noticed their attentions were not focused on Cinnia, now lying on the grass. They were focused on him.

He glanced down at his hands and cried out, then staggered up. The gasping crowd shuffled away from him, muttering words of shock and pity. Ruairi held his hands up and inspected them. They looked strange, rough and black, red and blistered, but he could not quite understand why. He laughed nervously. Were they burned? Curious how they did not hurt.

The horrific pain of his injuries suddenly matched the terrifying realization of them. His stomach lurched and his legs went weak. He fell to his knees, shaking, and dropped onto his back. The world spun wildly as his mind struggled to cope with the pain that enveloped him. He forced his gaze to the star-filled sky above, anywhere but the disgusted faces staring down at him.

Wings. Dear gods, please just give me wings.

Then he saw it, for a fleeting moment, a great gold and red light blazing across the heavens. His eyes widened and he wondered dreamily whether the vision might be the wings he so desperately wished for. Then his eyes closed and he felt himself drift into blackness.

It would be a long time before he looked into that sky again.

3
The Dread of It

Dayn sat on a chair by the hearth, nervously tapping his feet. It wasn't his usual habit, the tapping of his feet, but this morning he felt more than a little anxious. He leaned his head against the chair's high back and gripped the arms as though clinging for dear life. He had promised to go to the Summer Fires Festival to see his sister crowned Maiden, and there was no getting out of it now.

He stared into the hearth and narrowed his eyes. The dying embers and mountains of charred log looked like miniature landscapes. Perhaps like those of Aredyrah a thousand years ago when the mountains spewed fire and rock, or perhaps like that place where the demons lived now. He shivered, reminded of what he was.

It had been a year since he had been accosted by Sheireadan and his pack on the path, a year since he had over-heard his father and the Spirit Keeper on the porch. He never spoke a word of it to anyone, not even to Alicine in whom he once could have confided anything. He chose to keep the secret tucked deep within his heart and isolated himself at the farm instead. Strangely enough, his parents allowed it. His mother no longer sent him on errands to Kiradyn, not since he had told her months before that he refused to go. Even his father didn't argue the point anymore, although it was clear he noticed a disturbing change in his son. But now, weakened by his sister's tears, Dayn found himself going to the biggest festival of the year. And the dread of it was unbearable.

The festival started at sunrise, as most did, but his father insisted they not leave in the dark. Dayn was relieved; that meant less time to endure the ordeal ahead. They were just waiting for Alicine now and, thankfully, she was taking longer than usual to get ready.

Dayn looked down at himself and surveyed his clothing from chest to toe. Determined to go to the festival looking his best, he had bathed in the pre-dawn hours, gritting his teeth against the chill of the bath water. He'd rubbed his shivering body with quince lotion, and even put sweet-smelling herbs under his arms (something he usually scoffed at.) His pale, shoulder-length hair was parted and tucked behind his ears. His face was scrubbed as clean as he could get it; even the birthmark on his neck seemed paler. He wore his best tunic, the forest green one with the decorative plaid border, and had pinned it with a bronze curvilinear brooch. His best boots were polished, their long leather straps wrapped in a meticulous pattern up his brown woolen trousers. He had never looked better and maybe Falyn would think so, too. That is, if he got up the nerve to approach her.

Dayn watched as his mother strolled from the bedroom to the kitchen. Beads tinkled and petticoats swished with every step she took. Her indigo dress was the only nice one she owned, but in it she looked truly lovely. It was long-sleeved and high-collared, as was the fashion with Kiradyn women, and the gold-braided bodice hugging her waist outlined her slender figure. Colorful ribbons were woven into the two long plaits of her hair, and she had lined her eyes with black pencil. Dayn could not help but smile as she fluttered about the room. He had not seen her this happy in a long time, nor this beautiful.

A clamor directed Dayn's attention to the front door. His father's voice could be heard on the other side of it, grumbling about the fool horse. Gorman burst through, dressed in his festive best but still complaining about the horse, when he broke into a wide grin. He strutted over to Morna and pulled her close; then he lifted her up and swung her around. The beads that adorned her boots tinkled a playful tune as she twirled.

"You're as beautiful as the day I first laid eyes on you," Gorman said. He set her down and planted a kiss on her lips. It wasn't a common custom for people to show this type of affection in front of others, even their own families, but Gorman was clearly in love with his wife and this morning he did not seem to mind whether his son witnessed it or not.

Watching his parents laugh and dance across the room, Dayn felt a sudden admiration for their devotion to each other. He wondered if he would ever feel a love like theirs, but he pushed the thought from his mind. There was no sense in thinking about such things now. He was only sixteen and it would be months before he was old enough to court. That is, if anyone would have him.

"Isn't your mother beautiful, Dayn? Have you ever seen her look so radiant?" Gorman asked.

"Yes . . . I mean, no . . . I mean, she looks very beautiful, Father."

Morna blushed and slapped her husband playfully on the chest. "You boys are embarrassing me. Now then, are we all ready?" Her eyes scanned the room, then she headed toward the stairs. "What could be keeping that girl? Alicine, it's getting late, dear," she called up the stairwell. "Do you need some help with your dress?"

"No, Mother," Alicine's muffled voice called from the room above. "I'm almost ready."

Morna strode over to a three-legged stool and pulled it next to Dayn. She fluffed her skirt and sat down in a billow of blue. For a moment she seemed hesitant, then she said, "You look very nice today, son."

Dayn smiled and nodded but did not reply.

"I know you don't want to go, Dayn," she said, "but I think you'll have fun. Surely things have settled down between you and

Sheireadan this past year. Just stay with us, dear, and everything will be fine. You'll see."

Dayn looked back over at the hearth, tracing the outline of the imaginary mountains with his eyes. "Just stay with us, dear," his mother's voice echoed in his mind. *Like a child.*

"Son?"

This time it was his father's voice and Dayn was surprised by its unusually gentle tone. He glanced up to see his father standing next to him with something cradled in his hand.

"Son, I want you to have this," Gorman said. "Now that you're sixteen, I feel it's time you had it."

Gorman stared into Dayn's face with such intensity that for a moment Dayn felt alarmed. Dayn turned up his palm and waited with uneasiness for the token of his father's generosity to drop into it. Gorman paused as though having second thoughts, then placed the object onto his son's outstretched hand.

Dayn sucked in his breath. It was the brooch, the one of the cat-like beast he had admired for as long as he could remember. The beautiful ornament was gold and molded with the finest detail into the shape of a mythical beast: a four legged creature somewhat like a large cat, with a long tufted tail, fangs, and a great head of hair. It was eternally poised to pounce, claws outstretched, its mane blowing in the imaginary wind. It was the most valuable thing his father owned; Dayn couldn't believe the man was actually giving it to him. He hadn't even been allowed to see the thing since he was a child.

The only time Dayn had ever seen the brooch was when he was six years old, but he had never forgotten the details of it. He and Alicine were playing a hiding game in the house one rainy afternoon when he stumbled upon it while pushing himself behind the dresser in his parents' room. In his haste to move the cumbersome piece of furniture, he knocked over his father's jewelry box, the intricately carved one that held his brooches, belt buckles, and torques. He remembered fingering the brooch that tumbled out amongst the other baubles onto the floor, mesmerized by the shine of its gold, intrigued by the beast depicted in its design. But his father had grabbed it from him and tossed it back into the box, ordering him never to touch it again. He hadn't been allowed to see it since, but he remembered it well enough to make up childhood stories about it. On more than one occasion he had found himself at the end of his mother's wagging finger for drawing chalk pictures of it across his bedroom wall.

Dayn stared down at the brooch, unable to take his eyes from it. An overwhelming guilt washed over him. He had treated his father so coldly this past year, and now the man was giving him this precious gift. "Father, I . . ." But a rising lump in his throat prevented him from saying the rest of the words, words he didn't know how to express anyway.

"You don't have to say anything, Dayn," his father said. "It's yours now."

"Here, son," his mother said, leaning toward him. "Let me help you pin it on." She reached over and removed the bronze brooch Dayn had pinned to his shirt earlier and replaced it with the gold one. She stood and stepped back, smiling, but there was a hint of sadness in her eyes.

Dayn gazed down at the shiny beast clinging to his breast and traced it with his finger. "Thank you," he whispered.

Alicine descended the last few steps of the stairs, holding her full skirt up over her slippered feet. Dayn rose, grinning, and glanced at his parents who were staring, misty-eyed, in their daughter's direction. His little sister did look radiant.

"You look very nice," Dayn said. He felt his face blush. He wasn't accustomed to complimenting his sister on her appearance.

Alicine displayed a smile of satisfaction. "Well, I should. I certainly worked long enough on this dress. Goodness knows how many bottles of potion I had to sell to buy the material for this thing." She laughed and strummed her fingers across the skirt.

The dress was of harvest gold and decorated at the bodice, hem, and sleeves with hundreds of tiny white flowers each meticulously embroidered. She had worked on them every day for months. The back of the bodice was laced with a dyed yellow cord pulled into a bow, accentuating her developing bust. Delicate, ivory lace trimmed the collar that reached to her chin as well as the tips of the long sleeves that stopped in a point at her wrists. Her ebony hair was braided into one long plait woven with colorful ribbons and embellished with flowers strategically placed. She had even dotted her lips and cheeks with pink and outlined her eyes in black as her mother had.

Dayn felt an uneasiness in the pit of his stomach as he watched his sister. She was no longer a girl, but a young woman, and he wasn't particularly pleased about it. It would only be two short years before Alicine was seventeen and allowed to court. She would have no difficulty finding a beau; Dayn was certain of that. But what of himself? He might never find someone willing to accept his differences. What would he do then? Spend the rest of his years with only his aging parents to keep him company?

"Well, what are we waiting for?" Alicine said. "It's getting late." She lifted her skirt and pushed open the front door with her foot, taking herself, as well as the flowing yards of golden material, through it.

Dayn followed his sister and helped her up to the bench of honor in the back of the wagon. The wagon was hitched to the stubborn mare that snorted and stomped the ground. The old gray was the only horse they owned, and for a moment Dayn wondered if the poor thing would be able to manage the load. In addition to the four passengers, the wagon was loaded with food, water, and bottles of remedy to sell at the festival. Dayn shook his head. They could get to town faster by walking, but he plopped himself on the open gate of the bed anyway, and dangled his feet into the dirt.

Gorman flicked the reins and the horse lurched the wagon forward. Dayn faced out the back, his feet dragging, but he lifted them in a hurry when he noticed the damp dirt of the road begin to replace the polished shine of the leather. He folded his legs in front of him and propped an elbow on his thigh, leaning his chin onto his fist. His body rocked back and forth to the rhythm of the wagon as it made its way through the bumps and ruts of the road.

As they lumbered along, Dayn watched the house grow distant. Dwindling tendrils of smoke rose from the chimney. Porch rockers swayed to the rhythm of the chimes in the morning breeze. A strange feeling washed over him. He could not seem to take his eyes off the place. It was as though he would never see it again.

4
Dark Talk

The much anticipated wedding of the young prince and his bride was but three days away and the great city-state of Tearia was in a festive mood. For months the possibility of the union had been in doubt; the royal household had been in turmoil ever since the fire the year before. But now, after much speculation, the couple was to marry, and the continuation of the royal line was all but assured.

There was great joy for it in Tearia, but there was also dark talk. Some felt the wedding would not, or should not, take place. Surely the gods would intervene and put a stop to it. Others cheered the event, believing the gods had already intervened on the prince's behalf. But one thing they all agreed on was that a royal union needed to take place soon. The king had not been well these past months, his body grown weaker and his mind more confused by the day.

The illness had come upon Sedric quickly, too quickly some said. There were whispers that something, or someone, sinister was behind it. The healers held little hope for him, and everyone knew it was just a matter of time. There was nothing now, short of an act of the gods, to stop the son's ascension to the throne. The entire week had been proclaimed a holiday, and whether one agreed with the union or not, it had not kept anyone from taking advantage of the celebration.

The royal family had feasted and toasted around their own great table for days now. They were eager for the marriage that would bring some happiness to an otherwise dismal year. But just as not everyone in the streets believed the union was a good one, not everyone at the royal table did either.

Brina had sat through it all, day after day, night after night, but was weary of the soreness of her tongue where she had bitten it in silence. Tonight, surrounded once again by the royal revelers, she found she could bear it no more.

"This is a travesty," she said, pushing up from the table. She glared at the pasty-faced guests across from her, their mouths agape at her unexpected words.

"Brina, sit down this instant," her husband ordered. "This is neither the time nor the place for you to air your opinions." Mahon grabbed her by the elbow and yanked her back down to her seat.

Brina wrested her arm from his grasp. "Get your hands off of me, Mahon. I told you never to touch me again, or have you forgotten?"

Mahon's face paled, then deepened to shades of red. He pulled her toward him. "You will cease this now, Brina. Do you understand? This is a day of celebration."

"I have sat by for days now and endured this so-called celebration," she said. "But what, dear husband, are we supposed to be celebrating?"

"The wedding of our prince of course," he replied. "It is a joyous occasion for everyone in Tearia." He eyed the squirming guests across from him, and raised his goblet in an awkward solute.

"Everyone? No, I think not," Brina said. "Reiv, for one—" But before she could say another word, Mahon squeezed her arm, digging his nails into her flesh.

"You will not mention that name at this table," he hissed.

Brina scoffed, then scanned the faces around her. Those seated at the table were family and friends she knew well. Once she could have said anything to them without fear of repercussion. But things had changed this past year and the subject of Reiv was one carefully avoided. Brina felt the grip on her arm tighten as Mahon leaned in closer. The heat of his breath on her face and the antagonism of his tone surprised her. He was not a hostile man, but even he had changed this past year. She raised her head defiantly and worked to release her arm. "No," she said. "Let us not mention the one person's name that *should* be mentioned."

Brina jerked her arm from Mahon's grasp, then rose and rested a cool, critical stare on every person seated there. Some ignored her, as her sister the Queen did, and a few scowled at her insolence, but most simply looked away in embarrassment. Brina turned her gaze to the elaborate feast before her. Dozens of golden goblets, once carefully arranged, were scattered throughout a maze of food, their purple spills bleeding into the white tablecloth. Plates of half-eaten food sat ignored while others were piled with second and third helpings. Some guests did not even bother with plates, choosing to pick from the serving platters instead. It occurred to Brina as she stared at the abundance of discarded food that most of it would be thrown away. So many hungry people outside the city walls, yet this would be tossed into the gutters rather than sent to feed them.

With that thought in mind, she realized that angering the guests would only serve to prevent her from doing what had to be done—what she had been doing for years now—and, even more importantly, what had to be done tonight. She did not excuse herself, but turned and walked silently from the banquet hall.

Brina was almost to her room when a noise from behind alerted her. She glanced over her shoulder and frowned, then quickened her pace. It was Mahon, come no doubt to settle with her. He was at the far end of the long corridor that led to her private chamber, but even from that distance she could tell he was primed for battle. She clenched her jaw and kept on walking.

"How could you have behaved like that," Mahon said upon reaching her. "How could you have mentioned Reiv's name at a celebration of your nephew's wedding?"

"The fact that it is a celebration of my nephew's wedding is the very reason I felt it needed to be mentioned," she said. She continued toward her room, her eyes averted from her husband's exasperated face. He would not follow her all the way. He would not dare.

Mahon followed at her heels, his long strides keeping up with her short, quick ones. "Brina, you must listen to reason," he said. He increased his pace to round her and planted himself between her and her chamber door. Brina reached for the door handle, but he positioned himself in front of it.

"Out of my way, Mahon," Brina said indignantly. "I am tired and wish to go to bed." She attempted another reach for the handle, but he moved once again to block her.

Mahon cocked a brow and narrowed his eyes. "Tired? Or is this just an excuse to sneak out and see Reiv?"

Brina shot him a glare, then fumbled for the handle and shoved the door open. She brushed past him and entered the room. He followed her inside.

She spun to face him, her hands balled into fists. "Get out!" she shouted. "You have no right to be here."

Mahon closed the door behind him and secured the lock with a *click*. "I have every right to be here."

"No, you do not, not since . . ."

Mahon's jaw went slack. "Brina, please."

"Please what? Please do not remind you of what you did to our child? Or please let your murderous hands touch me?"

"You know what happened to our child had to be done," he said.

"Do I detect a tear, husband? And who would it be for? Our infant son, or his executioner?"

"You know I did not kill our son, Brina!"

"Perhaps you did not kill him with your own hands, but your insistence that it be done took him from us just the same."

Mahon grabbed her by the shoulders. "You're right. It was not done by my hands. It was done by yours! You would allow no one else to touch him. It was you, not me that—"

"Do not turn this on me," Brina said, pulling away.

"I am turning this on you. You know I would have had someone else do it. Why did you insist on carrying the burden yourself?"

"I would not have the last eyes my child ever saw be those of a stranger!" Brina turned aside. "Please, let us not talk about this. It is too painful and it will not bring Keefe back to us."

Mahon nodded and reached out to embrace her. She rebuked him and stepped away. "It is time you left," she said.

"You still have not answered my earlier question. Are you planning to see Reiv tonight?"

"Yes," she replied.

"I will not allow it!" Mahon exploded in fury, raking perfume bottles, hair clips, and combs from the dressing table, sending them crashing to the floor.

Brina winced and backed away, wondering if she, too, would be raked to the floor. She lifted her chin with shaky determination. "I will not be kept from him, Mahon. He needs me."

"*He* needs you? What about me? I am your husband. I need you."

"The sort of need you have is neither so great nor so important as the one Reiv has." Brina walked slowly toward him, noting how his body was poised as though in a fight for his life. She placed a hand on his arm. "Mahon, please try to understand," she said with forced control. "You did not sit by the boy's bed night and day listening to his screams as the bandages were pulled from his hands. You were not there when we thought the fever would surely take him. You were not there to listen to his pleas for Cinnia and his mother, neither of whom even bothered to come and see him. You were not there to see his face when he learned Cinnia was betrothed to Whyn, his own brother. And you were not there to hear his sobs when he found out he had been disinherited by his family in a mock court that took not only his inheritance, but his future. How do you think he feels to have lost everything, including his very name? To have been called Ruairi, the Red King, for fifteen years, then to be forced to take the name 'Reiv', the name of a servant. Gods, Mahon, where is your compassion? Have you no room in your heart for the boy?"

"What happened he brought upon himself."

"Brought upon himself? Gods, he was saving Cinnia's life."

"From a fire he started!"

"It was an accident, Mahon."

"Perhaps, but he had a history of so-called accidents. No, he got what he deserved." Mahon paused, surveying Brina's stricken face. "I am sorry that Ruairi—that Reiv has suffered," he offered. "But what is done is done. Just be thankful Labhras provided him with a respectable job. Foreman over the fields would be considered an honor for any Jecta."

Brina cringed at the word.

"Brina, Reiv is Jecta now," Mahon said. "You have to face it. Things could have gone much worse. You know this. At least he was not banished to Pobu. Considering the boy burned down Labhras' house and endangered everyone in it, I would say the man has been more than generous. Reiv has been provided an apartment within the city walls and he will certainly never go hungry. What more does he need?"

"He needs his life back," Brina said.

But in her heart she knew he would never get it, and after the wedding of his brother, Whyn, to Cinnia in three days time, she wasn't sure Reiv would want any life at all.

5

Peace Offering

Another terracotta pot streaked across the atrium, trailed by a spinning ball of dirt and a once well-rooted marigold. The clay missile found its mark and crashed against a pillar that divided the centrally located courtyard from the rest of the tiny apartment. Shards of pottery, clumps of soil, and what remained of the plant exploded against the stone, the noise of it nearly drowned out by the scream of the boy who had hurled it.

Reiv stood, trembling hands clenched beneath leather gloves, his face feeling as red as the hair bound at his back. He grabbed up another plant and raised it above his head. His eyes narrowed as he readied for another onslaught. In that instant he felt as though he could kill somebody. Anybody would do, although a few familiar faces came immediately to mind. If only he could run those faces through with his sword and make them suffer as much as he had, perhaps he could breath a little easier, or at least get some sleep. But he knew he never would, no matter how great the insidious fantasy seemed at the moment. He no longer owned a sword, and it was unlikely he would get another anytime soon; Tearian law forbade him to even own one now. He released the pot with a scream of anguish, sending it soaring through the air and into a table of zinnias. For now, killing plants would just have to do.

He reached for another, but realized the foolishness of his actions. It wouldn't change anything. He knew that. And he would be the one to have to clean it all up. There were no longer servants to do his bidding. "Ruairi, the prince who wanted to slay lions, now Reiv, the slayer of marigolds," he muttered. He shook his head and looked around at the messy atrium. Of all places to take out his frustrations, this probably had not been the best choice.

The atrium had actually become his sanctuary the past several months, after his hands began to heal and he was forced to relocate there. The plants at least gave him something to do when he wasn't working the fields. Before, when he was prince and didn't have to tend to such menial tasks, he had thought of cultivating plants as woman's work. But Brina helped him start a garden in the atrium on the pretense they could work together to develop healing lotions for his hands. Between the two of them they had grown an assortment of herbs and flowering plants, and had tried their skills at a number of homemade medicinals which he rubbed into his burns every day.

But the medicinals had not had the effect on his hands he hoped for. The scars were bad enough to look at—he almost always wore gloves to hide them—but it was the lack of sensitivity and decreased mobility in his fingers that annoyed him the most. Areas of his hands were all but numb, the burns so deep that damage to nerves could not be undone. With exercise he had managed to maintain some dexterity, but his grasp on things would never be the same. Picking tiny leaves off plants didn't require much strength, but his fine motor skills required concentration and patience. And it was patience he was most lacking.

Reiv stormed over to the mess that littered the once spotless floor and groaned. If only he had stopped with one plant, but he hadn't, and now there were not one, but several piles of broken clay, dirt, and wilting leaves to clean up. He gathered up a few shards of terracotta and cradled them in his hand, then threw them back down, smashing them into smaller pieces still.

"Oh, I do not care!" he shouted. "Just stay there!"

He marched toward the living area, threw back the dividing drape, and plopped down on the chaise in a huff. The room was usually dark, as was the rest of the apartment. There were no windows facing the streets on any side of the place, which suited him just fine. He didn't care to look out into the streets anyway. The only light that ever entered any of the rooms was from the central courtyard. That is, if he bothered to pull back the heavy drapes that separated it from the rest of the house. Many days he didn't bother to pull them back at all, preferring to exist in the darkness. He didn't know why he felt that way. Perhaps the darkness desensitized him. But he had left the drape open when he stormed into the room just now, and the annoying light of morning was filtering in.

He was housed in the outer quadrant of Tearia, near the Jecta dormitories, the stables, and the buildings that housed some of the Tearian Guard. The general Jecta population was not allowed within the walls of Tearia; only employed laborers and certain skilled craftsmen could even step foot there. Few Jecta lived there permanently, except Reiv, who by definition had become one. But he did not consider himself Jecta and swore he never would.

He glared over his crossed arms and down at his barely clad body. To look at him one would have certainly taken him for a Jecta. His hair was not blond, his skin was no longer smooth, and he seldom wore a tunic anymore. Now he was usually clad in a cloth tied about his hips. It was the most sensible thing to work in; he had learned that early on. Over time, his skin adjusted to the sun, though it never turned the golden brown of a Jecta. It preferred to stay a rosy pink.

Reiv didn't like his job, nor the fields, but it was the days when he was away from them that he hated the most. On those days he found himself stuck in the apartment, bored and restless. Today was one of those days, as had been the past five, and it was taking its toll. The entire week had been proclaimed a holiday, so all the Jecta laborers and craftsmen had been sent home to Pobu. Even Brina was not able to come and see him as much as she usually did. She was obligated to attend a multitude of festivities with the family and had explained to him she would not be able to slip away easily. The family, Reiv knew, did not approve of her visits.

What now? He scanned the meager contents of the white-washed room: the old chaise he was sitting upon; a cross-legged stool pushed against the wall near the door; a small marble table, scrubbed rough from use and misuse; an old oak table in the kitchen, its two low benches pushed beneath. His mouth compressed with displeasure. Not very princely quarters, but then again, he was no longer a prince. No longer was he Ruairi, the Red King. Now he was Reiv: Reiv the Foreman, Reiv the Jecta, Reiv the Nobody. He crossed his arms, tucking his gloved hands beneath them and fought the hollow feeling in the pit of his stomach.

What now?

He asked that same question almost every day, but the answer rarely changed until now. "Well, fool, now you have something to do. You can clean up the mess you made," he said. He trudged to the atrium, then stopped to scowl at the first pile of debris that lay at his bare feet.

A sudden rap on the door startled him and he spun around. He wasn't expecting anyone; no one other than Brina ever came to see him. She said she would come, but not until much later, and this rap was loud, not soft like Brina's. He thought not to answer it, to deny he had even heard it. But a second, bolder knock alerted him to the possibility that maybe, just maybe, someone had come bearing good news for once: news that Cinnia could not live without him, news that his family wanted him back, news that he was Ruairi again, Prince of Tearia.

His heart lifted at the possibility of it, and he found himself sprinting to the door. He reached for the handle, then closed his eyes and whispered a prayer. *Please dear gods, let it be good news.* Pulling open the door, he found himself face to face with the very person most frequently found at the tip of his imaginary sword—Whyn, his brother. But Whyn was now more than his brother. He was his enemy. *So much for prayers*.

Reiv shoved his hands against the door. He could not bear to face Whyn, not today, and considering the evidence of his own temper scattered about the place, he couldn't trust himself not to throw his brother against the wall as well. But Whyn's quick foot blocked his attempt, and pushed its way, along with the rest of him, into the room. Reiv stepped back, fists and jaw clenched.

Whyn faced him and scanned the dimly lit room. He was dressed in his usual royal finery, a golden silk tunic draped down his body, jeweled adornments pinned at his shoulders. Reiv looked down at the faded black cloth that covered his own hips and felt the crimson rise to his cheeks. Whyn had never come to see him here before and now here he was, eyeing the dismal apartment and his outcast brother, the former Prince of Tearia, now a Jecta look-alike.

"Ruairi, we need to talk," Whyn said.

"And you need this many guards to do it?" Reiv said, motioning to the several well-armed Tearian Guard at Whyn's back.

"Oh . . . well, there has been some unrest as of late and the Guard felt it necessary." Whyn turned and murmured to his escorts who nodded and departed the room, but not before they shot a look of warning Reiv's way.

"Ruairi—" Whyn began.

"Reiv . . . my name is Reiv. Great pains are taken to see that I do not forget it, so—"

"I am sorry, Reiv," Whyn said.

"What is it that you wish, lord?" Reiv thought he would gag.

"Please, do not call me that. It is not necessary."

Reiv shrugged. "What is it that you wish then, Whyn?"

"To talk. That is all."

"I suppose it is a good thing that is all you want, as I have nothing left to give you."

Whyn's face went gray. Reiv felt a surge of satisfaction.

"I—I—" Whyn stammered, "I want us to mend the bad feelings between us, Reiv. Especially about the marriage. I want . . . I need to tell you that it is not what you think." Whyn stepped toward him, an expression of desperation shadowing his face. "The wedding was not my idea. I swear it, Reiv. I fought against it. I did! But Cinnia and her father insisted. She had been promised the role of future queen. Father and Labhras worked out the details and the Priestess approved them. I had no say in it, Reiv. Please believe me; I had no say."

Reiv stared dumbly, his lips unable to respond to his brother, the great Prince of Tearia, now begging his forgiveness. He twisted his mouth in disgust. Had Whyn come expecting pity from him? Surely he knew he would get none, no matter how heart wrenching his story. Reiv shook his head. "No. You could have stopped all this. I am here by your will."

"Gods, Reiv, is that what you think? That I wanted this?"

"I think, and I know."

"But, it is not true," Whyn insisted. "I swear I wish everything was back the way it was. I wish you were the one getting married tomorrow, not me. But there is nothing I can do about it. You do not understand the position I am in." Whyn stepped closer. "Remember how you used to complain that you never had any say in anything? Remember? Well, it is the same for me. Do you not see? I have to marry Cinnia, and I do not even love the girl."

"But I do."

"What can I do, Reiv? I cannot give you Cinnia. You know that. If I could change all of this, I would. But the Priestess . . ." Whyn swallowed hard. "You are still my brother."

"No, Whyn. Ruairi was your brother. And he is dead now."

Whyn narrowed his eyes and studied Reiv's face. "My brother may be lost, but he is not dead," he said.

Reiv turned his face from the discomfort of his brother's probing eyes. "I think it is time you left, my lord. I am sure you have more important things to do than talk to a ghost."

Whyn nodded. "Very well. But before I go, I want to leave you this. It is yours and you should have it."

Whyn snapped his fingers at a guard who stood outside the door, then reached for the scabbard held out to him. He pulled the sword from within it and held it out to his brother.

Reiv's breath caught audibly. It was The Lion! He could only stare in disbelief. Whyn was actually giving it back to him? He felt utter joy at the thought of it, and found the rare emotion almost unnerving, but as much as he wanted to take the sword, he could not reach his hand out to it. It was a peace offering on his brother's part and were he to take it, he would be accepting the gesture. Reiv folded his arms across his chest.

Whyn laid the sword and scabbard across the marble table and moved his gaze to Reiv's conflicted eyes. "It is rightfully yours," he said. "Keep it."

But Reiv did not move.

Whyn pursed his lips, then walked to the door. He stopped with his back to his brother, and stood silently for a moment. "You are still my brother, Ruairi," he finally said. "When I am King, things will be different." He lifted his head and stepped into the street. He did not look back.

Reiv closed the door and bolted the latch, then turned and leaned his back against it. His body was trembling now. The hostility he had managed to keep at bay during Whyn's visit was erupting again, but this time killing a plant would not appease him.

He marched over to the sword and picked it up, trying with all his might to tighten his hand around the leather-bound handle. He swung it, slicing the air, but the sword flew from his grasp and landed with a metallic *clank* against the floor.

Tears of anger welled in his eyes. "Even your gift brings me nothing but grief!" he screamed.

He stormed over to the sword and picked it up, clenching it in both hands this time, his brow tightening as he focused his attention on the grip. Taking a deep breath, he swung the sword, its gold adornment dimly reflected through the scant rays of light streaking through the room. He tightened his jaw, then thrust the blade forward with a twist of his wrist. A grin stretched across his lips as he straightened up, the weapon still held out before him.

"Yes, some day things will be different," he said. "Some day I will see my enemy's throat at the tip of my sword."

6

Summer Fires

The wagon stopped atop the last crest as its passengers paused to take in the view. Pastel meadows spilled down the mountainside, assimilating into geometric fields of barley and corn. Golden wheat danced to the beat of a symphonic wind while azure waters shimmered in the distance. But Dayn took no pleasure in the beauty of the landscape. He could not seem to drag his eyes from the festival grounds just a short distance away. Even its colorful tents, spinning costumes, and snapping banners brought him no cheer. It was just a well-orchestrated whirlpool destined to suck him into a day of misery.

He turned his attention beyond the festival grounds to Kiradyn located on the other side of them. The city was a place of religious blessings and frequent celebration, but to Dayn the high-pitched roofs of its dark buildings looked more like daggers, poised to kill any new idea that drifted upon it. He shifted his gaze to the waters beyond the harbor. There white-capped waves beat silently, but mightily, against rocks that rose from the sea like monstrous spines. As Dayn scanned the distant horizon, he realized he was searching for something out there, though he couldn't imagine what. There was nothing beyond the rocks, only eddies that would suck you down, beasts that would swallow you whole, and tides that would pull you over the edge of the world. No, there was nothing to find out there. He would do better to look in the other direction

He slid off the wagon, relieved to stretch his back. Leaning his body to the side, he pulled the tightness from his muscles, and moved his gaze to the mountains. Fear still stirred within him when he looked at those peaks, but these days it was a different kind of fear. No longer was it fear of the unknown. Now it was fear of what he knew to be true.

He turned away and bent to brush the dust from his boots. But an unsettling sensation took sudden hold of him, and he straightened back up. He felt as though he were off balance, like the ground was rippling beneath his feet. A peculiar image flashed behind his eyes, then faded to darkness. He shook his head in an attempt to retrieve it, but only a foggy illusion and a queasy feeling remained to indicate it had been there at all. He clutched his stomach and stared at the ground.

"Are you all right?" Alicine asked. She was watching him from her perch in the back of the wagon, her eyes wide with concern.

Dayn reached for the side of the wagon and took a deep breath. "I—I'm fine, I think. Just got dizzy there for a minute."

Alicine rose from her seat, lifted her skirt, and stepped across the bundles of supplies. "Mother, I think Dayn's sick," she called out to Morna who had moved with Gorman to a nearby scenic overlook.

"I'm fine, Mother," Dayn shouted in their direction. He didn't want his mother to dote over him. It was probably just something he ate.

A cold wind whipped at his neck, its bite reawakening his senses. He pulled his collar close to his ears. The breeze felt oddly cool for this time of year. He turned to reach for the coat he had tossed at the last minute into the back of the wagon, but a deep rumble, so subtle at first he was not sure he had heard it, diverted his attention. He glanced up at the sky. A storm certainly would be welcome; then they could turn around and head home. To his profound disappointment the sky was as cloudless as he had ever seen it.

"Did you hear that?" he asked Alicine.

"Hear what?" she replied.

Dayn twisted his mouth. Perhaps he hadn't heard it either. Perhaps he had felt it rather than heard it. "Did you feel it, then?"

Alicine cocked her head and eyed him with suspicion. "Are you sure you aren't sick, Dayn? Your face is slightly green and—"

"No, I'm much better. Really." He took another cleansing breath. The queasiness of his stomach and the fogginess of his brain were lifting, but he could not shake the uneasy feeling that still lingered. The fleeting image had left a faint imprint of a distant memory. If only he could remember what it was.

Morna and Gorman approached the wagon and stared at him with expressions of concern. Dayn assured them he was fine, much to their obvious relief. They climbed up to the front of the wagon and Gorman took the reins. "You ready to go, son?" he asked.

"I think I'll walk, Father," Dayn said. Maybe getting his blood pumping would clear his head.

Gorman snapped the reins and the horse began the slow descent. Alicine settled herself back onto her perch, her body swaying to the movement of the wagon. The wind ballooned up her skirt, and she pushed it down with one hand while she battled wayward curls with the other. Dayn followed behind and eyed her warily. She looked especially pretty dressed in her festive best, or would have were it not for the suspicious scowl planted on her face, a scowl no doubt placed there for his benefit.

They pulled up to a cluster of wagons parked on the south side of the festival grounds. Their family always started their festival days there. That was where Gorman's clan met to catch up on the comings and goings of the family, to discuss the weather, the crops, and any topic they hadn't touched on since their last visit.

Dayn lingered by the wagon and watched his father embrace his older brother, Nort, a burly man with steely features much like Gorman's. Both had their long black hair pulled into the popular single braid, and wore similar tunics of forest green, a favorite color of the clansmen. From a distance Dayn could barely tell the two apart, they looked so similar. As he glanced around the crowd of people that milled about the wagons, some family, some not, it occurred to him that they all looked the same: same hair, same skin color, same style of clothing. For a moment, the realization took him by surprise. He was almost bored looking at all the sameness, and yet, more than anything he longed to be just like them.

"Dayn."

Dayn glanced over to see Haskel, his least favorite uncle, heading his way.

"We haven't seen you in months," Haskel said upon reaching him. He arched a dark brow. "Have you been hiding out? Ah well, I suppose it's for the best."

"No, Uncle. I've been busy."

Haskel looked Dayn up and down and frowned. "You've grown taller, boy. Didn't think it possible." He shook his head. "I suppose you can't help what you look like; it's not like you chose it."

Dayn winced and nodded. He didn't appreciate the reference to his height, but with Haskel he knew to expect nothing less. The man had never been one for courtesies, but who could blame him. He and his wife Vania were not skilled when it came to social protocols. For too many years they had lived in isolation on their farm, caring for a son who wasn't quite right. How the boy "wasn't quite right" was not clear to Dayn; he had never been allowed to meet his cousin. But it was common knowledge that Eyan was dangerous, and no one dared breach the subject whenever Haskel or Vania were around.

"Dayn, Dayn, Dayn! My goodness, what a handsome young man you've become!" Aunt Vania wrapped her short, chubby arms around his waist, and squeezed him so tight he thought the contents of his stomach would squish into his throat. He grimaced at the pressure to his gut, but hugged her back without complaint.

After the family exchanged greetings and gossip, they dispersed and made their way in small groups toward the tents beyond. Dayn was grateful for the departures. If he had to lift one more little cousin 'higher, Dayn, higher', he was certain his arms would drop from their sockets.

Alicine shifted her weight from foot to foot. "Hurry up, I've got to get to the Pavilion," she said. "The crowning is one of the first events scheduled and I have to get ready. My hair's a mess."

"You look fine," Dayn said.

"Oh, what would you know. You're a boy," she said. The smile playing across her lips revealed she knew she looked fine. She just needed the reassurances of a mirror, that was all. Obviously a brother wasn't quite the same thing.

Dayn laughed. "Fine. What do I know? And, by the way, your hair looks ugly."

Alicine slugged him, making sure the knuckle of her middle finger was extended. Dayn grabbed his arm in feigned agony, twisting his mouth and rolling his eyes. Alicine's face reddened at his dramatic display, but he kept up the act, even soliciting the aid of their mother against his sister's cruel assault. Morna scolded Alicine absentmindedly, but Alicine puffed up nonetheless. Dayn grinned a victorious grin. The blow to his arm hadn't even hurt, at least not as much as Aunt Vania's stomach squeezing, but it was so much fun seeing his sister riled.

"I'm sorry," he said through the laughter that burst from his throat. "Really, you look nice. And your punches didn't even hurt. You're such a weakling." He hooked his arm and bowed, but he wasn't being sarcastic. "I would be honored to escort you to the Pavilion, oh beautiful Summer Maiden."

Alicine smiled and looped her arm in his. "And I would be honored to have you as my escort, handsome sir," she said through girlish giggles.

They walked arm in arm down the hill toward the great tent known as the Pavilion. It was massive in size, ten times the size of any tent on the grounds. Its color was a brilliant blue and its roof would have faded into the nearly identical sky had it not been decorated with red and green symbols and its posts not been topped with snapping flags. Along its sides were cracked and faded paintings that depicted scenes of the Written Word, from Daghadar perched on a feather-like cloud, to a flood of fire and rock swallowing a screaming white-haired demon. Dayn had seen these pictures on the Pavilion walls so many times in his life that he seldom took notice of them any more. But this time he paused to look at the crudely depicted demon more carefully.

"Saying hello to your cousin?"

Dayn spun around and spotted Sheireadan leaning against a nearby support post. The boy's muscular arms were folded across his chest and a cruel smirk was smeared across his face. Dayn's first impulse was to run—that was always his first impulse when he saw Sheireadan—but Alicine was on his arm and his pride would not allow it.

"Leave him be, Sheireadan!" Alicine said. "He's done nothing to you."

"He came here, didn't he? That alone is enough to make me want to puke," Sheireadan said.

Alicine removed her arm from Dayn's and took a threatening step forward, her hands clenched.

Sheireadan curled his lip. "What are you going to do? Hit me in front of all these people? Oh, that would be grand. The Summer Maiden, picture of feminine beauty, fighting with a boy." He laughed.

"Come on Alicine," Dayn said. He took her by the arm, attempting to usher her away, but she resisted and stared Sheireadan hard in the eye. Dayn tightened his grip on her. "I said, come on. There'll be no fighting today." He pulled her along behind him and headed toward the flap that led to the back of the Pavilion.

"You can't hide, you know," Sheireadan shouted after him. "That would be impossible for someone who looks like you, now wouldn't it?" He laughed even louder than before, his delight apparent.

Dayn gritted his teeth and muttered under his breath, while Alicine twisted around to shout a select comment of her own. He yanked her arm, then continued to drag her after him.

"I can handle him, Alicine," Dayn said, stopping and jerking her to a halt. "You won't fight him on my account. Understand?"

"But Dayn—"

"No excuses! He's my problem, not yours." He glared at Alicine with tempestuous eyes, determined to get his point across. But then he spotted another problem, and it was walking in their direction. The thought of flight returned to his mind momentarily, but the fact that he was melting into a puddle made it impossible.

Dayn stared dumbly as Falyn headed their way. The girl looked as though she were floating toward them on a soft, dreamy cloud. The scenery behind her seemed to blur as strands of nut-brown hair played in slow motion around her head. Her lavender dress drifted around her body in hazy abandon, accentuating her feminine curves. Dayn sucked in his breath as a quake of nerves rippled through him. He felt shackled by his large immobile feet. If he could just get them moving there might still be time for a graceful escape.

As Falyn drew nearer, Dayn noticed a strand of hair whip across her face. She pushed it back, then reached both hands up to secure the curls that had freed themselves from the thick braid draped across her shoulder. A gust of wind grabbed the ruffled hem of her skirt and floated it up, revealing bits of white petticoat and shapely legs beneath. She pushed the sailing fabric down and held it there.

Dayn felt his throat go dry as forbidden thoughts rushed into his brain. He groaned, realizing his feelings for her would soon be all too apparent. He stepped behind his sister, but knew his sinfulness would not go unnoticed by the Maker; Daghadar was surely planning a terrible punishment for him at that very moment. Dayn crossed his arms and studied his boots. Maybe if he and Alicine just ignored the girl she would simply walk on. He glanced back up and felt his belly tighten. Alicine had stepped aside and Falyn was now standing in front of him, looking straight at him.

Dayn grinned sheepishly. Falyn was so beautiful; he could not help but stare. His eyes followed the skin that peeked over her collar to the thick braid cascading down her breast. The sun danced off her hair, highlighting the rare and subtle strands of copper that wound throughout the dark. He turned his gaze to her face and lost himself in her eyes. The golden specks within the brown seemed to sparkle like tiny autumn stars, and for a moment he imagined they were sparkling for him.

"Dayn, where have you been?" Falyn said. "I haven't seen you in such a long time." She reached a hand out and touched him on the arm.

"I—buh—the—um—I." God, he sounded like an idiot.

Falyn laughed. "What did you say? I didn't quite catch that."

Alicine nudged her brother in the ribs, then leaned in toward Falyn, her brows raised. "Oh that's just Dayn talk for 'I'm a stupid boy'," she said.

The two girls burst into giggles. Dayn's face went hot.

"Oh, don't pick on your brother so," Falyn said. She turned her gaze to Dayn who was now eyeing her up and down. "I know, I look silly in all this, don't I?" she said, twisting her body and twirling her skirt about her ankles.

"No! No, I—I think you look very—very nice," Dayn stammered. Why were the words so hard to get out of his mouth?

Falyn blushed and looked down at her feet, then up into his eyes. "Well, I am your sister's handmaiden today, so I had to look special." Her lips parted in a genuine smile.

"You always look special," Dayn said. He bit his lip. Those words had come out easily enough. "*No*, I mean—"

"No? I *don't* look special?"

"No—I mean—*yes*, you *do* look special. I mean, you *usually* look special. Like now." If only the earth would open up and swallow him whole.

"Why, thank you, Dayn. I think," Falyn said. "You look very nice, too." Then she smiled at him, the deep kind of smile that goes beyond everyday courtesies, the kind that holds special meaning, maybe even affection.

His mind raced. What did she mean? What was she saying? Was she just being nice? Did she really think he looked good? Before his befuddled brain could form another question, Alicine interrupted.

"We'd better get ready. It's almost time," she said. She grabbed Falyn's hand and pulled her toward the dressing area that was draped for privacy behind the stage. The girls waved back at Dayn as they made their way toward it. He lifted his hand in weak response.

Dayn walked over to the flap to the right of the stage and peeked inside. The stage was carpeted with cloths of yellow and green and was decorated with massive bouquets. The air was filled with a concoction of floral scents mixed with the aroma of ginger cakes and spicy meats. People, all dressed in their colorful finest, filled the massive tent. Some sat on cross-legged stools, others on picnic blankets scattered along the grassy auditorium floor. Still more stood against the back and sides of the cavernous room. The wind billowed the Pavilion walls and roof with low moans followed by quick snaps of canvas, but it could barely be heard over the loud and excited voices of the crowd.

Dayn saw his parents sitting up front on a blanket with Vania and Haskel. Spotting him, his mother motioned for him to join them. He smiled and declined with a polite wave of his hand.

A small group of musicians sat to the left of the stage as they plucked and strummed their instruments in preparation for their performance. The crowd hushed as the bandleader held up

his hands, signaling the ceremony was about to begin. A ripple of
nervous excitement made its way across the room one final time,
ending in hushed whispers.

The crowd watched with rapt attention as Eileis the Spirit
Keeper, escorted by a young man who held her arm in his, made
her way up the plank steps to the stage. The young man guided
her to the center of the platform where he bowed and backed
away, leaving her to make her usual greeting to the crowd. Her
hands were clasped in front of her and a smile stretched across
her crinkled face. The sparkle in her eyes could be seen even from
the back of the enormous room. It was always the Spirit Keeper's
role to introduce the girl who had been selected and it was apparent to everyone that she took particular delight in making the
introduction this year. Alicine had been her apprentice for years
in the art of the herbs, and the girl's skills were well known. It
was Eileis who had recommended her for Maiden.

Dayn scanned the room from his spot behind the flap, then
glanced over his shoulder at the sparsely populated grounds. He
didn't see Sheireadan amongst the crowd inside the Pavilion and
wondered if the boy was still lurking about. But he shook the
thought from his mind. What could possibly happen? There
were people everywhere.

"Let us begin with an entreaty to the Maker," Eileis said.
The crowd bowed their heads and folded their hands. "Our most
illustrious Daghadar, Maker of all things, source of all life, foun-
dation of all knowledge, please grant us on this festival day, hope
for a future."

Members of the crowd glanced amongst one another.
"What did she mean by that?" whispers could be heard asking.

She continued without pause. "Open our minds to the
truth so that we may follow in the path you have in store for us.
Lift the blindness from our eyes, the ignorance from our minds,
and the hatred from our hearts. We have feared the fire and hidden ourselves away in darkness for too long. Please, show us the
light so that we may continue in your grace." She looked up

from her folded hands and scanned the room. No one said a word.

Her eyes rested on Dayn for a moment, not long enough for anyone else to notice, but long enough for him to. She held his gaze in hers with such intensity, it became clear to him that it was for him she had been searching. He replayed the strange words of her prayer in his mind and wondered what in the world they had to do with him. His mind raced back, back to the last time he had seen the Spirit Keeper, that night almost a year ago. She had been a part of it, the conversation that revealed the truth to him. He had managed to push Eileis to the back of his mind since then, instead funneling all his resentments in the direction of his father. But now she was looking at him almost in secret communication, and the memory of her role in it swept over him like ice water.

He stared at the Spirit Keeper as though under her spell. She looked like a bent silhouette against the huge background of fluttering drapes that enshrouded her tiny frame. Her mouth was moving, yet he could hear no sound other than a droning noise like that of a great swarm of bees. The throne-like chairs, floral bouquets, and festive banners that decorated the stage began to blur into a whirling spiral. The rest of the room and everyone in it became nonexistent. Dayn was no longer where he was.

The room grew dark and eerily quiet. Dayn's common sense told him he was still standing in the Pavilion, but his mind said he was at his bedroom window, its shutters open wide to the night, the cold air playing at his neck. He pulled the blanket around his shoulders and leaned his elbows upon the sill, gazing out at the once-bright stars now pale in the approaching light of morning. He looked down, startled by voices on the porch. It was his father and Eileis, and they were arguing. He felt uneasy, as though this had happened before.

"How can you even suggest such a thing, Eileis," his father said. "No! I can't do it."

"It's time to tell him," Eileis said.

"Why? What good could come of it?"

"He already suspects."

"But he doesn't *know*. And as far as I'm concerned, he never will."

"Dayn must be told the truth. You can't keep the secret buried in a cave forever," Eileis said.

There was an uneasy hush. Dayn leaned further out the window and held his breath.

"I can't do it," Gorman said, "I couldn't bear to hurt the boy."

"He hurts every day. If anything, you would ease his pain."

"But to tell him . . ." Gorman's voice cracked.

"It will be difficult, but you knew the day would come when you would have to."

"But to tell him he's not our child, not our flesh and blood?"

"He's your child in every way that matters," Eileis said. "He'll recognize this. You must have faith in him. If he learns the truth from someone other than you, the damage could be worse, much worse."

"How do I make him understand, Eileis? Do I defend it? Tell him I rescued him from his demon-witch mother? And what if he wants to go back to the mountains? What then?"

"Gorman, you must leave Dayn's fate to Daghadar. The Maker has a plan for him, as He does for us all. But we must be patient. We must let it play out."

"Play out?" Gorman's anger was clearly building, but he kept his voice low. "I've carried the burden of this for fifteen years and can barely live with myself for it. And now I'm to just tell him and then sit back and let it play out? He's only a boy. What will this do to him?"

"It will free him," Eileis said.

Dayn felt the familiar pain return, the old wound re-opened. He stumbled back across his room toward the bed.

"So," his inner voice whispered, "it's true. I am—"

"Demon spawn!"

The hissing voice at Dayn's back jerked him back to reality. He whirled around, trembling, and stared into the face behind the voice—Sheireadan. The boy stood before him, his beefy fists clenching and unclenching as his jaw readied for a cruel assault of words. Dayn's chest rose and fell to the drumbeats of the music playing in the background.

"You here to spy on my sister?" Sheireadan asked. He took a threatening step forward.

"No, I'm here to see Alicine," Dayn replied, taking a step back.

Sheireadan glanced past Dayn toward the platform where the Summer Maiden and her entourage stood. "I saw you talking to Falyn earlier, cave slime. I've warned you to stay away from her, haven't I?"

"She just came up to talk to Alicine. I hardly said anything. Barely three words."

The music skipped to a new tune, a traditional folksong. The crowd cheered and clapped, crooning the well-known lyrics.

"Well, it doesn't really matter, I guess," Sheireadan said, his voice straining to be heard over the increasing noise. "From now on you'll not have more than a few words with her or any other girl for that matter."

"What—what do you mean?"

"Simple. My father, as well as every other father in Kirador, has already decided it."

The merriment of the music began to build. Strange, Dayn thought, how it didn't match the dread building in his gut. "Decided what?" he managed to ask.

"No man will ever let you court his daughter, much less marry her. It's already been decided. Everybody knows it. I'm surprised your father hasn't mentioned it. He'll have a farmhand for life." Sheireadan laughed. "Too bad the only girl you're ever going to have in your life is your sister. No marital bed for you with her. But then again, since she can't be your real sister, I suppose it's possible you and she *could*—"

Dayn's eyes bulged. An uncontrollable heat washed through him as well as an uncontrollable hatred. He had never felt this sort of rage before. At that moment he felt as though he could kill the boy right then and there. Dayn puffed his body up and raised a fist to strike.

Sheireadan's face went gray. "Stay back!" he ordered. His eyes darted around.

Dayn laughed, the same kind of cruel laugh he had heard from Sheireadan so many times before. "Stay back? Stay back? No, I will not stay back! You say I'm a demon. Well, you're right, Sheireadan. I *am* a demon. It's true. I'll not deny it." Dayn twisted his face into an evil grimace and moved in as though for the kill. "Do you know what happens when a demon gets angry?"

Sheireadan shook his head and stepped back slowly.

"He reaches into a man's chest and rips out his soul by its very roots. And then do you know what happens? The demon grinds it between his teeth and he swallows it . . . piece . . . by piece . . . by piece." Dayn grinned a wicked grin, his face contorted into demonic proportions.

Sheireadan's eyes widened, further fueling Dayn's desire to see him suffer at last. "And what becomes of the poor victim?" Dayn continued. "He roams the mountains for all eternity, a minion of the demon who devoured his soul." Dayn leaned in. "Would you like to be my minion, Sheireadan? A slave to do my bidding? *Would you?*"

Sheireadan jumped back and lost his balance, falling hard on his backside into the dirt. "Get away from me!" he cried as he crawled back in crablike motions.

Dayn straightened up, his fists still primed. "You're not so brave when your pack isn't with you."

Sheireadan scrambled up and headed for the path that led from the Pavilion. Then he stopped and turned, pointing a threatening finger Dayn's way. "I swear, demon, you'll regret forever that you ever stepped foot in Kirador. My father and the others will see to it you and your family never come around decent folk again!" And with that he ran through the sparse crowd and out to the festival grounds beyond.

Dayn closed his eyes and worked to calm his ragged breathing. He couldn't believe he had just beaten Sheireadan, but his joy was short-lived when he realized that what had been said between them was true, except for the soul-eating part. He glanced between the crack of the flap and saw Falyn on the stage. His heart fell like a stone.

The inevitability of his future flashed before him and it was terrifyingly lonely. He would never be allowed to take a wife or have a family of his own. He truly would be a farmhand to his parents for life. Now that he had revealed himself as a demon, he was more certain of it than ever. Word was sure to spread—Sheireadan would see to that—and Dayn knew his family would be made to suffer. The clans and councils would hold meetings; decisions would have to be made. Would Eileis be able to defend him and his family? He couldn't take a chance. He couldn't risk harm to his family, no matter what his parents had done.

He pushed the flap back and turned his gaze to the stage, expecting to see his sister beaming at the crowd. But her eyes were focused on him, and she was not beaming. She raised an inquisitive eyebrow in his direction, then turned her attention back to the audience, forcing a brief smile for their benefit. She looked back at him and mouthed a silent word of inquiry.

Dayn could tell from the expression on Alicine's face that she had seen something of the altercation; the slit in the canvas would have revealed bits of it to her from where she sat on the throne. He knew he must have looked demon-like and hated that she may have seen him, seen him for what he really was.

"Please try to understand, Alicine," he whispered. He raised his hand up in farewell, fighting back the tangle of emotions pulsing through him. This was probably the last time he would ever see her.

Alicine widened her eyes. She seemed to understand that he was leaving, but she was trapped by her maidenly duties. She was not yet crowned, and for her to leap from the stage and rush toward him would be unacceptable, especially in front of all these people. She fixed her eyes upon him as though by doing so she could prevent him from leaving.

Dayn tore himself away and let the flap drop behind him. For a moment he stood transfixed, consumed by the reality of what he was about to do. He looked toward the outskirts of the festival grounds, then to the meadowlands beyond. His eyes followed the sea of grasses that waved with the wind, then upward to the checkered hillsides that led to the mountains.

"That's where I'll go," he thought. "I'll follow the river to the mountains. Then I'll go to the cave where…"

He began to walk, forcing one foot in front of the other, slowly at first and then more quickly, past tents, vendors, and wagons. He dared not look anyone in the eye for fear of being stopped. Picking up his pace, he pushed his legs through the slender grasses, their tiny black seeds clinging to his trousers. He hunched his shoulders against the wind that howled through the valley. Its groping fingers and ominous groans filled his senses with dread.

He reached the top of the first crest and paused, then turned to gaze down at Kiradyn one last time. There was no future for him there. This he knew beyond a doubt. He turned his attention back to the mountains. His path would lead him there. A gust of wind spiraled around his body, whipping his hair and stinging his eyes. *Dayn* . . . it seemed to whisper. *Dayn* . . . He pulled his tunic up around his ears and forced his feet forward.

7
Revelations

Alicine pushed through the crowd, shoving bystanders aside in a most un-Maidenlike manner. The circlet of flowers on her head now sat askew, its pastel ribbons flying at her back. She bumped and dodged, oblivious to the indignant grumbles that followed, but quickly found herself halted by a wall of backsides bottlenecked at the exit. She cursed under her breath, something she never did, and bounced on tiptoes as she scanned the spot where she had last seen Dayn. The canvas flap was thrown back and a bright triangle of sunlight shone above the dark bobbing heads beneath. Surely if he were anywhere nearby she would spot him towering above the others. That is, if she could get out of the cursed place.

"Alicine! Alicine—wait!"

She twisted around toward the voice at her back and frowned. It was Falyn, elbowing her way through the crowd in her direction.

"Where are you going?" Falyn asked upon reaching her. "Your parents are looking for you."

Alicine shot Falyn an impatient glare, suddenly aware of a hostility creeping into her gut at the sight of the girl. "Tell them I'm looking for Dayn," she said coolly. She wheeled back around, shoved against the nearest back, and pushed her way between two particularly broad patrons. They growled, but she was gone before they could protest to her face.

"What do you mean, looking for Dayn? What happened?" Falyn called as she wriggled through the throng that filled Alicine's wake.

"What happened?" Alicine snapped over her shoulder. "Why don't you ask your brother that question?"

"Ask my brother? What does he—"

Alicine spun around and planted her hands on her hips. "What does he ever have to do with it, Falyn?"

Falyn took a startled step back, her eyes wide, but then they narrowed to their normal cat-like shape. "Don't play word games with me, Alicine. What did Sheireadan do to Dayn?"

"What do you care?" Alicine said. "You never cared what your brother did to him before. Why trouble yourself with it now?"

Falyn scanned the crowd, then grabbed Alicine by the arm. "We need to talk. Privately."

Alicine felt herself pulled and pushed toward the stage and the makeshift curtain that hung at its side. She would have protested had she not been so startled by the urgency of Falyn's voice and surprisingly strong grip.

"Now, tell me what happened between Dayn and Sheireadan," Falyn ordered.

Alicine shrugged her arm away. "All I know is I saw them over by the exit during the ceremony. I could just see them between the break in the flap and they were having words. I couldn't hear them over the music, thank goodness. If I had, then everybody else would have, too, and once again Dayn would have ended up taking the brunt of it. He's had enough of that in his lifetime, don't you think?" She shot Falyn a penetrating glare, determined to drive her point home.

"Of course he has. You make it sound as if I don't . . ." Falyn glanced around. "What do you think they were talking about?"

"I don't know, but from the expressions on both their faces it looked bad. What was really strange was that it was Sheireadan who ran off this time, not Dayn."

"So why are you looking for Dayn if he wasn't the one who ran away?"

"Because of the way he looked at me. He didn't have to say a word. I just knew. I could see it in his face; he was leaving."

"You make it sound like—"

"Like maybe he's going away forever or something? Why do you even care, Falyn? You barely ever paid him any attention, even when . . ." Alicine paused. She knew she should not speak for her brother, but perhaps it was time it be said.

Falyn stepped in closer. "Even when *what*?"

"Even when he was trying so hard to make you like him."

"What?" Falyn asked, drawing the simple word out slowly. "But he never had to try. I always liked him."

"Too bad you never bothered to tell him."

"How could I? I mean, I'm not allowed." Falyn looked down at her feet, clearly shamed by the words.

"I don't know why you're not allowed, but I tell you this, you'll never be the cause of Dayn's grief again. Not you, not Sheireadan. Now, if you'll excuse me, I'm going to go look for my brother."

Alicine turned and took a step, but Falyn yanked her back. "You make this out to be all my fault. You know full well why I'm not allowed."

"I know no such thing," Alicine said.

"Yes, you do. You know it's my father. That it's *all* the fathers. You know they're afraid of Dayn fraternizing with their daughters. You've heard the talk. There's no way you couldn't have."

"That sort of talk is too ridiculous to be taken seriously," Alicine said.

"Listen, Alicine, I know it's hard, but you need to take it seriously. Most people have a part in them that likes Dayn, but it's the fear of him that stays utmost on their minds. He's not a child anymore. He'll soon be of the age to court, and folks aren't going to risk him marrying and fathering more of his kind. Can't you understand that?"

Alicine clenched her shaking hands at her side. She would have knocked the girl into the dirt right then and there had her heart not reminded her that Falyn was only telling the truth.

"I've heard the gossip," Alicine said, "but after hearing it most of my life, I've learned to ignore it."

"Well, maybe this time you shouldn't have ignored it," Falyn said.

Alicine folded her arms and rolled her eyes.

"You can act all high and mighty if you want, Alicine, but isn't it possible that you just wanted it to go away? That you didn't want it interfering with *your* life anymore? Didn't you feel some sense of relief when Dayn avoided town these past several months? Wasn't it nice not to have to worry about him for a change?"

"How dare you say that to me."

"You think I don't know how it is? You think I don't know what it's like to live in the shadow of a brother's reputation? Turning a blind eye will do you no good. Trust me, I know."

"You're one to talk about turning a blind eye, Falyn. I don't recall ever seeing you stand up to Sheireadan. Where were you all those times he was beating up my brother?"

"If I'd defended Dayn it would have only made things worse for him. I couldn't bear to see him hurt anymore than he already was. If I'd defended him, Father would have found out, then he would have suspected . . . You know Father sits on the Council."

"A word from you to your father, just a word might have—"

"You don't have to live with the man, Alicine. You have no idea what it's like. Why didn't your father ever go to mine about it, or to any of the other fathers for that matter? Why didn't anyone? Why didn't you? I don't recall hearing you complain about the talk recently. Maybe you were too busy with your Summer Maiden ambitions to be bothered."

Alicine gasped, stung by the words.

"You knew it would come to this," Falyn said, eyeing Alicine's stricken face. "That one day Dayn would be forced to realize he will never fit in, no matter how hard he tried. That people will always say that he is—"

"Don't you dare say it!"

"That he's a demon. You know that's what they say."

"And what do *you* say, Falyn?"

Falyn looked around, then bent her head close to Alicine's ear. "I say he is the nicest boy I ever met," she whispered. "Even though I'm not supposed to say it."

"But you're saying it now."

"Yes, I'm saying it now. But only to you. The truth is, I like Dayn. I've always liked him. Very much." Pink rushed to Falyn's cheeks, revealing more than her words had said.

Alicine stared for a stupefied moment then sputtered, "You mean . . . you . . . care for him?"

"Sshhhh! Please, this is between us."

"He doesn't know?"

"Of course not! I couldn't tell him. I couldn't tell anyone."

"So why did you risk speaking with him this morning? What made you so brave all of a sudden?"

"I hadn't seen him in so long. I couldn't help it. I thought since you were with him it might go unnoticed. I had to see him, but now this has happened and all because of me."

Alicine calculated Falyn's pained expression, and for the first time realized that Dayn wasn't the only injured party. "I'm sorry, Falyn. I'm just scared. What if something happens to him?"

Falyn grabbed Alicine's hand in hers. "We'll find him. Come on."

They rushed toward the exit and made their way out into the blinding daylight. They didn't expect to find Dayn quickly, but it was clear that word of him had spread throughout the crowd. Patches of twittering patrons dotted the grounds, voices all aflutter with the latest gossip about the strange white-haired boy. Eyes, some dancing with delight, others dark and threatening, turned in

their direction. Swells of excited voices rose and fell. "Dayn . . .
demon . . . attacked . . ." Words Alicine could hear all too clearly
now. She and Falyn froze in their tracks, aware of the stares
aimed in their direction.

Alicine clenched the fabric of her skirt to keep her hands
from trembling. In the distance she could see Sheireadan, his
face contorted, his arms gesturing in the air. The crowd of spectators around him *oohed* and *awed,* entranced by the animated,
and no doubt exaggerated, tale he was spinning. Sheireadan
looked at Alicine and mouthed an indecipherable comment. He
pointed a shaky finger in her direction and all heads turned. It
was clear Sheireadan's encounter with Dayn had involved more
than just hurt feelings.

"My god, Dayn," Alicine whispered. "What did you *do*?"
She and Falyn looked at each other, their eyes wide.

"Alicine!" a voice called.

Alicine's heart leaped in her chest. It was her mother, calling for her through the bustling crowd at her back.

"Alicine!"

"Here, mother! Here!" She turned and rushed toward her
mother's voice, then threw herself into her arms.

"Child, what is it? Are you all right? Where's your
brother?" Morna asked as she glanced around.

"Mother, I don't know where Dayn is and people are saying
things. I don't know exactly, but I think he's run away."

"Run away?" Morna exclaimed. "But he was just watching
you get crowned, wasn't he? Didn't you see him?"

"No, Mother, he didn't see me get crowned. Sheireadan
came and—"

Morna stiffened. "Sheireadan?" She glanced toward the
boy ranting in the background, then took Alicine by the shoulders and stared into her face. "What happened, Alicine? What
did Sheireadan do? Tell me!"

"I—I'm not sure. It was hard to tell from where I was. But
Dayn looked strange, like he was going to hit Sheireadan or
something. He never did, but Sheireadan ran off anyway."

"Dayn looked strange? How? How did he look strange?"

"I don't know, his face, twisted or something. Like he was someone else, not himself. But I told you, I couldn't see it all that well."

"You say Sheireadan ran away. That doesn't sound like him."

"I think Dayn's left the festival, Mother. He looked at me odd, then waved goodbye. The next thing I knew he was gone, but there was no way I could stop him. I was up on that stupid stage." Alicine yanked the circlet off of her head and threw it to the ground. "I should have never made him come today."

"There is no time for laying blame," Morna said. "We have to find him. But first we must find your father." She ushered Alicine in front of her, then turned her head toward Falyn. "Falyn dear," she said, "you'd best be getting back to your family. Everything will be fine. You'll see."

Falyn nodded, then said, "Alicine, if you see, I mean, *when* you see Dayn, please tell him—"

"Don't worry," Alicine said, "you'll see him soon, I promise. Then you can tell him yourself." She smiled and Falyn smiled back.

Alicine and Morna made their way through the crowd as swiftly as they could, casually greeting pedestrians so as not to draw unwanted attention.

"There's your father!" Morna said, pointing in his direction.

Gorman could be seen storming toward them, his face ashen. He reached them in an instant and grabbed them both by their elbows, then spun them around in the opposite direction. "We're leaving now," he said and pushed them forward.

"But Father, what about Dayn?" Alicine asked.

"I don't think Dayn's here," Gorman said.

"But, where—" Morna started to ask.

"No questions. Just get to the wagon," Gorman ordered. He steered them between two tents, away from the crowded main corridor, and toward the hill beyond.

"But where are we going? Do you think he's headed home?"

"We're going to see Eileis," Gorman said.

"But isn't Eileis here at the festival?" Morna asked.

"No. She took ill and went home." Gorman continued to usher them toward the cluster of wagons ahead.

Morna hurried her feet to keep up the pace. "But if she's ill, should we bother her?"

"Good god, woman! Dayn knows! We have to find him!"

Morna let out a startled cry but was not allowed to break her stride. "He knows?" she cried. "He knows?"

"Knows what?" Alicine asked. But there was no reply. "Knows *what*?"

"I said no questions," Gorman barked as he steered them through the maze of rigs. "There!" He let go his grip on their arms and took off in a dead run, abandoning them entirely. Upon reaching the wagon, he leaned over the side and fumbled around, tossing blankets, bags of sundries, and baskets of food aside. Pulling out Dayn's jacket, he smiled and held it up as though it were a prize.

"He hasn't been here," he said. His face looked cautiously hopeful. "See? His coat, it's still here. Surely the boy would not plan a trek to the mountains without his coat." He scanned the hillside and the festival grounds below.

"Gorman, you know Dayn always forgets his coat," Morna said.

Gorman's face fell. He looked down into the wagon at the bags of lunch and bottles of water still sitting within it. "Get in the wagon. Now."

Alicine lifted her skirt and scrambled into the back, tripping over the debris scattered about. Morna took her place up front as Gorman leapt into the driver's seat, grabbed the reins, and whipped them across the horse's buttocks. He shouted at the horse which then took a great leap forward, jerking the wagon as well as its passengers up the bumpy hillside toward the even bumpier road beyond. Alicine clung to the box that had served as her perch, then lowered herself to the floorboards. She grabbed the side of the wagon and hung on.

The Spirit Keeper did not live far from the festival grounds and they soon arrived at her tiny cedar dwelling located at the edge of the forest. Gorman barely waited for the horse to come to a complete halt before he jumped from the wagon and ran around it to help Morna down. His hands shook as he held them out to his equally shaky wife.

Alicine rose from the lopsided pile of sundries in the back and stepped toward the end of the wagon's bed.

"No, Alicine, you stay," Gorman said.

"But, Father . . ."

"You heard me. No arguments." It was clear from his tone there would be no debating it.

Alicine scowled and crossed her arms, glaring in her parents' direction as they raced toward the house of the Spirit Keeper.

Gorman leapt over the single plank step that led to the porch and rushed to the door. He banged his fist upon it. "Eileis!" he shouted. "Eileis, open up!" He pounded again more feverishly. "I know you're in there woman! Open this door!" But he didn't wait for a response and kicked the door open with his foot.

Alicine could hear her mother's shocked gasp even from where she stood in the wagon, but her mother was not the only one shocked by Gorman's sudden irrational behavior. Alicine had seen him angry on more than one occasion—he was famous for his temper—but never like this. Then she realized it wasn't anger, it was fear, and she had never seen her father afraid of anything.

Alicine shaded her eyes from the sun and scanned the hut as well as the surrounding area. There was no sign the woman was home, no smoke from the chimney, no sounds other than the tinkle and clank of chimes fighting against the wind. Even the windows were shuttered. Alicine's trepidation was suddenly replaced by aggravation. Eileis probably wasn't even home. They should all be back at the festival looking for Dayn, not wasting their time here.

She jumped off the wagon, her legs trembling, and took a step toward the house. Nervous butterflies battled against the walls of her stomach. Her father had ordered her to stay and she knew better than to disobey, but she also knew she could not stand by.

She made her way to the side of the house nearest the wagon, careful not to be seen from the open door, and crept toward the window along its wall. Positioning herself beside it, she scanned the path that led back to the wagon. She would need a quick route of escape should her parents decide to leave. She leaned her head in toward the window. The shutter was pulled closed, but it was, as were most things around the place, hung crookedly, which left a tiny space perfect for spying. Closing one eye, Alicine peered through the crack with the other.

Eileis's entire house was one great room without walls or partitions to obstruct Alicine's view. It was dim inside, only a few lit candles scattered here and there, but she could see the Spirit Keeper clearly. The woman was sitting cross-legged on a mat in the center of the room and before her was Gorman, on his knees and pleading.

"Please, Eileis, you must help us," he said. "Dayn revealed himself at the festival. He—"

Eileis lifted a hand and silenced him. "Dayn has revealed nothing," she said. "He has always shown us his true self. Can you say the same?"

Gorman looked over at Morna who now knelt beside him and shook his head.

Eileis sighed, raised herself up from the floor, and hobbled to an overstuffed cabinet across the room. She reached in and shuffled and restacked parchments as she dug to the bottom of the pile. The great leather-bound book she pulled out was old, its pages brittle and yellow with age, its leather cover held together with a bit of frayed twine. A grin spread across Eileis's weathered features. "At last," she said, her eyes twinkling. "At last." She walked over to Gorman and Morna and laid the book before them, then settled back down on her mat.

Alicine watched her parents as they stared down at the book, their faces a mixture of fear, curiosity, and confusion. It was clear they did not know what the strange book was, but Alicine knew. It was ancient writings of Kirador, writings whose histories dated back even before those of the Written Word. Eileis had shown it to her once, but that was years ago, and Alicine could remember only bits and pieces of it now. There were stories in it, that much she recalled: stories about people of old, strange tribes of races long gone, consumed by the fire and rock of a wrathful god. Some were historical while others were fiction, based on legends and ridiculous prophecies, prophecies that had never come true, prophecies long since forgotten. Alicine leaned her ear in closer. Why was the Spirit Keeper showing her parents the book now?

"Now, Gorman, you shall have *your* lesson," Eileis said.

"We have no time for lessons, Eileis!" Gorman said. "Dayn revealed himself and is now missing. We have to find him."

"You will not find him and you must not try to," she said. "Dayn is not missing. He is returning to the cave."

"What?" Gorman gasped. "To the cave? How do you know this?"

"It was told to me. I knew it before he left."

"Then I'll find him!" Gorman said.

"No," Eileis said, "you will not." She unbound the twine that encircled the ancient book and opened it, then turned back brittle page after brittle page. "Aha . . . here," she said, pointing a gnarled finger.

"We don't have time for this," Gorman said.

"Silence!" Eileis said. She shot him an angry look then turned her gaze back down to the parchment. "Now, read."

Gorman moved his eyes over the page for a moment. "An old folk song. What does this have to do with Dayn?"

"Perhaps a great deal. I think there's more contained in these words that most realize."

"What nonsense are you talking?" Gorman said.

"These verses contain a message. A message of truth." She eyed him darkly. "But you seem to have difficulty with that concept, don't you Gorman?"

"What are you implying?" he said.

"Didn't you tell your wife that you saved the infant Dayn from a demon-witch?"

"That's the truth," he said.

"Is it?" Eileis asked. "Are you so certain the demon was not simply a woman? A woman like any other?"

"Impossible. She was white-haired and pale-skinned. Only demons are like that, made that way from years of living in the darkness."

"But Dayn's white-haired and paled-skinned, and he never lived in the darkness, except that which you made for him. But you insist a demon gave you this child. Curious thing for a demon to do. What, may I ask, did this witch-woman think you were, Gorman?"

"What does it matter what she thought?"

"Answer my question," Eileis demanded.

Gorman swallowed deeply. "She thought I was a god."

"Are you?"

"Of course not!"

"But you let her think you were? You let her think she was giving her child to a god. Would a demon have done such a thing?"

"I don't know what a demon would do, but I do know Dayn revealed himself as a demon today."

"Who said Dayn revealed himself?"

"Sheireadan said—"

"Sheireadan-ha! His words are empty air." Then Eileis's face took on an expression of newfound concern. She looked down at the book, still open to the passage, and said, "All we can do now is wait."

"Wait? Wait for what?" Morna exclaimed. She had been quiet throughout the conversation between her husband and Eileis, but now her temper was kindled. "You accuse my husband of lies, then you tell us we can't look for our son? Are you mad?"

"I believe this passage contains a message, a kind of prophecy. I believe Dayn has a part to play in it. The fact that he was brought here—by you, Gorman—and the fact that he may be going back to where you found him tells me something's at work here."

Gorman and Morna stared at the Spirit Keeper as though she herself was a demon-witch. Then Gorman turned the conversation back to his utmost concern. "Regardless of what that passage says, we can't let Dayn go to the cave. He won't know how to get there! He'll get lost! There are night creatures, there are dem—"

"He'll know to follow the river," Eileis said.

"My god, the boy doesn't even have the sense to take a coat, or food, or—" Gorman was suddenly on his feet. "I can't just stand by and do nothing! I have to find him. He won't survive out there."

Eileis rose and Morna followed her lead. Alicine watched as the three argued in the shadows. They argued about the validity of the passage Eileis had read, over whether or not they should look for Dayn, about the boy's chances of survival. Alicine listened to their words, but the meaning was only beginning to register in her mind. Dayn was born of a demon-witch? Impossible. Perhaps their father had rescued him from some strange woman, but her brother was no demon. And what was this nonsense Eileis was saying about him having a part in some old prophecy? The Spirit Keeper was surely confused. And to simply sit back and allow Dayn to go to the forbidden cave alone? Alicine straightened her spine. That would not happen. Not while she could stop it.

She turned from the window and looked toward the mountains. It did not matter what her parents did or did not decide. It did not matter what the Spirit Keeper commanded. She would find her brother, with or without their approval.

She raced back to the wagon, reached into it, and fumbled for the bag that contained the lunch her mother had prepared that morning. She slung it over the horse's back, then threw a water pouch and Dayn's coat up next to it. She unhitched the horse and led it forward a step or two. The horse twitched its ears and flank nervously. Alicine ran back and dragged out the box that had been her perch. Climbing onto it, she hiked her skirt up to her hips, then swung her legs over the horse. She grabbed hold of the reins.

"Horse, you'll have to go just a bit further today. We have to go find Dayn," she said.

The horse rocked its head, and before Alicine could kick her heels in, it took off full speed. Alicine leaned in, her legs clinging to the horse's sides with all her might, her golden skirt swirling behind her like a tempest. She would find her brother and she would bring him home, home where he belonged.

8
Flight of Fantasy

The blanket was pulled up over Reiv's head, daring even the smallest ray of light to trespass beyond it. The sanctuary he had created in his bed was a necessity, at least to his way of thinking. The moon was annoyingly bright, and the invasion of its rays upon his dark mood warranted additional protection. Even the drape that separated his room from the atrium had failed to deter the glow creeping beneath the hem, and he was left no choice but to sweat beneath his hot cocoon.

As he stared into the emptiness, the only sound was that of his breath quickening to a pant. Perhaps the nausea creeping into his gut was from the heat, or lack of air, but he didn't care. It would be morning soon, and then he would just as soon be dead anyway. When the sun rose in all its glory, Cinnia and Whyn would be wed, and he would have nothing left to live for.

Gods, Reiv thought, *just push it from your mind. It does no good to dwell on it.* He tossed onto his side, hugging his knees to his chest. *Push it from my mind? How can I? Today Cinnia will belong to Whyn. He will put his foul hands upon her and . . .* Reiv clenched his eyes, willing the image of them to disappear, but it was no use.

Maybe there is still a chance. Maybe with The Lion. Cinnia is probably waiting for me at this very moment, waiting for me to save her. His eyes flew open to the darkness, but his mind saw a far brighter vision. The fantasy consumed him, and for a moment his delusion brought him solace. But then a cold voice whispered: *You know he already has her.*

Reiv flung the blanket to the floor. "Enough!" he shouted. "Enough!" His body was drenched with sweat, and the air that rushed to envelope him felt cold and clammy against his skin. He shivered and raised himself up, then twisted around to the edge of the bed. He sat there, his bare feet planted on the tile, his hands clinging to the side of the mattress.

"You need to get a hold of yourself," he said, shaking his head to clear the foolishness. "There is nothing you can do about it." But the voice that had nagged him earlier returned, and the thought of rescue turned to that of revenge.

He rose and moved over to the trunk at the edge of the bed. It was old and large, with intricate depictions of ancient tales and children's stories carved into its graying wood. Its original owner was unknown—Reiv had inherited the trunk along with the rest of the furnishings in the apartment when he moved in—but in a way the carvings gave him comfort. There were no lions, much to his disappointment, but he still gazed at it at times, staring at it the way he used to stare at the fresco in Labhras's guestroom. But that fresco was long gone, burned to the ground with the rest of the house, and the trunk was the only source of fantastic adventures he had anymore.

He lifted the lid and leaned it against the wall, taking care to scuff neither. The Lion lay within its scabbard, wrapped in a faded tunic he rarely wore, hidden beneath a second blanket the temperature seldom warranted. He reached in and pulled the bundle out, then unwrapped it and slid the sword from its sheath. He held it up and rotated it, the imagined power of the weapon surging through him.

Reiv set the sword down and pulled on his gloves, determined the focus of everyone's fears would be on the sword in his hand, not the burns upon them. He took no time to don appropriate attire, the cloth around his hips would have to do. Snatching the weapon, he stormed through the doorway of his room, then into the blackness of the living area. He headed to the front door, needing no light to guide him. He would stop the wedding. He would save Cinnia. Then he would get his life back.

He jerked the door open and paused. The street was empty and draped in pre-dawn shadows. Tightening his grasp on the hilt, he took a determined step forward, but a burly arm threw itself in front of him and knocked him back a step.

"Oh, no you don't," a gruff voice ordered. "Get yourself back in there now."

Reiv felt his body go rigid. Guards were posted at his door!

"How dare you order me about," Reiv said with forced authority.

"I dare at the behest of the Commander," the guard said. "And his orders are that you are not to leave here 'til next morning."

"I am no prisoner! I have committed no crime. Now, out of my way." Reiv pushed against the guard and took a step past him, but a second guard grabbed him by the arm and yanked him back.

"You heard the man," the guard growled. "Get yourself back inside."

Reiv clenched the sword in his hand and eyed the guards with an open desire to murder them both where they stood.

The burly guard looked at the sword in Reiv's hand and the crazed expression on his face. "You are not supposed to have that," he said. "You know Jecta are not allowed." But he ceased the reprimand when the other guard mumbled something in his ear.

Reiv panicked. What if they tried to take the Lion from him? What if he lost it again? "It was a gift from the prince himself," he said. "He is well aware I have it. Do you question his authority?"

"No," the burly guard said, "I do not question my prince's authority. Only yours."

"I have been in here for six days now," Reiv said in a suddenly contrite voice. "I have to get some air. I am smothering."

"What does a sword have to do with getting some air?" the second guard asked.

"Nothing, I—I will put it back," Reiv said. And he would, too, if they would just let him go. He still had two hands to strangle Whyn's scrawny neck with, didn't he?

"You will put your whole self back," the burly guard said, shoving him back through the doorway. "Now, no more nonsense from you."

Reiv staggered back, struggling to keep his balance. His face went hot with humiliation and his chest ballooned with rage. Before he could think what he was doing, he rushed toward the guards, a scream of unrestrained fury escaping his throat. But he quickly found himself on his backside on the floor, the sword knocked from his hand and slung beneath the chaise some distance away.

The guards laughed as Reiv lay sprawled on the ground before them. "Settle yourself down, Jecta, or we will settle you for good," one of them said as the other pulled the door closed between them and their confrontational prisoner.

Reiv rose and threw himself hard against the door, banging it with his fists, but he knew it would only serve to entertain his captors. He stopped and leaned his forehead against the wooden barrier, then glanced over his shoulder toward the atrium. He turned and forced his feet to the partition. Pulling it back, a knot of realization welled in his throat. The sky was peach-colored now; the sun had risen. The wedding would take place soon; perhaps it already had.

As Reiv stared up at the dreaded morning sky, it occurred to him that the opening above the atrium might be a way to escape his troubles. If he could just climb over the roof, he would be free from this miserable place. He felt desperate to flee, even though he knew there was no hope of stopping the ceremony now. The temple was located in the inner quadrant, much too far to reach before the sunrise ceremony concluded. But regardless of the wedding, he refused to be anyone's prisoner. He would take himself out of there. Out of the city. Away from the memories and the painful knowledge of what had happened. What was still happening.

He rotated his body and scanned the opening above. It was too high for him to reach without help. He twisted around and searched for something, anything, to stand on.

There, the table!

A rickety thing, the atrium table's plank top was bowed by the weight of plants covering almost every square inch of it. Reiv rushed over and extended his arm, intent on sweeping the thirty or so pots to the ground. He stopped. The crash of pottery would surely draw the guards' attention. One by one, then two by two, he removed the plants and set them upon the ground. Then he dragged the table toward the corner of the atrium, gritting his teeth at the noise it made as it scraped the floor.

He moved it beneath the roof's edge and eyed its location from the perspective of where best to swing himself up. Lifting a knee to the table's edge, he glanced down and realized he did not have the sword; it was still where he had dropped it. He rushed over to the chaise and spotted the golden Lion's head jutting out from beneath, then grabbed it and scrambled back through the atrium. He skid to a halt.

"Gods, the scabbard," he said, realizing he would need both hands to pull himself up to the roof. He laughed to himself, almost amused by the fact that he had stormed out the front door earlier without it.

The drape to his room was still drawn and he threw it aside and made his way over to the bed. The scabbard was nestled in a pile of clothing he had pulled out of the trunk earlier. He secured it at his waist and slid the sword in.

He headed back to the atrium and climbed onto the table's top. He reached his arms up, but his fingertips barely reached the edge of the tile roof. Then, on tiptoe, he stretched as far as he could. No good. He was tall, but not tall enough.

Now what? There was that old familiar question again. He jumped off the table and headed back to the bedroom. The trunk would give him the additional height he needed to pull himself up to the roof. Tunics and under-things went flying as he emptied it. The container was surprisingly light, much lighter than the table, so he picked it up awkwardly and carried it out. He set it atop the table with a *thunk*.

He clambered up, balanced himself upon the arched lid, and grabbed hold of a row of terracotta tiles. Pulling himself up to the edge of the roof, he swung a leg over and rolled onto his back. With the other leg pulled up, he lay for a moment on the slanted, lumpy tiles. He eased himself into a sitting position, then assessed his surroundings. He would have to go to the right, then back toward the alley behind the apartment building. Otherwise the guards would see him. And if they did, he would end up right back where he started, albeit probably stripped of any furniture to stand on, or even worse, tied to a chair.

Reiv rolled onto all fours and crawled across the tiles, struggling to secure his gloved fingers along the cracks between them, but a sudden landslide sent him scrambling. He grabbed for anything he could cling to as his fingers, toes, and knees fought the perilous descent. Tiles crashed to the floor beneath him. He held on and squeezed his eyes against the inevitable. To his profound relief, the landslide slowed, and he was left prone and motionless. He opened an eye, barely daring to breath.

"Gods, please don't let them have heard that," he whispered. But there was no sound from the apartment. Perhaps the guards thought he was having a fit. Perhaps this time his reputation for temper had paid off.

He continued his ascent, testing each tile first, and made his way to the other side of the roof. He eased down, feet first, on his belly. Somehow going up had been much easier. He slid to the edge of the roof where he stopped himself with his toes, then peered over his shoulder to scan the alleyway below. No one was there, but neither was there anything for him to climb down onto. He contemplated his next move, then lowered his body over the edge and hung on for one precarious moment. Squeezing his eyes shut, he released his fingers and plummeted to the ground.

He landed hard, hitting the ground with his heels, then fell back and banged his head against the earth. For an instant he thought he saw stars and the strange memory of a bright light flashing across a night sky. But then it was gone and the certainty of the early morning sky above him, as well as the hard cold ground beneath him, jarred him back to reality.

He brushed himself off, then surveyed the alleyway. The stables were located at the end of it so he hobbled in that direction. He would get Gitta, the horse in his care, and he would ride out of there. But he needed some sort of plan. There would be guards posted at the gate and he would be riding a horse that didn't belong to him, with a sword he wasn't supposed to have.

The stables were quiet as Reiv crept into them. His feet barely made a sound as they padded across the floor. The sweet smell of hay mixed with the pungent smell of horse filled his senses. He breathed it in deeply.

"Gitta," he whispered as he rounded the wall to her stall. "There is my girl." He opened the half-door and entered her enclosure. The horse whinnied and stomped her foot.

"Shhh, quiet there now," Reiv cajoled, stroking her black velvety nose. "We are going on a little adventure. Would you like that?" The horse nodded as if to say "yes". Reiv laughed and hugged her neck. "Of course you would, but you will have to play along now. I might have to do a bit of fibbing."

Gitta snorted, blowing a wad of warm snot on his arm. Reiv scowled and eyed her with playful contempt. "Oh, yes, like *you* have never fibbed about anything. I seem to recall a time when you acted like you had not been fed when in fact you had." He pulled her ear affectionately.

He bridled her, but did not bother with a saddle. He rarely did; he loved the feel of her muscled girth between his thighs when he rode. Grabbing a handful of mane, he leapt atop her back, then kicked his heels into her ribs. She headed out of the stall and through the stable doors. Reiv reined her to a halt and scanned the street before him. Empty. He would have been grateful for that fact except he knew it was because everyone was at the temple grounds, there to celebrate the wedding of Whyn and Cinnia.

Thoughts of the wedding stirred the hostility in his blood; the need for escape became overwhelming. He envisioned the horse, he on its back, streaking through the streets, crashing through the gates, carrying him to the fields and the forbidden mountains beyond. He kicked again at the horse's ribs. "Hyahh!" he screamed. The animal reared up on its hind legs and danced about for a moment, startled by the harshness of her master's command, but no doubt equally thrilled by the promise of a swift run. She bolted forward, kicking dirt from behind her hooves, and sped down the narrow street.

They rounded the last corner full speed, Reiv leaning into the horse and clinging to the black mane that blew in such contrast to the red one at his own back. They must have been an incredible sight, the two of them racing like a comet toward the gate.

The stupefied guards fell over themselves as they scrambled to swing open the gate for the approaching storm of horse and boy now screaming for them to make way. The guards jumped out of their path, one falling onto his back, another left with mud splattered across his startled face. The men could only stare in disbelief as the cyclone of red, brown, and black sped past them.

Reiv whooped and hollered, delighted at how simple it had been to escape the city gates.

"Well, Gitta," he shouted as though she could understand him over the sound of her pounding hooves, "we did not even have to fib, now did we?"

He felt quite pleased with himself and pushed all doubts from his mind. He was out of the apartment, he was out of the city, and he was free—for now.

No Turning Back

"**S**tupid, stupid, stupid."

Dayn shook his head and scowled at his once shiny boots. For two days now they had wrapped his feet in agony and he couldn't wait to peel the things off. He hobbled over to a ledge alongside the river and eased his aching body down. The cold hardness of the rock reached through his trousers, adding further discomfort to his misery. He worked to unwind the knotted bootstraps, then finally managed to kick them off. Moaning, he peeled off his cold soggy socks. His feet were in a poor state, white and shriveled and covered with angry blisters. Glaring at the boots, he plotted a diabolical scheme for their disposal. But he knew he had no choice but to keep them, and turned his attention back to his wounded feet instead.

Wincing, he tugged at a bit of skin on the back of his heel, then dabbed the blood pooling around it. He wiped the sticky redness across his trousers, muttering to himself. "I'm such an idiot. Why didn't I wear the old ones?" He shook his head and continued to pick at the sore. "You know why, dolt; in case saw *her*. A lot of good it did you. Now here you are, out in the middle of nowhere with injured feet, no coat, *and* no girl!"

He wiped at the blister, but his efforts to clean it succeeded only in exposing more raw skin. He stared at his toes, then twisted his mouth in consideration of the tender bubbles that covered them. Maybe if he just soaked them for a while. He scooted down the rock and lowered his feet into the river, gasping at the frigidity of it.

Dayn laid back and propped his hands behind his head. The sun peeked out from behind a smattering of clouds, bathing his face with warmth. He knew he should continue on, but somehow he could not will his limbs to move. His eyes grew heavy and his mind drifted. Images of home floated through his consciousness, tempting him to turn back from his folly . . . *curled up in a nice warm bed, covered with fluffy blankets . . . or sitting by the fire . . . with clean, dry clothes . . . and a heaping plate of . . . of lamb and potatoes . . . and . . .*

"Dayn! Dayn! Where *are* you? Daaayn!"

He awoke with a start, the rhythm of his heart pounding in his ears. For a moment he dared not move, but a faint voice echoed in his mind, reminding him of the reason he had awoken in the first place. Dayn sat up and shook his foggy head, then looked all around. He saw no one. It must have been a dream.

He glanced toward the bend where the river disappeared behind a cluster of trees. The mountains that peeked over them were closer now; the cave could not be much further. He rose and stretched his body, forcing the stiffness from it, then reached down for the boots. Glancing between them and his blistered feet, he regarded them both warily. Determined to give his feet a reprieve, he stuffed the socks into the boots, tied the long leather straps together, and swung them around his neck.

He picked his way among the pebbles and sharp jutting rocks of the shoreline, then turned, deciding it best to head for the embankment. The stickers of the woods would be less painful than the pointy rocks now forcing him to dance with pain. He struggled up the bank and groaned. There were brambles as far as the eye could see.

"Dayn! Dayn!"

He swiveled toward the voice in the woods, his heart both leaping and sinking at the same time. It had not been a dream after all; it was Alicine. A fleeting surge of joy coursed through him at the thought of rescue, but then he realized his sister would not be alone, so rescue might not be worth it. His father would surely be with her, there to order him back to the farm.

Hide. Just hide until they leave. There're plenty of places . . .

But it was too late. Alicine spotted him and leapt off the horse. She sprinted toward him, her filthy Summer Maiden gown tearing through brambles and branches as she fought her way through the thicket. She threw her arms around him, burying her face in his chest and between the dangling boots. "Dayn, I've been looking for you everywhere," she cried. "I was so afraid we'd lost you."

But Dayn could only stand there with his arms at his side, muted by the enormity of his sister's sentiment and the realization that his father would soon be rounding the nearest tree to cuff him about the ears and drag him home. He pushed her away and took a step back. "What are you doing here?" he asked.

"What? Why, I came looking for you." She looked at him with startled eyes, caught off guard by his cool reception as well as by his foolish question.

"Well, I didn't need finding," he said. "I'm fine."

Alicine looked him up and down. "You certainly look fine."

But Dayn knew he didn't. His clothes were damp and smeared with dirt, and his hair was cluttered by bits of leaf and twig; his feet were covered with bleeding blisters, and his fingers and toes were noticeably blue. But he didn't need her sympathies or her help. "Go home, Alicine," he said.

"What?" she said, drawing out the word. "Go home?" Her eyes changed from the redness of joyful tears to the scarlet of acute annoyance. "Fine, but you're coming back with me."

"Oh no I'm not." Dayn turned to walk away, but she grabbed him by the back of his tunic and tugged, tearing the hem.

"Now look what you've done," he said, twisting to inspect the damage to his best shirt.

Alicine's eyes widened in mortification, then she cupped her hand over her mouth to stifle her laughter.

Dayn fingered the tear in the material. "Well you're going to be the one to mend it," he grumbled. But one glance in his sister's amused direction and he was soon laughing along with her.

"What happened to your feet?" Alicine asked, her humor subsiding.

"Oh, these stupid boots," Dayn said. "I should've worn the other ones."

"Well, I guess that proves you didn't plan this adventure."

Dayn's face turned serious. "No. I decided at the festival."

Alicine took him by the hand and tugged. "Please come home, Dayn. We can make things right. I know we can."

Dayn removed his hand from hers, then crossed his arms and lowered his eyes to his feet. "I can't go back."

"Of course you can. You just walk over to the horse, get yourself up on it, and ride home with me. It's simple."

"No. It's not."

"Dayn, listen, I know why you left. Sheireadan told you what the fathers have been saying, didn't he? About not wanting you to court their daughters and all. But they could change their minds. They could. And Eileis could help."

"It's more than that. It's . . ." He paused. How in the world was he going to tell her. He gathered her hands in his. "It's more than the issue of courting, Alicine. There's something else. I overheard Father and Eileis, that night a year ago when she stayed at the house. The night I was beaten up on the path by Sheireadan. Remember? Well, I heard them talking. Father said I wasn't his son, that he'd gotten me from a demon-witch in the cave. Do you understand what that means? I'm demon-kind, Alicine. I'm not your real brother."

"I know that's what Father and Mother think," she said, "but—"

Dayn threw her hands from his. "You *knew*? You knew all this time and said *nothing*?" He turned and stormed away.

"No! I didn't know until just a couple of days ago! Please, Dayn, I only just found out!"

Alicine ran alongside him, clutching at his arm, but he shrugged her away and kept his eyes averted, focusing them on the barely navigable path instead.

"After you left we went to Eileis," Alicine continued as she worked to keep up with his long, determined strides. "Father told me to stay in the wagon, but I snuck up to the house and listened anyway. I heard them talking about how he took you from a woman. Father said she was a demon, but Eileis didn't think she was. I don't think she was either, Dayn. I think she was just a woman like any other, except—"

Dayn spun to face her. "Except she looked like a demon? And she just happened to be in the cave? Right, Alicine, she was a woman just like any other."

"But Eileis doesn't think she was a demon. And if you come back, maybe she can convince the others, too."

"And did she manage to convince Father and Mother?"

"I—I don't know."

"Well, if she can't convince them, she sure won't be able to convince anyone else, now will she? No, Alicine, there's no point in me going back with you. It'll just be more of the same."

A strange expression crossed Alicine's face. Dayn cocked his head and eyed her suspiciously. "Is there anything *else* you haven't told me?" he asked, knowing full well there was.

"Yes," she said. "Falyn."

"Falyn?" Dayn felt his empty stomach wrench. "What about Falyn?"

"I talked to her before we left the festival. She's frantic with worry about you."

Dayn laughed. "Oh, sure she is. She can't get poor Dayn off her mind, now can she?" He turned to continue his retreat.

"A matter of fact—"

"Enough of this, Alicine! I'm not going back with you, do you hear? I'm going to the cave, back to where Father found me, or rescued me, or whatever it was he did." He paused and scanned the woods around them. "Where is he anyway?"

"Home, I guess. I don't know. I came here alone."

"Alone? You came here alone?" He grabbed her by the shoulders and shook her. "Are you mad? What were you thinking?"

"I had to find you, to make you understand, to bring you home. Eileis was arguing with Father and Mother, something about them not coming after you. She thinks you are part of some . . ." She chewed her lower lip for a moment. "She thought you just needed to work things out for yourself. That Daghadar would look after you. But Dayn, you didn't even take your coat, or food, or anything."

"Did *you*?" Dayn blurted, suddenly reminded of how long it had been since he'd eaten.

"Did I what?"

"Bring food or anything?"

"Of course, right over there, it's with the—" Alicine's face fell.

"Don't tell me you've lost the horse." Dayn groaned as hope for some food in his belly slipped away.

They ran to the spot where Alicine had left the animal and searched the leaf-strewn ground for a sign of its tracks.

"There!" Alicine said. "It went that way!"

"Well, at least it's headed in the right direction," Dayn said, pleased to note the horse had gone in the direction of the mountains.

Alicine scowled. "Well, it will soon be going in the other direction."

"No, it won't," Dayn said.

"Yes, it will."

"No, it won't."

And so the argument continued as they picked their way along the thorny path that wound along the river toward the mountains.

The horse had wandered much further than they expected, surprisingly far for such an ancient animal. They had no choice but to trudge after it, even if it took them away from the river. The animal did, after all, have the food with it, and Dayn would have followed the creature to the ends of Aredyrah for a bit of sustenance in his rumbling stomach.

Alicine spotted the horse grazing in a nearby clearing and she and Dayn took off running. When they reached it, she grabbed hold of the reins and with the other hand pulled the bag that contained what was left of the food off its back. "Here," she said, handing the bag to Dayn.

He grabbed it, thrust in a hand, and pulled out an apple, then bit into it with the passion of a starving man. "Wad-els-iz-enhere?" he asked through a mouthful. He rummaged around in the sack, not caring what else was in there. Anything would do. Even beets, which he despised, would have been welcome at that point.

He gulped down another apple, a chunk of bread, and a bit of cheese before realizing he hadn't offered his sister anything. Looking at her guiltily, he noticed she was watching him. He paused mid-chew, then looked down at the bag still clutched in one hand and the chunk of cheese in the other. He held the bag out to her. "Sorry, Alicine," he mumbled.

She smiled and took it. "You're going to make yourself sick, you know, wolfing your food down like that."

Dayn glanced toward the horse and his eyes lit up—his coat! He stuffed the last bit of cheese into his mouth and wiped his dirty hands down his even dirtier pants.

"Old coat," he said, wrapping it around himself in grateful relief, "I never thought I'd say this, but I think I'd rather have you wrapped around me right now than Fal—" He froze, horrified by the wickedness of his thoughts, and turned his back to his sister, ashamed and praying she had not realized his words.

"You know, Dayn," she said, "I never did get a chance to finish telling you about her."

"Who?" Dayn asked stupidly.

"You know who. When I said she was worried, I wasn't lying."

"I don't want to talk about it." Dayn gazed out at a nearby clump of bushes, reminded of other bodily needs. "I'm very relieved to learn you weren't lying, Alicine, but right now there's something else I need to relieve." He managed a feeble laugh, aware his attempt to change the subject was a weak one, then turned and excused himself to the shrubberies.

"You can't evade the issue forever," Alicine called after him.

"Oh, yes I can," he shouted back.

Dayn made his way between the brambles and branches, but glanced back in Alicine's direction. Although they had always shared a bedroom, matters such as bodily functions were kept strictly private, and he did not intend to change that custom just because they were out in the wilderness. He twisted through a vine that had latched onto his leg, then stopped midway down a sloping bank. He finished his task, worried Alicine might come looking for him, and turned to scramble back up the embankment. But a moan, deep pitched like wind in a hollow, filled his ears. He paused, then turned to scan his surroundings. He drew a sharp breath. Down the slope, barely visible through the underbrush, yawned the wide black mouth of a cave.

He scrambled up the embankment, through the undergrowth, and back to the clearing, screaming Alicine's name the whole way back.

"There—the cave—over there—behind the—" he shouted between gulping breaths.

"No," Alicine whispered.

"Yes! Just behind those trees! I saw it!" Dayn recognized the disappointment on his sister's face. "Alicine, that's why I'm here. I have to know what's in there."

"Please, let's go home. What is there to know? The woman is surely no longer there. And if there are demons, why would you want to meet them, Dayn?"

"Because I'm one of them!"

As Dayn stared into Alicine's tearing eyes, it occurred to him that she was not a demon, so how could he even consider taking her into the cave with him? The creatures might be willing to accept him, but what of her? "You have to go back," he said.

"No. If you're not coming with me, then I'm going with you," she said.

"It's too dangerous. I don't know what I'm going to find in there and I won't risk you getting hurt. You don't belong in there."

"Well, you don't belong in there either, Dayn."

"Yes, I do—"

"No," she interrupted, "you don't. Regardless, I'll be going with you." She placed her hands on her hips and narrowed her eyes into tiny slits. Dayn knew only too well what that meant.

"Listen," she continued, "you can go on in there by yourself if you want to, but I'll just follow you."

And Dayn knew she would, too. As much as he didn't want his sister going into the cave with him, or back alone, he wanted to return home with her even less. It occurred to him that in the past Alicine had always come to his defense, but never he to hers. Maybe it was time he became the man he had always wanted to be. Maybe with his own kind he wouldn't be so afraid anymore. He clenched his jaw. If she insisted on coming, so be it. And if the demons dared threaten her, he would make them sorry they'd ever been born.

"Come on then," he said, removing the reins from her hand. "But the horse stays."

They took the water pouch and the food bag and released the horse to graze. They didn't know how long they were going to be gone and did not expect the animal to be there when they returned. But there was no sense in taking a horse into a cave, and if they weren't able to make it back, it wouldn't have been right to tether it.

They headed across the clearing, through the brambles, and down the hill toward the cave. As they grew closer, moss covered stones could be seen slanting toward the cave in a semicircular pattern. Dayn and Alicine wound their way down and in between them, and after a time reached the base of the hill. There they stopped and surveyed the area that stretched across the mouth of the cavern. As Dayn recalled the stony benches at their backs, it occurred to him that the place was an amphitheater of old. There was one similar to it in the hills of Kirador, mostly used for religious purposes. Who could have constructed this one? Surely not the Kiradyns who dared not venture to this place. But then again, evidence of them was all around. There were chimes everywhere, clinging to the surrounding trees and shrubs. They were old, many lying on the ground, broken and scattered, others barely clinging to the branches, but the chimes were obviously Kiradyn.

Dayn stared into the cavernous mouth, the musty stench of its breath assailing his nostrils. He shivered; even his coat could not protect him from the chill. It was hard to believe he had come from such a place, but he would never know for certain if he didn't venture in. He took a bold step toward it.

"Dayn, wait. It's too dark to go in there without some kind of light," Alicine said.

"Oh, I didn't think—" Dayn started to say.

"Think what? That we would need some light? What do you think demons do, glow in the dark? I don't recall you ever keeping me up at night with your radiance."

Dayn's face went hot. "Well, I don't know exactly what demons do, now do I!" he said. "It's not as though I was raised by them." But then he wondered if a demon would take a baby from its mother and not tell it the truth its whole life.

Alicine stood quietly for a moment, then her face lit up with a flash of inspiration. "I think there's something in the bag with the food." She grabbed the bag from Dayn, then set it on the ground and rummaged through it. Pulling out an amber bottle, her mouth stretched to a victorious grin.

"Look. Herbal oil. For the bread," she said.

At first Dayn thought his sister had lost her good sense, but then he realized the oil could be used for fuel. He scrambled about, looking for some firestone, bits of kindling, and a branch long enough to fashion a torch. He eyed Alicine's skirt regretfully.

"We'll need some cloth," he said.

Alicine nodded and lifted the hem of her skirt, then ripped strips from her petticoat. "Fine," she said, "but not the dress." She handed him the torn cloth.

Dayn wound the ruffle around the stick, tucked bits of grass and twig between it, and poured on some of the oil. Then he set about starting a fire.

"What about your feet?" Alicine asked.

"What about them? Drat!" He scowled, both at the reminder of his feet and the stones he was striking together with little success.

Alicine glanced toward the path that led down into the cavern. "It looks rocky in there and—"

"There!" Dayn exclaimed as a tiny flame leaped from the kindling. He lit the petticoat wick and held the torch up, grinning.

"You're going to have to put your boots back on, you know. Where are your socks?" Alicine asked.

"Soaked, and tucked in my equally soaked boots."

"Here," Alicine said. She reached down and pulled more strips from her petticoat. "Sit. Let's see what we can do about wrapping your feet."

Dayn sat down on a boulder, wriggling to get comfortable, and stretched his long legs in front of him. Alicine frowned at his feet and wiped them with a strip of the material, then went about wrapping them with the remainder.

"Well, it's not as good as warm, dry socks, but at least you should be able to put your boots back on," she said.

"Let's not use up that petticoat too soon. We'll need to save it for the torch later. I'd sure hate to have to start using that dress of yours."

"Oh, no, the dress is off limits. Maybe we'll just have to start using some of that coat of yours instead."

Dayn clutched the coat with his free hand and shook his head. "I'm never taking this coat off again." He laughed and pulled the boots from around his neck.

The area that led into the cavern was rocky and slick with the excrement of birds or some such creature, but improved the further in they went. They picked their way down a spiraling path until they stopped before a bend that would take them from the light altogether.

Dayn held the torch out in front of him with a shaky hand and looked longingly at the sunlight that was disappearing at their backs. He hesitated for a moment, then took a deep breath. Grabbing Alicine's hand, he squeezed it tight and pulled her into the blackness.

10
Faces in the Dark

Dayn and Alicine approached yet another bend and cautiously slowed their pace. The path had thus far led them to many sharp turns, and with each it had been difficult to tell what lurked beyond. Dayn thrust the torch out and peered around the corner. Other than that which was illuminated by torchlight, he could make out little else in the darkness. He held his breath and listened for any sign of movement, but all he could hear was the melancholy drip of water nearby and a droning noise somewhere in the distance. He took a hesitant step forward, motioning for Alicine to follow.

They continued on slowly, startled by the occasional sound of a wayward pebble, jumping at shadows that seemed to lung out of nowhere. The droning grew louder and louder, until at last the sound of it was almost deafening. Dayn kept the torch extended, training his eyes on the farthest reaches of the light. The path was narrow and frosty with moisture, but appeared to widen up ahead. They stepped gingerly along until at last they found themselves standing before a large chamber. They had come across many others prior to this one, but the sameness of the rooms had become predictable. This space, however, held more than the usual milky pools and spiraling rocks; a rush of gray-green water could be seen plunging down an embankment on the far side of it. As they walked toward the falls, a gentle mist settled on their faces, but the power of the water itself vibrated through their very bones.

"Why, it's an underground river," Dayn said loud enough to be heard over the roar. He reached a hand into the water, then snatched it back. "It's freezing; probably melted snow from the mountaintop." He smiled and turned his gaze to Alicine, but she didn't look very impressed.

"It probably connects with the river back home," Dayn said. "You know, like a lifeline."

Alicine's expression brightened. "So if we follow it, it will take us back to Kirador?"

"Yes. Well . . . maybe." Dayn ran his eyes along the shoreline in both directions. If they followed the river to the left, it would lead them upward, but if they followed it to the right, the direction the water was flowing, they would end up facing a wall of rock where it plunged into an opening beneath.

"We'll have to go this way," Dayn said, nodding to the left.

Alicine sighed, clearly disappointed they would not be following the river out.

They trudged up the shoreline, occasionally slipping on the steep wet trail. After some time, the ground became level and the path easier to traverse. The river skipped in and out of the rocks, then eventually disappeared altogether. They continued in the same direction, but the course of the trek seemed monotonous without the river to guide them. Their surroundings were brown and dull, and there were few landmarks to mark the way back.

"How do we know we're going in the right direction?" Alicine asked. "And what is it we're looking for exactly?"

Dayn glanced at her and felt his insides squirm. Alicine had always been afraid of the dark, even to the point of climbing into bed with him when she was little and bad dreams invaded her sleep. Now here she was stumbling around with him in the bowels of a cave.

"I don't think it will be much further," he said, trying to sound optimistic. But in reality he was worried they might never find their way out.

"Let's go back," Alicine said, stopping. "What if we keep going and don't find anything? What if we get lost and never find our way home? What if we end up in here forever?" She grabbed his sleeve and attempted to tug him back in the other direction. "What about food and light? Dayn, please. This torch can't last."

"It can't be much further. It can't. Listen, if we don't come across something soon, we'll go back. I promise." But he hated making her that promise. To go back would mean returning to a life of lies and loneliness. He felt a renewed determination to press forward. What he saw next validated it.

He rushed to a nearby wall and ran his fingers along it. "Look," he cried. "Runes!" Alicine stared at the spot where Dayn had moved the torch for a better look. They glanced at each other in surprise. The runes were clearly Kiradyn.

"What does it say? Can you read it?" Alicine asked. She raised up on tiptoes and craned her neck for a better look.

"Rejoice," Dayn said. "It says 'rejoice'."

"What is there to rejoice about in *this* place?"

Dayn frowned. Surely if he were from this place there was something to rejoice about.

They continued on. Dayn was pleased to find more runes, no doubt written to mark the way. But the path didn't need marking as there wasn't much choice in the matter. The few times when there appeared to be an alternate path, they quickly found themselves blocked. As more runes appeared, however, Dayn felt assured they were headed in the right direction. The messages always put them back on course. So far the runes had said "rejoice", "heart", and "spirit." As they trudged on, Dayn continued his search. He was anxious to complete the message that would surely lead them to their destination. But he found himself disappointed.

A wall of tumbled rocks towered before them. Dayn pushed a hand against it, but it did not budge. "Now what are we going to do?" he grumbled. He passed Alicine the torch and pushed again, both hands this time, desperately and with great effort. Hope of finding any evidence of demons or of his real mother became fleeting. He pushed again and again, grunting and kicking, but it was no use.

Alicine watched her brother mutely, then spoke in a hesitant voice. "Maybe we should just go back."

"There has to be another way," Dayn said, inspecting the wall once more. "Maybe we just missed it."

"Maybe," Alicine said, "but—"

But Dayn didn't wait for any more opinions from his sister. He turned and brushed past her, taking the torch from her as he passed. Making his way back toward the last rune they had seen, he muttered to himself. Perhaps there had been a turn in the path somewhere. It had been a while since they had located the last message, and the two before that had been spaced fairly close together. That was it. They'd missed the turn. They had gone too far.

Dayn retraced the corridor carefully, searching for a missed rune or even the tiniest crack in the rocks which could lead them down another path. Then he sprinted forward. "Look, Alicine! Another message—here! We must've missed it!" He raised the torch closer to the spot on the wall where another rune could be seen etched into the rock. "Dag—Dag—Daghadar?"

"Rejoice, heart, spirit, Daghadar?" Alicine said. "What does it mean?"

"I don't know, but look—a passage! We missed it. I knew it. We missed it."

Dayn wormed into a narrow space between the rocks. Alicine followed at his back. The path widened and the grade began to descend steeply. Before long their feet were moving one in front of the other without any effort at all.

The foul stench of sulfur hit their nostrils and they both raised a hand to cover their noses. The air, noticeably warmer, wrapped them in a sticky mist that beaded on their skin. Everything was wet and slick, and the path oozed with slime. Dayn stopped, throwing an arm out to block his sister, and stared about the place. The chamber where they now stood was large and dank. Hissing coils of putrid steam rose from gaping pits in the ground. He lowered the torch and waved it back and forth at his feet.

"What are those?" Alicine asked, pointing at the pools that bubbled around them like cauldrons.

Dayn did not respond, horrified by the realization that they must be near the place where the demons lived. He shivered, what little nerve he had dissolving. Taking Alicine by the shoulders, he spun her back to face the corridor from which they had come.

"We're going back," he said.

They took a step toward the exit, but a sudden rumble brought Alicine to her knees. She screamed and grabbed at Dayn's coat. He reached for her, but a strange noise diverted his attention to the ceiling. A dark shape could be seen rippling along it, rising and falling like a great black canopy blowing in an underground wind. Dayn blinked and wondered whether his eyes were deceiving him. But before he could ponder it further, or deny its existence altogether, the canopy took sudden flight and descended upon them in a screeching, swirling vortex of wings and claws.

Alicine screamed again and covered her head with her arms. Dayn yanked her up and waved the torch over his head. He half-pushed, half-threw her forward, but the creatures that whirled and screamed around them had blocked the way. Turning his sister around in the other direction, Dayn pushed her again. He knew it would be a further retreat this way, but there was a dark crevice up ahead; maybe it could offer a hiding place until the fury subsided. He risked a glance behind them, then took a misstep and slipped. The torch dropped into the wetness; its flame hissed and sputtered, but managed to stay lit. Dayn retrieved it and pushed himself up, then grabbed hold of Alicine, who was twirling, waving, and screaming. They fled past the belching fumes and headed for the space between the rocks. It was barely visible in the distance, but it held the hope of sanctuary. If they could just get past the living nightmare that filled the room.

The corridor beyond the crack was narrow, and at first Dayn feared he might not fit into it. He pushed Alicine in anyway and twisted his body behind her, sucking in his stomach and lifting his arms. The flames of the torch crackled and cast distorted shadows in the constricting passageway. Dayn and Alicine made their way through as quickly as they were able, stopping only when confident the creatures had abandoned their pursuit.

Dayn leaned against the wall of the tunnel, his rapid breaths echoing with Alicine's in the eerie silence. "Keep going," he said, his voice trembling almost as much as his hand.

"But Dayn, it's too narrow." Alicine glanced between her brother and the walls that seemed to converge upon him.

"Keep going," he commanded.

They made their way laboriously, Alicine now with torch in hand leading the way. Dayn scooted along behind her, his body forced at times to turn sideways. The corridor narrowed and widened, then narrowed again. The walls continued to test him, forcing him to squeeze in his gut as his chest and back scraped along. At times he felt panic squeeze at his heart as if a cruel hand had reached inside of him. Then he would become nauseated and his body would break into a cold sweat. But he never spoke a word of it.

A surprisingly cool breeze wafted through the passageway, teasing Dayn's hair as well as his spirits. Alicine turned and smiled, an expression of relief replacing her once frightened visage. She increased her pace, her tiny frame able to move between the walls with ease. Dayn struggled behind, grumbling about the decreasing light from the torch that now moved away in the hand of his sister.

He reached the end of the corridor and found himself beside Alicine, standing atop a rocky outcrop that overlooked a massive chamber. But this chamber was unlike any they had seen before. The span of the place was so vast it could have almost housed all of Kiradyn.

"Is this it?" Alicine whispered.

"I don't know," Dayn said, but in his heart he knew it must be. There could be no grander place than this.

The great chamber was illuminated in a gold-green light, as though lit by a thousand tiny candles encased in emerald glass. The strange lichen and shiny mosses that coated the walls radiated a brightness all their own, and the glow of a hauntingly green pool added to the mysterious aura of the place. Across the distance, a thundering waterfall plummeted down a towering wall of stone and plunged into the pool. The pool spilled over its banks at either end and tumbled through a maze of boulders as it rushed out opposite sides of the chamber. The waters, it seemed, had not abandoned them.

As they made their way down the sloping, rock-strewn path toward the floor of the chamber, Dayn began to notice things, familiar things. There were massive paintings splashed across the walls, much like those that decorated the Pavilion back home. Cracked and faded by time, sections of them were difficult to make out. Fragments had broken free of their rocky foundations and crumbled to the earth below. But there were faces there—he could see them—golden-haired, pale-eyed faces. Faces like his. Then he saw on the opposite walls Kiradyn faces, with dark hair and eyes. Two peoples, light on one side, dark on the other, had been here together. But when, and why?

The chamber was like a great amphitheater, much like the one they had seen outside the mouth the cave. Stone benches once again sat in a semi-circular pattern around the stage-like area where Dayn and Alicine stood. The cascading falls and glowing pool served as a spectacular backdrop.

Alicine propped the torch against a boulder and wrapped her arms around herself. "It's cold in here," she said. "What is this place; those faces, that altar?"

"Altar?" Dayn said. "What altar?

"That, over there. Isn't that what that is?" Alicine pointed to a great marble table situated at the front of the stage.

Dayn hadn't paid the table much mind before, his attentions having been primarily focused on the pictures that adorned the walls and the breathtaking natural wonder of the place. But now he found himself drawn to the rectangular slab, although he found the idea of it being an altar somewhat disquieting. He walked beside it slowly and ran his finger along its top, tracing a line in the thick layer of dust that coated its surface. There were sacrifices, or perhaps gifts, placed upon it, all carefully arranged. Some looked very old, like a tiny faded blanket and bits of clothing obviously meant for a babe. Other things, such as a toy spinner wrapped with gray chord and a carved wooden horse with black eyes, looked to be for an older child. But a knife, its blade long and narrow and its handle carved with intricate designs, was surely meant for a young man. As Dayn scanned the items he noticed that some seemed to have been placed there more recently than others. A yellow tunic lay neatly folded and was barely dusty at all. He held it up and caressed the beautiful material. It had to be for a girl; the color was too bright for any boy to wear.

Then there was a bottle. The tiny tear-shaped container was covered with dust, but Dayn found his eyes drawn to it. Something about it made him feel uneasy, yet he could not help but reach for it. As he fingered it, his prints revealed it to be made of cobalt glass, the blue of it inlaid with decorative animals fashioned from shells. He inspected the tiny figures that encircled it and felt the shock of realization. The shell beasts were much like that of the brooch his father had given him, the very one his mother had pinned to his breast just days before. He opened his coat and gazed down at the golden beast clasped to his tunic, then back to those that decorated the bottle. They were indeed the same. An indescribable longing stirred within him, and he lifted the cork from the bottle's top and brought it to his nose. He sniffed, drawing in the sweet scent, and was reminded of something familiar, though he couldn't recall what it was. He replaced the cork, then moved to set the bottle down, but found he could not do it. He didn't know why, but he could not let it go. He tucked the bottle into his coat pocket.

"Dayn, is this the place?" Alicine asked.

"It has to be," Dayn replied. "But, I really don't know what we've found. Clearly Kiradyns made their way here a long time ago, just like we have. So Father would have been able to find his way here, too, I suppose."

"Those faces, the pale ones. They don't look like demons, do they," Alicine commented, gazing up at the great murals to the right.

"Who knows what one really looks like?" Dayn replied.

"The Word says they are a ghostly white with yellow hair and grinding teeth. These look more like you," she said.

"Yes. Like me," he responded.

"The woman was probably just a woman, Dayn, not a demon."

Dayn felt anger ignite within him. "Then where is she? Why did she turn me over to a stranger? Was I a curse to her?"

Alicine looked at her feet and remained silent.

"And what about my father?" he continued. "I had to have a father—a real one, I mean. Did he hate me, too?"

"They didn't hate you. How could anyone hate their own child? But it doesn't matter now, does it? They're long gone and you won't likely find them. You still have us, though, the family that does love you. Please, Dayn, let's go home. Please."

Dayn gazed around and realized she was right. His real parents, whoever or whatever they were, were long gone. What could he do about it anyway; search his whole life for faceless strangers who might not even be alive? Maybe Alicine was right. The family that raised him was the family that loved him. Maybe things could get better back there. If he told the others about the cave, about the beautiful golden faces, maybe he could convince them he wasn't a demon.

"All right," he said. "We'll go back." He glanced up toward the spot from which they had descended and realized they would have to return to the sulfurous chamber, the one with the flying creatures. Surely there was another way out. The Kiradyns could not have ventured to this place through such a narrow passageway.

"There has to be another way back," he said. He walked over to a great tumble of stone that lay beneath the mural of Kiradyns, and picked his way along it. The rocky barrier was hidden in darkness, making it difficult to tell if there was any sort of corridor beyond. He clambered over the debris, slipping in places as he made his way further back. As his eyes adjusted, he became acutely aware of the crunch beneath his feet.

He cried out and staggered back, staring in wide-eyed horror at the ground. The debris on which he was treading was not rock as he had assumed, but something that sent his stomach to his throat. Bones, ages old and barely identifiable, lay crushed and broken beneath his feet. It was clear that more than one creature had met its fate in this place. Then he noticed bits of clothing, shoes, and jewelry. The realization that the bones were human, not animal, raised new terror in his heart.

"What is it Dayn?" Alicine shouted over at him.

"Nothing! Stay back!"

He backed his way toward her, unable to take his eyes from the carnage scattered amongst the rocks. What had happened here? Were these people sacrifices, victims of the demons and their evil god? His answer came sooner than he expected.

The earth suddenly rumbled and shifted beneath their feet. Dayn staggered toward Alicine and pulled her into his arms. They clung to each other, not knowing what to do or which way to run. Rocks creaked on the walls above, then tumbled down in thunderous roars. Great clouds of dust billowed up around them, threatening to smother them where they stood.

Dayn's eyes darted around. The horrible demon that had devoured the others was now coming for them. "We have to get out!" he cried. He directed his attention to the passageway from which they'd come. A barrage of rocks crashed down upon it as an avalanche of debris rumbled in their direction.

Dayn pulled Alicine behind him, dodging the rain of death that tested their every step. The light of the cavern dimmed. Dayn grabbed the torch where Alicine had propped it by the pool, its once crystal waters now murky with mud.

"There!" Alicine shouted. "There!" She pointed toward a pitted area in the wall, the wall beneath the fair-haired faces.

The great mural above them crackled as lightning-shaped fingers crept across the golden features. Dayn pushed Alicine toward the passage, then shoved her in and dove behind her. The faces crumbled to dust, then crashed down behind them.

They curled up against the wall, Dayn covering his sister's body with his own. A thick cloud of dust followed them in and filled the air. Alicine sobbed while Dayn held her tight. This was the end, he was sure of it. They were going to die there and no one would ever know. Then the rumbling stopped and all went quiet.

"Alicine. Are you all right?" Dayn asked between coughs. He could feel her move beneath him, but she did not reply. He lifted himself off and rolled her over gently.

Silent sobs wracked Alicine's body. Dayn pulled her into his arms. "It's all right; it's over now," he whispered.

She opened one eye, then the other, and looked around. They were in a passageway, but not the one from which they had come. The torch that lay on the ground beside them flickered ominously. Dayn rose and grabbed it up, then pulled Alicine alongside him.

"We have to get out of here," he said. "It may come back."

"But where will we go?" Alicine asked between gulping breaths.

"I don't know, but look—there are markings—there on the wall." Dayn raised the torch to the marks etched into the rock, then frowned. "But I don't know what they say. They're some other kind of rune."

"Well, I guess it doesn't matter," Alicine said. "We'll have to go this way."

"You're right. There's no going back the way we came."

Dayn took her by the hand and forced a smile. He wanted to comfort her, but how could he when there was no comforting even himself. He had brought her into this dreadful place looking for answers, but the only answers he had found were winged creatures, death, and a murderous demon wandering somewhere in the mountain.

Dayn squeezed his sister's hand in his. "Come on, Alicine. We're going home."

He pulled her into the darkness, praying the strange runes would lead them back to Kirador, but if that was not to be, then anyplace but here.

11

Captured

In the cave, time was all but lost. The strange runes vanished from the walls by the end of the first day, if it had indeed been a day, and the journey became a series of missed passageways and rocky barriers. Dayn tried to be optimistic, directing frequent words of encouragement to his sister. But her response was usually a clear but silent communication of hopelessness. Over time he too fell silent, and the only sound left was the rumbling of their hollow bellies and the crunching of rocks beneath their feet. Boredom and repetition diminished their fear of the demon, but a new fear was kindled by the realization that they would soon be feeling their way in total darkness. Although the torch was still lit, the bottle that had contained the herbal oil was now empty.

The torch sputtered until its flame weakened into a tiny orb of glowing embers. Dayn stared hard into it, willing it to re-ignite. He blew some gentle breaths onto it, and the glow brightened momentarily. Then it grew fainter, until there was nothing left to it at all.

Their rapid breaths echoed in the nothingness. Dayn fumbled for Alicine's hand. "Put your other hand out to the wall," he said. "We'll have to feel our way."

Alicine replied with a sob, but did as instructed. Dayn pulled her along for a few steps, then let go and ordered her to latch onto his coat. He needed a free hand to find his way up ahead; there had been too many unexpected walls to risk his face to one. They made their way along, their pace slowing almost to a standstill. Not only did they have to feel along with their hands, but now with their feet as well.

The wall took a sudden turn to the right, and Dayn paused before rounding it. "God, please let this lead us out," he whispered. He took a few steps in that direction, then stopped dead in his tracks. A brilliant light could be seen flooding into a wide space in the corridor ahead, as though the very hand of Daghadar had put it there. At first Dayn thought it must be a celestial vision. Maybe he had died and was taking that eternal walk into the After Place. Memories of past transgressions left him with the sinking feeling he might soon be answering for them. He looked back at Alicine, wondering if she was seeing what he was seeing. From the expression on her face, if he was taking that walk, then she was taking it with him.

Dayn quickened his pace, drawing what was left of his energy into his legs. To his profound relief, the light was not that of the After Place but of wonderful, beautiful daylight. It spilled down through an ample opening in the rocks above and angled into the corridor. Crude steps could be seen carved into the wall, curving upward to the sky.

Dayn ushered his sister ahead of him, then stumbled out behind her. Their eyes squinted at the sudden stab of sunlight and they raised their hands to shield them from the brightness. The sky was a brilliant blue, not a cloud in it, and the sun was hovering above them in its slow journey to cross the mountains.

Dayn pulled the fresh air deep into his lungs and relished the warmth of the sun against his skin. He scanned the distant landscape. From where he stood he could see patterned hillsides and a river that poured from the mountainside below. It wound like a bright blue ribbon through miles of white cedars and disappeared into a pastel horizon. Dayn drank in the sight of it. It was as though he realized the beauty of the world for the first time.

"There, you see? I told you we'd get out," he said. He smiled and put on his most confident face, but in reality he was completely surprised they had made it out of the cave alive.

"But where did we get out *to*?" Alicine asked. By her expression it was clear she believed they had only gone from being lost in one place, to being lost in another.

They were standing atop an outcrop of stone that jutted like a tongue from the mountainside. Dayn stepped to its edge and searched the distance for a familiar landmark, but there was nothing recognizable to him. At first he assumed they had wound their way back to a different location on the northern side of the mountains, the side where they had started. The voice of Kiradyn reason reminded him there was nothing on the other side of the vast range. It had vanished generations ago, or so they had always been told. Yet, he knew in his heart they were not in Kirador, and though he felt somewhat disquieted by it, the biggest part of him felt jubilant. There was life on the other side of the mountains, not death as they had been taught.

The surrounding hills sloped steeply and were covered in part by forests not so old and dense as the ones in Kirador. A vast meadow also wound along the slopes and swept downward, painting the landscape in wild, vibrant colors. Dayn's heart leapt. He felt the overwhelming desire to run through tall meadow grasses again. His time in the cave had left him craving it. Too many times in the darkness he had feared he might never see the colors of a meadow again.

"Come on, let's go," he said, grabbing Alicine's hand and pulling her along behind him. She didn't say a word, but he could feel the tension in her grip and the hesitation in her step. "We can just follow the river. If we follow the river it'll take us home."

"I don't think it will take us home," Alicine said.

"Sure it will."

"We're on the other side of the mountains, Dayn."

"You can't be sure of that. Maybe it just feels like it because we're turned around. You know, confused because we've been in the cave so long."

For some strange reason he felt it necessary to keep alive his sister's hopes of getting home, but he knew she was too clever to be fooled by his arguments. He stopped and turned to face her. "Alicine, I'm sorry I didn't get you back to Kirador like I promised. But I will. Honest. For now, though, let's just see what's down there. Maybe we'll find some apples. I'm starving, aren't you?"

Alicine's eyes brightened and she nodded. She didn't wait for him to lead the way, but marched around him and headed down the shrub-strewn mountainside. Dayn smiled, noting a sudden perkiness in her step, but then he looked down and frowned. His own feet were feeling anything but perky. Blisters still tormented him, though he had at least been able to put his socks back on when they finally dried. He dreaded removing them, however. No doubt they were stuck to crusty sores and would not come off easily.

When they reached the meadow, the first thing Dayn did was plop down, reach up a foot, and untie the straps of his boots. He didn't care how much it was going to hurt to peel the things off; it couldn't hurt as bad as the good they were going to feel afterward. As predicted, skin came off with the socks. He squeezed his toes between the blades of grass and into the damp, cool earth, then closed his eyes and groaned. Alicine laughed at the expression on his face, then followed suit, kicking off her slippers. They, too, had proved to be a poor selection. With a renewed sense of energy, they bounded through the grass.

As they made their way further into the meadow, it became apparent the flowers were no longer growing wild, but were arranged in such a manner as to suggest someone had planted them. The flowers were in neat terraced rows now, not strewn about as was nature's way, and looped along the hillsides in well-organized patterns. Dirt paths criss-crossed between the rows and there were obvious signs of cultivation. They clearly had stumbled onto a well-tended crop. The concept seemed somewhat strange, as flowers, though valued by Kiradyns, were left to grow and reproduce at will. The meadows had never failed to provide them with all they needed, so man's interference had not been required. The realization that someone, or something, tended this place put an end to their frolicking.

Dayn stopped and Alicine moved to his side. They surveyed the area silently. No one else was there, only the two of them, standing in a peaceful and incredibly beautiful countryside. Surely there was nothing, or no one, to fear in a place such as this.

Dayn reached down to pick a bright yellow blossom. He rotated its stem between his fingers as he examined the tiny petals. It looked like a buttercup or perhaps a poppy, but it was trimmed with a strange, lacy design.

"What is this one called?" he asked, glancing at Alicine. She did not seem to hear him, and continued to stare at the horizon.

"I've honestly never seen a flower like this," Dayn said. He thrust it under her nose. "Have you?"

Alicine looked at the flower with sudden interest, then took it from him and examined it. "No, never," she said.

She reached down and pulled a handful up, her eyes alight with discovery. She gathered more and brought them up to her nose, inhaling deeply.

"Maybe Mother and I could use them to make a new potion," she exclaimed. "If I saved some to take back home, I could plant the seeds." She tucked them into the side-seam pocket of her dress, then headed off to skip between the patterned rows.

Dayn followed several paces behind. He smiled. "You look like you sprouted right out of the ground," he called to her.

"What?" she called back. She looked down at her dress and at the sea of tiny white blossoms at her feet, then laughed with delight. The embroidered flowers of her skirt cascaded to the ground, blending with the others. She gathered a corner of her skirt and curtsied, then plucked another handful of the flowers.

Suddenly her smile was replaced by a look of concern, the same concern that she recognized on her brother's face. "What is it?" she asked, turning her attention in the direction of Dayn's gaze.

Dayn stared out toward the hills. "Someone is coming," he said. He crossed over to her side.

From a distance Dayn could make out few details, but it was obvious a person on horseback was galloping full speed toward them. Dayn's first inclination was to grab Alicine's hand and run the opposite direction, but they would accomplish nothing if they avoided contact with others. They needed help: food, clean clothes, a place to sleep, directions back home. No one would deny them that, would they? No, they would just have to face whoever was approaching, and pray that the person was friend, not foe.

The great whirlwind of horse and rider reached them in an instant and surrounded them in a fury of dust and apprehension. The strange boy atop the horse reined the lathered animal to a halt, nearly trampling Dayn and Alicine beneath a battering of hooves.

Alicine screamed and grabbed Dayn's arm. He pulled her close, his blue eyes flashing in the direction of the angry violet ones now staring him up and down from atop the horse.

"Why are Jecta trespassing in the fields?" the boy on the horse demanded. He steered the animal around the two of them, circling them as though herding sheep. With each pass he made, he created an invisible enclosure. He glared down at them with an expression of simmering anger.

The horse snorted and brushed against Dayn and Alicine, nudging them with its nose. The animal seemed aware of the discomfort its closeness caused, and appeared to take some delight in it. But the boy's face revealed no such delight as he stared at them with steely eyes. His mouth was hooked down in obvious distaste at the mere sight of them.

"I said, what are Jecta doing trespassing in the fields?" the boy repeated more firmly.

"I—I don't understand," Dayn said, glancing around. He didn't know what a Jecta was, but thought perhaps he might spy one.

The boy narrowed his eyes. "The question is simple enough," he said.

Dayn could feel his legs shake and prayed the stranger did not notice. The boy expected an answer from him, but he wasn't sure he would give him the right one, and didn't know the penalty should he fail to tell the boy what he wanted to hear. "We're lost."

"Lost? Do not lie to me, Jecta. You will regret it."

Dayn felt a new uneasiness as the strange eyes bore into him. It was almost as though the boy knew him somehow. But Dayn was quite certain he did not know the boy, for never in his life had he seen such a boy as this. He was tall, almost as tall as Dayn was, and certainly taller than any Kiradyn. His hair was odd, the color of fire, and though it appeared an attempt had been made to pull it back, most of it was whirled about his head and shoulders as if blown by a great and furious wind. His skin was fair, yet obviously exposed to the sun, and his violet eyes, neither pale nor dark, were of a color Dayn had never seen before. The boy wore gloves, but little else on the rest of him. His feet were bare, and the only thing covering his body was a faded black cloth tied about his hips and a belt that appeared to have the handle of a long knife sticking out of it.

Dayn glanced down at Alicine still clinging to his side, and felt sudden concern for the fact that his little sister was standing before a practically naked boy. His common sense told him this was the least of their problems at the moment, but when he saw the expression on her face, he felt a new twinge of nerves take hold. He had expected her eyes to be modestly averted from the bold display of flesh atop the horse, but he was startled to see her examining the boy, her eyes full of wonder. It was all too clear that the wonder Dayn saw there was not just the question of what was going to happen to them, but the wonder of the boy himself.

Dayn pried Alicine from his side and moved her to stand behind him. He felt her bury her head in his back momentarily, but then she peeked around and continued her inspection of the strange boy who glowered at them from his lofty place of authority.

"We didn't mean to trespass," Dayn said. "We were just looking for food, that's all."

"Do you eat Frusensias?" the boy asked, eyeing the bundle of flowers still clutched in Alicine's hand.

"Frusensias? I don't understand," Dayn said.

"Frusensias—the flowers the girl has in her hand there. I am losing patience with your act of ignorance, Jecta. You had best answer me and be quick about it. I asked you a question. You were going to eat them?"

"No, she'd just never seen any like these and—"

"So, she stole them," the boy said.

"No! I mean, well, she didn't steal them." But Dayn began to realize the ramifications of the boy's words. He recognized that the plants were being cultivated, such as a farmer would a crop of corn or barley, but in his mind flowers were not such a crop. It had not occurred to him that they were stealing. Now, however, he was being forced to see it somewhat differently.

"I'm sorry," Dayn said. "We didn't know we were stealing. Where we're from flowers are for everyone to use and enjoy."

"Where you are from?" the boy sneered. "I know where you are from, Jecta, and you speak nothing but lies."

Alicine stepped out from behind her brother and placed her fists on her hips. "How dare you call him a liar!" she said. "He doesn't even know how to."

Dayn grabbed her by the arm to pull her back, but she shrugged it from his grasp and threw the flowers to the ground. "There, have them back," she snapped at the boy. "Eat them if you wish. I certainly have no desire to."

The boy's mouth dropped as though he had never been talked to in such a manner. He leapt from the horse and drew the long knife from the band at his waist, pointing it in Alicine's direction. Dayn took a step forward in her defense, but a quick wave of the blade tip under her chin stayed his approach.

The boy kept the weapon pointed at Alicine as he circled, surveying her up and down. His gaze lingered on the dress, and for a moment a look of puzzlement crossed his features. But he quickly regained his look of contempt and moved back around to face her.

"So, a Jecta thief dares talk to a foreman in such a manner?" he asked. He flipped her long braid across her shoulder with the tip of the blade.

Dayn felt unbridled fury explode within him; the knife became invisible to his eyes. He lunged at the boy with all his might. But in an instant he found himself pinned to the ground with the blade tip pressed against his throat.

"I said I would have my enemy at the end of my sword," the boy screamed, "and now I have!"

Dayn felt the blood trickling down his collar as he stared into the crazed eyes now inches from his. The boy's neck was bulging with fury, but his contorted face was almost unreadable. Was it recognition, hostility, or satisfaction? Dayn could not be sure, but the intent was clear enough; the boy meant to kill him.

"Please," Dayn rasped, "we didn't mean any harm."

"You lie, Whyn!"

Dayn felt the boy's hot breath on his face. "No, please, I can't win. You clearly are the victor!" He choked as the knife pushed in deeper.

"Let go of him!" Alicine screamed. She rushed over and grabbed the boy's arm, pulling the tip from Dayn's throat. "It's my fault! I took the flowers, not him! We'll do whatever you say; just let him go."

The boy's eyes fluttered and the glazed look melted as he turned them in Alicine's direction. He swallowed, then blushed as though caught doing something he should not have. The boy leaned back and eased the blade further from Dayn's throat. "Perhaps—perhaps you did not know," he said.

"We didn't; I swear it," Alicine said.

Dayn held his breath and kept his eyes on the weapon still clutched in the unpredictable hand.

The boy placed his hand on Dayn's chest to push himself up, but at that moment his expression turned to one of curiosity. "What is this?" he asked. He reached into the pocket of the coat and pulled out the tiny blue bottle, the one Dayn had found in the cave. He held it up, rotating and inspecting it, then leapt to his feet, his fury fully returned.

"So you are thieves after all!" he said.

"No, we're not!" Alicine said.

"Then where did you get this? No Jecta comes by a vessel with the lion emblem upon it, not honestly that is. This is stolen and it is you who stole it."

Dayn struggled up and wiped at the tiny stream of blood trickling down his neck. He yanked Alicine over to him. "I took it," he said. "She didn't even know I had it."

"Where did you get it?" the boy demanded.

"In the cave, but I didn't know it belonged to anyone."

"You lie, Jecta. No one goes to the cave. No one. It is forbidden for anyone to even step foot in the mountains. The gods would never allow it, especially someone like you. What Tearian home did you steal this from, thief? Tell me!"

The boy was shouting now, his face as red as his hair. He clenched the bottle in his fist as he waved it in Dayn's direction.

Dayn stood trembling, at a complete loss for words. His eyes darted between the bottle in the boy's one hand and the terrible weapon still grasped in the other.

"And just what is considered stealing where you are from, Jecta?" the boy ranted on. "Is not taking something that does not belong to you stealing? Or do you simply make up your own rules as you go along? No, I think you knew you stole the bottle when you took it, just as I think she knew she was stealing when she took the Frusensias!" He shoved the bottle back into Dayn's pocket, then ordered him to remove the coat.

Dayn complied, and the boy's eyes were instantly drawn to the brooch at Dayn's breast. The brooch glistened for a moment, the bright gold of it in such contrast to the dull cloth it was pinned to. The boy's face contorted. With a quick hand he snatched it from Dayn's tunic, leaving a jagged tear in its place.

Dayn grabbed for the beloved ornament, but a wave of the weapon forced his hand back down.

"And this?" the boy said. He thrust the brooch out, keeping it beyond Dayn's reach.

"My father gave it to me!" Dayn said. The defiance in his voice sounded strange even to his own ears, but he had no intention of letting the boy think he had stolen it.

The boy did not dispute him, nor did he accuse him further. He took Dayn's coat from him, thrust the brooch into the pocket with the bottle, and tossed the coat containing the incriminating evidence over the horse's back.

"You will both come with me," he ordered. Then he turned and grabbed Alicine by the braid of her hair.

She gasped with indignation as the boy pulled her toward him and backed toward the horse, his long knife pointed in Dayn's direction. He sheathed the weapon momentarily as he leapt onto the animal's back, Alicine's braid still in hand. She twisted in an attempt to get free, but a cruel yank stopped her efforts.

"Where are you taking us?" Dayn asked.

The boy smirked. "Where do you think I am taking you?"

"I—I don't know. That's why I'm asking."

"Watch your words, Jecta, or you will find yourself at the end of my sword again. Now, get yourself in front of the horse where I can keep an eye on you."

Dayn started to cross in front of the horse, then paused. "Can we get our shoes, first?" he asked.

"Your what?"

"Shoes—boots—to cover our feet."

The boy frowned down at Dayn's feet. "And what is the purpose of such things? To do further damage to your toes?"

Dayn looked down at the crusty blisters and realized he would probably be better off without the torturous things.

"Very well, fetch them," the boy said, "but do not be tempted to run off. I have a good grasp on this braid here and might forget to let loose should I need to go galloping after you."

Dayn nodded, then turned to scan the area for the shoes they had tossed into the grass earlier. To his relief, he spied them quickly and gathered them up. He handed Alicine her slippers, then sat down and pulled his boots on, lacing them up hastily. Alicine, unable to bend her head down far, was left to push her feet into hers as best she could. The boy watched her with obvious amusement.

Once finished, Dayn hobbled around to the front of the horse. "Which way?" he asked.

The boy scowled and motioned to the south, away from the mountains. "That way, to Tearia." From the sound of his voice, he didn't want to go there any more than they did. "What are you two called?"

"I'm Dayn and she's Alicine. What are you called?"

"What? You do not know?" The boy laughed, but whether it was due to genuine amusement or whether he was merely toying with their ignorance, Dayn was not sure.

"I am Reiv," the boy said. "Now walk."

12
March to the Gates

The walk to Tearia was painfully slow and Reiv became increasingly irritated at his own grandiose plan. The terrain was not rough, the hills from this point on were fairly easy to traverse, but to be slowed down by a girl whose braid was in his grasp, and a boy hobbling in strange foot coverings, was annoying. But even more annoying was the fact that Reiv found the Jecta boy strangely familiar, and it made him feel even more uneasy about his decision to return to Tearia.

That morning, when Reiv had stormed through the gates, the thought of starving in the wilderness seemed preferable to staying another moment in Tearia. But the further he rode from the city, the more he realized it was going to have to be preferable, as that was probably what he was going to end up doing anyway. He knew little about such things as surviving alone in the mountains of the region. Even out there he didn't belong.

But then he discovered two strangers in a field, and realized the gods had given him an opportunity to return with pride intact. The strangers were clearly Jecta thieves, and he, as foreman, had a responsibility to deal with them. Weighing what he had left

behind with what he faced ahead, Reiv realized he had a choice:
he could either take them back to Labhras with the hope of receiving some recognition for his loyalty, or he could continue
on, letting fate fall where it may. From the increasing growls in
his empty stomach, fate was looking none too pleasant. And so
he had chosen to take them back.

Now here he was, lumbering down the road to Tearia with
his two prisoners in tow. He kept a close watch on the boy, but
frequently found his eyes straying to the girl. His gaze trailed
down the long braid clenched in his hand to the head of the girl
struggling to keep a cool distance away. It was obvious she felt
contempt for him, but he sometimes caught her sneaking
glimpses in his direction when she thought he wasn't looking. As
she marched ahead of him, Reiv found himself staring at her
hair. It was shiny black and looked to be soft, although he could
not know for certain. The gloves prevented him from feeling its
texture, but even without them he would not have been able to
feel it. He imagined how long her hair must be unbound, left to
cascade down her back. An ache filled his belly as a lusty image
formed in his mind. He shook his head, flinging the foolishness
from his brain.

Reiv's curiosity shifted back and forth between the prisoners. There was nothing about them that was alike. What was
their relationship? Brother and sister? No, probably husband
and wife. It occurred to him to just ask, but then he thought
better of it. He did not want to appear too interested in them, especially the girl. It would not be proper for a foreman to behave
in such a manner.

Gitta nudged Dayn in the back, edging him forward a step
or two. He flicked her a look of impatience. She persisted and no
matter how many times he tried to sidestep her or scold her, she
always managed to find him with her nose. Finally he gave up,
and slowed his pace to walk alongside her. He looped his arm under her neck, and stroked her jaw as he assured her he was going
as fast as he could and would appreciate a bit of patience on her
part. She seemed satisfied with that, and bothered him no more.

Her attention eventually turned to Alicine, who walked a few paces back.

The first great lick caught Alicine full in the face, and she spat and wiped angrily. Reiv laughed, but Dayn went practically rigid.

"I think you'd better get your horse away," Dayn said over his shoulder to Reiv.

"Would you rather me tie the girl behind it? Or, is that why she needed her—what do you call them—shoes?" Reiv laughed again.

Alicine's face turned red.

"I am not jesting," Dayn said. "You'd best move the horse away. Alicine has a bit of a temper."

"I have yet to fear a girl, especially one so small as this. And I certainly have no fear of a Jecta," Reiv said.

Alicine's nostrils flared. "You've said that word to us over and over and I'm tired of it. What is Jecta? It's not our name, so why do you call us that?"

Reiv tugged her braid. "Are you not from Pobu?"

"What is that? A city?" Alicine asked.

"You know full well it is," Reiv replied.

"I know no such thing."

Reiv jerked her braid to rein in her lack of respect, but a third tug left him flat on the ground, staring up at the furious girl who had suddenly turned, grabbed his arm, and toppled him down from his lofty perch.

Reiv leapt up, hot-faced and furious. He dug his toes into the dirt and clenched his fists at his side. He could have struck her down, he had the right to, but he reached to regain his hold on the braid instead.

Alicine jerked her head and flung the braid from his reach. "I'm tired of you latching your dirty hands onto my hair!" She glared at his gloves, then at his face, the face that was struggling to regain some semblance of authority.

"You will do as I say, girl!" Reiv ordered.

"I don't even know you," Alicine snapped. "So why should I? You're no one to me, just some ridiculous boy who has nothing better to do than pick on innocent people."

"Ridiculous boy? I am foreman over these fields, and as such I am obligated to turn you over to the authorities for trespassing and thievery. As for your so-called innocence, the authorities will decide that issue. I think the evidence will speak for itself."

"Evidence? Ha!" Alicine said. "When the authorities, whoever *they* are, hear our story you'll come out looking like the fool you are."

"I have had enough of your insolence," Reiv said, exasperation creeping into his voice. He grabbed hold of the braid once more and pulled her toward the horse. "Now, settle yourself down and—"

"And what?" Alicine said. "You have a horse and a knife, and could run us down in an instant. I don't think it's necessary for you to leash me like an animal."

Reiv looked down at the braid clutched in his hand. Perhaps it wasn't necessary to hold onto it the entire way back. It was slowing them down and he had grown weary of it. He took a deep controlling breath and considered the possibility of a more diplomatic approach. After all, he had not forgotten all of his princely training. A bit of diplomacy might go a long way, although it was something he never thought he would use with a Jecta.

"Very well," he said, letting the braid drop. "You may walk unfettered. But not next to him." He motioned to Dayn who was now standing just steps away.

"Fine," Alicine said, tossing her braid over her back. She turned and walked a few paces ahead, then stopped, her arms crossed and her back to the boys.

"Well," she barked over her shoulder, "are we going or not?"

"I told you . . ." Dayn mumbled, as he resumed his place on the other side of the horse.

They walked for hours, no one speaking a word, and took an occasional break, but only to tend to personal needs. At first Reiv was nervous whenever Alicine slipped into the privacy of the shrubbery, but he soon relaxed his fears as he came to realize she would never leave Dayn who was always kept at Reiv's side whenever she was gone.

"Why is it so hot here?" Alicine grumbled, tugging the lace at her neck as she plodded back from her most recent visit to the thicket.

"Well, why do you wear such ridiculous—ridiculous—" Reiv waved his hand in the direction of her dress and shook his head in bewilderment.

"And why do *you* wear nothing at all?" Alicine sneered, eyeing him up and down.

Reiv steered the horse close to her. He leaned down and placed his lips near her ear. "Who was it that was complaining of the heat?" he said. He reined the horse aside and moved back a few paces, then stared hard at her back, hoping she would sense his telepathic attack. She stiffened her shoulders and marched on, offering him no satisfaction as to whether or not she did.

Night soon fell, and Reiv began to feel uneasy. The sun, which was barely over the peaks of the mountains when he first encountered the two strangers, was now almost vanished behind the horizon. Although the moon was bright, Reiv did not like the idea of making his way back to the city at night with two Jecta prisoners in tow. His nerves, however, were not nearly so apparent as those of the prisoners. The boy and girl looked frightened and could not seem to keep their eyes off the increasing shadows.

"What are you afraid of?" Reiv asked. It was a stupid question, of course, as there was plenty for them to be afraid of, thanks to him. But the discomfort of their expressions compelled him to ask anyway.

"Do—do the demons come here?" Dayn asked, his eyes darting around.

"Demons? What are those?" Reiv asked. He looked in the direction of Dayn's wide-eyed gaze, but saw nothing unusual.

"Well, if you don't know, then there must not be any," Dayn said. His voice sounded relieved, but he and Alicine exchanged nervous glances nonetheless.

Reiv cocked his head and watched them warily, then decided it was nothing more than a Jecta superstition. "Do not slow your pace," he said, "but do feel free to tell me if you see a demon."

Their arrival at the outskirts of the city of Tearia was marked by a sudden stop and a loud gasp from Dayn. Down the winding road, between a stand of shimmering poplars, the city could be seen nestled like an enormous opal in the hillside. The moon was high in the sky now, its light blanketing everything in silvery shades of blue and lavender.

Dayn stared at the city as though in a dream, the reflection of it playing off his eyes. "Is that Pobu?" he asked.

Reiv thought to be angry, to accuse the boy of lying again, but then he thought better of it. The strange Jecta was clearly entranced by the sight of the city and there was no hint of a lie on his awe-stuck face. Reiv found himself wondering if the girl was right. Perhaps Dayn truly did not know how to lie. Perhaps the boy was some kind of idiot.

"No, that is not Pobu," Reiv said. "It is Tearia."

"So Pobu is a city and Tearia is a city," Dayn said.

"Yes, and Tearia is also everything else."

"Everything else?"

"Yes, you know . . . *everything* . . . *else*," Reiv said impatiently.

"I think he means like Kirador is everything else," Alicine said to Dayn.

"Oh," Dayn said. He faced the road ahead and said nothing more.

"You there. Dayn. When we get to the gates, you keep quiet, understand?" Reiv said. "And girl, I would not recommend you attempt your temper with the guards. They are far better equipped to subdue it than I was earlier. It would not be pleasant, I assure you."

Alicine and Dayn looked back at him and nodded, then turned their attentions to the spiraling towers and snapping banners that flanked the massive gate before them. Two guards with spears in hand stepped forward and demanded that they stop.

"Why do you bar my path?" Reiv said crossly. "I have passage."

"You will not pass until you have been authorized to do so," a guard said.

"And who, may I ask, has the authority?" Reiv asked.

"I do," a voice from the shadows replied. A tall, golden-haired guard stepped out, a cruel grin stretched across white teeth, his blue eyes gleaming like hot stars. He marched over to Reiv and crossed his arms across his chest. "Well, if it is not the princeling."

"Crymm," Reiv said. "So you are still ordering the little man around."

"If you are referring to yourself, then yes," Crymm replied.

"No, I was referring to the less than illustrious guard under your command." Reiv curled his lip in the direction of the two guards flanking Crymm, both less than stellar examples of the military unit.

Crymm's grin turned to a frown. "What were you doing outside the gates, Reiv? The Guard had orders you were not to leave. I was notified you rode out of here this morning on a stolen horse."

"Gitta is under my care. You may ask Labhras if you have any doubts regarding that minor detail. As for my riding out of here, I received word there were trespassers in the fields and, holiday or not, it was my responsibility. As you can see I have brought the thieves back with me. Do you intend to keep me from my duties? I do not think Labhras would appreciate it."

Crymm walked over to Dayn and regarded him with a puzzled expression, then crossed over to Alicine who returned his critical stare with an icy one of her own.

"She looks too much for you to handle, princeling," Crymm said, laughing. "Perhaps you should leave the girl to me.

I will see to it she gets to Labhras. Eventually." He turned to the other guards who readily understood his implications. They returned his laughter with snickers of their own.

Dayn took a sudden step toward Crymm, but Reiv leapt from the horse, waylaying any intention Dayn had of defending her.

Reiv shoved Crymm back, and leaned in, nose to nose, with him. "You will stay away from her," he hissed.

Crymm saw Reiv fingering the weapon at his waist, and his face blanched. "What are you doing with that weapon?" he said, moving his hand to the regulation sword at his own hip.

"Ask Whyn. That is, if you wish to risk questioning your prince's judgment," Reiv said. "As for the weapon at your own side, I suggest you keep it hidden. I do not think you would like your legacy to be that of my murder. Or is that the ballad you would like to have sung of you?"

Crymm growled and stepped back, then straightened his shoulders and lifted his head with a renewed air of authority. "You may pass, but rest assured, if I find that you speak lies—"

"Then you may have my title," Reiv said as he remounted his horse.

They passed through without further interference from the guards, but Reiv could feel their stares bore into his back as they filed by. Crymm would check out his story with Labhras, but there was nothing to fear. He was, after all, taking the two straight away to Guard Headquarters where they would be detained and questioned. But a knot made its way into his gut as he realized a flaw in his plan. The Jecta would have to be escorted through the city; the main headquarters was located near its center. It occurred to him that this was the last eve of the marriage festivities. Tonight would be the biggest gathering of all in the inner quadrant and the streets would be teeming with revelers. The marriage would have been consummated by now; the topic on everyone's lips would be whether or not a royal heir had been conceived. For Reiv to go marching through the merriment would be seen as an act of defiance. True he had planned to stop the wedding earlier, but his head was clearer now. He knew such a bold disruption could hold dire consequences, not only for himself, but for the Jecta in his care. No, he would have to wait until morning, then he could transport them through the city. He groaned to himself as hopes of being free of the two prisoners evaporated.

Reiv directed Dayn and Alicine toward the stables where he ordered them to halt, then dismounted Gitta and led her hurriedly to her stall. Motioning the prisoners to stand against the wall, he got the horse settled, and latched the half-door behind her. He hated that he didn't have time to tend to her properly, but there was water in a trough inside and he had scooped out a bucket of feed and set it in front of her before he left.

He instructed his charges to turn left when they exited the stables, then directed them through a narrow street and down an alleyway.

Dayn, his face paler than the moonlight, looked back at Reiv. "What is going to happen to us?"

"What happens to all Jecta thieves," Reiv said.

"What's that?" Alicine asked, fear in her voice.

For a moment Reiv did not respond. How could he tell her that thieves usually lost a hand, or in some cases their lives? He felt an unexpected pang of guilt. Did she and the boy deserve such a fate as that? Other than their thievery, they seemed descent enough. He rolled the unpleasant taste of regret around in his mouth, then spat it out. Why should he care? It wasn't his fault they were criminals.

"What happens, Reiv?" Alicine repeated.

"You will find out soon enough," Reiv said. "You will be transported to Guard Headquarters in the morning. I will do what I can to encourage leniency, but I make you no promises."

He said nothing more and motioned Dayn to the left, down a main corridor, and then to the right. The side street was deserted and quiet, and the moonlight left menacing shapes in its wake. They eventually halted before a thick, wooden door that was stripped of paint. Reiv reached around them and pushed it open, then motioned them through ahead of him.

Dayn and Alicine hesitated in the doorway.

"Well, go on!" Reiv barked.

"It's dark in there," Alicine said.

"I like it that way," Reiv replied. Then he shoved them into the blackness that was his apartment.

13
Out of Control

Dayn shuffled through the threshold and into the darkness, his arms thrust out in front of him. The insistent shove of Alicine's palm against his back prodded him forward a step or two, where shin quickly met cross-legged stool. He cursed, rubbing at the latest in a series of injuries to his person, and threw an invisible glare over his shoulder.

"Slow down, Alicine," he said. "I can't see where I'm going as it is."

The door slammed behind them. "Don't go anywhere," Reiv ordered.

"Where do you think we would go?" Dayn muttered. The assault of Reiv's shoulder against his made it perfectly clear the remark was not appreciated.

Alicine stood next to Dayn, clutching his sleeve as though in terror of losing him. "It's as dark as the cave in here," she whispered.

Dayn wrapped his arm around her. "Don't worry, everything will be fine, you'll see." He could not see her face, but was certain her eyes were searching for his. Impatience welled in his chest. "Don't you have any light in this hole?" he called out. He struggled to focus his eyes, but could make out no shapes whatsoever.

A sudden flash directed his attention to a corner. Reiv's face could now be seen aglow, his features lit in a pattern of illumination projected from the lantern in his hand. Dayn recognized the boy's expression of dissatisfaction and wondered whether his own rude remark had been the cause of it. But Reiv made no reference to it, so Dayn turned his gaze to survey what little of the room there was to see.

"Further away from the door," Reiv instructed. He motioned them toward the center of what appeared to be the living area, a manageable distance from where he stood, and flicked Dayn a look of annoyance. "This hole, as you call it, is where you will be spending the night, so you had best get used to it."

Dayn winced at the remark, then guided Alicine over to where they had been instructed. He kept his eyes and ears attuned to Reiv, but more specifically to the weapon hanging at the boy's waist.

Reiv's piercing eyes remained raised to them, his brows knitted as he set the lantern in the middle of the table. "Are you thirsty?" His tone was flat and his face stern, as though the simple question was a gravely serious one. He turned his body to the side, his gaze fully upon them as he went about his task. He reached up to a cabinet along the wall, removed three mismatched mugs from its shelf, and poured an unknown drink into them from a jug. He then set two of the mugs at the end of the table nearest Dayn and Alicine while keeping the third for himself.

"I said, are you thirsty," he repeated. "I will not ask you again."

To Dayn the boy's simple act of offering drinks seemed out of place, as though he had not seen Reiv as a real person before, but some cruel enigma, incapable of common courtesies. Then Dayn realized his own manners, or lack of them, and replied, "Yes. Thank you."

Reiv instructed them to come to the kitchen table, its low, elongated benches tucked beneath. He did not appear to want them to sit, only to drink their drinks and return to where they had been standing. Alicine dallied for a moment, sniffing her mug with a crinkled nose. She dipped the tip of her tongue into it, then asked straight out if it was poison. Reiv puffed up and went to grab for her drink, but she plucked it from his outreached hand and sipped, eying him slyly. Dayn, on the other hand, gulped his down in one great swallow, delighted by the cool wetness sliding down his parched throat. If it was poison, so be it. At least it was wet.

Dayn wiped his mouth with the back of his hand and looked around the room with curiosity. He could see a few more pieces of furniture here and there, a few more odds and ends. It was clear they were in the strange boy's home, not some far worse place of confinement. The apartment was sparsely furnished and there was no sign that anyone else lived there, certainly no feminine touches. Yet Dayn detected the sweet scent of herbs and flowers, reminding him of the way their own kitchen smelled when Alicine and their mother started a season of potion making. Surely potion-making was not a craft a boy like Reiv would ever dabble in. But sure enough, along shelves and counters, tucked into every corner of the kitchen, were bottles and jars of various shapes and sizes, all containing potions of some unknown nature.

Reiv scowled as Dayn and Alicine eyed the contents of the room, seeming particularly annoyed when their attentions lingered on the bottles and jars. He ordered Alicine to finish her drink.

Alicine set her empty mug on the table next to Dayn's. The two of them stepped back to the room where they had been before. As they anticipated Reiv's next command, Alicine shifted her weight from foot to foot, tugging at Dayn's sleeve.

"What?" Dayn mouthed.

Alicine stared into his face with wide eyes and raised eyebrows. Dayn twisted his mouth. No doubt his sister was trying to communicate some sort of secret message, but her meaning was all but lost to him. Glancing over at Reiv, he leaned his ear down closer to her and whispered out the side of his mouth, "What is it?"

"Dayn, I can't wait," she said softly.

He became aware of his sister's legs crossing and bending in an obvious display of bodily discomfort. "Oh, by the Maker, Alicine," he said.

Dayn scanned the room. There were few areas of privacy, but the back part of the place was dark. Surely there was someplace... He turned his attention to Reiv, who was now removing the belt that held the weapon, and realized he did not feel comfortable approaching the unpredictable boy just yet.

"You're going to have to wait," he whispered in Alicine's direction.

"I can't."

Dayn puffed out his cheeks and released a slow breath. He was tired of them being watched every time nature called, and was becoming increasingly concerned for his sister's virtue. "Very well. I'll see what I can do." He took a step forward, contemplating a means of negotiation.

"What are you whispering about?" Reiv said crossly. He folded his arms, a clear indication that he did not really wish to know, and stared hard at Dayn who was slowly walking toward him. Reiv fingered the sword he had set on the table. "Stay where you are."

"You can't keep us prisoners," Dayn said, stopping and lifting his chin in an attempt to look brave. "You have no right, besides—"

"You are in no position to tell me what I can and cannot do," Reiv said. He pulled the sword from the sheath.

"At least allow Alicine to go," Dayn said, motioning toward her. "It's not proper for her to be here."

"Would you prefer she spend the night in jail?"

"Jail? What is jail?" Dayn asked. He knew they did not have them in Kirador, at least he didn't think they did. From the sound of Reiv's voice, however, it didn't sound like a good thing.

"You do not know what a jail is? Fine. Would you prefer I turn her over to the Guard then?"

This time Reiv's meaning was not lost and Dayn felt his stomach go sick. Glancing over at Alicine, he shook his head 'no'. The look of satisfaction on Reiv's face left Dayn frustrated at his own lack of backbone. He had already been silenced and he hadn't even addressed the question he'd intended to ask.

As if reading his thoughts, Alicine moved to Dayn's side. She scanned the room, then settled her eyes on a closed door tucked in the shadows to their left. "Please, we need that room very much," she said.

Reiv glanced toward the door with a look of surprise. "Marital comforts will have to wait, girl," he said with a snort. "Surely you and your husband do not expect to be accommodated here of all places."

Dayn's mouth dropped open at the implication while Alicine's body went noticeably stiff. She took a bold step in Reiv's direction.

"Dayn is my *brother*," she said.

"*Brother?*" Reiv said. He stared the two up and down and burst into laughter. "You must think me a fool!" But his laughter was halted when Alicine's palm met his face.

Dayn grabbed his sister's arm and yanked her back toward him. "What do you think you're doing, Alicine? Have you forgotten he has a weapon?"

Alicine's face colored to match the heat of her emotions, then she spun to face Reiv once more. His hand was pressed against his smarting cheek and his eyes were wide with disbelief.

"You struck me," he cried. "You actually *struck* me." He removed his hand and looked down at the glove as if expecting to find blood there.

"I'm . . . sorry," Alicine said somewhat unenthusiastically.

"If you wish me to plead leniency for you in the morning, this is no way to achieve it!"

Alicine lowered her eyes in feigned defeat, but not before wresting her arm from Dayn's grasp. Dayn grabbed it again.

"Alicine," he said, "we're not in Kirador and he's not one of the neighborhood boys. You'd best watch yourself or you're going to get us both killed!"

"Did you hear what he *said*?" Alicine said. "Who does he think he is?"

"I don't care who he thinks he is. All I know is we've been accused of stealing—*stealing*, Alicine. And in case you've forgotten, he has a weapon. A weapon I've met personally!"

Alicine opened her mouth, but Dayn stopped her short. "No!" he barked. "For once you'll do as I say!"

"Enough!" Reiv shouted. "The both of—"

But before he could say another word there was a loud knock at the door and a concerned voice calling his name on the other side of it.

Reiv risked a glance in the direction of the door and groaned.

"Oh gods," he whispered. "Brina, not tonight." There was no time to consider a plan to ignore her, however, for the door burst suddenly open.

"Reiv! What is happening here? I heard shouting."

Reiv closed his eyes in brief denial. How in the world was he going to explain all this? He glanced in the direction of the prisoners. Their expressions spoke of wide-eyed awe at the sight of the woman now standing in the doorway with her hands planted on her hips.

Brina marched over to Reiv, awaiting his reply. She raised an eyebrow in his direction, no doubt expecting the worst. Reiv turned his face away. She moved her gaze to the sword clutched in his hand and frowned her disapproval.

"Reiv. Explain," she ordered.

He lowered the sword as well as his eyes, humiliation bathing him. The handprint still felt hot against his cheek and he could tell from Brina's expression that she saw it. "I have everything under control," he said rigidly.

"Yes, I can see that," Brina said. She looked over at the motionless boy and girl who were half lost in the shadows, and nodded in their direction. "Who are your guests?"

"Jecta thieves." Reiv refocused his attention on the two criminals across the room. "I found them stealing in Labhras's fields."

"Why are they here?"

Reiv motioned Brina to the side in an attempt at private conversation. "Because of the festivities," he said in a low voice. "I couldn't take them to Headquarters tonight. You know that."

Brina slanted her eyes in Dayn and Alicine's direction. "But do you think it wise to bring them here?"

"I had to."

"And the sword? What could possibly necessitate that?"

"You do not understand, Brina. They are Jecta. They cannot be trusted."

Brina turned her attention to Dayn and Alicine who were still cloaked in the darkness. "Come out, you two. Let me see you," she said.

Dayn and Alicine looked at each other hesitantly, but as requested stepped forward and stood to face her.

Brina's mouth parted and her face went pale. "The boy?" she asked, throwing a look of inquiry in Reiv's direction.

"Do not be fooled by his resemblance to Whyn, Brina. He is a Jecta and a thief."

"Yes, of course . . . Whyn," she said. But from her expression the explanation was not a satisfactory one.

"Did he give you the mark?" she asked, indicting Reiv's cheek.

Reiv stiffened. "No."

"The girl then?"

"It was a misunderstanding."

"What sort of misunderstanding?"

"The girl said she required the bedchamber. I thought they were husband and wife."

Brina's eyes widened and she turned to study the precocious young woman in the corner. Then she broke into gentle laughter. "Reiv, do you not understand what the poor girl probably meant?"

"Probably meant?"

"Reiv, have you no sense at all?" Brina said, obviously surprised by his lack of it. Reiv's face reddened with sudden understanding. "What? I—Well, gods! She could have said it straight out instead of acting like it was some great mystery."

Chiding him for his masculine stupidity, Brina lit a second lantern and took it with her over to Alicine. "Come, child, I will help you tend to your needs."

Alicine went willingly, more concerned with bodily relief than any danger Brina might pose. As they walked past Reiv, Alicine curled her lip in his direction, but he kept his face averted, refusing to acknowledge her.

Reiv sat down upon the chaise and watched Dayn from the corner of his eye. Laughter could be heard through the lavatory door. Reiv scowled. What could they possibly find so amusing? He rose, muttering about how long it took women to do things, then paced a few steps back and forth. Feeling Dayn's gaze upon him, he glanced over to see an expression of amusement plastered across the boy's face.

"What do you find so amusing, Jecta?" Reiv snarled.

"Oh, nothing much, Reiv. That is your name, right? But we haven't been formally introduced, now have we, and since you don't seem to want to call me by my—"

"There is no need for formal introductions." Reiv lidded his eyes with indifference and half-turned his back to him.

"Well, I think there are. And, by the way, my name is Dayn, not Jecta. Where we come from—"

"And just where *do* you come from?" Reiv demanded, rounding on him.

Before Dayn could open his mouth to respond, Alicine and Brina returned from the lavatory.

"Reiv, enough of this," Brina said. "Your guests are tired."

She walked into his bedchamber and retrieved two blankets, the only two he owned, and handed them to Dayn and Alicine. "Here. Make yourselves a pallet on the floor there. Things will look brighter in the morning light."

"What am *I* supposed to use?" Reiv asked, indignant at Brina's sudden generosity with his blankets.

"Why nothing, dear." Brina turned her eyes to the strangers. "Boy, you are limping. Have you been injured?"

Dayn frowned down at the boots. "No, ma'am. Blisters. We walked a long way and these boots weren't a very good choice."

"Well, pull them off. Let us see what can be done. Reiv, fetch some salve so we can mend this poor boy's wounds. And bring some water and a cloth. It will do no good to treat feet covered in filth."

Reiv's jaw dropped, then snapped shut. He stormed over to the shelf and reached for a jar, then retrieved a jug of water and a rag. "What am I, some sort of servant?" he mumbled as he thrust the supplies into Dayn's hands.

Dayn wiped his feet, then rubbed the sticky ointment from top to bottom and in between each toe. "Thank you," he said. "They feel better already."

Dayn settled onto the pallet. For a long while he could feel Alicine fidgeting next to him. He glanced in her direction. Perspiration bathed her face and dampened her clothes in dark patches. She fanned her skirt, then saw him looking and stopped.

"Are you hot, dear?" Brina called from across the room. She made her way over to the pallets, then stepped around them and moved to the massive drape covering the wall behind them. Reaching up, she grabbed the great tapestry and pulled it back toward the corner of the room, securing it with a long, braided cord.

"There," she said, "that should help."

A sudden breeze drifted in, teasing at their hair. Dayn twisted around, realizing the drape served as a textile partition dividing one room from another. With the drape pulled back, he could see a large atrium revealed beyond, but in the darkness it was difficult to identify the shapes that filled it. As though on cue, the moon peeked out from behind a cloud, bathing the courtyard in bright, silvery light. Dayn's eyes widened and he nudged his sister to take a look. The atrium was filled with flowering plants, hundreds of them, all carefully tended. They both gawked at the atrium, then over at Reiv, then back at each other.

"Who'd have thought," Alicine whispered.

Dayn rolled over onto his back, determined to get some rest, but Alicine could not seem to cease her incessant movements. He nudged her and mumbled a word of complaint, but it did little good. Between her kicking of the covers and the battle going on in his mind, he doubted he would ever get to sleep. He moved onto his side and watched Reiv and Brina as they visited across the room. New questions came instantly to mind, but he just added them to the list of a hundred others he had asked himself that day. He shifted his body in an attempt to get comfortable and pulled the corner of the blanket up under his chin.

Brina watched the two strangers who were finally asleep across the room. She turned and sat down on the bench at the table, then moved her eyes to Reiv who was busy at the counter.

"Reiv, you have not removed your gloves," she said. "Do you intend to?"

"No," he replied.

"You need to apply the medicinals every night. You know that."

"What difference does it make!" He glanced at her guiltily. "I am sorry, Brina. I did not mean to snap. I will do it. Later though."

Brina rose from the bench and crossed over to him. Reiv tensed, sensing a lecture was in the making. "I was so stupid," he said, looking at his hands.

"You did what you had to do," Brina said.

"Did I?"

"Of course you did. Could you live with yourself if you had not?"

"I cannot live with myself now." Reiv stepped toward the table and sat down on the bench. He rotated his empty mug on the tabletop while Brina took her place across from him. For an awkward moment neither said a word.

"What was it like today?" Reiv finally asked. "Did Cinnia seem, you know, happy?"

"Yes, I think she is happy. She can thank you for that, my dear. If not for you, she would not even be here."

Reiv nodded, assessing whether or not it had been worth it, then telling himself for the thousandth time it had. "What of Father? Is he any better?"

Brina's face grew grim. "No. He still lingers."

Tears welled in Reiv's eyes, but he hurriedly wiped them away. "They won't even let me see him."

Brina remained silent.

"What of the rest of the family? Did anyone ask about me?"

Brina's mouth twisted as though dreading the words. "No, Reiv, they did not," she finally replied.

Reiv slammed his fist onto the table and rose, shaking. "Why did I even ask, Brina?" he shouted. "Why do I even care?"

Brina rose and walked around to him and placed a hand on his shoulder. He jerked away and stumbled against the bench, knocking it to the floor.

"I do not think I can bear all this!" he cried, digging his fists into his eyes.

But before Brina could make another move to comfort him, her attention turned to two pale eyes staring at them from the shadows.

"The boy," she whispered.

Dayn scrambled to his feet in embarrassed discovery, suddenly aware that Brina and Reiv's emotionally charged conversation was turned in his direction. Awakened by the rise and fall of voices, Dayn had found himself reluctantly eavesdropping. In the beginning he squeezed his eyes against the scene, trying to give Reiv and Brina the privacy they were due. But the passion of it was paramount, and so, like a moth to a flame, his eyes were drawn to the scene unfolding before him.

Reiv followed Brina's gaze to Dayn, now staring back at him from the corner, and lurched toward him. Reiv's face looked feral, as though his very soul lay bare upon it. Anguish, fear, anger; all radiated from him in an explosion of emotion. But it was the hatred that frightened Dayn the most.

"Reiv, stop!" Brina cried as she grabbed him by the arm.

He brushed her aside. "What did you hear?" Reiv screamed.

Dayn saw purple veins cord in the boy's neck, and he backed away. But a startling hardness rammed against his spine.

"I said what did you hear!" Reiv demanded, moving in closer.

Dayn pressed his back against the pillar and forced the saliva down his throat. "Nothing—I swear—I just woke up—the bench—the noise of the bench woke me!" He glanced down at Alicine and saw that she too was awake, her eyes as round as saucers. "Stay down," he whispered. She ignored him and rose to stand by his side.

Brina rushed to place herself between Reiv and Dayn, then turned and stared Reiv down. "Reiv!" she shouted. But his eyes did not seem to see her, even though she stood but inches in front of him. "Reiv, listen to me. He is not Whyn." Her voice became softer, more soothing. "Reiv, please hear me. He is not Whyn."

Reiv blinked in acknowledgement and took a deep breath, his jaw clenched tight.

"It is all right. The boy did not hear anything," Brina said.

Reiv regained his composure, although with obvious difficulty, while Brina offered him continued, quiet assurances and waited. Satisfied that he was no longer a prisoner of his rage, she turned to face the still quaking Dayn and Alicine. Folding her hands in front of her, Brina contemplated the two of them. Then she approached Dayn who was standing with rocking knees.

"What is your name, boy?" she asked.

"Dayn," he said. He stared at the floor, conscious of the woman's eyes upon him. It was as though she were examining him now, rather than merely looking at him.

"Dayn," she repeated.

"Yes," he said.

Reiv paced the floor. "Brina, I told you, they are Jecta thieves. There is no need to acquaint yourself with them further. The sooner they are out of here the better."

"We are not thieves!" Alicine said. "Please, lady, we didn't know we were trespassing. I did pick some flowers, but only because I'd never seen any like them before. I meant no harm; *we* meant no harm."

"Reiv," Brina said, "is it possible this was yet another misunderstanding?"

"Misunderstanding?" he practically shouted. He stormed over to Dayn's coat that had been thrown by the door earlier and grabbed it up, then pulled out the tiny bottle that was stuffed in the pocket. Holding it up, he said, "Do you call *this* a misunderstanding?"

Brina's hand fluttered to her breast and her breath caught audibly in her throat. "Where did you . . . get that?"

Reiv, shaken by her reaction, turned his eyes to the bottle clutched in his hand, then back to Brina's stricken face. "The same place as this," he said, pulling out the brooch. "I suggest you ask the thief where he got them."

Brina crossed over to Reiv, her hands trembling, and took the bottle from him, then the brooch. She held them on her outstretched palm momentarily, then wrapped her fingers around them. She spun around to face Dayn, and searched his face.

"Dayn," she said, "where did you get these?" Her voice was kind, not accusing, and her expression was not as one wanting details of a crime, but one who wanted answers to a much more important question.

Dayn was taken aback. Was the bottle hers? Had he stolen something that belonged to her? Bowing his head, he realized that he was indeed a thief.

"I found the bottle in a cave." He jerked his head back up to her. "But the brooch is mine. It was a gift from my father!"

"A cave?" Brina whispered.

"There were other things with it, but I only took the bottle." Recognizing the futility of trying to explain his thievery, Dayn's voice cracked. "I'm sorry. I shouldn't have taken it."

Brina moved closer and continued to study his face. "Are you . . . Jecta?"

"No, I'm Dayn."

Her eyes narrowed. "No, Dayn. I mean are you *a* Jecta?"

Dayn shifted awkwardly. "Forgive me, but I don't know what a Jecta is."

"Of course he is Jecta!" Reiv said. "Do not be fooled by him, Brina. He is marked somewhere, I can assure you."

"Marked somewhere," Brina echoed. Her eyes moved to Dayn's neck. "What is that there?" She motioned toward the tiny cut.

Dayn reached his hand up and fingered the wound. It was beginning to scab and was not nearly so tender as it had been. He glanced in Reiv's direction, not sure whether to tell the woman how he had come by it or not. He pulled the collar up over it and remained quiet.

Brina looked back at Reiv, obviously suspicious.

"He attacked me, Brina," Reiv blurted. "I had no choice!"

"You *cut* him?" She took a step toward Dayn. "Here, let me see it." She reached her hand toward him.

Dayn stepped back. "No," he said, "it's all right."

Brina looked down at the bottle and brooch still clutched in her hand, then back up at Dayn. An unreadable expression formed across her face. She took his hand in hers, pulling him gently. "Please, Dayn, there is nothing to fear. Let me take a look."

Dayn tried to remove his hand, but Brina squeezed it tight. He didn't want to go with her, but something told him he should. He was led to the table where he stopped and waited. Brina stared into his face, scanning every detail.

Reiv made a sudden move as though to intervene. Brina motioned him aside with a swipe of her hand.

"Please, Dayn, I have to know," she said.

Dayn swallowed hard. "Know what?" he asked.

Brina extended her hand toward Dayn's neck, but he leaned just out of her reach. She paused, coaxing him with her eyes, eyes that looked so much like his. Dayn willed his feet to back away, but they refused to obey his command. Brina's fingers brushed against his neck and pushed aside his collar. Dayn held his breath, praying the examination would be over soon.

Brina gasped and jerked her hand back as though she had been stung. There was clearly a wound on Dayn's neck, small and healing, but that was not where her eyes were focused; it was on the birthmark on the other side of it. She crumpled to the floor in a sobbing heap, crying out the word 'Keefe' as she wrapped her arms around Dayn's legs.

Dayn stared down in horror at the hysterical woman now clinging to him. He peeled her from his limbs and pushed her away, then stumbled back and fell into Alicine who had rushed to his aid.

Reiv charged over and knelt down before Brina. She was staring up at Dayn as though in a daze, tears streaming down her face.

"Brina! What is it?" Reiv cried. But all she would say between gulping breaths was "Keefe".

Brina rocked to and fro, both laughing and crying at the same time, seemingly oblivious to everyone but Dayn, who was quaking off to the side. Reiv took her by the shoulders and shook her. "Brina! Look at me! What is wrong?"

"It is him!" she cried out, pointing a shaky finger at Dayn.

"What did he do to you?" Reiv demanded, shooting Dayn an accusing glare.

Dayn's eyes darted between Brina and Reiv. Fear of Reiv's potential for violence was being rekindled. He felt a sudden urge to run, but found his legs, once again, were no longer in his control.

"Brina," Reiv said, "did he harm you? Please, tell me."

"No," she said, smiling at him through her tears. "Oh no, Reiv. He did not harm me."

"Come then, let us get you up." He lifted her from the floor and guided her to the nearby bench. Once she was settled, he knelt on the floor and faced her.

"Please, Brina. Tell me," he said.

She reached down and gathered his hands into hers. "Oh Reiv. He is back. My son is back."

Reiv pulled his hands away. "What—what do you mean?"

"It is Keefe. My son has returned to me." She gazed at Dayn, her face full of joy.

"Think what you are saying, Brina. You have no son."

Her expression changed from joyful discovery to guilty knowledge. "Yes. I do. Sixteen years ago I had a son, a beautiful son, but he was marked, here," she said, moving her fingers to her neck.

"But your child died, Brina. It died at birth."

"No, he did not die. I saved him. I gave him to a god. He said he would remove the mark. He said he would return him to me. And now, here my boy stands, come back to me."

All eyes turned to Dayn, standing as though frozen, his face unable to hide the horror of the words Brina had spoken. His mind raced and his head grew dizzy. "No," he whispered.

Brina smiled at him, her emotions evident, even if the truth was not. "Yes," she said. "You are Keefe."

"No," Dayn said, "I'm—"

His tongue grew still as he struggled to make sense of it all. Yes, he had hoped to find his mother, but this woman was not she. Wouldn't he know it if she were? Wouldn't he feel it? The birthmark was a coincidence, nothing more. The events that led him to this place could not have led him to his own mother, not so quickly as this. It was too impossible to even fathom. He looked at Brina, her face streaked with tears, yet radiant in the mistaken belief that she had found her long lost son. He felt sudden pity for her. "I'm sorry about your son," he said, "but I'm not him."

Brina rose and made her way toward him, holding out the brooch.

"You said your father gave you this. It was pinned to your clothing the day I gave you to the god. How did your father come by it?"

Dayn gaped down at the brooch. "He never said how he came by it. He just..."

His mind became a whirlwind of thoughts, mixed-up images swirling in his head, confusing him, toying with him, drawing him into the deception of this strange woman who for some unknown reason wanted him for her son. Maybe she was a demon-witch, disguised by sorcery to conceal her true self from him. Maybe she had some evil intent for him, some wicked plan for his disposal. No, he did not belong to this woman. He did not belong in this place. He had to get out. He had to go home. He backed away.

Brina reached her arms out to him. "Please, Keefe, my son, my child, I would never hurt you. I love you."

"Stay away from me," he shouted, "I'm not your son. I'm not! I'm Dayn . . . Dayn!" But his voice was not his own.

.

14
A Very Big Problem

I'm Dayn, I'm Dayn, I'm Dayn. The words echoed over and over in his mind, pounding like a hammer inside of his skull. Sweat ran down his face. He wiped his brow, then reached a hand to his collar. His eyes scanned the room. It all seemed so blurry. Where was he? What was he doing here? A tightness grabbed his belly. He remembered now. That woman. The one with eyes like his. She had touched his neck. She said he was—

"Keefe," the woman said.

Dayn shook his head. "This is not happening."

"Keefe, listen to me."

Dayn took a step back and glanced over at Alicine who was staring at him in stunned silence, then back at the woman who was approaching him with her arms extended.

"No!" he shouted. "Stay away from me!" He had trusted her. He had let her touch his neck. Then she lied to him. He thrust out a warning hand. "I said stay back!"

"Keefe . . . Dayn, please. Let me explain."

"Explain? Explain what? There's nothing to explain."

"Yes, Dayn, there is."

I have to get out of here. I have to go home. I don't belong here.
Dayn swiveled his eyes toward the door, but realized there would
be no escaping through it. Reiv was standing near it, too near.
Dayn glanced to his right, then left. There was no place to go but
back. He moved his feet in retreat, but suspected he was backing
into a trap. Familiar panic rushed through him as painful memories flooded his mind: memories of neighborhood bullies,
memories of a sword pressed to his throat, memories of lies—
from his parents, from everyone.

He twisted around and ran, but found himself stumbling
into a shadowy maze. He stopped and turned around in a slow
circle. Dark corners. Mysterious shapes. Fluttering walls of gray.
Which way? Which way? He took a determined step forward,
but stopped again. It led to nowhere. He changed direction and
snaked between rows of pots. A spindly plant grabbed hold of his
sleeve. He jerked his arm and sent it crashing to the floor. The
noise sounded like thunder. Too many obstacles. Trapped. Always trapped.

"What is this place?" he screamed. He turned round and
round, scanning the spinning room. Then he froze. There she
was. The woman. Standing at the edge of the atrium, moonlight
bathing her face in white.

"Dayn, please don't run." She was begging now, pleading.

"I have to run," he whispered.

A blur of dark braid and gold fabric rushed forward and
planted itself in front of him. Alicine balled her fists, a murderous expression splashed across her face. A familiar scene, Dayn
thought, his little sister, once again to the rescue. He ran his fingers nervously through his hair.

Alicine shook her fist in Brina's direction. "Lies!" she
yelled. "Lies!"

"No, girl, hear me," Brina said.

"He's my brother, do you hear me? He's not your son!"
Alicine took a threatening step toward the woman. "Don't touch
him," she said between clenched teeth. "Don't you dare!"

Reiv rushed to Brina's side and thrust out an arm to block her advancement. "Brina, stop! He cannot be your son. You must be mistaken."

Brina turned her face to Reiv. From the look in her eyes it was clear she had no doubt as to Dayn's identity.

Reiv directed his attention to Alicine who was still poised for battle. "Calm yourself," he said with forced control. "Brina means your brother no harm."

"Why should I believe you?" Alicine snarled. "You've caused us nothing but misery ever since we met you."

He nodded reluctantly. "True, but we need to get this sorted out, and Brina is the only one who can do it. Perhaps we should all just quiet down and listen to what she had to say."

Reiv no longer had the face of the scowling boy who had forced them at sword point from the fields to this place. The mask of hostility was gone, replaced by an expression of concern for a woman who had lost her handle on reality. Whether Reiv's suddenly calm exterior was sincere or not was difficult to determine, but Alicine lowered her fist nonetheless.

Reiv placed a hand on Brina's arm and motioned his eyes toward the kitchen. "If you and Alicine will wait at the table, I will talk to Dayn. There is some honey water in the jug there."

Brina smiled as though in agreement, then looked back at Dayn still transfixed in the atrium. Seeing her hesitation, Reiv said, "I will fetch him."

She nodded, then walked toward the kitchen. Alicine followed her reluctantly.

Reiv took a deep breath and approached Dayn. "Come to the table, Dayn," he said.

"No," Dayn said. He took a step back.

"I will not hurt you." Reiv said, pausing and turning up his palms. "See? No weapon."

Dayn glared at Brina across the way. "Well, lies hurt."

"I do not think she is lying. At least not in her own mind."

"I'm not her son. I'm not."

Reiv cocked his head and gazed at him for a moment. "Who are you then?"

"Who am I?" Dayn hesitated, then scowled at Reiv, suddenly angry with the boy, or perhaps at himself, for the seeds of doubt sprouting in his mind. He lifted his chin. "I am Dayn."

"I know that," Reiv said. "But is it possible you are more?"

"More? I—I don't know."

"Well," Reiv said, "we will not find out standing here, now will we? How about we go over to the table there and talk about it."

Dayn looked at Reiv as though he had never seen him before. He had, in fact, certainly never seen this side of him. But what Reiv said did sound reasonable and so Dayn took a small step toward him, and then another, and before long he was following him out of the maze and into the kitchen.

They gathered at the table and sat silently, cups of sweetened water sitting untouched in front of them. Dayn sat at the farthest end of the bench from Brina and stared down at the table, daring not even a glance her way. Alicine placed herself between them, while Reiv sat on the opposite bench, facing the three like a judge before a court.

For a long awkward moment there was only silence. Brina pulled a cup toward her and ran her finger round and round its rim. Finally she leaned around Alicine and looked at Dayn, trying in vain to meet his eyes. Then she said, "Dayn, I am sorry I frightened you. I know you have many questions."

Dayn lifted his gaze to her. "You're not my mother."

Brina rose from the bench and walked a few steps from the table, her back to the group. She folded her hands in front of her. "There is much to tell, Dayn. Please promise you will listen."

"I'll listen," he grumbled. But he didn't think he really wanted to hear.

Brina turned to face them. "Sixteen years ago I bore a son. He was so beautiful. We named him Keefe. That means 'cherished', did you know that? That perfume bottle there," she said, pointing to the counter where it now lay, "was a gift from Mahon. Mahon is my husband, Dayn. He is your . . . he was the father of my child."

Dayn looked down at the table, tracing the patterns of wood with his eyes. He hadn't even thought about the father. A new cause for alarm grabbed his gut.

Brina continued. "The bottle was an anniversary gift. Mahon gave it to me the year I carried our son inside of me. We had not been married long, only a year, and the gods blessed us quickly with a child. But he was marked, marked with a flower-shaped stain here." She raised a finger to the left side of her neck.

Dayn raised his hand and covered the birthmark clumsily with his fingers. He could feel everyone's eyes staring at him, at it. He had never considered the mark to be of any consequence before. No one in Kirador ever cared about it; there were too many other things about him to be concerned with. But here the mark seemed to mean everything.

Tears welled in Brina's eyes. "Mahon would not accept it. No one would have, of course, but I fought against the inevitable."

"The inevitable?" Reiv asked.

"The Will of Agneis," she said.

"The Will of Agneis?" Reiv said, shocked. "No, Brina, surely not. That only happens to people who are—"

"Inferior?" she said, completing the sentence for him. "Reiv, the Will of Agneis can happen to anyone. I am of superior blood, but my child was marked. According to Temple law, his fate was sealed."

"What is the Will of Agneis?" Alicine asked.

"When a child is born impure," Brina said, "it must be turned over to the gods. Usually that means taken out into the wild and left to fate. It is written as law, but few speak of it."

Alicine gasped and lowered her eyes. She did not ask any more questions.

"Gods, Brina," Reiv said, "I never realized. How could you do it?"

Brina walked over to him and looked him in the eye. "Reiv, you of all people should understand the value placed on physical beauty here."

Reiv winced and moved his hands to his lap.

She continued. "Reiv, you asked how I could do it. Well, in fact I could not. But my choices were few, so I made a plan to save my child. I told Mahon—I told everyone—that I would do what had be done, that I would allow no one else to do it. I left the next morning, taking only a handmaiden with me. But I did not go where they all thought I would."

"You went to the cave instead," Dayn said.

"Yes, Dayn, yes!" Brina rushed to his side and knelt down beside him. "I took you to the forbidden mountain to find the gods. To beg them to cure you."

"But you left me—I mean—you left the child there." His voice sounded pitiably small.

"Yes, but with a *god*, Dayn! A god who promised to remove the mark. Hear me Dayn. I could not let you die by the Will of Agneis or otherwise. I could not!"

"But you did not go back."

"Oh, Dayn, of course I went back. I went back for you the next year, and the next, and the next, and every year after that, just as the god instructed. But he did not bring you. He never brought you."

Dayn shook his head. "This can't be true."

Brina rose and grabbed the perfume bottle. "The gifts, Dayn! You saw the gifts. You said so! Look—the perfume bottle." She held it out to him. "It was a gift, for you, so you would remember me. Every year I brought gifts: blankets, clothes, toys, tokens. I brought them all for you."

"Maybe you did give your son away in the cave," he said, "but that doesn't prove I'm that son. Besides, I still have the mark, see?" He pulled the collar back, revealing the birthmark to her once more. "The mark's still there. No god took me. No god cured me."

Alicine rose from the bench and moved away, standing with her back to the others. She had remained unusually quiet during the entire conversation, asking few questions and offering no comments. "I think she speaks the truth, Dayn," she said softly.

Dayn cocked his head. "What are you saying, Alicine?"

"I think she speaks the truth," she said, turning to face him.

Dayn rose. "How could you possibly know whether she speaks the truth or not?"

"Because of what Father said."

"What do you mean?"

"Remember I told you how I sneaked up and listened when Father and Mother went to Eileis's, when we all went looking for you?"

"Yes."

"Well, I overheard Father admit he let the demon-witch think he was a god."

"He said that?"

"Yes."

"Those very words?"

"Yes, Dayn, he said them."

Dayn felt the truth come crashing down upon him like the rocks that had rained upon them in the cave. One by one the beliefs he held dear, as well as all his doubts and fears, tumbled around him. "Demon spawn," he whispered.

"What?" Alicine asked.

"Demon spawn. That's what the boys used to call me. How could they have done such a thing?"

"They were only cruel boys," Alicine said.

"No, I mean our parents! I knew I was not their real child, but it was their lies I hated more than anything. And now to find out that I was stolen..." Dayn began to pace, playing old questions and new answers over and over in his mind.

"Mother lost many babies in childbirth before we were— before we came," Alicine said. "Maybe Father was desperate."

"I didn't ask why, Alicine, I asked how."

"Dayn, if Brina thought Father was a god, maybe he thought she was of another world too. Maybe he thought you were a gift from Daghadar."

"Then why did he say he got me from a demon-witch?"

Alicine looked over at Brina and bowed her head. "I don't know."

"Regardless of what he thought she was or said she was, the fact remains that he made promises to her he did not intend to keep. He promised to remove the mark and he promised to bring me back to her. He did neither."

"Dayn, I don't know what happened in that cave, but I do know this—Father and Mother love you. And you know it, too."

She was right. His parents had always loved him in their way, seen to his every physical need, strived to make him happy as best they could. "Yes, I know it," he said, "but it doesn't make the pain of this any better."

Brina had stood silently to the side, watching Dayn and Alicine's faces, listening to their words. "Keefe, where have you been all this time?" she asked.

Dayn searched her face, then searched his heart. This woman believed her child had been left with a god, when in fact he had been stolen by a man. While Dayn's life had been difficult as an outcast, hers, surely, had been worse. "I've been in a place called Kirador," he said.

"Kirador? That is where the god took you?"

"Yes, but he wasn't a god. He was a man."

"But he said he was a god. He said he would remove the stain from your neck. He said he would return you to me. He said—"

"Yes, he said that."

Brina's face went stark. "Oh, Keefe. I am so sorry. I did not know."

"I was loved and cared for, Brina."

"Then why did you come back to me, Keefe? Why are you here now?"

"I had questions about who I was, where I belonged. I was different."

"Dayn," Alicine said.

"No, Alicine, you know it's true. You know what I went through." Dayn turned back to Brina. "I went to the cave to find out who I was, but when the truth began to reveal itself I wasn't ready. I'm still not sure I'm ready."

Brina nodded. "It will take time for all of us, but know this: you are my son. You are Keefe."

"Maybe, but I'm also Dayn."

"Then that is what you wish to be called?"

"Yes, I wish to be called Dayn. That is my name."

Their reunion was, at first, an awkward one, but gradually Dayn and Brina relaxed and before long they, along with Alicine, were seated at the table, trading quiet stories of their lives.

Reiv sat away from the group, slumped upon the cross-legged stool by the wall, watching from tired eyes. It was his choice not to join them, it did not feel right, and though Brina bade him over time after time, he preferred to ponder the events of the day from his solitude across the room. Within that contemplation, however, he realized a problem was in the making. A very big problem.

He headed over to the table, facing them with dread. "Brina," he said. "What are we going to do with them?"

"Do with them?" At first Brina looked puzzled, then her eyes widened. "Oh gods," she whispered. She rose and stepped from the bench.

"What does he mean, Brina?" Dayn asked with alarm. "Are we still going to be turned over for stealing?"

"No," Brina answered. "But we do have a problem."

Dayn stood and leaned across the table, his hands splayed across the top. "What problem?" He glanced from Reiv to Brina, then back again.

Reiv stood with crossed arms, his eyes fixed on Brina as she paced back and forth. "They cannot stay here," he said.

"I know," Brina said shaking her head. "Their safety; your position; Mahon . . ."

"What problem?" Dayn persisted.

"If we are found out . . ." Reiv said, now pacing beside Brina. "You know what the authorities would—"

"Enough!" Dayn shouted. "What problem?"

Reiv and Brina stopped in their tracks. They looked at Dayn, then at each other.

"A problem of my own making, Dayn," Reiv said stiffly.

Dayn crossed his arms and stared Reiv in the eye. "Tell me then."

"There is much you do not know about the way things are here, Dayn," Brina interjected. "You have learned some difficult truths here tonight, but not all."

"I have to know, Brina, but I swear, if I hear too many more difficult truths tonight I think my head will leap off my neck and roll across the room."

Brina smiled sadly. "I know, my dear, but I suppose your head must be risked."

"You and Alicine are Jecta," Reiv said. "*That* is the problem."

"That word again," Dayn said. "You've called us Jecta more times than I can count, but I still don't know what that is."

Reiv's mouth hooked in distaste. "Jecta is the name for those who are impure," he said.

"What do you mean 'impure'?" Dayn asked.

"I mean stained, deformed, of the wrong coloring, or . . . well, not good enough."

Dayn narrowed his eyes. "Explain 'not good enough'."

Reiv threw his arms up. "Enough! I do not know how else to explain it."

"Well, you *will* explain it," Dayn said. "I have the mark on my neck, so I'm stained. That much I can understand, but Alicine . . ." He motioned over to his sister. "She has no marks. How is it that she's not good enough?"

"She is dark," Reiv said.

"Dark? What do you mean by dark? You mean her hair?"

"It is not just the issue of her hair color. Most Tearians are blond, but those whose hair is not quite acceptable simply lighten it with lye. It is a common custom. But the eyes cannot be disguised, nor can the skin. Alicine is clearly not Tearian. Therefore she is Jecta."

"That's ridiculous," Dayn said.

"That is the way it is, the way it has always been," Reiv said defensively.

Dayn marched toward Reiv as though the prejudice were of the boy's own making. "How can you say such a thing?" he said. "How could you say such a despicable thing about my sister?"

Alicine also appeared taken aback, but she rose and placed a hand on her brother's arm. "Dayn, we aren't in Kirador. Things are different here."

"It doesn't matter. I can't believe what I am hearing."

"I remember a pale-haired, blue-eyed boy being beaten up by dark-haired, brown-eyed boys in Kirador," she said.

The memory swept across Dayn's face. "Yes, I do, too."

"I think we'd better get used to Tearian customs, whether we like them or not. I don't want to be the cause of anyone getting hurt." Alicine turned to Reiv. "Do you mean we can't stay in the city, or just not here with you?"

"Some Jecta are allowed to dwell within the city. But only some. You and Dayn would not be allowed. You are not employed laborers or craftsmen."

"Maybe since you're a Jecta," Dayn said, "we could pretend—"

"I am Tearian!" Reiv snapped.

"But your hair isn't blond and your eyes aren't that pale," Alicine said. "How is it that you're Tearian?"

"I am, or rather was, an exception," Reiv said, flustered. "Regardless, I made the mistake of declaring you thieves to the guards at the gate and I am expected to turn you over. Since I have not—"

"Then we must smuggle them out," Brina said, crossing over to him.

"How? And when? And where would we take them?"

Brina twisted her mouth and stared at the floor thought-fully. Then she looked up, her eyes alit with a plan. "Tomorrow. After breakfast. I will come back. Keep them here until then." She headed for the door.

"Then what?" Reiv asked, following at her heels

"Tomorrow is Market," she said. "Because of the recent celebrations, there will be more Jecta than usual invited to display their wares."

"And the more Jecta there are milling about the better chance we have of slipping them out."

"Yes. You will have to be the one to do it, Reiv."

"That sounds all well and good, but there is still one small problem—Crymm. He saw us enter through the gates and there were others with him. We had an altercation. He knows I was planning to take them to Labhras."

"Who is Crymm?" Alicine asked.

"The guard we encountered at the gate," Reiv said.

"Well," Dayn said, "the way I see it, Alicine hit you over the head and we escaped."

Reiv smirked. "A girl? Hit me over the head? Ha! Who would believe such a tale?"

"So you think no one would believe it?" Alicine said. "Well, I seem to recall a red mark splayed across your cheek curiously shaped like my hand."

Reiv touched the side of his face and felt humiliation rush to his cheeks. "Oh, fine then. We have no time to argue the point."

"Where are we to go? Back to Kirador?" Alicine asked.

"No!" Brina and Reiv responded simultaneously.

"Alicine," Reiv said, "you cannot simply walk out of here and go back to Kirador. I mean, it would not be so simple. Besides, do you really want to?"

"Well, I'm not ready to go back to Kirador," Dayn said. "At least not yet." He looked over at Alicine as though seeking support, but she just stared at him, her face expressionless. He turned his attention back to Brina.

"If we're not welcome here, then where are we to go?"

"You must go to the Jecta city of Pobu," Brina said. "But do not worry. You will be safe there and welcome, and we will be able to come see you. Reiv can move back and forth freely and I . . ."

Seeing her hesitation, Reiv added, "Yes, we can still see you, of course. I can go there if I choose. You just cannot come here."

"When will you be back, Brina?" Dayn asked.

"As soon as I can make my excuses from the breakfast." Brina turned her attention to Reiv. "Reiv, can you get them some more appropriate Jecta clothes, clean ones? They certainly will not blend in with the crowd dressed like that."

Reiv surveyed Dayn and Alicine while considering Brina's request. He circled Dayn, examining his height and build. "Well, he is a bit taller and broader than I am, but I suppose I have something he could wear, although it will fit him much more snuggly."

Dayn's face paled. "More snuggly?"

Reiv could not help but be amused, but then he turned serious. "Brina, I do not have anything for a girl to wear."

Brina assessed the full skirt and long sleeves of Alicine's dress. "I see no way of altering it in any way. Reiv you will have to go find her something. Can you do that?"

"Find her something? How do you propose I do that? What Jecta woman would willingly part from her clothes for me? I mean, I cannot simply remove a woman's clothes. I mean . . ." He sighed. "You know what I mean."

"Yes, Reiv, we understand your meaning," Brina replied. "What about the dormitories. Most, if not all, of the Jecta who stay there will either be at their homes for the holidays or at Market with their crafts. Perhaps you could find something there."

Reiv gaped at her, shocked at the suggestion. "Brina, do you realize what you are asking? You know the penalties for stealing."

"What other choice do we have? It would only raise suspicions and risk unwanted gossip if you, of all people, were seen

buying women's clothing? If we had more time I would try to secure something myself, but I fear I will be watched more closely
due to my lengthy absence tonight. Just coming here tomorrow
will be a risk in itself. It is up to you to get Alicine something
suitable to wear."

Reiv looked from Brina to Dayn then lowered his eyes.
"Brina, would you really ask this of me?"

"Reiv, look at me," Brina said. "We are all in peril if our
plan does not succeed. This must be done. I see no other way.
Let me assure you I have no intention of sacrificing you for the
sake of anyone else. Besides, were you not once called the Prince
of Insolence?"

Reiv's mouth dropped, then he nodded. "All right. I will do
it."

"Good, it is settled then." Brina put her hand on the door
handle, then turned to face them. "I regret that I must leave you
now, but my absence tonight will not have gone unnoticed and I
fear Mahon will not turn a blind eye to my visit here."

Lines of worry lingered on everyone's faces.

"Do not fret," Brina said. "Tomorrow I will go to Pobu and
find you a safe place to stay."

"How do you intend to do that?" Reiv asked, mortified by
the thought of it. "You know it is forbidden for you to go into
the Jecta city. You never said you intended to actually go there."

"Oh, do not worry yourself," Brina said with a wink. "I
have my ways. Besides, the Guard has become complacent about
the borders. They are more concerned about what comes in than
what goes out. There is always a risk, but I have been doing it for
years."

"Years? Gods, Brina! You will soon find my head lying
across the room next to Dayn's."

Brina laughed. "I hope not. I could not bear to lose two
sons' heads in one day." She turned and left, closing the door
quietly behind her.

"You are her son also?" Dayn asked, surprised.

"No. Her nephew actually," Reiv said. He arched a brow. "Did she not tell you? Ah, well, I guess she has left that story to me." He strolled across the room and gathered up the cups still scattered about the tabletop.

"Well?" Alicine said.

"Well, what?" Reiv asked.

"The story."

"Oh no, not tonight," he said yawning. "You may wish to spend the night telling more stories, but not I. I am tired and intend to get some sleep. We will leave new stories, as well as the finding of clothing, for the morning."

Reiv looked longingly toward his bedchamber, then at Alicine and Dayn who had turned to make their way to the blankets still crumpled on the floor.

"Alicine," Reiv said, "you may take my bed if you wish. I will sleep on the floor there with Dayn."

By the expression on Alicine's face, she was surprised by Reiv's offer, if not somewhat embarrassed by it. Dayn grinned at her and she tipped her nose in the air. "Well, at least *I* won't be sleeping on the floor tonight," she said.

"Actually, Dayn may have the chaise if he wishes," Reiv said.

Dayn's eyes twinkled with satisfaction, while Alicine's rolled with annoyance.

Reiv ushered Alicine toward his bedchamber, Dayn following close behind her. He entered the room and lit a candle on the stand by the bed, then motioned her in. "There, now you can see your way around." Reiv gathered up some clothes that were piled on the bed and tossed them into the corner, then moved over to the mattress and plopped down. "It is not too bad," he said, bouncing lightly upon it.

Alicine lingered outside the door, her eyes modestly averted; Dayn leaned with folded arms against the doorframe.

Reiv looked at them for a confused moment. "Oh, the blanket. Of course. Let me fetch it."

"No," Alicine said, "I don't think I'll be needing the blanket. I'm wrapped in enough material for tonight I think."

"That you are," Reiv agreed.

"Besides, you'll be needing it more than I will," she said. Reiv's eyes followed hers from his bare chest down to his uncovered limbs. "Oh, yes, of course. Well, if you need anything . . . ."

Excusing himself, Reiv brushed past Alicine and Dayn, his face feeling suddenly flushed.

Dayn watched with suspicion as Reiv exited the room. The subtle exchange between Reiv and Alicine had not gone unnoticed.

Alicine entered the room and Dayn followed her in. Turning to face him she smiled and said, "Do you think you will survive sleeping in the same room as Reiv?"

"Oh, I think I can manage it, unless he's prone to nightmares that require a weapon." He intended the remark as a joke, but found himself frowning at the possibility of it.

"Well, if you need rescuing, you know where to find me," Alicine said. Her expression froze at her words. "I'm sorry, Dayn. I didn't mean it like that."

"I know, but then again, you've always been my rescuer. Why should it be any different now?

"I think everything is going to be different now," she replied.

"Yes," Dayn said. But there were some differences he knew would be more difficult than others to accept. And the way Alicine looked at Reiv was going to be one of them.

15
The Plan in Play

Alicine awoke in a room of white walls bathed in bright morning light. It was peacefully quiet, except for the squeals of children playing in the distance and the soft, pleasant hum of the breeze sweeping the open drape. She groaned and rolled onto her back, then stretched her arms above her head. It was so nice to be in a soft, cozy bed again.

She sat up with a start and threw her legs over the side of the mattress. This wasn't her bed—it was that boy's! She leapt off and grabbed the catch in her spine. Surely the abuse her body had suffered these past few days was justification for her travesty. She leaned forward to release the tightness from her back, then frowned at her dress. The hem was rimmed with stains and the once beautiful material was dotted with sweaty splotches. Even the flowers were wilted from white to shades of gray. She brushed her hands down the wrinkled skirt, then ran her finger beneath the damp lace of her collar. As predicted, she had not required a blanket during the night.

She crept to the door and opened it, careful not to make a sound. Dayn was curled up on the chaise across the way, twisted around the blanket like a snake on a limb. His breathing was so noisy, she could hear it even from the doorway where she stood. To her profound relief, Reiv was nowhere in sight. She settled her eyes on the door past the living area. The services of the lavatory were sorely needed.

Looking to her right, then left, she stepped out and tiptoed past Dayn. But her attentions were directed by a *clank* in the kitchen. Reiv could be seen rummaging around in a cabinet, and Alicine could only stop and stare.

The boy in the kitchen looked nothing like the one who had left her standing in the doorway of the bedchamber the night before. The long, bright red hair she had only seen bound behind his neck now lay in auburn streams down his back, darkened by the water that had recently washed it. He wore a sleeveless tunic, once bright violet, now faded to soft lavender, and belted at the waist by a tawny leather braid. Much more conservative than the previous day's attire, the tunic covered him from shoulder to mid-thigh. His face was scrubbed clean and, lacking the mask from the day before, glowed with peach-colored skin. He was almost too beautiful to be a boy, but the tall muscular build of his body erased any doubts one might have about that. His hands were still covered by gloves, though not the same ones as the day before, and he was now busying them in the preparation of breakfast.

Reiv glanced up and spotted Alicine standing dumbly. "So you are awake. Good. You are in time for breakfast," he said.

"Yes, I was just—I was just going to the room there," she said, pointing to the door across the way. She continued to stare at him as though she had never seen him before in her life.

Reiv glanced down at himself, then back up at her. "What?" he asked.

"Oh, nothing." Alicine felt her face go hot. "You just look different, that's all."

"Nothing that a little soap and water could not help. I have drawn you a bath," he said, nodding in the direction of the lavatory.

"A *what*?"

"A bath," he repeated. "You certainly are in need of one. How long has it been?"

"Not that long," Alicine declared.

"I would think much longer."

"Well, you didn't smell so sweet yourself yesterday."

Reiv frowned and turned away. "It was a bad day."

"Well, thank you for the offer, but I think I'll just wait until Brina returns."

"Suit yourself."

Dayn raised up on an elbow and assessed the exchange going on between his sister and Reiv. It seemed inconsequential, so he yawned and stretched, then kicked the blanket from his legs. Spying the door to the right, he rose and headed in that direction. But he quickly found himself competing with his sister for the comforts of the little room.

"Fine, you go first then," he grumbled. He turned and leaned against the wall, arms crossed, waiting for her to finish, and watched Reiv busying himself in the kitchen. "What was all that ruckus between you and Alicine?" he asked.

"That sister of yours," Reiv said, shaking his head. "I merely suggested a bath. You would have thought—"

"A *bath*?" Dayn asked.

Reiv glanced up. "Yes, a bath. You know what that is, do you not?"

"Of course I do."

"Well," Reiv said, nodding in the direction of the lavatory, "there is one drawn in there. I suggest you use it. Your sister does not seem to want to."

"Use it? But I—"

"—took one a week ago or something. Yes, I know. You'd best use it, Dayn. Brina will expect it and she will have my head if I do not see to it."

"What is it about Brina and our heads?" Dayn muttered.

When Alicine finished, Dayn entered the lavatory and eyeballed the cask of bathwater. It did look inviting and he was dirtier than usual. Besides, Reiv said Brina would be expecting them to bathe, and he certainly didn't want to risk angering her this early in their relationship. He stripped off his filthy tunic and trousers, then lowered himself into the tub and leaned his head back against the rim. His arms floated in the sudsy water as his mind drifted.

A rap at the door brought him to his senses.

"Dayn are you all right? Reiv says you have been in there a long time."

Brina! He bolted upright and covered himself with his hands, sending a splash of water over the side.

"Don't come in!" he shouted, scanning the room for the nearest towel. "God, what does she want to see now?" he said.

"I heard that, Dayn," Brina said through the door.

"Sorry, Brina." He slunk back down.

"Well, come out when you are ready. Food is on the table."

When Dayn arrived in the kitchen he saw that everyone had already gathered around an enticing breakfast of fruit, eggs, bread, and honey. He sat on the bench beside Alicine, grabbed a chunk of bread, and shoved it into his mouth. He glanced at Brina; her eyes were scanning him with distaste. "What?" he asked her between chews.

"Reiv, have you not had a chance to fetch him some clean clothes?" she asked. "A bath does little good if it is followed by such grime."

"No, Brina," he said. "I have been too busy getting clean myself and, in case you have not noticed, this breakfast did not prepare itself."

"When you are finished, then," she said. "Oh, and did you take care of—"

"Yes," Reiv said, "in the bath."

By Reiv's cool expression it was clear he did not wish any further discussion regarding the mysterious matter, so Brina said nothing more.

When breakfast was over, Reiv rose and cleared his dish, then headed for the door. "Dayn, I will find you something as soon as I get back," he called over his shoulder.

"Thanks," Dayn replied as he followed him to the door.

Reiv put his hand on the latch. "Bolt this behind me and do not open it unless you are certain it is me. Understand?"

Dayn nodded. "All right. Be careful."

Reiv forced a smile. "I was once fairly skilled at getting in and out of tight situations. Perhaps I still possess the talent."

Brina walked up, her face speaking of gratitude. "Reiv . . ."

"Do not worry, Brina. I know what I am doing."

"Just act normal," she said.

"Oh, and what exactly is that?"

He opened the door a crack and peered out, then turned back to Dayn. "Remember, bolt the door behind me."

Reiv made his way down the narrow cobble street, scrutinizing every doorway, alcove, and alley. He dreaded the thought of meeting up with Crymm or one of the other guards he had confronted the night before. But if he did, he would need to be prepared. Gritting his teeth, he replayed the humiliating story he would have to tell.

He rounded the corner and strolled to the stables. No one of consequence was in sight, but even if there had been, his presence would not have seemed particularly unusual. He did, after all, spend a great deal of time with Gitta. For the past year she had been the only friend he had. Pushing open the double doors of the stable, he felt overwhelming remorse. He had sorely neglected the horse the night before.

He entered the stall and felt the familiar joy he always felt at the sight of her. He wrapped his arms around her neck and buried his face in her mane. "Gitta," he said. "How is my girl today?"

She snorted and stomped as she moved to nuzzle his neck.

He set a fresh bucket of oats down before her and she put her mouth to them immediately. His remorse returned.

"I am sorry, Gitta. Do you forgive me?" He grabbed a brush from a shelf on the wall, and brushed her with long, gentle strokes. She raised her head, snorted again, and returned to her oats.

"Well," he said, laughing, "at least you are thinking about it."

A sudden rustling was heard in the adjoining stall. Gitta jerked her head up while Reiv paused to listen. All went quiet. "Probably just a rat, girl," Reiv said. He patted her back and resumed the brushing.

On the opposite side of the stall's partition, Crymm crouched, silent and listening. He had spent the previous night drinking and gambling, and had found himself far too inebriated to make his way back to the bunks. He'd collapsed in a heap in the stables, barely caring about the consequences of the morning when a familiar voice in the adjoining stall raised him from his stupor.

He leaned back on his haunches and blinked his crusty eyelids. Could he be dreaming? Pressing his cheek against the boards, he slanted an eye between the crack. He couldn't believe his luck—it was the princeling.

"I am sorry for the neglect last night, Gitta," he heard Reiv say to the horse. "You know I had to tend to our guests."

Crymm's ears perked up. He huddled closer to the wall and peered between the slats.

"They were not as bad as we thought though," Reiv said. "Maybe we could get to know them better."

Gitta nudged her face against Reiv's chest and pushed him gently.

"Whoa, there, girl. I understand your concern."

Reiv continued to brush, his brow furrowed in contemplation. "Perhaps we could make more effort to go to Pobu. I know, I know. We are not particularly welcome there." He placed the grooming brush on the shelf and stood with his hands on his hips, watching Gitta devour a second bucket of oats. "Gods, girl, if you continue to eat like that you shall be the fattest horse in the stables." He laughed and ran his hand along her back, then said, "Well, I will leave you to it. There are things I must do."

The horse paused and stared at Reiv as though awaiting an explanation.

"Do not worry," Reiv said. "All will be well." Then he turned, walked out of the stall, and headed for the street.

Leaning around the partition, Crymm watched as Reiv exited the building. Rising on stiff knees, he glanced at the poor state of his attire. He ran his fingers though his hair, combing out bits of straw, and tugged at the tunic now stained with ale and manure. There was no time to freshen up. An unexpected opportunity had come his way and he could not afford to let it pass.

Crymm skulked past Gitta's stall, his cold blue eyes fully focused on the door. The horse suddenly reared up and thundered her hooves to the ground; the gate rattled as though it would burst from its hinges. Crymm staggered back, hissing and swearing. "Foul creature! When I have taken care of the princeling..." He eyed a whip that hung on a nearby peg. "If only I had time."

He crept to the stable doors and peeked out. Glancing to his right, he caught sight of Reiv's red hair weaving between the growing crowd of blond Tearians. More and more residents were making their way to Market and this, he knew, could work in his favor.

Dodging between shadows and shallow doorways, Crymm kept close to the buildings that lined the streets. On more than one occasion he found himself diving for cover as the red head paused and twisted around. But the boy never appeared to have seen him and each time turned and continued on.

Reiv rounded a corner and stopped before the Jecta dormitories, a cavernous two-story structure made of gray stone blocks. He glanced from side to side, then disappeared through the front door.

Crymm crept over and inched along the wall toward an open window. Strangely, the prince was making his way to the women's bunk area rather than to the men's. What in the world could he be doing there?

Reiv looked around, then hurried over to the nearest bunk. Opening a large wooden trunk resting at the foot of it, he peeked inside and frowned. He took nothing, and closed the lid before moving to another trunk nearby. The lid opened with a *creak*. Reiv winced and threw a glance over his shoulder. He reached in and pulled out a red and gray patterned sarong, then took a coin from the money pouch at his waist and tossed it in. He closed the lid and headed out the door.

Crymm's mouth curled to a devious grin. "I have you at last, you arrogant prince," he whispered. "First you harbor thieves, now you have become one. But, just in case there is any doubt as to it . . ."

His pale eyes narrowed; his sinister brows met. The plan was in play. And this time he would not fail.

16
Culture Shock

Reiv leaned his head against his front door and muttered a prayer of gratitude. How long had it been since he had thanked the gods for anything? He couldn't even remember. He glanced over his shoulder, then rapped on the door. "Open up, it is me," he whispered loudly. He leaned his ear in closer. Muffled laughter could be heard in a distant part of the apartment. "Gods," he muttered. He ground his teeth and rattled the handle. "It is me; open up." So much for being discreet.

The door opened a crack and a blue eye peered out. "Yes?" the voice behind the eye said.

Reiv shoved his way in, banging the door against Dayn's arm. He stormed across the room, tossed the bundle onto the table, and turned to his somewhat disgruntled cousin.

"Dayn, this is no time for jokes!" he barked. "You have no idea what is going on here, do you?"

Dayn massaged his aching elbow. "I'm sorry," he mumbled, "but I knew it was you."

"Listen, this is serious business and you need to treat it as such!" Reiv rubbed his temples and scrunched his face with exasperation. How in the world was he going to make him understand? As he looked into the wounded, boyish face of his cousin, he realized Dayn was just that—a boy. Though they were nearly the same age, Dayn had clearly not been forced into manhood as quickly as Reiv had.

"Assaulting your cousin again, Reiv?" Brina said as she swished into the room and made her way over to the bundle flung onto the table.

"Brina, he has no idea—" Reiv started to say.

"Of course not, dear. Did you expect him to?"

"But—"

"Reiv," Brina said, shooting him a look, "try a little patience, will you. Now, what did you bring us?" She untangled the bundle and held the sarong up for inspection.

"Where is Alicine?" Reiv asked, noticing she was not in the room.

"She is in the bath. I finally managed to convince her. Such modest children these two." She laughed. "Reiv, would you please go find Dayn something to wear now?"

"Oh, of course," Reiv said, realizing the quest for clothing was not yet complete.

He headed to his bedchamber and over to the pile of clothing he had tossed to the floor the night before. He had not yet returned the trunk to its rightful place and he made a mental note to do so later. Rummaging through the tumble of clothes, he searched for something that would fit Dayn's larger frame. This time of year most Jecta men wore loincloths, but he knew his cousin would never agree to that. He pulled a faded brown tunic from the pile and held it up for scrutiny, then shook his head. The fit would not be a comfortable one.

Reiv strode from the room and handed the tunic to Brina for her approval. Holding it up, she glanced from the tunic to Dayn, then back again.

"Here, Dayn," she said as she tossed him the tunic. "Try this on."

Dayn held it up, examined it, then glanced at Brina.

Brina sighed, turned her back to him and resumed her inspection of the sarong.

Dayn watched Brina from the corner of his eye as he yanked off his filthy tunic and replaced it with the Jecta-styled one. Rubbing his hands down the front of the surprisingly conservative top, he surveyed himself, a look of relief blanketing his face. The tunic was short and it did fit a bit snugly, but at least it wasn't a loincloth.

"This isn't so bad," he said.

Brina looked him over. "Those—off," she said, pointing to his trousers.

"Wha—Off?"

"Dayn," Brina said, "you need to dress like a Jecta."

"But what about . . . ?" Dayn glanced over at Reiv's bare legs, then back at Brina.

"What?" Brina asked.

"Britches!" Dayn said.

"Britches?"

"Leggings . . . *bottoms*!" Dayn grabbed hold of a pants leg and shook it.

Looking over her nose at the increasingly exasperated Dayn, Brina said, "Jecta do not wear bottoms, dear." She then turned her attention back to the sarong.

"But what am I supposed to wear under *this*?" Dayn cried, lifting his arms in the air. He gaped down at himself. The hem of the tunic was pulled almost to his hips.

"What are you wearing under those bottoms now?" Brina asked, gesturing toward his pants.

"Now? Nothing, but—" Dayn turned to Reiv, his eyes begging for support in the battle over fashion.

Reiv stifled a laugh.

"So, what are you wearing under *that*?" Dayn demanded, pointing to Reiv's faded tunic.

"Well, not *nothing* as you are," Reiv said. "Come with me. I may have something you can have. I don't normally share my bottoms, as you call them, but under the circumstances . . . ."

Grabbing Dayn by the shoulders, Reiv spun him around and pushed him toward the bedchamber. "Well, look at it this way," Reiv said as he entered the room behind his cousin, "at least you will not have to wear the boots."

"Alicine, dear, here is a change of clothes for you," Brina said through the closed lavatory door.

"Don't come in," Alicine called from the other side.

"I will not enter if you do not wish me to, but how am to get these clothes to you? Would you prefer I send your brother in?"

"No! Wait!" Alicine shouted. How could the woman even suggest such a thing.

Alicine scanned the room and was relieved to spy a bath sheet hanging on a nearby peg. Keeping one eye on the door, she raised up from the water, both hands clutching the rim. The sides of the tub were somewhat high for someone of her stature, but she managed to escape the slippery tub with a small degree of grace. She tiptoed across the wet, tiled floor, arms wrapped around herself, then grabbed the sheet and pulled it around her naked body. She flung her long, wet hair behind her and crept toward the door. Opening it only a crack, she peered out at Brina, who waited patiently on the other side.

"Here, dear," Brina said, threading the sarong through the tiny crack as Alicine pulled it through from the other side. "Let me know if you need any assistance."

"Thank you . . . yes . . . I will . . . thank you," Alicine said. She closed the door, almost catching the end of the garment in it.

Alicine held up the sarong and inspected it. It was nothing more than a long piece of cloth intended to be wrapped around one's body and secured. But with what? She had never seen a garment such as this and had no idea what to do with it. She twisted her face with disgust. There was not much to the thing, certainly not enough to cover her body appropriately, and the color—what was Reiv thinking?

"Brina," she said through the door, "I will not wear this thing. I simply will not."

"What did you say, dear? I could not quite understand you," Brina said back.

"I said I will not wear this. If this is Reiv's idea of a joke, you can tell him for me it's not the least bit funny." Alicine threw the swath of cloth onto the wet floor and crossed her arms.

"Alicine, Reiv selected a very suitable garment. That is what many Jecta women wear and if you intend to blend in, then that is what you will have to wear, too."

Alicine stared down at the rumpled heap. "I don't even know how to put the thing on," she muttered.

"Alicine, please, let me help you. I will make every effort to respect your privacy. I promise."

Dayn and Reiv strode across the living room and toward the lavatory, both wearing smug looks of satisfaction. Dayn, though still uncomfortable with the nakedness of his legs, as well as the swath of material now wrapped between them, was pleased to have at least some bottoms on; and Reiv was looking victorious at having found him some.

"What's going on?" Dayn asked, seeing Brina's perplexed expression.

"Dayn, help me with your sister. She needs help with the sarong, but will not let me in to assist her."

"Alicine," Dayn shouted through the door, "what's wrong? Why won't you let Brina help you?"

"If you could see this *thing* she expects me to put on." Alicine sounded completely exasperated.

"Well, you should see what I have to wear." Dayn frowned down at his long, pale limbs. "Just let Brina help you."

"No!"

Dayn winked at Reiv and Brina and said, "All right then. Reiv says he's coming in. You know he has absolutely no patience."

"He wouldn't *dare*! Dayn!" By then Alicine was practically screaming. "I know Reiv did this on purpose!"

"I did not," Reiv replied. "Did what?" He looked over at Brina, who pursed her lips and shook her head, silently assuring him it was nothing.

"Reiv didn't do anything, Alicine," Dayn said into the door. "But if you don't open up and let Brina help you, he's going to open it for you."

Dayn nodded at the others, confident his plan would work. Reiv took a step and extended his hand toward the door. Dayn shoved him aside and shot him a don't-you-dare look.

"I was only trying to help," Reiv said in a surprisingly playful tone.

There was a long silence from Alicine's side of the door. Dayn looked at the others and shrugged. If his plan did not work, their wait might be a long one.

"Oh, very well. Brina can come in," Alicine finally said. "But you and Reiv get away."

"Fine then. We're leaving," Dayn said. "We're going to the kitchen." He turned to Reiv and winked. "We're going there now. Right now." But neither of them moved.

Alicine opened the door a crack and peeked out. Seeing the two boys standing before it she promptly slammed it in their faces. "You're despicable! Both of you!" she screamed.

"I'm sorry, Alicine," Dayn said, laughing so hard that tears came to his eyes.

Reiv's expression brightened, he was obviously enjoying the banter, but Brina had had enough. She shooed the boys into the kitchen, her arms waving in the air as she scolded them soundly. "Out, both of you!" she said. "This is difficult enough without your foolishness! Now, sit yourselves down!"

The boys remained standing and stared at her reddening face. Reiv seemed amused, but Dayn was dismayed at the thought of being the cause of her temper.

"Now, I said!" Brina took a threatening step in their direction.

The boys sat down promptly and held their mouths in check. Brina scolded them with a wagging finger and an authoritative voice. The corner of Reiv's lip quivered in a battle to remain serious. Dayn snorted at Reiv's expression, but he stifled it in a hurry when Brina directed her attention to him instead of Reiv.

"Have a heart, Brina," Reiv said. "We did not mean anything by it."

Brina scowled, then turned and marched off to help Alicine.

The boys sat at the table, exchanging small talk as they waited. "What's taking them so long?" Dayn asked, eyeing the hallway leading to the lavatory.

"Women," Reiv retorted. "They take forever to do everything."

Brina reentered the kitchen, her face beaming. "Boys, wait until you see," she said.

"What?" Dayn asked.

"Your sister. She is just beautiful." Brina's eyes grew misty.

Dayn snickered. "I'm surprised you came out in one piece. When Alicine gets her mind set on something . . ." But then his eyes turned to the living area and his sister who was now standing in it. The muscles in his face went lax.

"Wha—" Reiv started to ask as his eyes followed Dayn's gaze. But the question evaporated on his tongue.

Alicine stood with the light of the atrium at her back. She was wrapped in the bright red sarong, the golden skin of her shoulders, arms, and legs exposed. Her thick black hair, normally braided and pulled away from her face, hung loosely down her back, reaching to her calves. Her arms were wrapped around herself and she stared at the floor with an expression of humiliation.

"Well, what do you think?" Brina asked the two boys who were sitting slack-jawed at the table.

Dayn stood and walked toward his sister. "Why, she's *naked*!" he proclaimed, one hand tugging down on the hem of his tunic, the other pointing a shaky finger in her direction.

"Do not be ridiculous, dear," Brina said

"Yes, she is!" Dayn insisted. He crossed his arms, but quickly uncrossed them when he saw it only served to hike his tunic up further. His face flushed. "No sister of mine is going to walk out in public looking like that."

Brina thrust her hands to her hips. "Dayn, this is how Jecta women dress. No one will think Alicine is naked. In fact, she is far from it. You are making this more difficult on your sister than it has to be." Brina then turned to Reiv for support. "Reiv, please explain to Dayn that—" But seeing the glimmer in his eyes, Brina glanced at Alicine as though to be sure the girl wasn't naked after all. "Reiv!"

"Oh, sorry, Brina," Reiv said. He cleared his throat and turned his gaze from Alicine to Dayn. "Dayn, I assure you Alicine is dressed appropriately. No man will even notice her."

Dayn knew Reiv's last statement was a boldfaced lie, but even more disturbing was the fact that Alicine was watching Reiv's face intently. Clearly she wanted his approval.

Brina motioned Dayn and Alicine to the table and quickly changed the subject. "Come," she said. "We need to talk. There are more important things that need to be discussed."

Alicine followed her over, walking in much smaller steps than she was accustomed to. Having always worn dresses with full skirts, the tighter fitting sarong was obviously an unpleasant adjustment for a girl used to walking in wide strides. "How do those women wear these things?" she mumbled.

Dayn sat next to her, his bare legs bouncing under the table.

"Quit tapping your leg," Alicine snapped. "It's annoying. Besides, it only draws more attention to *your* nakedness."

Dayn stopped immediately.

"Dayn," Brina said, "I know this is difficult for both of you." She slid onto the bench across from him and took his hands in hers. A grimace flashed across Dayn's face as he made a subtle attempt to remove his hands. But Brina persisted, no longer willing to be put off by her long-lost son.

"Dayn, time is growing short and there is much I have not said."

Dayn swallowed and nodded.

She fixed her eyes on his. "We have been apart our whole lives and now, by the will of the gods, we are reunited. We barely know each other, but there will be time for us to learn."

"Do Alicine and I really have to leave?"

"Yes, but we will visit you there very soon. I promise."

Reiv's face blanched. He rose and stepped away from the table, keeping his back to the group.

"What Reiv said about my going to Pobu is true," Brina continued, "but ever since I was forced to part with my child sixteen years ago, I have made it my mission to help the Jecta. Call it my own little crusade against the customs of Tearia. I have contacts there and ways of getting in and out. Now, listen carefully. I am going to go there to find you a place to stay."

"What will we do once we get there?" Alicine asked.

"Arrangements will be made, but do not concern yourselves with that now. I will return to you as soon as I can, but caution must be paid. If I am detected, I could be prevented from ever returning to Pobu, or worse. But do not worry. In sixteen years I have yet to be caught. I just want you to realize how important it is to be discreet." She then turned her attention to Reiv. "Reiv, I expect to return here soon, but if for any reason I am not back by High Sun, take them and leave without me. High Sun, no later. Understood?"

Reiv nodded, but did not turn to face her.

"What do you mean if you don't come back?" Dayn asked.

"Just a precaution. I have several people to talk to and one can never predict delays. But there is nothing to fear. Reiv will be there for you. As a Jecta, he can come and go freely."

Reiv's back stiffened. Brina rose and moved from the table to the door.

"Reiv, if for any reason I do not return, you must get them through the gates. When you arrive in Pobu, go to the town square. There is a blacksmith shop to the right of it. The smith is a friend; he will know what to do. I will meet you there as soon as I can."

"Yes, Brina," he said.

"Oh, and Reiv, while I am gone, you might take the time to explain some of the Jecta customs, including clothing." She opened the door slowly and peered out. "High Sun, no later."

She glanced back at the three who had followed her and now stood, pale-faced, at her back. She smiled assuredly, then stepped into the street.

Reiv closed the door and rested his hand on the bolt. For a long moment he did not move.

"Reiv?" Alicine asked.

He whirled to face them. "I have work to do," he said. And with that he brushed past them and headed for the atrium.

Dayn and Alicine looked at each other in bewilderment. Dayn shook his head and shrugged his shoulders. "Maybe I should talk to him," he said, moving to follow.

Alicine grabbed his arm. "Not yet," she said. "Maybe we'd better think this through. You've seen his moods." She pulled Dayn over to the corner, then put a finger to her lips as she motioned her eyes toward Reiv.

Dayn glanced at Reiv who could now be seen lifting a large trunk from a table in the atrium. "What's there to think through?" Dayn said. "He's been fine all morning. What could possibly have happened?"

"I'm sure it was something Brina said. I saw that look on his face again. You know, the one he wore all day yesterday." Alicine contorted her face into a scowl just in case Dayn needed reminding.

"I didn't see it," Dayn said. He cocked his head and struggled to examine Reiv's face from across the distance.

"Well, I did. I saw it just before Brina left, right after she talked to us about Pobu."

Simultaneously they craned their necks to watch Reiv as he walked swayback toward his room with the trunk. He paused and glanced over at them. Dayn and Alicine smiled at him, but he did not return the gesture and continued toward the bedchamber.

Alicine tightened her brow and directed her eyes to the kitchen where the last conversation with Reiv had taken place. "Dayn," she whispered, "I think I know what it was Brina said.

She said, as a Jecta, Reiv can come and go. Those were her exact words."

Dayn shook his head. "That can't be it. She probably just meant because he's foreman."

"I don't think so."

Dayn studied Reiv who had returned to the atrium and was now gathering up bits of broken pottery. "But he's not dark; he's not marked. And we've seen most of him."

"Not his hands. We've never seen his hands. He's never taken off the gloves, not once. Don't you find that strange?"

Dayn leaned around her and looked with curiosity at the gloved hands that now held crushed stems and shattered terracotta. "Well, he *is* a laborer."

"Dayn, do be serious. Who wears gloves all the time? I think I should be the one to talk to him."

"I don't know."

"I could handle it much more delicately than you and if we both went over he might feel cornered. Besides, I have knowledge in healing. I don't know what's wrong with his hands, but maybe there's something I could do."

Dayn thought for a moment. His sister was particularly gifted in the art of healing and her knowledge of plants and herbs was unsurpassed in Kirador. Maybe she was right about something being wrong with Reiv's hands, and if Reiv could be helped, Alicine was certainly the one to do it. He nodded his head reluctantly. "All right. If you think it will help."

Dayn walked into the nearby kitchen while Alicine strolled into the atrium. Keeping one eye on his sister and the other on the unpredictable Reiv, Dayn reached for a mug and poured himself a drink. He leaned against the table's edge while he sipped and watched.

Reiv glanced up and spied Alicine weaving her way between the numerous plants that crowded the floor in front of her.

"Now what have you come to complain about?" he muttered. He moved away, pretending to concentrate on a shrub across the room.

Alicine changed her direction and worked her way toward his new location. But he only moved further away. Her face grew red with frustration as his attempts to avoid her became more than a little obvious.

"Reiv!" she said loudly. Then her voice softened. "Reiv," she repeated.

He stopped and turned to face her. He wanted very badly to be angry with her. He needed to be angry with her. It was simple. She was going away. Dayn was going away. They were Jecta. He wasn't. They would be living in Pobu and he couldn't imagine visiting them in that place. He had thought that he could, but now he realized he didn't have it in him. He had been fooling himself to think he could have family again, much less friends. If he could just hate them.

"What *is* it, Alicine?" Reiv said impatiently. "I am very busy."

"Your plants are so beautiful. I thought maybe you could show them to me."

"Well, I do not have time to take you on a tour," he said. He turned his face away for fear she would see the regret written across it. Grabbing a potted seedling, he eyed it with distaste, then pulled the shoot out and tossed it to the ground.

"I'm really good with herbs," Alicine said, stepping around to see what he was doing. "Even medicinals. Maybe I could help you."

"Help me?" Reiv forced a laugh. "I do not need any help."

"Don't you?" She slanted her eyes toward his hands.

"What do you mean by that remark?"

Alicine brushed her hand across some pink blossoms, stirring their scent. "What I said. I could help you."

"I did fine before you came. I do not need your help. For that matter, I do not need anything." *Hate her. That is all you have to do. Just hate her.*

"Well, we need you, Reiv. Very much. Dayn especially. I just don't see how we'll get through this without you."

"Well, you had best get used to it. I will get you as far as Pobu if I must, but after that you will see little of me."

"What do you mean 'see little of you'?" Alicine asked. "Brina said—*you* said—you could come and go there freely. That you would be there for us."

"Well, Brina was mistaken."

"And you? Were you lying to us then?"

Reiv's eyes flashed. "No, I was not lying. I thought I could, but . . . Listen, Alicine, I cannot visit you in Pobu. I will go there only if I have to take you there. Otherwise . . ." He turned his back to her.

"Cannot visit us or will not visit us?"

"Cannot—will not—both! Quit asking so many questions. Gods!"

He stepped away, but she rushed to block his path, and faced him down. "Why is that, Reiv? Enlighten me."

"Because it is Jecta."

"But Brina said as a Jecta you could go there."

Reiv's shoulders stiffened.

Alicine continued, "And if you are Jecta—"

"I am not Jecta!" Reiv shouted. He grabbed her by the shoulders and pulled her toward him. "Never call me that! I am Tearian! Do you hear me? Tearian!" He pushed her away, then turned and attempted, once again, to distance himself.

Dayn took a step in their direction, but Alicine motioned him back with a wave of her hand. "Prove it," she called to Reiv's back. "Prove you're not Jecta."

Reiv stopped in his tracks, startled by her sudden challenge. He spun to face her. "Prove it?"

"You heard me. Prove you are not Jecta. Show me that you have no marks, no imperfections."

"Jecta do not have to have marks. I already told you."

"So you have no marks? Then why do you always wear gloves?"

"That is none of your concern," he said. "You know, I cannot wait until I am rid of you."

"You're a liar."

"I told you, girl, I am no liar."

"Then tell me. Why do you always wear gloves?"

"Because I choose to."

"Tell me the truth, Reiv."

"No, I said! No . . . No . . . No! Do you understand me now?"

"Yes, I understand. You're afraid."

Reiv's jaw dropped. "I am afraid of nothing."

"A liar *and* a coward."

"Coward? How—how dare—I am no coward, girl. *That* I can assure you."

"Then take off your gloves, unless you're afraid to." Alicine smiled smoothly and folded her arms across her chest.

"I am not afraid!" Reiv screamed, his face an instant mask of rage. "I am not!" He grabbed a nearby plant and flung it over Alicine's head. It crashed into a hundred pieces against a nearby pillar.

Alicine jumped. "Reiv," she said, her voice cracking.

He stepped toward her, his fist clenched in the air.

"Reiv, please."

Dayn sprinted toward the atrium. Reiv saw him fast approaching and suddenly realized why. He froze and looked at his own trembling fist, then at Alicine's stricken face. "Gods, what am I doing?" he whispered. He lowered his fist and backed away, his eyes darting between Alicine and Dayn.

"Don't you dare touch her!" Dayn shouted. He planted himself between Reiv and his sister.

"No, I—" Reiv gulped.

"Alicine was right," Dayn said, his usually calm voice fraught with hostility. "You have been lying to us, pretending to be our friend, saying you would be there for us when you had no intention of it. It was all just a big show for Brina, wasn't it? You don't care a whit about us, do you?"

"No, Dayn. I mean—yes—I mean . . ." Reiv stumbled over the words, frantically searching for the right ones to say. "You cannot possibly understand."

Alicine stepped around and stood at Dayn's side. "We can't understand if you don't explain it to us."

Reiv stared hard at the floor in front of him, then tucked his hands beneath his folded arms. "I do not want you to see. Can you understand that?"

"You don't have to show us, Reiv," Alicine said, sounding genuinely remorseful at her earlier insistence that he do so. "But can't you at least tell us?"

Reiv stood silently for a moment, then looked into their curious faces. He unfolded his arms and held out his hands, struggling to set his face with indifference. "Burned. They were burned. That is all you need to know."

Alicine took a step toward him, her eyes full of sympathy. "Maybe I can help."

"No one can help," Reiv replied.

"But there are treatments."

"Everything that could have been done, has been done." Reiv waved his arms around him. "Do you not see all the bottles? Do you not see all the herbs? Brina and I have been working for a year now to try to make my hands better. No, Alicine, there is nothing else that can be done."

"It's been a year since it happened?" Alicine asked.

"Yes," he said.

"And that is why you are called Jecta?" Dayn asked hesitantly.

Reiv's eyes shot in his direction. "Yes. But I am *not* Jecta. I was born Tearian. That is what I am, not Jecta!"

"What of your family?" Alicine asked.

"Brina is my only family. Well, and now Dayn; and you, I suppose."

Dayn drew in a breath. "Reiv—" But before he could finish they were startled by a loud knock at the door.

"Brina!" Dayn exclaimed, his voice full of hope. He turned and ran in the direction of the door.

"No, Dayn! Stop!" Reiv shouted.

But it was too late. Dayn reached the door and threw open the latch.

17
Princes and Warriors

Brina paused in the shallow alcove and scanned the river of faces winding past. She wasn't supposed to be there, royals were not allowed this close to Market without an escort. But she had lied that morning, claiming she was going to see an ailing friend who lived nearby. She did indeed call on that friend, justification for the falseness of her words, but stayed only long enough to solicit the woman's silence and a change of clothing. The promise to bring her friend back a Shell Seeker trinket had sealed the agreement between them.

She pressed her back into the shadows as two members of the Guard strolled past. Although she was dressed in pastel green in place of royal yellow, Brina could not risk the guards' attentions upon her. Were they to recognize her face, and they very likely would, there would be no explaining her way out of it. She eased from the wall and watched the guards as they disappeared into the crowd. Pulling in a steadying breath, she stole into the mass of bodies and made her way out the gates toward the Market grounds beyond.

A large Tearian man, blinded by a tower of purchases teetering in his arms, pushed into her, almost knocking her off her feet. Before he had a chance to finish his half-hearted apology, Brina turned and disappeared into the crowd. With growing impatience, she craned her neck to see over the throng ahead of her. The Shell Seeker tents were just up ahead. That would be her first stop.

The Shell Seekers always had the greatest number of customers at their booths, for they were the most sought-after crafters at Market. They were the only ones who dared dive into the sea, so the goods they brought were considered a luxury. Over the years, the Tearians valued the shell wares so greatly that they came to regard the Shell Seekers more highly than the other merchants. But there was still no denying what the Shell Seekers were—Jecta.

A shell pink awning caught Brina's eye and she worked her way to it. Shouldering her way between a wall of haggling customers who crowded the booth, she moved to the back where a dark-haired young man was speaking with a patron. Brina strolled along the tables, fingering shells here and there, all the while eyeing the young man. His business finally completed, she motioned him over in her most authoritative manner.

"Young man," she said, "I am looking for a special vessel, a gift for my sister."

"Of course," the young man said. "As you can see, we have many. What did you have in mind?" He ushered her over to the display of intricately designed bottles, vases, and urns that lined a shelf along the back of the booth.

"A perfume bottle," she said.

"Here is a nice one," he said, picking up a beautiful pink bottle inlaid with a swirl of bird-shaped shells.

Brina took the bottle and examined it, commenting on its beauty as she rotated it in the light. "It is lovely, but not quite what I had in mind." She sighed and handed the bottle back to him, then bent down to inspect the row of bottles more carefully.

"I see nothing here that is to my liking. Have you anything else you could show me?"

"Well," the young man replied, "there is one you might be interested in, but it is in the back still being crafted. I could not risk handling it to bring it to you here."

"Take me to see it then," Brina said.

"Very well," he said, motioning toward a flap dividing the stall from the tent at its back. "Please, allow me..." He bowed and held the flap back as Brina brushed past him. Glancing over his shoulder, he stooped and made his way through the low portal and disappeared with her to the other side.

Brina grabbed the young man's arm. "Torin," she whispered. "Where is your sister?"

"Here is the bottle you wanted to see," Torin said somewhat loudly. Then he whispered, "She's here, somewhere. What's wrong, Brina?"

Brina hesitated. She knew she could confide in him. She had known him since he was a child and knew him to be trustworthy. But she wanted his sister Jensa to be there before she divulged her plan. She studied his worried face for a moment. Torin was a handsome young man, tall, with a striking mane of jet-black hair braided and pulled away from his face. He was dressed in a loincloth, and his chest was covered with strands of colorful shells. Tattoos encircled his muscular arms and black kohl lined his dark brown eyes. Nothing about him could be mistaken for Tearian, except perhaps his pride.

"Tell me Brina," he said. "What is it?"

"I will tell you, but I want Jensa to be here when I do. This will concern you both."

Torin placed a hand on Brina's shoulder and nodded. "Wait here and I'll fetch her." And with that he slipped through the flap and went back to the stall.

Brina fingered a half-finished bottle that lay amongst the shells and tools littering the worktable. The flap opened behind her and she wheeled around, then smiled with relief.

Jensa strode into the room, her presence filling it. Tall and lithe, she stood nearly the same height as her slightly older brother, Torin. Her hair was dark, though not as dark as his, and was piled up in braids and ringlets. The shells decorating her ears cascaded down her long neck and across her barely covered breasts. The green tattoos around her arms gave the impression of ocean waves dancing across her golden skin. Her kohl-lined, pale blue eyes darted in Brina's direction. "Torin says you need some assistance with a bottle," she said.

"Yes, this one here," Brina said.

"What is it, Brina?" Jensa said in a hushed voice. She ushered her to the back of the tent.

"Who is watching the booth?" Brina asked.

"Mya is watching it for us," Jensa replied. "What—"

"I need your help," Brina said. "There are two Jecta I need smuggled out of the city."

"Smuggled out? Who are they?" Jensa asked.

"Strangers. Reiv brought them to his place last night."

"Reiv—humph!" Torin said. "Since when does he take in Jecta?"

Brina's mouth compressed momentarily, then she said, "Torin, please, can we keep our personal feelings out of this?"

"But Brina, you know how Reiv is. Why would he have Jecta at his place?"

"He thought they were thieves. He intended to take them to Headquarters, but was delayed due to the wedding." She shot Torin a cool look to remind him the previous day's festivities would have been particularly difficult for her nephew.

"Are they thieves?" Jensa asked.

"No. Reiv made a mistake."

"Reiv *is* a mistake," Torin muttered under his breath.

"Torin," Brina said, struggling to keep her voice down. "Reiv made a mistake and he is doing everything in his power to rectify it. May I remind you that he is at risk also? They were seen by the guards last night. They know he had the Jecta with him and that he was planning to take them to Headquarters.

What do you think will happen to Reiv when they discover he never turned them over?"

Torin moved to speak, but Jensa put a commanding hand on his arm. "Torin, put your hostilities aside and listen to what Brina has to say."

He nodded and folded his arms. "What is it you need us to do, Brina?"

"They need to be smuggled out. I am planning to go to Pobu to see Nannaven. I need to find them a place to stay."

"That still doesn't answer what you want us to do," Jensa said.

"If Reiv could get them this far without being detected by the guards," Brina said.

"Then they could leave with us," Torin added, piecing her plan together.

"Yes, and you could escort them to Pobu. Of course there could be some risk to you. The guards might recognize them, but they are dressed as Jecta now so perhaps—"

"Dressed as Jecta? But you said they *were* Jecta. Brina, who are these people?" Jensa asked.

"A boy and a girl. They are very special. That is all I can tell you now."

Jensa and Torin looked at each other in bewilderment.

Brina continued. "I told Reiv that if I was not back by High Sun he was to take them to Pobu himself and wait for me at Gair's shop."

"Reiv? To Pobu?" Torin was shocked. "Gods, they *must* be special. He would never go there if they weren't."

"Exactly. That is why I need to get back from Pobu before too long to tell him to come here instead. I did not want to send him here unless I had spoken to you first. His presence in Pobu would raise too much suspicion, by both Tearian guards and Jecta." Brina narrowed her eyes at Torin. "All the more reason to give Reiv some credit, Torin. He knows that if I do not return he is to take them to Pobu himself and he is willing to do it."

Torin stiffened his back. "I'm sorry, Brina, you're right."

Brina looked around the tent and toward the flap. "We do not have much time to talk. Jensa, do you have a wrap I might borrow? I was watched with much more scrutiny than usual this morning. Even though I managed to borrow this frock, the color might still draw unwanted attention."

"Of course, Brina, whatever you need." Jensa walked over to a large trunk and pulled out a lightweight cloak.

"Oh, and a trinket for the owner of these clothes," Brina said. Jensa lifted a strand of shell beads from around her neck and handed it to her. Brina pulled the beads over her head and draped the cloak around her shoulders. "I noticed more guards than usual milling about today. Something is afoot and I pray it does not involve Reiv or the Jecta he is harboring. Is there perhaps a way one of you could watch his place, just to make sure they are safe until I return?"

Torin frowned and shook his head. "Jensa and I would be noticed in that area of the quadrant. Shell Seekers don't go there."

"I know," Brina said, "but—" An energetic boy bounded into the room and rushed toward her, his short arms suddenly wrapped around her hips.

"Brina!" he exclaimed. His eyes twinkled as his grinning, freckled face turned up to hers.

Brina reached down and tousled his sandy-colored hair. "And how is my little warrior today?"

"Good Brina! Why are you here? Are you going to stay? Are you? *Please* say you will! " The boy looked pleadingly into her face and grabbed her hand, jumping up and down.

"Kerrik, settle yourself down this instant," Jensa ordered. She grabbed him by the shoulders and pulled him away.

"But Jensa," he protested. "I only want—"

"I don't care what you want," Jensa said sternly, squeezing his shoulders even tighter. "Brina did not come to see you."

"Oh, Jensa," Brina said, "I always have time to see my favorite person." She smiled sweetly at the boy who was struggling to remove himself from his sister's firm grasp.

"Jensa," Torin said, his voice strangely level, "couldn't Kerrik spy for us?"

"Torin!" she cried. "Are you mad?"

"He's seven years old now. I was younger than that when I started taking up the cause and you were even younger still. Remember?"

"What are you saying?" Brina said.

"What I'm saying is that Jensa and I can't go undetected to the place you want us to go. But Kerrik—"

"No, absolutely not!" Jensa stomped her foot. "I will not have it!" She looked over at Brina for support, but Brina revealed no sign of it. "Brina, surely you don't expect—"

"Torin, do you think the boy could manage it?" Brina asked, glancing down at Kerrik's twisted right foot.

Kerrik's eyes, wide with anticipation, darted between Brina and Torin. He wrenched free of Jensa's grasp and bounded over to his older brother. Lifting his head, he puffed out his chest in an attempt to look bigger.

Torin laughed. "Have you ever known anything to slow this boy down? Besides, I've been working with him and, as you know, our little warrior has been most anxious to be just that. Maybe this would be a good first job for him."

Brina looked over at Jensa whose hand had risen to her mouth. "Jensa, you know how much I love Kerrik. I would never risk him. But, this is so important."

Brina knelt down in front of Kerrik and placed her hands on his shoulders. Staring him in the eye, she took a very serious tone. "Kerrik, I need your help. Do you know where Reiv lives?"

"Yes, Brina."

Jensa gasped. "How could you possibly know?"

"I've been there," Kerrik replied matter-of-factly.

"*Been* there?" Jensa exclaimed.

"Of course," he replied, "What do you think I do all day at Market while you and Torin are flattering Tearians?"

"But to *Reiv's*?" Jensa said.

"He never knew I was spying. Nobody saw me. I just wanted to see the Prince."

Brina stifled a smile. Why wouldn't the boy want to see him? Reiv was famous, after all, especially amongst the Jecta boys who thought being a prince must be the greatest thing in the world. "Kerrik," she said, "all I need you to do is watch Reiv's place. Nothing more. Can you do that?"

"Of course."

"If anyone goes there, anyone other than me, you must come back and tell Jensa and Torin immediately, do you understand?"

"I understand."

"And Kerrik, if anything happens there, under no circumstances are you to interfere."

"I will be the best spy the Jecta have ever known," Kerrik said bravely.

"I know you will," Brina replied. Then she pulled him into her arms and hugged him tight.

"Brina, please," Kerrik whined. He squirmed from her grasp. "I'm not a baby."

Brina took a deep breath and rose, then turned her attention to Jensa and Torin who were standing silently to the side. "Here is what we must do," she said. "I will go to Pobu. Kerrik will keep an eye on Reiv's place. After I have secured a place for them with Nannaven, I will return here to let you know all is well, then go to Reiv and instruct him to bring the boy and girl here. You can then take them with you when you leave Market."

Torin and Jensa nodded.

"And if you don't come back?" Jensa asked.

"If Kerrik sees Reiv leave with them, he is to follow and give him the message to come here." She looked over at Kerrik. "Can you do that Kerrik?"

"Yes, Brina. I know what to do," he said.

Brina smiled. "I knew I could count on you."

Brina tightened the cloak around herself and pulled the hood up over her head. She walked toward the rear exit of the tent, then paused. "There are no words to tell you how grateful I am," she said over her shoulder. Then she slipped through the portal and left them standing in awkward silence.

Jensa pulled Kerrik over and spun him around to face her. "First, we must get this kohl off of you," she said, scowling with disapproval. She reached for a rag that was draped across the workbench and scrubbed it across his face.

"Ow, Jensa, that hurts!" Kerrik cried, trying to jerk his face away from the harsh wipes that were only replacing the black marks with red.

"Be still!" Jensa barked.

Torin stepped toward them. "Are you trying to wipe off his entire face?"

Jensa shot Torin an icy glare. "And you! I cannot believe you suggested this." She turned her attention back to the wriggling boy and continued to rake the rag across his skin.

"He'll be fine, Jensa. It's time."

"Time? Time for what? Time to risk his neck?"

"No, time for him to grow up."

Torin yanked Kerrik from Jensa's grasp. "Let him be," he said as he ushered the boy away from her.

Jensa stood staring at Torin, her blue eyes now black with rage. She threw the kohl-smeared rag to the ground. "Fine, but this will be on your conscience, Torin, not mine!"

Torin frowned at his sister, then placed his hands on the boy's small shoulders. "Kerrik, you are a man now. Be brave. Be smart."

"Yes, Torin," Kerrik said, looking up at his big brother proudly.

Torin stared into the boy's sparkling eyes, the blueness of them now surrounded by streaks of pink and gray. For a moment Torin hesitated, then he took the small chin into his hand and shook it firmly. "Be careful," he stressed. The boy nodded enthusiastically and Torin straightened his shoulders. "Off with you then." He escorted Kerrik across the room and out of the tent.

"I don't like this. Something's not right," Jensa said.

"Brina needs us, sister, and she's always done for us. What would you have us do, ignore her pleas for help?" Torin walked over to her and placed an arm around her shoulder. "Kerrik will be fine. You'll see."

"No, Dayn, wait!" Reiv shouted from the atrium. But it was too late. Dayn had already thrown open the door.

Dayn froze in the portal and felt the color drain from his face. Before him stood Crymm, flanked by several Tearian Guards, all with swords drawn. Dayn grabbed the door in a desperate attempted to shove it closed, but quickly found himself knocked to the ground. Crymm took a menacing step toward him and seized hold of his tunic, yanking his head from the floor.

"Where is the princeling?" Crymm demanded.

"I don't know!" Dayn cried, grabbing Crymm's wrist.

Crymm slapped Dayn across the mouth. "Do not lie to me!" he barked.

Dayn felt warm blood pool on his lower lip. His eyes darted around for a sign of rescue.

"Crymm!" Reiv shouted as he rounded the drape and ran into the room. "Let him be!"

Crymm threw Dayn to the ground and stepped over him, then marched, sword drawn, toward Reiv.

Reiv stopped and stood fast.

"So I have you at last, Jecta," Crymm said, grinning.

Dayn's eyes shot to Reiv's, searching for the reaction that would surely come from his being called Jecta. But Reiv's expression indicated no acknowledgment of it.

"Why Crymm, whatever do you mean?" Reiv asked. He folded his arms across his chest.

"You know full well what I mean. You are harboring Jecta thieves, are you not?" Crymm tightened his grip on the sword and took a step toward Reiv.

"They are not thieves," Reiv said.

"Oh, but *you* are," Crymm said. "I saw you stealing from the dormitories this very morning. Do not deny it. I watched you."

"I do not know what you think you saw, but I stole nothing."

Crymm slitted his eyes in Dayn's direction. "Oh really? I seem to recall your guests were dressed in some rather odd attire last night."

"What of it?"

"Do you normally keep women's clothing in your apartment?" Crymm motioned to Alicine who was now being shoved into the room by another guard. "I'm sure Labhras, as well as the Commander, will have some choice words for you and your thief friends." Crymm strutted over to Alicine and fingered a long strand of hair that cascaded across her shoulder. He glanced at Reiv, no doubt expecting a reaction. Alicine jerked her head away, while Dayn scrambled to his feet and made his way toward her.

Reiv threw out a stiff arm and blocked his cousin's path. "I will handle this," he said. He took a step toward Crymm. "Take your hands off of her, or I will be sharing a few choice words with Labhras about *you*."

Crymm smirked and released Alicine's hair, then wiped his hand down his chest. He strolled around the room, lifting an item here and there, and examined the meager contents with a critical expression. "Not exactly a palace, is it?"

"What is your point, Crymm?"

"My, but your arrogance does land you in the worst sort of places. Well, compared to the jail cell you will soon be visiting, this will seem like a palace."

"And just why do you think I will be visiting a jail cell?" Reiv asked coolly.

"Stealing, for one thing," Crymm said, eyeing Alicine's red sarong.

"I stole nothing. It was a purchase, nothing more."

Reaching into a small pocket, Crymm pulled out a coin and flipped it into the air, then caught it in his hand. "Is that so?"

"Your pay for the month, Crymm?"

Crymm's face grew red. Snapping his fingers, he motioned one of the guards toward him. The guard stepped forward with a bag clutched in his fist. He handed it to Crymm who shook it in the air, jingling its contents. "It seems you dropped something in your mad dash from the dormitories, princeling." He opened the bag and held it up. Turning his hand over slowly, he poured the contents of the bag out. Beaded necklaces, bronze bracelets, and a decorative belt of shells, cascaded down and danced across the floor.

Reiv's jaw went slack. "You know full well I did not take those things!"

"Oh, but I saw you drop them. Of course that is what I will tell the Commander."

"Why should he believe your lies?"

"Why should he believe yours? We will let him be the judge of who is lying and who is not." Crymm then turned to the guards. "Take them," he ordered. And with that he turned on his heels and strode out the door.

18
The Other Side of the Bars

Brina pushed her way against the chattering flow of Jecta and kept her eyes on the dirt road ahead. The cloak she had borrowed concealed her hair and upper class attire, but her face was still at risk for recognition. Over the years she had made the acquaintance of many of the Jecta bustling past, but she dared not make eye contact with any of them now.

The crowd began to thin and Brina found her advancement to Pobu less trying. She quickened her pace, rehearsing in her mind what needed to be said to the Spirit Keeper. Nannaven would not be expecting her, and Brina prayed the old woman would be home, not tending to a sick child or some other task that befell her status in the community. There was no time to search for her, and little time to explain.

Pobu was just up ahead, nestled in the valley at the end of the dusty road. It was nothing like the great metropolis Brina had left behind. While the pastel outline of Tearia's buildings was impressive, Pobu's was dull by comparison. Its buildings were low and tightly packed, the mud-brick walls of them blending into the dirt as though they had simply risen from it. There were no gates, no guards, no banners, nothing to indicate pride in its identity or any desire to maintain power and security for its residents. It was dusty, and crowded, and filthy compared to Tearia, for the Jecta had long since given up hope of improving their lot in life.

The rutty road stretched into the city until it was assimilated into a huge courtyard, leaving Brina to select any one of the narrow lanes that disappeared between the sameness of the buildings. Normally she would have been met by the noises and smells of vendors selling their wares: dried fruits scavenged from Tearian orchards, flatbreads and sweet breads, unknown meats hanging from hooks, blankets and trinkets and crafts. But today the courtyard was unusually empty, except for the beggars and those too old or sick to make their way to Market. Brina scurried past them without her usual offering of assistance. Her errand would allow her no time for charity today.

She made her way down several narrow, winding streets before reaching the weatherworn door of the Sprit Keeper's house. She knocked, then pushed open the creaky door and peered inside. "Nannaven?" she said. She stepped through the threshold and glanced around. The room was dark and cool and smelled of sweet herbs and onions. The Spirit Keeper always had something cooking in the great black pot that hung in her hearth.

"Is that you, Brina?" The elderly voice from across the room was soft and calm and did not seem terribly surprised, although it should have been. Nannaven was sitting on the floor in front of the hearth, reweaving the grasses of a well-worn mat. She ushered Brina over with a wave of her hand. "Sit child," the old woman said. "Tell me."

Brina gathered her wits and sat as instructed, then stared into the ancient face of the Spirit Keeper. The crinkles around the woman's eyes deepened with her smile.

Brina worked her mind to find the words to explain, but she suddenly felt afraid. It surprised her, for she had never feared the wise old woman seated across from her before. But she had lied to the Spirit Keeper, and now had to face her for it.

"Nannaven," Brina said, "I have come to beg your help. There is a boy and a girl I need you to shelter."

Nannaven tilted her head and eyed Brina curiously as she continued to work the reeds of the mat. "What is so unusual about that, my dear? You have spirited many an unwanted Tearian child my way over the years."

"But these are not Tearian children."

The old woman paused. "Your face is flushed. Here, let me get you some refreshment." She went to raise herself up, but Brina motioned her to stay.

"There is no time for the luxury of drinks," Brina said, the pace of her words quickening. "Will you shelter them?"

Nannaven furrowed her brow. "Who are these children?"

"There is a boy, sixteen years old, and a girl younger. They are at Reiv's and must be smuggled out."

"Reiv's? But how did—"

"It is a long story, but I will say this much, I would give my life for them."

"You did not answer my question, Brina. Who are they?"

Brina's gaze moved from the Spirit Keeper's questioning face to the fire dancing in the hearth. "The boy is my son," she said.

"I see," the Spirit Keeper replied.

Brina's eyes shot to hers. The tone in the woman's voice had not contained the shock or confusion she had anticipated. It had, in fact, sounded almost as if the Spirit Keeper expected it.

"Nannaven," Brina said, "I lied to you in when I told you my son was dead. That night sixteen years ago when I took him to do what was expected of me, I found I could not do it. I went to the mountains instead. I took him to be saved, but I sinned in so doing it, this I know. I defied the laws of my people and of my gods, but I did not care—not then, not now. I took my baby to the sacred mountains, searching for the gods, but in my ignorance I left him with a man."

"A man?" Nannaven said. She set the mat aside.

"I thought he was a god, but he was a man. All this time my child has been with strangers, raised in an unknown place, a forbidden place. Now he has returned to me, but his life is in great danger. Please, Nannaven, will you take him?"

"Of course I'll take him. Did you think I would not?"

"He has been falsely accused of thievery, but I have no time to explain. I must get back to Reiv's."

A sudden shadow darkened the doorway and the jingle of shells mixed with the sound of labored breathing entered the room.

"Brina, Spirit Keeper," Torin said, bowing hurriedly. "You must come back now, Brina. Guards have taken them!"

Brina gasped and rose quickly from the floor. "Guards have taken them? Oh gods, oh gods." She paced back and forth, wringing her hands. "What am I going to do? What am I going to do?"

"Calm yourself!" Nannaven said, rising also. "Torin, what do you know?"

"Kerrik was watching them. The guards came and took them—Reiv, the boy, and the girl."

"Were they all right? Were they hurt in any way? *Were* they?" Brina demanded.

"I don't know," Torin said, but his expression said otherwise.

"I must speak with Mahon." Brina brushed past him and headed for the door.

"Stop this instant, Brina," Nannaven ordered. "You are not thinking clearly. You are letting your emotions dictate your actions. Exercise some common sense, my girl. You mustn't reveal too much too soon. What would you say to Mahon?"

"I do not know, but he is the boy's—" She glanced over at Torin, then rephrased her statement. "He is the Commander of the Guard and would have some say as to their treatment. Perhaps I could persuade him."

"To do what? Let them go? Why should he?" Nannaven asked. "No, you mustn't reveal any of what you have told me, Brina. Not to anyone, especially to your husband. Talk to

Mahon if you must, but no matter what he sees, or suspects, or thinks he knows, he mustn't know the truth. Not yet. Do what you can, but watch your words."

Brina nodded.

"You must get them here to me, all three of them."

"Reiv would never."

"He'll come," Nannaven said. "I do not think he'll have a choice."

Reiv threw a scowl in Crymm's direction, sending an extrasensory dagger into the guard's arrogant back. The man was strutting up ahead, his golden head held high, his sword of power clutched in hand. From the cocky bounce in his step, he had a prize catch indeed.

A throng of spectators lined the streets, making way for the small parade of guards and prisoners walking down the middle of it. Anxious voices traded theories about the two Jecta, particularly the pale-haired boy. His features were whispered to look like that of the Lord Prince. But it was the red-haired prince-turned-Jecta that held most of their attentions.

Reiv twisted his wrists to ease the pain of the straps that bound his arms at his back. He glanced at the crowd on either side of him. Hundreds of judgmental eyes scraped over him while comments punctuated with laughter assaulted his pride. He swallowed the nausea that had edged up his throat, and worked to slide a brave mask in place. But even a mask would not disguise his fear if he vomited it onto his feet.

Crymm glanced back at Reiv, who refused to meet his eye, then stormed back toward him and thrust a boot in his path. Reiv tumbled into the dirt while Crymm displayed exaggerated surprise. The crowd reacted with cheers and laughter, although a smattering of boos and hisses could be heard as well.

Crymm grinned and raised his arms up as though he was a performer on a stage. He placed his hands on his hips and leaned down toward Reiv. "Are you tired, princeling? Here, let me help you." He grabbed Reiv by the hair and forced him up, eyeing the crowd with a cruel gleam.

"Show some respect to our prince," an angry voice shouted from the crowd.

"Is that not what he is doing?" another said, laughing.

"Don't spoil his pretty face," a woman's voice exclaimed.

Reiv spit the dirt from his mouth and forced his eyes forward. His stoic mask slid back into place while his belly burned with humiliation. He could ill-afford to let loose his proud temper. It would do him little good bound like an animal, and he could not risk Dayn and Alicine over it. He marched forward, a guard prodding him in the back.

The crowd thinned as the parade neared the inner quadrant. No doubt most of the spectators realized they would see nothing more once the prisoners were secured within the walls of Guard Headquarters. They would find out soon enough what was going on, so most turned back to enjoy what was left of their holiday instead.

Reiv glanced back at Dayn and Alicine. They were walking a few paces behind him, their hands bound at their backs, their mouths agape as they drank in the sights. This part of the city was different from that which they had passed, certainly nothing like where Reiv lived. Evidence of great wealth could be seen in every inch of this quadrant. The buildings were a harmonious blend of white, blond, and pink stone, and there were towering pillars carved with flutes and scrolls and tiny god-like faces. Baskets of flowers dangled from looming archways and fountains sprayed water amongst marble statues. More than once Dayn and Alicine tripped over themselves as they looked at everything but their feet.

"Surely no such place exists in this world," Dayn said, pausing momentarily in his tracks.

Reiv turned his eyes to the source of Dayn's awe and felt his legs go momentarily weak. Before them stood a soaring peach-colored building, so tall it seemed to touch the clouds. Terraced with floral gardens, the massive structure was built on a hillside and surrounded by cascading streams and bubbling fountains.

Reiv struggled to divert his attention, but the pull of the place was too overwhelming to ignore. There, in all its radiance and beauty, was his former home, the home of his family, the place where he had been born and raised. A lump of realized sorrow filled his throat, but he pushed it down. That was in the past, and there was nothing he could do about it now.

They were escorted up a pathway that wound through a great greenway, landscaped and clipped to perfection. From there they continued up the hill toward Headquarters, a handsome structure that housed the business dealings of the Guard. Frescoes decorated its vast, cream colored portico where scenes of Tearian guards atop great horses could be seen, their manes and flags forever waving.

When they reached its entrance, Crymm ordered them to halt. A guard pushed the door open while Crymm strode back to Reiv with a cruel grin plastered across his face.

"It has been a while since you were last here, has it not, little lord?" he said. "Well, this time you will be seeing it from the other side of the bars." He turned on his heels and marched through the doors, signaling the guards to follow with the prisoners.

Reiv, Alicine, and Dayn were ordered to stand off to the side while the Commander was summoned. They gazed around the room, from its clean-whitewashed walls to the simple but elegant furnishings it contained. The brown terracotta floors were polished to a shiny glow that accentuated the light shining down from the casements above. Crymm stood in the filtering light, his back to the group, legs spread apart and hands clasped at his back. He lifted his head as voices could be heard echoing down the corridor to his right.

Dayn and Alicine glanced at Reiv, who could not disguise his anxiety.

"What is it, Reiv?" Dayn whispered.

"Nothing," Reiv said quietly. But it was not nothing. Mahon was approaching; he recognized his voice.

Mahon stormed into the room, red-faced at the obviously unwelcome interruption. An impressive man, Mahon was tall and well built, with a golden mane of curls that reached to his shoulders. His gray eyes flashed in Crymm's direction. "What is it Crymm?" he said. "I was in the midst of some pressing business and was told there was some sort of emergency."

"Sir," Crymm said, standing at stiff attention, "I have brought Jecta prisoners per orders of Labhras, sir."

"Prisoners?" Mahon said. He turned his attention to where they stood. "What are the charges?"

"Thievery, sir," Crymm replied.

Mahon marched past Crymm and approached the three, his eyes narrowing in recognition of Reiv. He stopped before his former nephew and scowled. "By the gods!" he said. "What—" Then his eyes fell on Dayn and the words dissolved on his tongue.

Mahon moved toward Dayn, his realization of the boy's resemblance to Whyn all too apparent. He walked around the prisoner, looking him up and down.

"Who is this?" Mahon asked sternly, staring hard into the face of the boy now quaking before him.

"A Jecta thief, sir," Crymm said. "I do not know his name."

"Well, boy, what is your name?" Mahon demanded.

"Dayn, sir," Dayn's barely-level voice replied.

"Where are you from, Dayn?" Mahon asked, moving in for a closer inspection.

"I—we—"

"He is from Pobu," Reiv interjected.

"Silence from you," Mahon shouted, glaring at Reiv's suddenly downcast eyes. Mahon turned his attention back to Dayn. "I said, where are you from, boy?"

"Pobu, sir," Dayn said.

Mahon turned to inspect Alicine. "So, Jecta thieves, eh?" he said. Then he returned his gaze to Dayn alone, and stared at him intently.

Dayn averted his face, and the rose-colored birthmark on his neck suddenly surged into view. Mahon's breath caught audibly as an expression of horror swept his face.

"I thought the same thing," Reiv said, stepping forward. "He looks much like the Lord Prince, but I assure you, it is coincidence only. Nothing more, sir."

Mahon narrowed his eyes at Reiv, then nodded, grim faced. He turned and marched back to face Crymm, who was still standing at attention. "Crymm, you say you have brought them here on Labhras's orders. I need to speak to him immediately. Take the prisoners to the holding cell while I send someone to fetch him." Mahon glanced momentarily back at Dayn, then turned and walked briskly from the room.

Crymm grinned at the three as he approached them. "This way, thieves," he said. "Or shall I let the princeling lead you there? He certainly knows the way."

Reiv pushed past and led Alicine and Dayn down the dim, narrow corridor. He shot a glare over his shoulder to Crymm who now wore an expression of fury.

"Here it is, is it not, Crymm?" Reiv said as he stopped in front of a tiny barred room.

Crymm reared his fist as though to strike. Reiv lifted his jaw, challenging him to go through with it.

"No!" Alicine shouted.

Crymm smiled. "Perhaps you are right," he said, relaxing his fist. "I would not want to be considered cruel now would I?" He pulled down a cluster of keys from a peg on the wall and shoved his way past Reiv, almost knocking him off of his feet. "In you all go," he said, pushing them into the small, sparsely furnished cell.

"What about our hands?" Reiv said as Crymm pulled the door closed. But the man only laughed and turned to walk away.

"What will the Commander say to you not letting your prisoners see to their personal needs?" Reiv shouted through the bars. Crymm could make up a variety of excuses for why he needed to leave bruises on them, but even he would have trouble explaining why he left their hands tied at their backs in a holding cell.

Crymm halted with a growl, then stormed back and unlocked the door. He pulled his sword from its sheath and strode in Alicine's direction, all the while watching Reiv.

"Shall I just cut the ropes?" Crymm said, eyeing the tip of the blade. "Or shall I . . ."

Dayn rushed forward and pushed his body into Crymm, shoving him against the wall.

"Why you piece of—!" Crymm cried, lurching toward him.

Reiv leapt between them, his eyes flashing. "Let me remind you, Crymm, that I may not be what I once was, but I still have enough information on you that notice will be paid!"

Crymm gnashed his teeth, no doubt understanding Reiv's implication, and marched over to Alicine. He grabbed her by the arms, spun her around, and sliced the ropes at her back. Then he turned to Dayn and ran the sword between his bindings, cursing him under his breath as he did so. Lastly he cut Reiv's ropes, but not before digging the blade tip into the back of his arm. "We will see who pays notice to what," he hissed into Reiv's ear. Then he shoved Reiv away, knocking him against the wall, and stormed from the cell, slamming the door behind him with an echoing *clank*.

Reiv grabbed his forearm and held it tight.

Alicine rushed over to him. "He cut you? Here, let me take a look." She reached her hand to his arm, but he pulled away.

"It is nothing," he said.

"Don't be stupid, Reiv. Let me see."

Reiv removed his hand and lifted his arm so both he and she could take a closer look. Dayn walked over and leaned in, staring at the trail of blood now dripping into the straw.

"God, Reiv," Dayn said, his face looking rather queasy.

"It is not that bad," Reiv said.

Alicine reached down to the hem of her sarong and tore off a strip of cloth, then glanced up at Dayn. By the startled expression on his face, he was thinking the sarong was short enough as it was.

"It's only a knee," she said. "What am I supposed to do? Let Reiv bleed into unconsciousness?"

Dayn gulped and nodded, clearly embarrassed that the thought of her exposed knee had taken precedence in his mind over the welfare of Reiv's wound.

Alicine looked around. "Did he leave us without water?" She shook her head and wrapped the strip of cloth around Reiv's arm, binding it tightly. "We'll need to clean this soon."

Reiv looked down at the brightly colored tourniquet. "Well, this is certainly the most decorative bandage I have ever seen." He watched as the pattern grew darker and wider.

"Sit down and keep the pressure on it, for goodness sake," Alicine said.

Reiv jumped at her command then slumped down against the nearby wall, squeezing his arm. "How long do I have to hold it?" he asked impatiently.

"Until I tell you to stop."

Reiv rolled his eyes.

"You'd best do what she says, Reiv," Dayn said. "You know her temper and you've no place to run." He laughed weakly and gazed around the small, depressing cell.

Dayn started to the sound of creaking hinges. He rose from his spot in the straw and peered between the bars. A tall, blond-haired boy was walking toward them, flanked by two well-armed guards.

The boy motioned for his escorts to wait outside the door, then stepped to the cell. The guards hesitated and remained at his back. A stern look coupled with a loud command from the boy prompted their immediate departure.

Alicine moved next to Dayn and the two of them stared speechless at the visitor. He was truly impressive with his yellow silk tunic, jeweled brooches, and ornately decorated belt. But it was not his clothes that held their undivided attention.

As Dayn faced the boy, he felt as though he was looking at himself. The visitor had the same pale hair, though much neater, and his eyes were the same bright blue. But it wasn't just his coloring; it was every feature on his face.

Dayn glanced in Reiv's direction, noting his cousin had moved to the far side of the cell. The boy stepped back and moved toward Reiv. Reiv glared at the visitor, but did not say a word.

"Reiv," the boy said, "are you not going to acknowledge me?"

Reiv rushed over and grabbed the bars, jerking them with his fists. "Oh, yes, *my lord.* I forgot. It is only I who am not to be acknowledged." He pushed away and bowed with formal sarcasm. "There, is that acknowledgement enough?"

"That is not what I meant," the boy said sternly. "I only meant we need to talk, and it cannot be done with you snarling at me from across the room."

"What is there to talk about? I am here and you are there. I will be convicted of thievery and you will live happily ever after."

The boy's mouth compressed with irritation. "I need to know whether or not you are guilty of the charges."

"Guilty of the charges?" Reiv said, his voice building. "Do you actually think that of me? Gods, I thought you knew me better than that."

"I do not know you at all anymore, Reiv, and I cannot help you if I do not know the facts."

"Here are the facts, dear br—" Reiv glanced over at Dayn and Alicine. "Here are the facts," he said. "I stole nothing and they stole nothing. Who was it that brought us here? Could Crymm *possibly* have it in for me? Think! Or have you erased all recollections of your childhood?"

"I have forgotten nothing," the boy snapped. "And I never will. I am not your enemy and it would be in your best interest not to forget it."

"Enemies come in all forms."

The boy's face reddened and he opened his mouth to speak, but then he shut it with a snap. He and Reiv stared at one another in stony silence until at last the boy said, "You are wrong, Reiv." Then he looked over at Dayn. "There appears to be some mystery at work here. Perhaps some mysteries are best left unsolved." The boy glanced back at Reiv and shook his head, then turned and exited into the corridor, closing the door quietly behind him.

"Who was that?" Dayn asked. "Who, Reiv?"

"Nobody," Reiv said.

"Oh, no," Alicine said. "He is definitely somebody. Tell us, Reiv, who is he?"

"I told you." Reiv heaved a sigh of resignation. "Fine. That was Whyn."

"Whyn? I've heard that name before," Dayn said. "You and Brina said something about my resemblance to him." Dayn approached Reiv and looked him hard in the eye. "Why do we look so much alike?"

Reiv motioned off-handedly. "A coincidence, nothing more."

"I don't buy that," Dayn said. "Who is this Whyn and how do you know him?"

Reiv slumped against the wall and cradled his arm. "Can we discuss this another time?"

"No!" Dayn and Alicine shouted.

Reiv looked up at them with welling eyes. "If you must know, he was my brother. There, satisfied? Now, leave me be. I cannot think anymore." He curled up on the straw, leaving Dayn and Alicine to contemplate his words in stunned silence.

19
The Hearing

Brina rushed into her husband's office like a woman possessed. "What have you done with my nephew!" she shouted.

Mahon lifted his gaze from the parchment on his desk to the face of his exasperated wife. "What does one normally do with a thief?" he said calmly.

Brina gripped the edge of the desk and leaned in toward him. "That is a lie and you know it. Reiv is no thief!"

Mahon returned his attention to the parchment, dismissing her with indifference.

"Mahon!" Brina said, marching around the desk. "Do not disregard me. This is serious."

Mahon drew in a breath of forced tolerance and rolled the parchment into a scroll, then set it aside. "You are correct, wife. It is serious." He stood and stepped over to a table located against the wall behind the desk and picked up a bag, then turned and poured the contents of it upon his desk. "This is evidence of Reiv's thievery. Would you deny it now?"

Brina's eyes widened as Jecta jewelry and trinkets danced across the marble desktop. "What do you mean 'evidence'? Reiv did not take those things. I know it for a fact."

"Oh, do you now? How is it that you know it?" Mahon took a step toward her and stared hard into her face, searching for evidence of a lie, or perhaps the truth for once.

She turned away. "I just know."

"Well, it does not matter what you think you know," he said. "There is also the issue of the Jecta that Reiv had with him."

Brina's eyes darted back to his. "Is Reiv all right?" she asked, refocusing the subject of the debate back to her nephew.

"Of course. He is in a cell where he will remain until the hearing. It could be any time now."

"Any time now? Surely not so soon."

"As soon as Labhras arrives I will be summoned. Sedric is too ill to attend of course, but Whyn will be there, and Crymm unfortunately." Mahon shook his head. "This whole sordid incident is going to have to be handled quickly. The Priestess—"

"The Priestess?" Brina exclaimed. "What does she have to do with this? Gods, Mahon, petty issues such as this are not normally handled by the Priestess. Only issues that warrant consultation with the gods. Why would—"

"Because she ordered it, that is why," Mahon said, cutting her short. "The situation is exceptional, surely you understand that. Important decisions need to be made. You know full well there has been talk in the streets about the boy's Unnaming. And that fool Crymm marching him through the crowd like some sort of prize."

Brina laid a trembling hand upon his arm. "What is going to happen, Mahon? Please tell me."

Mahon pursed his lips. "It is a difficult situation."

"Who will have the ultimate say?"

"You know the answer to that, Brina."

"The prisoners will not be made to appear before her, will they?" Brina asked, digging her nails into his arm.

"Under law there is no obligation to allow Jecta to speak, but since there are extenuating circumstances . . ."

"Surely you have some influence, Mahon. I do not think it wise to parade them before the Priestess. They are only children."

"They are hardly children," he replied crisply. "Regardless, I will have no say in what happens. If the Priestess wishes them brought to her, I will have no choice but to do so."

"I must see them, then," Brina said, making to leave.

"Them? Why must you see *them*? I should think you only need to see Reiv. Or is it Dayn you really need to see?"

Brina felt her face go stark, but she rearranged it quickly. "I said I need to see them. That is all you need to know."

"No, I think there is more. This boy Dayn. He looks so much like—"

"Whyn. Yes I know. Coincidence only."

"So you know him?"

Brina shrugged. "I have seen him at Market."

"How did you know it was he who was arrested with Reiv?"

"I went to see Reiv last night and the boy was there. The talk in the streets was that one of the Jecta was tall and fair, so I just assumed."

"Since when does Reiv entertain Jecta? No, Brina, I think there is more to this boy than you are telling." He paused and forced her eyes to his. "I saw the mark on his neck, and it is exactly like—"

"Do not say the words you plan to speak," Brina said. "Do not dare say them to me, Mahon."

"I *will* say them! He is marked just as our son was marked and he looks like our nephew, your sister's own son! Do not dare say it is coincidence." Mahon grabbed her by the shoulders. "No more lies, Brina. Tell me! Is this boy our son? Is he?"

"No! Our son is dead."

"Are you certain? Did you watch him die? Do you know for a fact he is dead?"

"Of course I know it."

"How can you be so sure?"

"Because I killed him myself!" A sob escaped Brina's throat. "I told you I left him for the gods, but I only said it to spare you, Mahon. I killed him with my own hands. He is dead I tell you. Dead."

The falseness of Brina's words could not prevent the overwhelming emotion she felt at having said them. Her body went weak.

Mahon pulled her into his arms and held her close. "Forgive me," he said. "I did not mean for you to tell me. I only thought that if the boy—"

Brina pushed away. "Our son is not coming back, Mahon. No matter how much we want him to. He is gone forever. Please."

Mahon nodded slowly. "You have lied to me so many times, Brina, that all we have between us now is the lies, and the loss, and the painful memories of our child. When I saw the boy I thought there was a chance he could be ours. Perhaps I even hoped he was. But even if he were my son, he might as well be dead to me. I would never be allowed to be a father to him. You are right. Our son is gone forever."

He turned to leave, then paused. "I would have given you a hundred children had you asked it of me," he said softly.

"How can you say that to me?"

"Because it is true, dear wife. You see, I am a foolish man who can love only one woman, even if that love is not returned." He did not wait for a response and disappeared through the door.

Whyn hustled up the path as two guards struggled to keep pace. The Priestess did not like to be kept waiting and he knew the others had already arrived. He reached the temple quickly, then paused to gather his wits.

Waving the guards back, he made his way in. His lone footsteps and rapid breaths echoed down the corridor. Before him loomed two great double-doors, their towering surfaces decorated with gold filigree. There were images of torture and sacrifice molded upon them, ancient images, but images not forgotten. Whyn set his jaw and shoved the doors open.

The Room of Transcension was large and illuminated by an eerie glow. Immense statues reached from floor to ceiling and lined the perimeter of the room. The images stood cold and silent. Even the torchlight that flickered off their brindle faces provided no sense of warmth. Each statue stood shoulder-to-shoulder alongside another, and all stared with dark, unseeing eyes toward the center of the room. No two were the same. Some were human in form while others were animal, and there were male and female, and some that appeared to be both, or neither. Only one was greater than the rest, and it stood predominantly at the center of the room. The statue's feminine face, made of purest white marble, seemed to be lit by a light from within. It was Agneis, Goddess of Purity, the supreme deity of Tearia.

The Priestess, almost an exact replica of the goddess at her back, sat before it in a high-backed chair centered upon a raised platform. She was dressed in a sleeveless tunic top that sparkled like precious stones, her breasts clearly revealed beneath the pale, shimmering fabric. A wide belt accentuated her slender waist and from it descended an elaborately embroidered apron, each colored thread meticulously woven into a design of unsurpassed splendor. Beneath it she wore a flounced skirt made of overlapping layers of pastel material, each with a different design, each layer adding to the pattern of the next. Her feet were bare, but her nails were painted gold, as were her lips and the lining around her eyes. Her white hair was pulled back by a band that wound around her head, and streams of beaded jewels and feathers trailed down her neck and across her shoulders. Her eyes were icy blue and so pale they glowed like a cat's against the flickering dimness of the room that surrounded her.

"Welcome, our Prince," she said in a smoky voice as Whyn entered the room.

All but she bowed to him, their heads almost touching the floor. He strode past, paying little notice to their respectful display, and kept his gaze fully upon the Priestess. He went before her and bowed low. She reached her hand to his chin and tilted his head up toward her, then stroked his cheek lightly with her fingers. Chill bumps rose on his arms immediately and a shiver crept down his spine. But he showed no sign of discomfort at her touch. He dared not.

Whyn stepped off the platform and made his way to a row of seats that faced the Priestess. He settled himself into a velvet-cushioned chair. On either side of him were cross-legged stools and in front of them stood Labhras, Mahon, and Crymm. Four priests, older men with shaved heads and white linen togas, stood with heads bowed behind the stools.

All waited silently, but the Priestess did not speak for quite some time. It was as though she relished the awkward silence that permeated the room. Finally she rose, and motioned them to sit like a master to her dogs.

Slowly, gracefully, she descended the steps and walked as though floating along the row of men before her. As she passed them, her hand brushed along their faces, necks, and shoulders with a feather-like touch against their skin. Her gaze fell upon them each, one by one, and she searched their faces with pale, piercing eyes.

"There is much emotion here," she said as she walked along. "Hatred . . . jealousy . . . gratitude . . . and—ah . . . what is this?" She held her gaze momentarily on Mahon, then stepped back and surveyed the row once more. "I do not believe a fair judgment can be made amidst so much emotion," she said, shaking her head. "For how could the decision be an unbiased one?" Then she turned her eyes to Whyn alone. "I fear, my dear Prince, that it may be up to the gods to decide the fate of the Unnamed One."

Whyn's eyes widened. "Great Priestess . . . the Unnamed One? To whom do you refer? Do you speak of the prince unnamed, or the Unnamed One of the Prophecy?" His voice trembled slightly as the words left his lips, and all eyes other than hers turned to him in mute, but obvious surprise.

"Perhaps they are one in the same," she said, her features suddenly hard. "If the one the Prophecy speaks of is indeed real, Tearia is at risk." Then she smiled and relaxed her expression. "Of course, who is to say whether the Prophecy is fact or fiction. It was given in the age of the Purge by an impure one, a dark witch, no one of consequence. Regardless, caution must be paid. Things such as prophecies cannot be taken lightly. Belief in them can be powerful."

The Priestess walked back to the platform and returned to her great chair, where she eased herself down and rested her arms upon the golden scrolls beneath them.

Her voice grew loud, the sound of it resonating against the walls. "It would not do for us to ignore such things, just as it would not do for us to displease the gods. History well proves their wrath can be terrible. As you know, Aredyrah was once a larger place, but it grew lazy in its pride. Its people fraternized with the lesser creatures of the land and impurities were allowed to infiltrate. The gods were not pleased. And for that sin, the ancient fires were sent up and the great Purge began." She sighed and rolled her crystal eyes, shaking her head. "Alas, Mercy intervened, but we have done well to keep the impure ones apart, and will continue to do so. As for the Prophecy, the danger is in those who believe it. For that reason alone we must take care not to stir the pot of superstition."

Whyn rose and bowed, then said, "Great Priestess, if it is believed the Unnamed One of the Prophecy walks among us, what would our duty be toward him?"

"That is difficult to say. Acknowledgement of him would only serve to give him power."

"You said one of the prisoners could be he. You know of whom I speak, but I will not utter either of his names in this sacred place. There is talk in Tearia of his treatment, and much unrest has come about because of it. Now he is accused of thievery and there is evidence of it. The other two prisoners trespassed and may have stolen as well. They appear to be friends of the first. Examples should be made, of course, but considering the circumstances—"

The Priestess interrupted him briskly. "I know the circumstances and were it my decision alone, I would execute the one and maim the others." She smiled cruelly. "Alas, I fear the Goddess will need to be consulted. We can risk no error in this."

She leaned her head back and her eyes fluttered closed as her body began to glow with an ethereal light. Whyn sat down quickly and clenched the arms of his chair. The room became strangely silent.

A moan, low and deep like that of an approaching gale, rose from the marble Goddess. The torches along the walls hissed and sputtered, the flickering of the flames accentuating the expressions of apprehension plastered across the faces of those in the room. The Priestess jerked her head and her eyes shot open. They were no longer pale, but black as the darkest night, and she stared out as though unseeing. She spoke from the hole that was her mouth, and her body writhed in the chair like a snake coiled to strike. Then she said in a voice not her own:

The Unnamed One is among us. He has been renamed. He is weak, yet he is strong. The truth could give him power, though he would deny the existence of it. Allowed to survive, others would show him the way; yet, were he to die, the reach of his power would be greater still. He must not be allowed to live, yet he must not be made to die. He must simply fade away . . . fade away . . . fade away . . .

Then the ground rumbled and the room went black.

Dayn fell hard to the floor, suddenly on all fours, and retched noisily into the straw.

"Are you all right?" Alicine cried as she rushed to his side.

Dayn spat the foul taste from his mouth. "Did you feel that?" he asked.

"Feel what?" Alicine asked.

Reiv walked over and stared down at Dayn. "Well, I hope I do not feel it, whatever it is," he said, a mixture of humor and sympathy in his voice.

Dayn scowled at him, then pushed up from the floor. But he immediately found himself falling into Reiv's arms as his legs went out from under him. He landed on one knee, Reiv still holding him by an arm, and grabbed at his queasy stomach.

"Gods, Dayn, what is wrong with you?" Reiv said. He released Dayn from his grip and allowed him to sink to the floor.

"Don't you feel it?" Dayn asked, annoyed. "Like the ground is shifting or something?"

"I do not feel anything," Reiv said. He glanced at Alicine who returned his look of concern, then knelt beside Dayn who was clutching the straw for support. Reiv placed a comforting hand on his back.

"Is this the same feeling you had the other day?" Alicine asked. "You know, when we were going to Summer Fires. Your face is definitely the same color."

"Yes. The same. But it's been happening more and more."

"You didn't tell me it had happened since," Alicine said.

Dayn waved his hand to disregard her concerns. "Just a couple of times. You weren't around. Besides, I didn't want you to worry. It never lasts long anyway."

"This has happened before?" Reiv said. "You mean you have been ill?" He stood and took a step back.

"No, not ill. Something else; I don't know. But if it's like before, it'll leave quickly."

A long moment of silence passed. As Dayn predicted, the queasy feeling left him almost as suddenly as it had occurred. He took a deep cleansing breath and pushed himself up, then wiped his mouth with the back of his hand.

"I'm fine now. Really," he said.

In the darkness of the temple, all that could be heard was the labored breathing of men. Whyn shivered; the air felt like ice against the sweat now coating his skin. The torches on either side of the room suddenly relit, and the room became instantly warm again. The Priestess sat on her chair, as pale-eyed and beautiful as before.

"You have heard the words of the Goddess," she said. "The Unnamed One is to fade away. And that he will do in Pobu, where all people are nameless and faceless to Tearia. As for the other two, an example of their execution will serve our purposes well enough."

Mahon sprang from his stool. "No!" he shouted. He glanced at the others, then bowed his head. "Priestess, please," he said. "I mean no insolence. But if there is a friendship between the three, such harsh punishment might serve as a catalyst for the Unnamed One."

The Priestess stared hard at him, but did not say a word.

Mahon continued hesitantly. "And . . . and the Jecta boy looks much like our Lord Prince. If he was put to death, it could be seen as a bad omen. I do not think any citizen of Tearia knows the reason for their arrest, and I could see that the Guard make no mention of it."

The Priestess studied him in silence, then spoke. "There is much emotion in you, Mahon, yet there is some wisdom in your words." She directed her gaze to Whyn. "What does our Prince say?"

Mahon sat back down as Whyn rose and eyed the row of men. "Labhras," he said, "the two Jecta trespassed against you, and it is from your fields that the thievery took place. What do you say as to their punishment?"

Labhras squirmed in his seat for a moment, his expression that of contemplation under pressure. "Let them fade," he said finally.

Whyn then turned to Crymm. "Crymm, I thank you for your loyalty to Tearia and your prompt handling of the matter of the thieves. Do you feel you would lose face were the punishment of the two Jecta less than maximum?"

"My Lord Prince," Crymm replied, "there could be some question from the Guard under my command as to whether my decision had been a rash one. Might that lessen their respect for me? I do not know, but it is certainly not a risk I would wish to take, not for myself or for Tearia."

Whyn nodded. "Well, Crymm, I would not wish you to lose any respect from your men. You know, you are long overdue a reward for your years of faithful service. Perhaps a promotion would stay any doubt from the minds of the guards under your command. Of course, you understand one of your first responsibilities would be to quash any talk. Nothing more could be said of the three or of the circumstances surrounding their arrest or of their disposal. I am sure word of it has already spread somewhat amongst the guards, but with your skills and new position of authority, I have no doubt such talk could be obliterated. Do you agree?"

Crymm grinned. "Yes, My Lord, of course. I will see to it."

"Very well," Whyn said. He turned to face the Priestess and nodded. "They will fade."

"So be it," she said. Then she rose and left the room, followed by the priests who had not moved or said a single word during the entire proceeding.

"Crymm," Mahon barked when they reached Headquarters, "you will see the prisoners escorted to Pobu tonight, after it is dark and there is no one in the streets. Take only enough guards to ensure security, no more, and see to it they say nothing of this to anyone. Do you understand?"

"Yes, sir."

"And no more grandiose displays."

"Of course not, sir."

Mahon dismissed him and returned to his office, his eyes searching the room as though expecting to see Brina still there. He gathered up the Jecta trinkets scattered across his desk and shoved them back into the bag. The evidence would need to be destroyed or discarded; there was no longer a need to keep it. Of course, the ornaments could be returned to their rightful owner, but what would be the point in that?

He paced around his office, pausing at times to stare out the window, then returned to his seat, only to rise and pace once more. He could not seem to settle his nerves or the constant movement of his legs. Lifting a brow, he wondered if Whyn had seen to it that Reiv was told of the sentence. No, not likely. That would be a sign of interest on the Prince's part, and he had already risked that with his visit to the cell earlier. A groan escaped Mahon's throat. He would see to it himself. It was, after all, the right thing to do, even though he had not always been one to do the right thing.

He walked down the corridor to the holding cell, determined to keep his emotions in check. Resentment had a way of creeping into his heart when it came to Reiv. The boy had pushed the wedge of contempt deeper between him and Brina this past year.

He stormed into the cell area and slammed the door against the wall. "Well," he said in a firm voice, "the sentencing has been made." He paused to momentarily enjoy the expression of terror on Reiv's face, then relaxed his stiff shoulders and allowed the pleasure to diminish. "You are to be banished to Pobu. Tonight."

Reiv closed his eyes and breathed a loud sigh of relief, while the other two stared at Mahon in startled silence.

Mahon caught Dayn's eye and looked away awkwardly. "That is all," he said as he turned to leave.

"Sir," Dayn called out. "Please, may I ask you something?"

Mahon stopped in his tracks. "What is it?" he said over his shoulder.

"Before, you looked at me so strangely. I just wondered why."

Mahon turned to him, his face slack. It was though every muscle had grown weary from years of sternness. "You reminded me of someone."

"You mean Whyn?" Dayn asked.

Mahon bristled at the boy's casual use of the Prince's name. "No," he said harshly.

"Someone close to you?"

Reiv grabbed Dayn by the arm. "Do not ask the Commander of the Guard personal questions! It is not allowed."

"I—I'm sorry," Dayn said.

"No, it is all right," Mahon said. He walked back to the bars and scanned Dayn's face for a moment, then said, "Yes, it was someone close to me. Someone I lost."

"What happened to him?" Dayn asked.

"He died."

"Are you . . . are you . . . Mahon?" Dayn asked, barely able to complete the simple question.

"Yes. And you are Dayn."

"Yes. I'm Dayn."

"Well, Dayn, I will not be seeing you again. You will be escorted from here tonight and will not be allowed back within the city ever again. Do you understand?"

"Yes, sir. I understand."

Mahon stared at him for a brief moment more, then turned and left, closing the door quietly behind him.

Dayn walked to the back corner of the cell, where he sank down upon the floor and stared at the opposite wall. Alicine knelt down and wrapped her arms around him, hugging him tight.

"That was my father," Dayn said.

"I know," she said.

No one in the cell said another word for a very long time.

20
As Good As
Nowhere

It was the middle of the night when Reiv, Dayn, and Alicine were dumped onto the streets of Pobu. The Tearian Guard who escorted them had made a point of insulting and humiliating them every step of the way. Only Reiv had reacted to the treatment, and he quickly found himself face down at the behest of a Tearian boot. Crymm eventually notified his men that no more grandiose displays were to be made. And so they stopped and simply left the three standing in the dark.

The sound of the guards' horses faded into the distance, and the street was left eerily quiet. All Reiv could hear was the hollow tinkle of a reed chime blowing somewhere in the distance. It was most unsettling. The mud-brick buildings on either side of them were a golden color by day, but it was dark now, and they were only distorted silhouettes of gray.

"Now what are we going to do?" Reiv said. He turned in a slow circle, surveying the gloom of their surroundings. "Brina said there was a blacksmith's shop to the right of the town square, so that is where we should go, I suppose. But I do not know where we are exactly. I have not been here since I was a child."

"Well, we came from that direction," Alicine said, pointing behind them, "so let's just go to the right from this point and see where it takes us."

"I was going to suggest that," Reiv said.

"Of course you were," Alicine said.

Reiv scowled an invisible scowl and turned to lead them in the agreed upon direction. He carried himself with stiff grace, determined to look princely, at least somewhat. In truth, he knew he was worse than a nobody here, and the thought of it terrified him.

His entire life he had heard stories about this place, about the filth and crime and people so low they prowled the streets like animals. Of course he had been around Jecta in the past, those who worked for him as well as the merchants invited to show their wares at Market. But those were the exceptional ones, not like the others who were allowed nowhere near the city of Tearia. The others were the diseased and deformed ones, the ones with dark painted faces and even darker thoughts. Panic flooded through him. By the light of day he was going to stand out. Even if the residents of Pobu did not recognize his face, his hair would surely give him away. And then what? He could only imagine what they would do to him for their own twisted pleasure. He quickened his pace, fighting the building knot in his belly.

"There!" Dayn said excitedly. "I'd know a smithy anywhere. I've spent enough time in one."

"Keep your voice down," Reiv snapped.

Dayn brushed past him and made for the door to the smithy. He rattled the handle.

"Dayn," Reiv said, "I said keep quiet."

"What's the problem?" Alicine asked. "Are we not supposed to be here or something?"

"I do not think we need to make a grand announcement."

"Well, it's locked," Dayn whispered loudly. "But smiths usually arrive early, so we'll just wait 'til he gets here."

"Not in the front, though," Reiv said. "Around the back or something."

"Reiv? Are you all right? You sound scared," Alicine said.

"Do not be ridiculous."

"Then what are you not telling us?"

Reiv sighed, resolved to the fact that he would have to tell her the truth, or part of it anyway. "I will not be welcome here. You and Dayn will be fine, but as for me—"

"Why are you not welcome here?" Dayn asked, moving closer.

"It is a long story and I do not wish to go into it. I just think it would be best if we stay hidden until the smith gets here." Reiv stepped around Dayn and Alicine and headed down the alleyway at the side of the building. In the darkness he could just make out the shapes of crates and barrels stacked alongside the wall. He made his way over to them while Dayn and Alicine followed at his back.

"Look, we can settle ourselves behind these," Reiv said. "Maybe we can get a bit of sleep while we wait."

"Fine," Alicine said curtly. "You know, Reiv, one of these days we are going to get all of these stories out of you."

Reiv did not respond and lowered himself next to a barrel. He wrapped his arms around his bent legs and rested his chin on his knees. His mind raced with the events of the previous day, as well as the previous year, and pondered how his life had come to such a sorry end. What had he done to deserve it all, he wondered. He placed his forehead on his knees and closed his eyes, willing the questions and the images to go away. If he could just sleep, maybe he could get a respite from the noises in his head, at least until dawn when he knew the real nightmare would begin.

Reiv opened his eyes and realized it was daylight. He jumped up and pressed his back against the wall. A crowd of people could be seen gathering in the alleyway, staring at the three of them as though they had dropped from the sky. Reiv kicked Dayn with his foot and Dayn responded with a grunt and a grumble. Then he, too, jumped up and pressed himself against the wall next to Reiv.

"Alicine," Dayn said in a raspy morning voice.

She frowned in her sleep and muttered some unidentifiable syllables. Dayn reached down and shook her, then yanked her up by an arm. Rubbing at grainy eyes, she stared in bewilderment at the curious onlookers.

A small gang of Jecta men joined the crowd and pushed their way through, scowling in the direction of the three newcomers standing against the wall. The men eyed them up and down, muttering and whispering, then crossed their arms and cocked their heads. Reiv inflated his chest, determined not to look like a coward.

"Well, what new trash have the illustrious Guard plopped down in our midst now?" one of the men sneered. He eyed the three with a look of disgust, but clearly the look, as well as the remark, was intended for Reiv.

A second man took a bold step toward them and stopped, leaning in toward Dayn and examining him. He eyed the birthmark on Dayn's neck and laughed loudly. "So, you are not so pretty as you first appear." His eyes narrowed as he looked between Dayn and Reiv, noting their fair features and extraordinary hair. "Even royal birth lines do not prevent the treachery of the Tearians. They throw their purebloods into the garbage with the rest."

Reiv seethed at the remark, then ushered Dayn and Alicine behind him. They edged down the alleyway, navigating a maze of crates and barrels at their backs, but it did little to distance them from the throng that continued its approach. Two small boys darted up, one touching Dayn's arm and the other Reiv's hair. Reiv reproached them and one of the boys jumped back, laughing, while the other bowed in feigned reverence. Alicine huddled closer to Dayn who wrapped an arm around her. The noisy chatter of the crowd cramming its way into the narrow alley became louder as questions and comments were passed back and forth. The wall of dark-haired, tattooed faces pressed forward.

Reiv clenched and unclenched his fists at his side. A confrontation was in the making; he could feel it. Dayn, who must have sensed it too, moved next to him. Reiv motioned him back impatiently, and planted himself before the approaching crowd. He held his arms back in a protective gesture, and flashed his violet eyes in the direction of the approaching dark ones. Some of the Jecta snickered, but others just stared mutely, no doubt wondering what the former Prince of Tearia intended to do. But then a rumble of voices swelled from the back of the crowd and all eyes shot toward it.

The mob parted like two great waves in a sea of bodies. Faces turned upward to stare at a huge man shouldering his way between them. The man bellowed orders for the onlookers to step aside, then stopped before the three young strangers and folded his great arms across his burly chest.

Reiv gulped, his Adam's apple lodged like a boulder in his throat. Staring up at the towering man, he felt dwarfed by the sheer magnitude of his size and nervously impressed by the numerous scars that crisscrossed his tawny skin. The man's black and gray streaked hair was pulled back from his ruddy face and revealed a line of intricate tattoos that outlined his forehead and trailed down his jaw.

The man raised his thick, black eyebrows and eyed the three of them intently, then grinned in amusement. He uncrossed his massive arms and rested his fists on his hips.

Reiv reached to his side, but knew it was a foolish move. There was nothing there to grab. He struggled to form a defense in his mind and looked around for anything he could use as a weapon. But there was nothing, other than his own fists, and they were not strong enough to stop a man such as this. The giant took a step toward them, and Reiv retreated, pushing Dayn and Alicine along as he went. He quickly found himself at a stop, pressed against the two of them. They had backed into a wall.

"Well, if it isn't the Prince," the towering man said.

Reiv tightened his jaw and glanced from the man to the faces in crowd. Hundreds of eyes could be seen boring into his, some hating him, some pitying him, and maybe even a scant few respecting him. But then he spied a pair of strikingly blue ones and the face of the beautiful girl behind them.

The girl held his gaze in hers as she worked her way between the mass of bodies. She stopped when she reached the man who was still looming over them. "Gair, you are frightening our young guests," she said. She turned her face up to him, and he leaned down while she whispered into his ear. The man lowered his eyes in contemplation and nodded, glancing at the strangers. He murmured something back to her; then they turned their attentions to the three.

Reiv felt his face grow hot. "We tire of your Jecta welcome," he said. "Speak your business or leave us be."

"I should have expected a response like that," the girl said. "After all, some of the residents have been less than courteous." Her eyes darted back to the crowd, settling momentarily on a few who lowered their heads in response. She looked back at Reiv, then said, "I'm Jensa. I have been sent to fetch you."

Reiv opened his mouth, then snapped it shut. Jensa was unlike anything he had ever seen before. Tall, willowy, and golden skinned, she stared at him with pale eyes that were elaborately outlined with Shell Seeker kohl. Her arms were tattooed with repeating patterns of ocean waves from just below the shoulder to midway to the elbows. Breathtakingly beautiful, she was dressed with only a strip of material wrapped around her breasts and another draped about her hips.

"I am Jensa," she repeated, appearing somewhat baffled by their silence. "Come; follow me. I'll take you to the Spirit Keeper." She motioned them to her, then turned and walked toward the crowd.

For a moment the three hesitated, but then Dayn pushed at Reiv's back. "You heard her. She's taking us to the Spirit Keeper. Go!"

Dayn and Alicine shoved past the still dumbfounded Reiv and followed Jensa into the crowd. Dayn shot a mischievous look back in Reiv's direction. "Come on, fool," he shouted.

Reiv watched as his cousin caught up with the beautiful Shell Seeker, then he sprinted forward, quickly finding himself at Dayn's side. The two boys walked behind Jensa, watching her backside as though under a spell. Her hair, in both braids and ringlets, bounced to her stride, and the shells that adorned her body sang the melody of her movements. The two boys looked at each other momentarily, but neither said a word, then returned their attentions to her backside.

Gair took up the rear of the group, making sure the crowd kept a safe distance, but that didn't prevent the spectators' comments from reaching their ears. "Ruairi . . . prince . . . royalty." Words that could be heard all too clearly now.

Alicine and Dayn looked at each other, expressions of bewilderment blanketing their features. They glanced in simultaneous curiosity over at Reiv, but he did not acknowledge their stares, just as he did not acknowledge those of the crowd.

Jensa led the little brigade through the winding, dusty streets. The original crowd of onlookers began to lag, mostly due to Gair's hostile glares and threatening gestures. But new, equally curious faces moved in to take their place. Some paused along the sides of the street while others stood in doorways or leaned out windows. Many merely stopped and watched as they passed, but most dropped what they were doing and followed the peculiar group. Children chased the visitors, laughing and darting excitedly between the strange newcomers. But most ran alongside Reiv, their small eyes staring up at him in wonder. "It's the Prince!" young, excited voices were heard saying over and over again.

"Reiv, what does 'prince' mean?" Alicine asked.

Reiv remained momentarily silent, not knowing how to answer her. She would find out soon enough, but later would be better than now. "It is intended as an insult, Alicine. That is all you need to know," he said.

"What kind of insult?" Alicine persisted.

Jensa turned her head around and looked at Reiv as though surprised he had even been asked. But he did not look at her, nor did he answer the question.

"Shall I tell them then?" Jensa asked, a touch of amusement in her voice.

Reiv's eyes shot over to hers. "No!" he snapped. "They will know soon enough." He marched on furiously.

"But Reiv," Dayn called out, "why can't—"

"No!"

Dayn looked down at his feet, clearly aggravated by Reiv's dismissal of him once again. "You're always so impatient," he grumbled. "You'd think after all we've been through together. . ."

Gair followed them all like a great watch dog, no longer a force to be feared, at least not by the newcomers. Any brash comments he now made were directed toward unruly members of the crowd, not the strangers themselves. Hearing the brief but emotional exchange between Reiv and the others, he said, "Be patient, little ones. The gods choose when they wish to make things known."

Alicine looked up at the man, a giant from her perspective, and seemed startled by the gentleness of his voice. "What do the gods have to do with this?" she asked.

Gair looked down at her and smiled. "The gods have a plan for every person and every living thing, and even some things not living. Usually we don't understand their plan, if we're even aware of it at all. But sometimes the plan is so great, the gods decide to share the knowledge of it with us."

"What plan?" Alicine asked.

"In due time."

Alicine stopped in her tracks and stomped her foot. "Why is the answer to every question either 'later', or 'in due time'? Dayn and I are tired of being kept in the dark about everything."

Gair laughed, amused by her sudden display of temper. "Keep walking, girl." He turned her around by the shoulders and nudged her forward. "Like I said . . . patience."

"Patience, indeed," Alicine hissed under her breath. But she resumed her march, now several paces behind the others, struggling to keep up with Gair's wide strides.

The walk through the streets seemed to take forever. The actual distance was probably not far, but it was difficult to gauge since frequent interruptions by curious onlookers slowed their pace. Reiv, realizing he was getting ahead of Jensa and had no clue as to where he was going, dropped back reluctantly and resumed his pace alongside Dayn. Alicine seethed behind them. They ceased further discussions and walked silently, each deep in their own thoughts.

The sun was higher in the sky when they rounded what seemed like the hundredth corner and found themselves standing before an earthen dwelling. It was much smaller than most of the ones they had previously passed, but it looked cozy and inviting. Clusters of fragrant herbs and colorful flowers surrounded its dull walls, and a bent woman stood in the doorway, her long, gray hair blowing in the breeze. The knowing smile that graced her lips spoke a silent greeting to the dusty group that now stood before her.

Jensa approached and bowed politely to the woman. "Nannaven, I have brought them to you as requested."

"Praise to the gods for your safe arrival," the woman said, looking the newcomers up and down. She stepped from the doorway and hobbled over to Reiv. Reaching out she motioned him to bend down to her, then placed her small, wrinkled hands upon his cheeks.

"We are so blessed that you've come to us, Reiv. Thank you, my dear, dear boy."

Reiv opened his mouth to respond, but wasn't sure how to. "Oh, you—you are welcome— I think," he managed. He glanced over at Dayn and Alicine, then shrugged his shoulders in confusion. The woman said nothing more, but continued to stare at him, her hazel eyes twinkling. For a moment Reiv found himself searching her face for a hidden message. Finding none, he looked to the ground, praying she would move her probing eyes to someone else.

As if reading his mind, the woman moved over to Dayn and Alicine, who stood side by side. "I'm Nannaven, the Spirit Keeper of Pobu," she said, motioning them down to her. They looked at one another, then complied. Nannaven placed her hand on each of their cheeks. "You have been through so much.

Come, let's go indoors where you can be refreshed." She ushered them toward the house.

Nannaven turned to see Reiv lingering, his arms crossed. He shifted his weight and stared at the ground.

"Come, Reiv," she said, motioning him forward. "You must walk beside us." Seeing his hesitation, she approached him and hooked her arm through his.

He forced a smile, but it turned to a scowl in a hurry when the crowd began to snicker. He yanked his arm away, and folded it back across his chest. What was he, some sort of red-tufted parrot doing tricks for their entertainment?

"Shush! Off with you all now," Nannaven said, waving her hand to scoot the spectators away. Most lost their grins of amusement and bustled off, heads bowed timidly.

"Come, Reiv," she coaxed.

"No, I think I should go now," he said.

"Go? Where would you go?"

"Well, I was only meant to get Dayn and Alicine to Pobu and then—"

"Then?"

He looked back at his feet. "I do not think I can stay. I mean, this is your home and I am Tearian. I do not belong here."

"And where, may I ask, do you belong?"

He paused for a long moment, then said, "Nowhere I suppose."

"Then here is as good as nowhere." She looped her arm back through his. "Come. You must be hungry."

The scent of herbs and roasting fowl greeted the three as they entered the house. It was a welcome relief from the stench of the cell and the streets that still lingered in their nostrils. Nannaven ushered them over to a plank table, not particularly large, but adequate for the hungry group, then she and Jensa poured them each a mug of water topped with a leafy sprig of mint. They gulped the drinks down eagerly and held their mugs out for more, finding their thirst quenched only after having received two more fills. Nannaven served them up plates of meat and cooked carrots, and placed a warm loaf of bread at the center of the table.

Alicine and Dayn did not wait for an invitation to sink their teeth into the food, but Reiv hesitated and stared at it suspiciously. Dayn took a great mouthful and groaned with pleasure. Alicine laughed in his direction and wiped a trickle of greasy juice from her chin. Reiv continue to examine his share; he wasn't certain what animal the meat came from. But he could bear his hunger no longer and was soon shoving it into his mouth with as much passion as the others.

"It is good," he said, his mouth full and his words muffled. He smiled up at the Spirit Keeper, revealing an emotion almost resembling that of happiness. She expressed instant delight and rushed over to spoon an extra helping onto his plate. Whether it was the compliment for her cooking or the genuine smile he had flashed her was not clear, but after that she seemed to pay him particular attention. Before long he was politely declining her offer of a third helping. Dayn readily volunteered to take it in his place and held his plate out time after time until he, too, was pushing his plate away, his belly full at last.

"Nannaven, what does 'prince' mean?" Alicine asked, watching Reiv from the corner of her eye. He scowled and flashed her a warning, but she persisted. "I mean, we've heard that word many times, but no one has explained it to us."

Nannaven looked at Reiv as though confused. "Reiv?"

He moved the dregs of food around on his plate with his fork and remained silent.

"He hasn't told them about himself," Jensa said. "He said they would learn soon enough, or something like that."

Nannaven shook her head. "So many secrets with you people."

"What is that supposed to mean?" Reiv asked.

"What I said. You don't have secrets?"

"No."

"Well, then, tell them what 'prince' means."

"Yes, Reiv, tell us," Dayn said eagerly. He rested his weight on his elbows and leaned across the table toward his grumpy cousin.

Reiv rolled his eyes with great drama. "Oh, very well," he began. "A prince is a non-reigning male member of a royal family, traditionally the son of the monarch, who is usually destined to inherit the sovereignty. That is all."

Dayn's jaw dropped. "I don't know what you just said."

Alicine cocked her head. "And?"

"And I am, I mean, I was once a prince."

Dayn and Alicine looked at each other then back at him, clearly confused by the definition of the word as well as his statement following it.

"Reiv," Jensa said, "may I rephrase it a bit so they'll understand?"

Reiv shrugged with indifference.

"In Tearia there is a royal family," she said. "They possess the highest political power in the land, other than the Priestess, and we'll discuss *her* later." She frowned instantly, then refocused her attention and her expression back to the subject of royalty. "The king is the ruler and the princes are usually his sons and grandsons. The King of Tearia is Sedric and he has two sons, Reiv and Whyn. The oldest son inherits the monarchy, or kingship, upon the death of the father."

Her eyes moved to his, and for a moment Reiv thought he saw pity there. He turned his gaze to the tabletop, and swallowed down the emotion that was mushrooming in his throat.

"So, Whyn is the prince who will be the king because he is older," Alicine said.

"No," Reiv replied, "I am older, but by one minute only." He glanced at her questioning face. "We are twins."

"So why then—" Dayn began. His attention moved to Reiv's gloves. Reiv moved his hands to his lap.

"Why aren't you still a prince, Reiv?" Alicine asked.

"Because I became impure."

"Impure?" Dayn exclaimed. "You mean your hands? Your family disowned you because of your hands?"

"Yes. I was Unnamed because of them."

"But you still have a name," Dayn insisted.

"It was once Ruairi, but that name was taken from me because it meant 'Red King'. Since I could no longer be the Red King, I was given a servant's name."

"Well, that's just wrong," Dayn proclaimed.

Reiv gaped at him, somewhat stunned, then smiled a smile of weak appreciation. "At any rate, there is nothing that can be done about it. I will have to remain the nobody I am."

"There are no 'nobodies' here," Nannaven said. "Especially not you, Reiv. Everybody has a purpose."

Reiv forced a laugh. "I am sitting in a hovel surrounded by Jecta with no place to go and nothing to do. I do not see what great purpose there could be in that."

"How did your hands get burned?" Alicine asked.

Reiv's expression went dark. "I do not wish to talk about it. Do not ask me again." He turned his attention to the Spirit Keeper. "Nannaven, I was wondering if you might take a look at my arm. I have a small wound that probably should be treated."

"Lands, what am I thinking?" the old woman exclaimed. She moved to his side and eyed the cloth still tied around his forearm. "Come, let's move over by the fire where I can get a better look." She motioned him over to the hearth, and pulled out a stool, then pressed him down and untied the bandage, careful not to pull tender skin. "Who did this to you?" she asked with disgust.

"That guard did it," Dayn said. He moved to stand next to them and eyed the blood-encrusted slice in Reiv's arm.

"Shameful," Nannaven muttered. "Well, don't worry, it will be mended before you know it." She instructed Jensa to fetch her some fresh water, herbs, and a clean bit of cloth. She cleaned it carefully and pressed the herbs onto it, then bound it with the cloth. "By morning you'll not even know it's there. Now what about your hands, do you need—"

"No!" Reiv practically shouted. "I mean no, thank you. They are fine."

"Very well. Take a seat on one of those mats there while I finish up here. Dayn . . . sit."

"Wha—Why?" he asked.

"Your lip, dear boy. Let's take a look."

Dayn felt along his lip with the tip of his tongue, seeming to have forgotten it had even been split. He sat down and leaned his face up to Nannaven, slanting his eyes aside to spy on Reiv.

Reiv picked at his new bandage, inspecting it to see what it was the woman had put into it. He caught Dayn's eye and grinned. "Bet you never had your lip split by a Tearian guard before."

"No, but I've had it split by worse."

"Worse? Who could be worse than Crymm?"

"Sheireadan," Dayn mumbled as the Spirit Keeper dabbed some ointment onto his lip.

"And who, may I ask, is that foul creature?" Reiv asked.

"Oh, he's the brother of the girl Dayn likes," Alicine said.

"Girl? Well, tell me about her, little cousin." Reiv leaned in with sudden interest.

Dayn scowled and pulled his face away from Nannaven's probing. "There are some things I don't want to talk about either," he said coolly. "So don't ask me about her again."

Reiv was startled by the chilly reply and dropped the subject immediately. The room became uncomfortably quiet as Dayn's tending-to continued at the hands of the Spirit Keeper.

After Nannaven finished with him, she invited them all to sit on the mats laid out before the hearth while she took her place on the stool. They sat where instructed and waited. Alicine struggled to adjust herself in the sarong, while Reiv sat next to her with criss-crossed legs. Dayn threw himself onto his back, arms tucked behind his head, and closed his eyes in noticeable satisfaction of his pleasantly full stomach.

Nannaven eyed the three. "Before we begin," she said, "is there anything else you need?"

"Before we begin?" Reiv asked.

"We have things to discuss. What must be done with you, for one thing."

Dayn sat up quickly. "What do you mean, done with us?"

"Well, you must earn your keep, and though you are welcome to stay here for a time, eventually permanent accommodations will need to be made."

"We will not be in Pobu permanently," Alicine said.

"Oh?" Nannaven said.

Dayn and Alicine exchanged glances and remained silent.

"I know you are from another place," Nannaven said. "Brina told me you are her son, Dayn, and that you and your sister made your way here through the forbidden mountains. Quite a feat for two so young as yourselves, I must say."

"Brina said we aren't to speak of it," Dayn said.

"The Tearians must not know, of course. Were word of it to get to the Priestess, there could be dire consequences for all of you." Nannaven's eyes settled on Reiv. "Great pains have been taken by Tearian leaders, the Priestess in particular, to hide the truth of our histories. They have all lived a lie for far too long."

Reiv turned his face from her, wounded by the attack on his heritage.

"You can deny it, Reiv, if you wish," she continued, "but you'll learn the truth of it soon enough."

"The only truth that needs telling I already know," Reiv said haughtily. "There are people living on the other side of the mountains. What of it? They are obviously stragglers from the Upheaval. The gods took mercy on them, that is all. They are just a few misplaced Jecta, nothing more."

Alicine's jaw dropped. "Is *that* what you think we are? Jecta leftovers living by the pity of your gods? Well, we don't even believe in your gods."

Reiv gasped. "You do not believe in the gods? Why—why that is—"

"Is what?" Alicine said, her voice heated. "Blasphemy? Well, we believe in one god only. Daghadar the Maker. He teaches us that there is only one true god. Where we are from it is a sin to believe in any others but Him."

Reiv opened his mouth to speak, but Nannaven interrupted. "Enough. We can debate the issues of religion later. Right now we need to discuss the issues at hand." She turned to Dayn who had not participated in the discussion between Reiv and his sister. "Dayn, what skills do you have?"

"Well, I'm good with farm work: plowing, tending to livestock, planting, that sort of thing. But I also have some skill at blacksmithing. I was friends with the smith back home and he showed me things."

"Gair is our smith and I'm sure he would be pleased to have you help him there," she replied.

"Gair is the smith?" Dayn gulped. Gair hadn't been mentioned since they entered Nannaven's house, but the memory of the intimidatingly huge man flooded back.

Nannaven laughed. "Don't worry. Gair is a lamb in a bear's body, unless he becomes angry, that is. Then, well, let's just say you'd best pray he's on your side."

Dayn nodded. "I guess that would be all right. I think I'd rather work with the smith than till the fields at any rate."

"Then it's decided," Nannaven said. Then she turned to Alicine, who had her arms crossed and her frowning face turned away from Reiv.

"Alicine, what skills can you offer?"

"Oh, that's easy," Dayn said. "She is the most talented person in all of . . ." He paused and glanced over at his sister, then continued " . . . in all of Kirador with herbs and potions. She can do anything with them."

Nannaven clapped her hands with delight. "Excellent! We're in desperate need of healers here. I would be so pleased if you would help me make and administer medicines to those in need, and I fear there are many."

A smile crept into the corners of Alicine's compressed lips.

"And you, Reiv? How about you?" Nannaven waited patiently, but he did not respond for a very long time. "Reiv?" she repeated.

"I do not know," he said, stabbing the dirt with his finger.

"Couldn't he work with me at the smithy?" Dayn asked.

"No, Dayn," Reiv said, "I do not have the strength in my hands to do that kind of work."

"You could stoke the fire or—"

"I do not think that would be much of a job, Dayn," Reiv said. "I admit to being skilled at starting fires, but I do not do well to stay out of them. Besides, I doubt Gair would need the both of us. I think I had better find something else to do."

"Well," Nannaven said, "something will turn up. It always does." She rose, pushing her frail body up from the stool. "Reiv, Jensa will keep an eye on you until I can make other arrangements for someone to watch you."

Reiv's face fell. "You do not trust me."

"It is others I do not trust. The people of Pobu have not forgotten you were once Prince of Tearia and while some may sympathize with your plight, there are those who would try to do you harm."

"I understand," Reiv replied, but he wasn't happy about it.

"Nannaven, when will we see Brina again," Dayn asked.

"Oh," Jensa said, "she gave me a message for you all. I saw her yesterday when she told me there was the possibility of your banishment and that I was to be on the lookout for you. Let's see, she said to tell you she would try to rescue the lion, retrieve Alicine's flowers, and secure Dayn's bottoms, whatever that means." She giggled at that, although she did not seem like the sort of girl who giggled.

Dayn blushed and tugged at his tunic.

The rest of the day was somewhat uneventful. Alicine wiled away the hours puttering with Nannaven in the herb garden, while Dayn sat at the table, cutting vegetables and visiting with Jensa who seemed to have taken a great interest in him. Reiv, on the other hand, slept curled up on a mat in the corner, as was his usual custom when the problems of life invaded his mind. Sleep, which had become his only respite during the past year, proved to

be no different today. But he arose in time for dinner, which
Dayn proudly proclaimed at having had his hand in.

Afterward, they all lounged by the fire while Nannaven told
them about herself, and Pobu, and the Shell Seekers. And there
was much to tell. They learned that Nannaven was a great healer
and humanitarian, much like the Spirit Keeper of Kirador. She
lived alone, except when she was sheltering those in need, such as
she was now. No one went homeless or hungry if Nannaven
could help it. Pobu was crowded and dirty and poor, for the Jecta
were forced to live off the leftovers of the Tearians and were
placed under a great many restrictions. They were not allowed to
own land, or gather for public meetings, or write, or sing, or
carry weapons or hunting tools, although some simple utensils
were allowed for cooking and gardening. There were horses, but
not many, and even those were the ones considered too old or too
ill for use by the Tearians. At one point Dayn asked what it was
the smith actually did without horseshoes and hunting tools to
forge. To his obvious disappointment he was told the smith fashioned mostly nails, eating utensils, hinges for doors, and tools
for gardening.

Jensa, they learned, lived in another town, Meirla, with the
others of her kind. Her village was nestled along a palm-treed
beach that overlooked the ocean to the south of Pobu. The tales
of the sea snakes and treacherous waters proved to be exciting,
and Dayn asked Jensa question after question. She was only too
happy to respond, delighted by his profound interest.

Dayn and Alicine listened with rapt attention as Nannaven
and Jensa told them about the ways of things for the Jecta, but
Reiv at times found himself mentally closing off their voices. A
part of him hated hearing about the oppression his people im-
posed on others, while the other part of him struggled to justify
it. But he never said a word in defense, nor interjected his opinions or excuses. These women had, after all, fed him and housed
him, and he wasn't totally without manners.

"Come, it's getting late," Nannaven said at last. "You all
need to get some rest. I'm sure you have much sleep to catch up

on." She tottered over to a cupboard in the corner and removed three rather worn blankets and handed them to Dayn, Alicine, and Reiv. "You'll sleep on the roof. There's plenty of room there and the night air will be pleasant. But even better than that, you'll sleep with a canopy of stars above you. A wondrous show, don't you think?"

"Thank you, Nannaven, for your hospitality. And you too, Jensa," Dayn said as he moved toward the ladder leading to the trap door above.

Jensa looked at him with surprise. "It was my pleasure, but you do not have much to thank me for, I think."

"Yes we do," Dayn insisted. "You saved us."

"Saved you?" Her expression took on a look of curiosity as her gaze lingered on his face. Then she smiled. "Get some rest. I'll see you in the morning. Oh, and you'll help me with breakfast?"

Dayn grinned broadly and nodded his head in the affirmative.

Nannaven and Jensa sat at the table, sipping tea and visiting quietly. "I don't think the Prince will do well here," Jensa said.

"No," Nannaven agreed. "But if he's here, then he's meant to be."

"But what purpose could there be in it? He's a Tearian of royal blood, son of a king who continues to oppress us." She pursed her lips and shook her head. "Few will welcome him, Nannaven. I fear he'll find little happiness here."

"I doubt he had much happiness in Tearia either. Maybe he's due some."

"Well, he'll get little sympathy from me. He's had every opportunity for happiness. He was born a prince and given everything he could possibly want."

Nannaven reached out and patted Jensa's hand. "Tough words from a girl who wouldn't kill a spider. Reiv didn't pick his lot in life any more than the rest of us. Just remember, falls from high places hurt worse than falls from low ones."

Jensa nodded. "I suppose. Well, he's here now, so there's not much we can do about it. How long do you need me to stay?"

"Just a few days, until we see what unfolds. I'll send word to Torin that you're staying a while to help me with things."

"All right," Jensa said. Then she smiled. "Dayn is sweet, isn't he? He and Reiv are so different—like fire and light."

Nannaven's eyes shot over to Jensa's. "What did you say?"

"I said Reiv and Dayn are like fire and light; one red haired and hot tempered, the other with a goodness in him that shines like starlight."

Nannaven's gaze moved past Jensa's shoulder to the fireplace beyond. "Fire and light," she whispered.

Jensa glanced over her shoulder, then back to the Spirit Keeper who stared out as though in a daze. "What is it, Nannaven?"

The old woman's attention returned to the table. "Nothing, dear. I was just thinking." She rose and headed for the cabinet along the wall. "I have to go check on a fever patient. Won't be long."

She gathered up a few potions and placed them in her bag, then exited the hut muttering to herself.

21
Blurred
Perceptions

Nannaven allowed her guests to sleep in later than she normally would have, even against the protests of Jensa who seemed sincerely disappointed that Dayn was not up to help with breakfast. Eventually the three awoke, their faces puffy from almost too much sleep. They tended to their personal needs, ate their breakfast, and listened as plans were made for the day.

Nannaven, they learned, would escort Dayn to the smithy and deposit him into Gair's care. She and Alicine would then continue on to make the morning rounds. Meanwhile, Reiv was to go with Jensa to make inquiries about employment. Dayn and Alicine reacted with excitement at the thought of seeing Pobu in a new light, while Reiv made numerous excuses in a transparent attempt to postpone the inevitable. Before long Jensa was simply walking out the door, demanding that he follow.

Dayn and Gair bonded immediately and, just as Nannaven had said, the day was spent mostly making forks and spoons and barely-sharp knives. Alicine and Nannaven wound their way through the city, tending the frail and those in need of medical attention. There was much illness in the city and few with the skills to treat it. As planned, Jensa took Reiv to meet numerous merchants, hoping someone might have need of him. But he was rejected time after time, sometimes due to prejudice, but more often for fear of reprisal. Few dared risk the ire of those who would just as soon see the former prince dead.

After several frustrating hours Reiv insisted they return home, complaining he felt ill and needed to lie down. It would have been the perfect ruse if it hadn't been the truth. They went back to Nannaven's where he did sleep, and when he awoke he trudged over to the table where Jensa was peeling potatoes. He helped her as best he could, but found working the small knife awkward, and ended up cutting more potato than peel. Afterwards, he dusted and swept the floor and cleaned some dishes. But he found it humiliating. It was as though he were a housemaid.

On the evening of the third day, Reiv, still unemployed and growing more frustrated by the minute, found himself alone in the hut with Jensa once more. Dayn had stayed late at the smithy to work with Gair on a surprisingly large job, while Alicine and Nannaven had been kept longer than expected caring for a woman in labor. Jensa sat by the window, working on a bit of mending before the light grew too dim. Reiv paced across the room, cursing his worthlessness. He could not help with the mending, nor could he repair the mats or peel the potatoes waiting to be peeled. For that matter, there was little of value he could do.

He plopped down on the stool by the fireplace, facing the flames, and opened and closed his fists in an attempt to work the discomfort from them. Since coming to this place his hands had been sorely neglected. There was little opportunity for privacy and he was far too proud to ask for medicine. No one spoke to him of it, they obviously did not wish to risk his temper, and so he had endured it in silence.

Jensa rose and set the mending aside, then stretched her arms and arched her back. "I think I'll step outside for a bit and get a breath of fresh air. Would you like to come?"

"No," Reiv replied in a none-too-friendly tone.

"Suit yourself," she said, and walked out to the yard beyond.

Reiv glanced past the open doorway. The sun was setting and the once vibrant colors of the flowers were barely clinging to their petals anymore. He muttered something about his matching mood, then twisted his body away from the outside world.

He worked his hands, first one and then the other, balling his fists, clenching and unclenching his fingers. But it did little good. They needed release from the sweaty confines of the gloves, but somehow he could not bring himself to do it.

A figure shadowed the doorway at his back and Reiv paused momentarily. He could feel someone's presence, but did not turn to see who it was, and continued his task, keeping his focus upon it. Soft footsteps padded across the room toward him. From where Reiv sat, he could not tell who it was, not even from the corner of his eye which he eased in that direction. The sound stopped directly behind him and waited.

"What?" Reiv barked.

"I'm sorry, I didn't mean to interrupt," Alicine said.

Reiv rested his hands on his knees and looked over his shoulder. He flicked a strand of hair out of his eye and shot her a look of annoyance. "What is it, Alicine?"

"Your hands are hurting, aren't they."

Reiv opened his mouth to speak, but Alicine interrupted him. "Don't bother to deny it," she said.

He rose from the stool and turned to face her. "Well, it should come as no surprise," he said.

"What does that mean?"

"What I mean is they always hurt." Reiv shrugged his shoulders, then turned and sat back down on the stool. "Do not concern yourself, Alicine. Really. They have been much worse." He glanced up and saw the pained expression on her face. He hadn't meant for her to feel sorry for him. He had only meant— "I am sorry. I did not mean to sound unappreciative." He kept his hands on his knees and dared not move them, but he could feel them twitching and hoped she did not notice.

"You haven't taken your gloves off in how many days now? They need to be cared for. Brina said—"

"Well Brina is not here, is she?" he said. Then he realized his tone. "Do not worry about Brina. She would understand." Leaning over, he rested his forearms on his knees and slowly opened and closed his fists. He could feel Alicine watching them, but for some strange reason he was beyond caring.

Alicine sighed and turned aside, then walked toward the window. She stared out for a moment, then glanced along the wall toward a narrow table and the lamp that sat upon it. "It's getting dark in here. This lamp needs refilling." She rummaged through the items on the table and on the shelf above it, searching boxes, baskets, and bottles.

Reiv looked up. "Try that amber bottle, the tall one there behind the jug. I think I saw Jensa with it the other night when she was looking to light the lamp." He turned his attention back to his hands.

"You and Jensa have been spending a lot of time together," Alicine said. She lifted the bottle up and examined it.

"Yes," Reiv replied.

"Do you like her?"

Reiv wrinkled his brow, confused by the question. "Yes, of course. Do you?"

"Of course." Alicine tipped back the barely burning wick of the lantern and trickled some oil into the reserve. The flame grew bright. She smiled over at Reiv, who did not smile back, then pulled in a deep breath. "Reiv, I know we've only been here a short time, but I've become familiar with the potions Nannaven has and I've been working on a few of my own. I've mixed up a salve that might ease the pain in your hands. I thought you might want to try it."

Reiv was certain his eyes would betray his eagerness. He lowered them in an attempted show of disinterest. "Well," he said, "I could try it, I suppose. If you really want me to."

Alicine's face lit up. "I'll fetch it. Take off your gloves." She turned to retrieve the remedy tucked in the cupboard across the way.

Reiv rose and stood motionless, his face pinched with worry. Take off the gloves? Now? He would have to eventually, but privately of course. Surely she didn't expect him to do it with her here. He folded his arms and tucked his hands beneath. How could he possibly let her see them? She would never look at him the same way again, and the pain of the hands would be nothing compared to the anguish of that.

Alicine walked over to him, a skip in her step. She was practically beaming. Their eyes met and Reiv could not disguise his trepidation. Alicine's smile wavered as she turned her gaze to the jar. For a moment neither said a word, then she held out her hand.

"Come on," she said. "Let's sit over there on the mats." Her voice sounded cheerful, but cautious. She kept her hand extended to him, but he did not take it.

"Where is Jensa?" he asked, glancing toward the door.

"Nannaven sent me home early, so since I'm here now, Jensa left for a while. I think she needed a break from you." She laughed.

Reiv nodded, but found his lungs had stalled. What was he so afraid of? It was only Alicine, not—

"Do you want to move over there?" she asked, motioning to the mats.

He nodded again and studied Alicine's face. Golden firelight danced across her cheeks, alerting him to the unexpected beauty of her features. For a moment his perception of her blurred, as though she had transformed into someone else and was luring him through some mysterious female power. He forced his eyes from her face, only to find them staring at the rich streams of hair cascading down her breasts. A strange sensation wound through his body, twisting its way through every fiber. He forced his lungs to exhale, but the air escaped raggedly. Before he could think what he was doing, he reached his hand out to hers and she took it.

They knelt and faced each other on the mat, Reiv looking down nervously at the gloved hands splayed across his thighs,

Alicine at the bottle of salve clutched within her own. Neither spoke, muted by the awkwardness of the situation. Reiv stirred restlessly. There was still time to change his mind. He could simply get up and run full speed out the door.

"You'll have to take them off," Alicine said, motioning to the gloves.

A million thoughts and fears flooded his mind. He did not attempt to remove the gloves. He did not have the courage.

"Here, let me," Alicine said, taking one of his hands in hers. She tugged gently at the glove, but he balled his fist and tried to pull it from her. She held fast, as though waiting for him to reconsider. He swallowed, then cautiously relaxed his fingers. One by one she opened them, until his hand lay unmoving in hers. Then she removed the glove.

Reiv went cold at the realization of Alicine looking at his hand, his hideous, deformed, impure hand. His eyes shot to hers, expecting to see horror there, or pity. But he saw neither. She was looking at his hand as though she had seen it a thousand times. He frowned down at the mottled hand cradled in her perfect one, and felt as though he was going to be ill. He bit back a moan, but did not remove his hand. He found he could not move at all.

Alicine took his other hand and removed the second glove, then reached for the jar at her side and opened it. She dipped out some of the sweetly scented ointment and took one of his hands in hers, then massaged the thick lubricant into it.

He winced. "I can do it myself," he said softly.

"I know, but I need to see how the treatment reacts to your skin."

Reiv watched as Alicine's small slender fingers caressed his badly damaged ones, working the lotion in between them, massaging the tender skin and tight muscles. He thought her hands must be soft, though he could not know for certain. So many parts of his hands were numb from the injuries, and of those parts not numb, he usually felt only discomfort. But he had not forgotten what it felt like to be touched so tenderly. He knew the pleasure touch could bring. He closed his eyes as his thoughts returned to Cinnia.

Cinnia had touched his hands many times, and he found himself imagining her doing so now. He recalled the feel of her hand in his, the featherlike touch of her fingertips as they explored his body, the softness of her lips as they brushed across his. He always took pleasure in Cinnia's touch, just as she always took pleasure in his. But the touch of her hands and her lips was all he had ever known of her. It occurred to him that had they been wed, he would have known so much more of her by now. He envisioned her in his arms and a lusty passion took root.

The awakenings of his body forced his eyes open, and he realized it was not Cinnia caressing him so tenderly; it was Alicine. He thought to pull away from her, to deny it was even happening, but then his eyes trailed along her arms and up to her bare shoulders. Her skin was a rich tawny gold, nothing like Cinnia's, and he found himself fascinated by it. His gaze moved to her lips, and he watched them, imagining how they might feel against his. He told himself not to think of her that way, to turn his thoughts away. But the power of her femininity was far greater than any power he had within himself. Cinnia was gone from his life, but Alicine was not. She was here; she was now. He squeezed her hand in his. "Alicine," he whispered.

Alicine blushed and looked away. She made to remove her hands from his, but this time it was he who held fast.

He leaned in closer and felt her rapid breaths upon his face. He reached out to her, then hesitated. She would surely be revolted by his touch, and he did not know if he could bear it. To his complete surprise, she took his hand in hers and raised it to her cheek.

Reiv cupped Alicine's face in his hands and stared into her eyes; he felt as though he was falling. He clenched his jaw with weak determination, but it was hopeless. He could not distance himself from the bottomless pit into which he was plunging. He brushed his lips across hers, his kiss light and sweet. To his delight she returned it. Then his passion intensified, and he covered her mouth with his, kissing her hard and deep. Her warm breath against his cheek quickened to match the rhythm of his own. He ran his hands down her neck and along her shoulders, entwining his fingers in her hair, willing himself to feel the silkiness of it. He buried his face in her neck, breathing in her scent. His senses blurred and his mind raced. He felt her lips searching for his, and he met them with a passion he had not felt in a long time. For a moment he was terrified it was only a dream, and yet he prayed more than anything it was. He knew he should stop, that he had to stop, but she was kissing him back. Wasn't she making it clear she wanted him? His body reacted to the thought of it and he leaned further into her, wrapping her in his arms, drinking in the pleasure of her. It all felt so familiar.

"Cin . . ." he whispered, tracing his lips along her bare shoulder.

Her hands moved between their bodies and inched their way up his chest. His heart beat wildly at her touch. He felt her hands press against him, pushing with gentle but obvious effort. At first he did not recognize her signal, or perhaps he only denied it. She was telling him to stop, but he felt desperate to ignore it. The needs of his body were more powerful than his common sense.

"Please . . ." he whispered as he pressed his body hard against her.

He felt her tense then, and she shoved her hands against him with a strength he could no longer deny. She did not want him. He realized then that she was shaking and her eyes were wide as though in terror of him. He stared at her, breathless and bewildered, then leaned away in sudden self-loathing. What was he doing? How could he have forced himself on her like that? He felt overwhelming shame consume him. He had misunderstood. He had gone too far. He struggled to his feet. "Alicine, please forgive me."

Her chest was rising and falling. "I'm—I'm sorry if you thought—but you said it yourself," she said haltingly. "Sin. And it is a sin, outside of marriage I mean."

At first Reiv didn't know how to respond, then he realized he had called her 'Cin'. He shook his head and backed away. "No, that is not what I meant. I mean, when I said 'Cin' I was thinking of—" He stopped mid-sentence as his mind scrambled. Was it better that she think he had spoken another's name during the heat of passion, or that somehow he was taking pleasure in the idea of committing a sin? Then he realized it didn't matter either way. There could never be a future between them. Neither of them belonged here, she least of all. She was only here for Dayn, and it would be Dayn she stayed or left for, not him.

"I am sorry, Alicine," he said, his voice strangely level, "I should not have done it. Not with you. Never with you." He hated the words as he spoke them. He wasn't even sure he believed them, but he had to make sure she did.

"I have to go," he said, and bolted through the door and into the gathering darkness.

Dayn strolled through the door and froze, startled by the sight of his sister kneeling before the hearth, sobbing into her hands.

"Alicine? What's wrong?" He rushed over and knelt to face her. She lowered her hands and turned her face away.

"Alicine, tell me." He glanced at the jar by her side, then noticed the gloves lying on the floor nearby. A mixture of fear and fury grabbed his gut. "Did something happen with Reiv?"

For a moment she did not respond, then she took a gulping breath and said, "Don't be concerned, Dayn. I offered Reiv an ointment for his hands. That's all." She picked up the jar with a trembling hand and placed the lid back on it.

"What happened?"

"He, I mean, I helped him take off his gloves and—"

"He *let* you?"

"It was very difficult for him, but I managed to convince him."

"And?" Dayn persisted.

"And I treated them with some salve."

"So why are you crying?"

"His hands, Dayn. It's so sad what he's been forced to endure."

Dayn did not respond for a time as his eyes scanned her face, her neck, and her shoulders. His face grew hot.

"What is it?" Alicine asked. She moved her eyes from the intensity of his gaze.

"Your face," he said, but it sounded more like an accusation than a statement.

Alicine wiped the back of her hand across her cheek, smearing the ointment that lingered there. "Oh, it's from my own hands, nothing more."

But the shine of it wasn't just on her face.

"Did he touch you?" Dayn asked, his voice rising at the thought of it.

"Dayn, please."

"He did! He touched you!" He rose abruptly and stormed toward the doorway. "He'll rue the day he dared touch my sister!"

"No, Dayn, wait!" Alicine threw herself out to stop him.

Dayn stopped and turned, shocked by the despair in her voice, alarmed by the sight of her desperation. He rushed back and put his arm around her, then guided her up and over to the stool.

"I'm sorry," he said. "I won't leave. I promise."

"I want to go home, Dayn. I want to go back to Kirador."

"Back to Kirador?" Dayn choked, startled by her sudden change in the subject. Surely she didn't want to go back now; they had only just arrived. She had to give him more time. He wasn't ready. He shook his head. "No, I can't go back. Not yet. Please."

Alicine grabbed his hands in hers. "We don't belong here, Dayn. We're too different."

"I'm not different here. It's only in Kirador that I'm different."

"But you belong with us. You belong with your family. It doesn't matter where you were born, does it? What matters is that Father and Mother love you and that I love you. You belong with us."

"But Brina loves me, too."

"She barely knows you," Alicine snapped. "Besides, where is she? She's not here, and likely never will be."

"She's my mother, Alicine. My true mother. Are you implying she doesn't care?"

"No. I'm sorry. I didn't mean that." Alicine stood and stepped away, her back turned to him. "I just want to go home."

"Alicine, you know I would do anything for you and I promise, you will return home. I'll take you there myself, I swear. Just, please, not yet."

Dayn held his breath. Would she accept that? Would she be willing to cling to that promise for just a while longer? Or would she insist that they leave now? And if she did insist that they leave, how could he possibly refuse her?

Alicine stared out, her face void of emotion. "All right, Dayn," she finally said. "We'll stay. For a while." She wiped the wetness from her face. "I'm sorry I upset you. It was selfish of me. I know it's too soon."

Relief flooded through him. "I promise, Alicine, I'll take you home. Soon."

Reiv did not come back that evening, nor did Jensa. Alicine and Dayn ate silently at the table, neither saying a word until Nannaven returned. The thick and silent aura of emotion blanketing the room could not have escaped the Spirit Keeper, but she asked no questions. She watched the two of them warily, but went about her business, allowing them to work it through at their own pace.

It grew late and eventually the two of them excused themselves to their bedrolls atop the roof. As usual Alicine tossed and turned, then ended up on her back, staring up at the sky. Across the way Dayn awoke from a disturbing, but forgotten, dream and glanced over in his sister's direction, noting the blanket twisted between her feet. He raised up on one elbow and watched her silently.

He felt movement behind him and turned his head to focus his eyes in the darkness. It was Reiv, making his way to his own mat nearby.

"Reiv?" Dayn asked quietly. "Where have you been?"

Reiv stopped in his tracks and stiffened his back. He looked in Dayn's direction, then turned and knelt down to rearrange the wool blanket that was his bed. Plopping down onto his back, he leaned his head against his arms and gazed at the stars. "I had some business to attend to," he replied after some time.

"What sort of business?" Dayn asked.

Reiv didn't respond and continued to stare at the sky.

Dayn sat up and studied his cousin's shadowy shape. "What sort of business, Reiv?" he repeated.

Reiv turned his head to face him. "I will be leaving in the morning."

"Leaving?" Dayn staggered up from his blanket. "What do you mean, leaving? Where are you going?"

"I am going with Jensa to Meirla. She invited me to stay with her and I think I should."

Dayn took a step toward him. "You are leaving us? Just like that?"

Reiv sat up, poised for a debate. "No, not just like that. You must understand, I do not belong here and . . ." He paused and took a deep breath. "I have no skills, Dayn. Nothing I can offer here. Anyway, Jensa—"

"Jensa!" Dayn interrupted, "What sort of skills does *she* offer you?"

Reiv stood and faced him. "She has offered to teach me how to hunt for shells. At least there I can earn my keep. Here I will be nothing but a burden."

"You are going with Jensa?" Alicine asked, rising from her place. Both boys spun to face her.

"I think it is for the best," Reiv said.

"But things could be different here," she said. "You haven't given it enough time."

"No!" Reiv said, "I have made my decision and I will not discuss it further. I leave in the morning." He threw himself down on his bedroll and squeezed his eyes shut.

"Fine, then, leave!" Alicine said, her anger ignited. "I don't care. Go to your precious Jensa. I'm sure she has much more to offer you. Besides, we won't be here that much longer either." With that she, too, threw herself upon her mat and turned her back to him.

Reiv sat back up. "What do you mean you will not be here much longer?" he asked with alarm. Alicine ignored him, so Reiv turned to Dayn, who still stood silently to the side. "What does she mean, Dayn? You are leaving? Not back to Kirador. Not so soon."

"I promised Alicine I would take her home. I can't make her stay forever, Reiv. She doesn't belong here."

"You cannot simply walk back to Kirador. It is far too dangerous. Plans would have to be made. Precautions taken." Reiv's voice was stern. "No. Impossible. You cannot do this."

"We are not leaving tomorrow as *you* are," Dayn said dryly. "We know plans will have to be made. But don't worry about us, cousin. When the time is right, I'll take my sister back home. By then you'll be a Shell Seeker and will have forgotten about us anyway."

Dayn marched to his bedroll, threw himself down, and pulled his blanket up over his ears. No one spoke or moved for the rest of the night.

The next morning Alicine awoke at the first hint of daylight and looked in the direction of Reiv's bedding. Both he and it were gone.

"Dayn, wake up!" she shouted as she ran past him toward the ladder leading to the kitchen below. She almost lost her footing as she struggled down the wooden rungs that were damp with morning dew. The speed of her feet did not seem adequate for the urgency of her task. She jumped past the last two rungs and twirled toward the door, then stopped, breathless and flush-faced.

Reiv was leaning against the doorframe, watching the morning sun creep over the horizon. In his hands, once again covered by the gloves, he held a mug of tea. His bedroll and a knapsack were on the floor by the wall. He turned to acknowledge Alicine who stared at him with her mouth agape.

"Did you think I would leave without saying goodbye?" he asked.

"No. Well, yes," Alicine stammered, "I thought you might." She shoved a strand of wayward hair behind her ear.

Reiv looked into the last dregs of tea that floated at the bottom of the mug. He tilted it as he studied the remaining bits of leaf. "You know, they say Nannaven can read the leaves. Maybe she could tell me my future." He walked into the kitchen and set the mug on the table.

"I think she would say you have a very good future," Alicine said.

Reiv shook his head. "I doubt—"

But before he could finish, a barely awake Dayn came sliding down the ladder, his face creased with the folds of the blanket he had lain upon. He hit the ground hard and his legs almost went out from under him. "What's going on?" he sputtered, rubbing his puffy eyes in an attempt to focus them. "You're not leaving now are you? Surely not so soon!"

"I am ready to go. As you can see there was little packing for me to do." Reiv motioned to the bedroll and knapsack. "Nannaven let me keep the bedroll and was kind enough to give me a water pouch and some food. Otherwise all I have is this." He tugged the material of his tunic.

"Where is Nannaven?" Alicine asked.

Reiv shrugged. "She left right after I got up. Said something about letting things play out. I did not understand what she meant. But then again I rarely do. She always speaks in riddles."

"And Jensa?" Alicine asked.

"She is with her. Said she would wait for me down the road a piece, so we could say our goodbyes here privately."

"Jensa's not even going to say goodbye to us?" Dayn exclaimed, clearly wounded that the Shell Seeker had disregarded their friendship so easily.

"She will be back; we will both be back. Next month; at Market time," Reiv said.

"Do you really have to go?" Alicine said. "I still don't understand why."

"I swear I would not if I did not have to, but you must realize this is right for me. In a day's time you both found ways to earn your keep here; Dayn, you at the smithy, and Alicine, you with the Spirit Keeper. Do you recall what I said when Nannaven asked me what skills I had?"

Neither responded.

"I said nothing, because there is nothing." He laughed. "Oh, I know how to wield a sword. Not much use in a place where they are banned. And, yes, I am particularly gifted at ordering Jecta around, a valuable talent in a place where I have no authority." His smile faded. "No, the only skills I have, the trade of my father and his fathers before him, are of no consequence here."

"But you could learn something," Alicine insisted. "Someone could teach you."

"Teach me what? And who?" Reiv's voice rose. "No one wants me here, Alicine. Do you not yet understand that I am not welcome."

"But you *are* welcome," Dayn said. "Nannaven cares about you, and you know Alicine and I do."

Reiv folded his arms and looked at his feet. "Listen, I told you I would get you to Pobu. I never said I would stay."

"But you made us think you would," Alicine said. "It was just another one of your lies wasn't it."

"Fine, Alicine," Reiv said. "I am a liar. Does that satisfy you?" He whipped around and grabbed the bedroll and knapsack, then moved hastily toward the door.

"Don't go," she cried. "Please, stay. We need you."

Reiv froze in his tracks, his back stiffening. "What is it you need of me?"

"We need to know why you're really leaving."

"I told you. There is no reason for me to stay."

"No reason to stay? We're not reason enough for you? You drive me mad, Reiv, I swear. First you accost us in a field and practically kill Dayn. Then you drag us into Tearia, accusing us of thievery. You have shouted at us, threatened us, called us names, but is that enough for you? No; then you feed us, clothe us, risk your life for us, only to turn on us by deserting us. By your gods, Reiv, what is *wrong* with you?"

Reiv turned and looked between Alicine, a pillar of fury, and Dayn, standing mute to the side. "Nothing," he said, "and everything."

He stepped outside the door, then paused and looked over his shoulder at Dayn. "Goodbye, little cousin. I will come back to see you both soon, I promise." Then to Alicine, "I kept the lotion you made, Alicine. I hope you do not mind." He held up the knapsack, indicating it was there.

"No," she said, "I made it for you, to help you feel better."

"It did make me feel better. Very much." He blinked back the emotion in his eyes and forced a smile. "I will see you soon— at Market." His gaze lingered on Alicine a moment longer, then he headed down the path that led from the house.

22
Difficult Lessons

It had been two hours since Reiv and Jensa departed Pobu, and Reiv had expected them to be in Meirla long before this. It was not that they were not making good time; the well-trod road wound pleasantly downward through the foothills that sloped from the city to the sea. The greens of the landscape had long since changed to the dull, scruffy browns of a more salt-loving fauna, and while it gave Reiv hope they would reach their destination soon, his feelings were torn as to whether he actually wanted to. As he played the probable reception he would receive in Meirla over in his mind, it occurred to him that he had probably only jumped from the waters of Nannaven's stew pot into the sacrificial fires of the mysterious Shell Seekers.

"Gods. How much further?" Reiv grumbled. "I had no idea it would take so long."

"Are you never satisfied?" Jensa said.

"My apologies for asking."

"You know," Jensa said, "if you would watch your words more carefully you wouldn't have to apologize so often."

"So I have begun to realize."

"Well, in answer to your question, it's just over the rise there." Then Jensa flashed him a look of warning. "You'd best watch that mouth of yours, and your temper. My brother Kerrik wants nothing more than to be a warrior and will have little toler-ance for the likes of you."

Reiv felt a case of nerves take hold of his gut at the thought of what awaited him, and suddenly found it necessary to excuse himself into the shrubberies. After some time he returned, refus-ing to meet Jensa's amused stare. He slung his pack back over his shoulder. "Well, what are we waiting for? Let us get on with it," he snapped.

They continued on in silence until they reached a rise pro-viding a scenic view of the waters in the distance. Jensa stopped and pointed a finger toward the shoreline. There a tawny land-scape merged with white sand that wrapped the teals of the shal-lows like a bright, rippling ribbon.

"There, you see? Almost there," she said.

Reiv gazed out, the warm sea air whipping his hair, the salt-iness of it settling on his lips. The vast ocean seemed enchanting to him, almost magical. He had only seen it once in his life and that was when he was very young. It seemed odd, even to him, that a prince whose family actually owned the sea rarely ventured to it. But most of the coastline was rocky and impenetrable, and even the accessible areas were of a violent nature, with dangerous tides and flesh-tearing rocks, and evil creatures that lurked be-neath the surface. The Shell Seekers had always harvested the seas for their masters, so there was no point in the Tearians going there.

"The water is so beautiful," Reiv said as though surprised by it.

"Don't be deceived by its beauty," Jensa said. "It's treacher-ous, but it gives us a living."

"Where is the village?"

"There. Don't you see it?"

Reiv squinted his eyes and scanned the mottled shoreline. At first he saw only sand and water, but then a scurry of move-ment caught his eye and he realized he was looking straight at it. The beach was dotted with palms, and the roofs of the tiny huts huddled beneath were made from their fronds and formed into the same star-like shapes. It was only the barely detectable movement of people that revealed the place to be a living village. Reiv found himself smiling, but his elation dissipated quickly. "Jensa, is there anything I should know before I get there? I mean, will it be the same as Pobu?"

"Does it look like Pobu?"

"Well, no, but I mean the Shell Seekers are still—"

"Still what? Jecta? We are Jecta only to the Tearians," she said crisply. "We are Shell Seekers."

She marched onward and Reiv hurried after her. "Please, I did not mean to offend. I just meant do your people hate me as much as the Jecta do?"

Jensa spun to face him. "Hate you? What reason would they possibly have to hate you?"

Reiv took a step back, startled by the acerbity of her tone.

"After all," she continued, "it is by the generosity of your family that we are allowed to hunt in your seas, is it not? Of course we cannot keep much for ourselves. Only that which we make from crafting the shells and the pittance we get for bringing the best fish to Market. We could just steal them from the sea and keep it for ourselves. Who would ever know?" Jensa eyed him darkly. "Well, I'll tell you who would know. The spies who would betray us for a bit of Tearian coin pressed into their palm! Now in answer to your original question—"

"Never mind," Reiv said, "your point is well taken." He said nothing more as they walked down the hill toward the village, choosing to follow several paces behind her in silence instead.

As they drew nearer, the old familiar feeling of being led to an execution returned. Curious faces turned in his and Jensa's direction and distant voices shouted as groups of villagers rushed from huts and various corners of the place. Reiv cringed and prayed they were all just happy to see Jensa. But he knew it was his blaring head of red that was what they were all pointing at.

He forced his eyes to Jensa's back instead of toward the gaping faces that surrounded them, but a determined movement fast approaching diverted his attention. He sucked in his breath and felt his body go rigid. Storming up the path toward them was a man with dark flashing eyes, his expression not merely that of anger, but of pure fury. The man's hands were balled into fists at his side and his hostility shimmered off his muscular body like heat off the sand.

"Is that Kerrik?" Reiv asked, his face blushing at the realization his voice had cracked in the asking.

"No," Jensa replied, "that is Torin, my other brother. He does not cause near the trouble Kerrik does."

Reiv stopped in his tracks, hesitant to take another step. But then he forced a foot forward and prepared himself for the blow to his face that was surely coming.

"Why is he here?" Torin demanded upon reaching them.

"Calm yourself, Torin," Jensa said. "I'll explain it all to you later—in private if you don't mind. Do you have to make a spectacle out of everything?" She continued walking, Reiv close at her back.

Reiv avoided eye contact with anyone, although he periodically glanced over his shoulder in case anyone decided to come at his head with a rock. He heard the usual comments, but they soon become predictable, and he came to feel almost unfazed by them all.

A highly energetic boy came suddenly bounding full speed toward them and leapt to Jensa's side, grabbing her hand and tugging at it impatiently.

"The Prince!" the boy said. "You brought the Prince! You didn't say you were bringing *him* with you. Why is he here, Jensa, huh? Why?" The boy hopped alongside her, still tugging at her hand and staring wide-eyed at Reiv. A grin of pure joy was stretched across his freckled face.

"Settle down, Kerrik," she said. "I'll tell you later. Let's get home first."

"This is Kerrik?" Reiv asked, astonished.

"Yes, I'm Kerrik!" the boy said, abandoning Jensa's hand to walk alongside him.

"I heard you wanted to be a great warrior," Reiv said. He looked the boy up and down. Kerrik was tiny and bore the face of a child and the foot of a cripple. Not very warrior-like material.

"Oh, I *am* a great warrior," Kerrik said eagerly. "And I'm a really good spy, too. I've spied on you even."

"Is that so? And why would you have ever had need to spy on me?"

"The day you were arrested. I saw you and the others. Brina sent me. She said I was the bravest warrior she ever saw. And I *was* brave! You were brave, too, Prince. And the girl . . . she was *real* brave. The other boy was *kind* of brave, but not as much as you and—"

"Enough, Kerrik!" Torin snapped.

"But, Torin—"

"You heard me! Now come up for some air, will you." He shot the boy a look, daring him to say another word.

The further into the village they went, the more Reiv felt like he had stepped into another world. The huts that were almost invisible from a distance, proved to be quite unique and colorful up close. Decorated with shells that streamed down in iridescent colors, the houses seemed to sing melodious songs of the sea. Perhaps the people were forbidden to sing, but the shells that tinkled in the breeze certainly were not.

As he turned his eyes toward the people crowding around them, Reiv noticed the Shell Seekers delighted in their own personal adornment as well as that of their homes. Their intricate tattoos were tinted in shades of the sea, and the jewelry that cascaded down their ears and necks danced to their movements like shimmering waterfalls. Their hair and eyes were of every color, and their skin would have been, too, had it not been bronzed by the sun. Everybody and everything was clean, and much care and effort had been taken in the appearance of things. The people may have been poor, but they were proud and appreciated the beauty of their surroundings.

Reiv gazed around him in awe, no longer aware of the painted faces that watched and whispered in his direction. He had even almost forgotten about Torin, whose face still wore an expression of acute ferocity, and Kerrik who continued to barrage him with questions and comments.

They eventually halted before a hut much like any other. Jensa pulled back the shell beads that hung in the doorway and motioned Reiv in before her. She eyed Torin and mouthed a silent threat in his direction. He responded with dark, knitted brows and clenched teeth.

Kerrik danced around his brother and darted into the hut, tugging at Reiv's hand as he attempted to usher him around.

Reiv jerked his hand away. It didn't feel right being touched by a Jecta, even one so small as Kerrik.

"Here's my bed, Prince," Kerrik announced. He motioned Reiv over to a cot framed with reed poles, its mattress that of a faded flax coverlet stuffed with soft grasses. Bouncing himself upon it, he said, "You can have my bed if you want. I'll sleep on the floor. I don't mind. I would like to sleep there. Would you like to—"

"Kerrik, gods!" Jensa said. "Leave him be for goodness sake."

"Thank you, Kerrik," Reiv said, "but I will be fine on the floor, somewhere."

Reiv twisted his body and inspected the interior of the hut. It was simple and neat and the rooms, if you could call them that, were separated by nearly transparent drapes of pastel cloth that billowed in the breeze wafting through the open doorway. There were two sleeping areas, one for Jensa and the other for her brothers, and there was a kitchen consisting of a wooden counter and a small baking hearth formed out of mud brick. Grass mats sat around a small, centrally located fire pit that appeared to be where they ate. The only table in the place was littered with tools and surrounded by baskets overflowing with shells. It was a pleasant place, bright and clean and full of feminine touches, and for a brief moment Reiv thought he might truly find some happiness there. But then Torin spoke and the blissful fantasy evaporated.

"By the gods, Jensa! What were you thinking of, bringing him here?" Torin demanded.

Jensa regarded him with indifference. "He needs a skill. I offered him one."

"A skill? What skill would that be, pray tell?"

"Seeking shells, of course. He and the other two were banished to Pobu, but no one would give the Prince work there. We inquired everywhere. What else could I do?"

"And just what makes you think he'll be accepted here?"

"Do not concern yourself with me," Reiv interjected. "I will just stand over here in the corner and pretend I cannot hear you insult me." Reiv regarded Torin with distaste. He was growing increasingly impatient with the man's ill manners.

"Don't mind my brother," Jensa said to Reiv. "He frequently forgets himself. Here. You can set your bag over here and bed down against that wall. I'll move a few things out of the way. Perhaps in time we can get you a real bed put together. Now, let's see about getting some refreshment."

"He is *not* staying!" Torin insisted.

Kerrik stood to the side, remaining surprisingly quiet while his eyes darted back and forth between his sister and brother. Unable to hold his silence any longer, he rushed over and planted himself in front of Torin.

"Oh, pleeeaaase, let him stay, Torin," Kerrik begged. "I'll look after the Prince. I will! I'll teach him how to seek. You won't have to, honest you won't. And he can have some of my share of the food; I won't mind. He won't be any trouble. Please? I promise he won't." He gazed up at Torin with pleading eyes of liquid blue, and his bottom lip jutted out just a bit, no doubt a well-rehearsed act of innocent manipulation. From the weakening expression on Torin's hard face, it appeared to be almost working.

"Yes, *please*, Torin," Reiv mocked. "I will be a good prince, I *promise*."

Torin stormed over to Reiv and leaned his face to his. "There is no promise you could make that I would believe," he said. "Your whole upbringing has been based on nothing but lies. Why should it be any different now?"

Reiv clenched and unclenched his fists at his side. He wanted to strike the man down right then and there, and had every intention of doing so, when Kerrik suddenly wedged his way between them, nudging Torin back a step.

"Out of the way, Kerrik, this is between the Prince and me!" Torin said. He didn't take his eyes off Reiv for a single second, not even when he grabbed his little brother by the arm and swung him roughly to the side.

"That is right, Torin," Reiv said, his temper flaring. "Twist the boy's arm off if it will make you feel like a man. I will not be moved aside so easily."

"We'll see about that!" Torin said as he moved in Reiv's direction. But a great wave of water suddenly washed over them both, leaving them gasping and sputtering, their eyelids flickering at the unexpected shower.

"That should cool you both off," Jensa said, one hand holding an empty bucket, the other fisted on her hip. "I've had enough of this nonsense. Torin, Reiv will stay. Reiv, you will watch your mouth. And Kerrik, you may take care of the Prince, but first please go fetch me some more water."

Kerrik drew in his breath as though he had just been given all the riches of Tearia. "Oh, thank you Jensa! When can I teach him? Today? Is today all right? Or would tomorrow be better? Oh, I can't wait!" His still chattering voice could be heard trailing off into the distance as he ran to refill the bucket.

"Are you hungry, Reiv?" Jensa asked, changing the subject. She motioned him toward the mats and picked up a basket filled with chunks of palm nut and held it out to him. "I hope you like these; we eat a great deal of it around here."

"I am sure it is very good," Reiv said. "But I think I would rather have some dry clothes at the moment if you do not mind." He remained standing, shaking the water from his outstretched arms.

"Well, you should have thought about that before you insulted my brother," she said.

"Insulted your—but—"

She shot him a non-verbal warning and he closed his mouth immediately.

Torin smirked, obviously feeling a taste of victory at his sister's defense of him. His face fell, however, when she added, "Poor Torin can't help his weaknesses, Reiv. He was born that way and it's difficult for him to be reminded of them by a Tearian."

"Weaknesses?" Torin cried.

Then it was Reiv's turn to smirk, but he knew it would be a short-lived triumph. The sudden drenching of cold water may have temporarily cooled down their bodies, but the hostilities within their guts still smoldered hot and deep. It would only be a matter of time before the fires were rekindled.

Because Kerrik desired it more than anything in the whole wide world, he was given permission to take Reiv to the beach that afternoon to train him in the work of shell seeking. Torin argued against leaving their little brother alone with the former prince, but Jensa assured him the boys would not be alone, as most of the village would probably be spying on them anyway. After some debate, she and Torin marched out the hut to continue their heated discussion in private. But it was clear Jensa had already won.

Kerrik began the lesson by telling Reiv he would need to strip off his tunic and gloves. Reiv responded with a gasp and a great knot in the pit of his stomach. The tunic was no problem, but removing the gloves was something else altogether.

"You can't hunt for shells in *those*," Kerrik said, eyeing the gloves.

Reiv removed them reluctantly and tossed them to the floor by his bedroll. Strangely, Kerrik did not act surprised by the scars on Reiv's hands, though he did comment that they must have *really* hurt when they got burned. Reiv nodded silently in response and poised himself for the barrage of questions that was surely coming. To his surprise, none did. He pulled off his tunic, leaving only the undercloth beneath, and waited for the next instruction.

"Now, we have to blacken your eyes to protect them from the sun," Kerrik said. He reached over to a small, carved box and removed a bit of kohl. "Here, I'll do it for you."

Reiv frowned. "No, I will not need that."

"Yes, you will," Kerrik insisted. "The sun's very bright and it reflects off the sand and the water. This keeps the reflection down. All the Shell Seekers wear it."

"Well, I am not a Shell Seeker," Reiv said, but then he noticed the boy's downcast expression. "I mean, I am not a Shell Seeker *yet*. Perhaps later, when I am truly one of you."

Kerrik sighed like a parent with an unruly child. "Very well, but you'll regret it." He gave Reiv a small knife for digging snails out of shells and prying them from between rocks, then handed him a belt to tie around his waist with a cloth bag hanging from it. "To put the shells in, of course," Kerrik said in response to Reiv's puzzled expression. The boy inspected him up and down, his arms crossed in serious contemplation. "Your skin is very pale, Reiv. We should put something on it."

"Do not worry about it," Reiv said. "I have spent many hours out of doors and my skin always looks like this. It will be fine."

With that, Kerrik appeared resolved to accept Reiv's stubbornness and so he headed out the door, motioning for his pupil to follow. As Reiv walked behind the sprite of a boy who was more hopping than walking along the sand, he could not help but stare at the tiny twisted foot. It turned inward and arched in a very peculiar way, but it did not slow him down, and Kerrik seemed unaware that he should have any difficulty with it at all. Reiv looked down at his own hands and wished he could be as accepting of his imperfections as Kerrik was of his, but he doubted he ever would be.

When they reached the beach, several villagers gathered, clearly intent on enjoying the show. Kerrik marched over to them and barked an order for them to leave. "We will require some privacy during our lesson," he told them. "Torin and Jensa said so." With that, the disgruntled audience muttered their disappointment and walked away. Reiv could only stare in disbelief that one so small as Kerrik could command a group of adults so easily as that. But then he realized the boy was, after all, the brother of Jensa and Torin.

"We'll start there," Kerrik said. "The water's not too deep, so you can reach the bottom quickly."

"Reach the bottom? Why do we need to reach the bottom?"

Kerrik jerked his head with bafflement. "To get the shells of course."

"Can we not just pick them up on the shore here?"

"On the shore?" Kerrik laughed. "Oh, no. Only the babies pick up the shells off the shore, and there are not many shells that make it to shore anyway. We have to dive for the shells out there," he said, pointing to the dark, gray-green of the deep.

Reiv felt the blood drain from his face. "We are going out there?" he asked.

"Yes, but today we'll start closer in, though we may not find so many shells."

Reiv paced along the water's edge, eyeing it with consternation. A wave pushed its way in and lapped at his feet. He jumped back.

"It's not cold, come on!" Kerrik said, bounding into the water. He turned and stared back at Reiv who was still pacing back and forth. "Come on! What are you waiting for?"

Reiv put in a foot and pulled it back, shaking his head. The water was not cold; it was in fact quite warm. But as it wrapped around his feet, it seemed to him like a living thing, its gritty fingers reaching out to pull him into the murky depths.

Kerrik plodded his way through the water and back to shore where he stopped before his reluctant pupil. "Can't you *swim*?" he asked.

"Of course I can! But . . . well . . . actually . . . I have never swum in water so deep as this, and I have certainly never been in water so—so—" He didn't know how to finish the sentence without sounding like a complete idiot.

"So . . . what?" Kerrik asked.

"I just do not like it, that is all."

"Well, then how are you going to hunt for shells? You don't want to be a baby, do you? You don't want everyone laughing at you, do you?"

"No, but..."

"I thought princes were brave," Kerrik said. He cocked a brow in Reiv's direction. "Well, I guess I'll just have to tell Torin and Jensa that you're scared."

The image of Torin's laughing, smirking face flashed into Reiv's mind. "Oh, very well, I will learn to dive, but you had best teach me to swim better first. Is there someplace where the waters are a bit calmer?"

Kerrik's expression brightened. "I know just the place! There's a pool near the rocks a ways down and no one will see us, unless they really try. We can do it there."

They made their way along the shoreline and between the craggy rocks that lay tumbled along it. Kerrik hopped across them easily, oblivious to their jagged edges and sharp ridges. Reiv on the other hand, picked his way along, frequently stopping to inspect his feet, expecting to see blood leaking out of them. They reached the pool, a reserve of calm surrounded by rocks against which the sea pounded thunderously. A great crashing wave occasionally sent a spray of water over the pool, settling upon them in a fine mist. But the pool itself was calm and not too deep and would suit their needs well enough.

Reiv waded in as instructed and stared down through the clear water. The sand felt gritty and crunched and shifted beneath his weight. Tiny, silver fish darted about his ankles and nipped at his feet. An orange-shelled crab sauntered slowly alongside him. He didn't like the strange creatures at all, and kicked a foot toward the fish and moved in the other direction of the crab.

"They won't hurt you," Kerrik said, recognizing Reiv's look of discomfort.

"Oh, I know, I just do not wish to harm them," Reiv lied. In truth, he wouldn't have minded if the crab was good and dead.

From that point on Reiv practiced putting his face, then his head, then his whole body under the water. He kept his feet firmly planted in the sand, ducking under in a sort of squat. But that plan did not go well as the buoyancy of his body jeopardized his balance and he soon found himself struggling back up. During one such attempt he felt something brush across his cheek. He reacted to it with a gasp, not a good idea under water he quickly learned. He pushed up frantically, coughing and gagging and throwing up salt water. It burned his throat and left a bitter taste in his mouth, and his belly felt sick afterward. But Kerrik, who seemed to possess a sort of ruthlessness as a teacher, would allow him no rest, insisting that he go back under as soon as he recovered himself.

Eventually Reiv floated face down and stroked his arms back and forth as he paddled across the water. He learned to ignore the fact that he was sharing the pond with pinching claws, ridged mouths, and sharp fins. It helped that he didn't open his eyes, but then he was told he would have to do that as well. A Shell Seeker would find few shells with his eyes closed.

The first time Reiv opened his eyes under water they stung and felt as though someone had thrown a handful of sand into them, and he wondered how in the world he was ever going to get used to it. For a moment he considered giving up his foolish attempt at being something he obviously could not. But then he forced them to stay open and saw the fishes swimming in their synchronized dances, and the crab meandering across the sand, its beady-black eyes turned up to him in mutual curiosity. He began to feel somewhat of an appreciation for the strange creatures and found himself thinking that perhaps he could become a Shell Seeker after all.

They practiced for hours, floating, and diving, and competing with one another for who could hold their breath the longest. Kerrik always won, of course, but with each attempt Reiv increased his time, and before long he became bound and determined to win, although he never did. After a while they took themselves to the beach to rest for a while.

"I think you're ready to go to the deeper water," Kerrik said. "Maybe tomorrow. We won't go out too far though. It's harder with the waves, but even if you're not so good with strokes, at least you can float. But first I need to tell you about the snakes."

Reiv sat up quickly. "The snakes? What snakes? You mean the sea snakes? Oh gods, I forgot about the sea snakes. Surely we will not be swimming with them! Are they poisonous? Do they attack? What happens if—"

"Yes," Kerrik said.

"Yes what?" Reiv asked, his voice squeaking somewhat.

"Yes, I'm talking about the sea snakes. Yes, we'll be swimming with them. Yes, they're poisonous, some of them. And yes, they'll attack if you make them mad."

Kerrik seemed indifferent about it and for a moment Reiv could only stare at him, his satisfaction at the day's accomplishments washed out with the tide.

"Don't tell me you're afraid of snakes, too," Kerrik said. "Well, you better get used to them. They live out there and there's no way to avoid them. Don't worry, Reiv, I'll protect you." The boy who seemed so childlike when they first met had taken on a maturity beyond his years since they had begun their lessons. He now spoke about diving with snakes as though he had been doing it for a hundred years.

"How old *are* you?" Reiv asked.

"Why, I'm seven!" Kerrik replied.

"Seven? And how long have you been diving for shells?"

The boy twisted his mouth and rolled his eyes to the sky as he worked it out. "Three years . . . ever since I was four."

"Four! Gods, they let a four-year-old dive with snakes?"

"I *told* you, only the babies pick up the shells on the shore. Don't worry, Reiv, the snakes are not so big. But there is *one*—" Kerrik sat up suddenly alert, and his eyes took on a look of profound wonder. "I'm going to slay it one day. Then I'll be the most famous Shell Seeker ever known!"

"How big is this snake exactly?" Reiv asked.

"Oh, it's *huge!*" Kerrik jumped up and spread his arms out wide. "It's longer than anything! It's Seirgotha, the most evil creature in all the deep." Then he began the story, his face full of animation, every limb moving in the telling of the tale.

"It is she who stirs the waters and makes the whirlpools that would swallow us and the tides that would drag us out to sea. And she has magic in her, for she can disguise herself and no one ever sees her until it is too late. Legend says she will someday show herself and try to take us all down into the depths. But *then* a great warrior will slay her, and because of his bravery the warrior will be given power by gods. It's said the warrior will be given great knowledge and with that he can save everyone." Kerrik paused and fixed his face with determination. "I will be that warrior. I will slay her, and then I will know how to heal!"

The initial fear of the huge snake evaporated from Reiv's mind. He could not help but smile at the boy whose tiny body was poised for battle with an imaginary sea monster. "Perhaps you will slay it, Kerrik," he said. "Perhaps you truly will."

Kerrik grinned at Reiv's words of optimism. "Oh, I *will*," he said.

"You certainly have your brother and sister's feisty temperament."

"Oh, Torin and Jensa are not my real brother and sister."

"No?"

"No, my parents are Tearian, but they couldn't keep me because of my foot." He looked down at it and shrugged. "I don't see why though. It doesn't bother me at all and I wouldn't have been any trouble."

For a moment Reiv's heart went out to him, but then he realized the boy did not seem terribly upset by it, so he held off saying any words of sympathy. "What brought you to this place, then?"

"Brina saved me and then she took me to Nannaven and then *she* took me to Jensa and Torin."

"Brina? Saved you?" Reiv couldn't believe it.

"Yes, she saves lots of babies," Kerrik said matter-of-factly. Then he noticed the shocked expression on Reiv's face. "Didn't you know that?"

"No. I did not."

"Well, anyway, that's why I want to slay Seirgotha and become a great healer. Because that way I can make people well and the babies, too, and then people won't have to give them away. Then everyone will be happy and no one will be sick or sad anymore. That's what I want more than anything!"

Reiv stared silently out at the horizon for a moment, contemplating the boy's noble words. For the first time in his life he felt a twinge of guilt at having ever been called Tearian.

Kerrik eyed him curiously. "Reiv, are you all right? You look funny." Then he glanced in the direction of Reiv's gaze. "It's getting late. We'd better go home now. Jensa gets really mad if anyone's late for dinner and if you think Torin's got a temper . . ."

Reiv pushed himself up. "Well, I certainly do not wish to meet that temper tonight."

They trudged toward the village, or rather Reiv trudged while Kerrik hopped along. Reiv's muscles were beginning to stiffen and his eyes and skin were starting to sting. By the time they reached the hut, his lids were swollen and his back had erupted in blisters.

Jensa gasped at the sight of him. "Gods, Kerrik, why didn't you rub some kohl around his eyes," she exclaimed.

"He wouldn't let me," the boy cried.

"And his back!" She walked around Reiv in a circle, eyeing him up and down. "We have lotions you could have put on him."

"He said he was used to the sun," Kerrik insisted. "He said his skin always looked white."

Torin laughed from where he sat at the work bench. "Well, he's not so white now," he said, clearly enjoying the Prince's discomfort.

Reiv went to contort his face with displeasure, but found it too painful to move. Jensa ordered him over to a stool, then pulled out a jar of salve and lathered him all over with it. He winced and groaned as she rubbed it across his swollen lids and tender back.

"I told you you'd regret it," Kerrik mumbled.

"He's going to get sun poisoning," Jensa said.

She mixed up some water with a powdered herb and ordered Reiv to drink it. He complied, all the while insisting he was fine. But after he ate and laid down on his mat for the night, he was overtaken by chills and a deep, painful itch that tore at every inch of his flesh. He got no sleep at all, and neither did anyone else.

In the weeks that followed Reiv became a much better swimmer. Although he was still not as adept as he needed to be, he had begun to dive to the deeper rocks. The first time he emerged with a shell, he strutted up and down the beach as though he had discovered a great jewel. Kerrik laughed and clapped and danced around him with glee. As the boy had said, there were indeed sea snakes, but Reiv learned to avoid dark crags in the rocks where they liked to hide and knew to move cautiously when near them. In time he grew accustomed to the snakes as well as to the multitude of other sea animals that shared the waters, just as his skin grew accustomed to the sun, and his eyes to the salt water.

He also became more comfortable with wearing kohl, not only because it did indeed protect his eyes from the glare, but also because he noticed the girls in the village paid him more attention with the kohl than without. The black smudged around his eyes seemed to accentuate the rare and beautiful color of them, and Jensa, convinced his eyes were his best feature, began to experiment with marking the kohl around them in various patterns. He allowed her to do so, mainly because all the other boys his age had some signature design on their faces. Before long Jensa settled on a pattern that was unique. Reiv tested the waters, so to speak, by strolling casually through the village, intent on seeing what reaction he might get to Jensa's artwork. Much to his delight, many a feminine head turned and smiled in his direction. Thereafter, he was never without his kohl.

By the third week he seemed to have become more accepted by the villagers, although the young women had warmed up to him much more quickly than the men. Torin was still cool toward him and avoided confrontations only by avoiding him altogether. Jensa, on the other hand, invited Reiv to accompany her whenever possible and introduced him to many a young female Shell Seeker. After a while he became suspicious and joked that she was trying to get rid of him by marrying him off to the first girl that came along. She responded to his jests with denials, but the sly grin on her lips told him he wasn't too far off.

Torin went to Pobu two days out of every week, but rarely came home with anything other than news. When he returned, he always reported to Jensa, speaking directly to her whether the news concerned Reiv or not. But this week Torin had not make his usual trip—Market was but two days away—and a Jecta messenger had come seeking him out.

Reiv stood at the flap of the hut, watching Torin and the messenger across the way. Even from that distance, it was clear the conversation was an emotional one. Torin turned and suddenly stormed in the direction of the hut, sending a lump of dread Reiv's way. Torin shoved past, screaming Reiv and Kerrik out of the hut with such fury that neither of them dared protest.

They hustled out and away from the hut. Kerrik didn't seem particularly surprised by it all, but Reiv was deeply concerned. He had seen Torin angry many times, usually at him, but this time it was different, though Reiv was sure he played a role in it somehow.

He and Kerrik took themselves to the beach to do some seeking while they waited. Reiv found himself mostly pacing the sand, his mind playing possible worst-case scenarios. After some time they headed back, and there they met Torin rushing from the hut, glaring more heatedly in Reiv's direction than usual.

"What was that about?" Reiv asked as he entered and set his nearly empty bag of shells on the table. Kerrik tossed his bag down also, then grabbed a handful of nuts and dashed out to play.

"Don't stay out long, Kerrik," Jensa called after him. "It will be dark soon." She made her way over to the table and emptied the bags, then raked through the shells, sorting them by color and size.

"That one is particularly good," Reiv said, motioning to a bright orange shell with swirls of iridescent blue. But his eyes were on Jensa, not the shell.

"Yes, it's very nice," she said.

Reiv moved to her side. "What is wrong, Jensa? Tell me."

"Nothing for you to worry about."

"You are not a very good liar," he said.

She turned her face away. "A friend of ours was killed yesterday. By the Guard." A sob escaped her throat.

Reiv was startled by Jensa's sudden display of emotion. She had always been so brave, so stoic. "Who was it?" he asked, rounding to face her.

"Eben. You didn't know him. He was a good man, a potter with a wife and three children."

"But why? What did he do?"

"The Guard wanted information. Word in Pobu is that Eben found something of value, though no one knows what. The guards took him and questioned him. When he wouldn't, or couldn't, tell them what they wanted to know, they decided to make an example of him. His body was found by his wife on their own doorstep."

Reiv took the shells from her shaking hands and ushered her to the bench. Then he filled a mug with cool tea and a pinch of lavender and handed it to her. "Here. Drink. It won't take away the grief, but it may calm your nerves."

She drank the tea down, then handed the mug back. "Thank you. I'll be all right. But Torin . . ." Her gaze drifted out the door. "His heart is more fragile than you know, Reiv." She sighed. "Well, there is some good news. About Dayn and Alicine. Would you like to hear it?"

Reiv felt his heart leap. He nodded and sat on the mat before her, eager for the information.

"It seems your cousin is doing so well at the smithy that Gair has decided to expand the business. Dayn's actually teaching Gair a thing or two about metal work. They've recently taken on a particularly big job, so it's just a matter of time before the two of them are rolling in the coin."

Reiv could not help but grin.

"And Alicine . . ." She paused and smiled.

Reiv's eyes lit up.

"Well, let's just say you won't have to worry about her leaving Pobu anymore. She has found herself a beau and decided to stay forever."

Reiv's face fell. "She what?"

Jensa tilted her head back and laughed. Though it did Reiv good to see her momentarily cheerful, he could not share in her amusement.

"Aren't you happy?" she asked.

"About what?" he grumbled.

"Oh, Reiv. You are so transparent. I was only joking. How can Alicine have found a beau when she's probably still pining for you."

"Pining for me? Do not be ridiculous." But he could no longer bear the suspense. "Do you think she is? Really?"

"Of course. I hear her transparency is as obvious as yours." She rose and placed a hand on his shoulder. Thank you for the laugh, Reiv. It felt good.

"You are welcome. Any time you feel the need to torture me with your humor, feel free." He was only jesting, but for the first time he realized any torture would be welcome if it renewed his hopes with Alicine.

23

Promises to Keep

The day before Market had finally arrived and the Shell Seekers were slowly making their way up the road leading from Meirla. Reiv found himself strangely thrilled at the thought of returning to Pobu and at times wanted to leap for joy at the thought of it. He forced restraint, but it was obvious from his unusually happy mood that his reunion with Dayn and Alicine could not come soon enough.

He ducked into the hut one last time and paused to check himself in the reflective plate. That morning he had bathed and styled his hair, braiding it with long strands of white cockles that wound between the red. The kohl around his eyes was painted most meticulously, and his faded tunic was accessorized with numerous strands of colorful shells. He had worked particularly hard to make himself look attractive for Alicine. Maybe his hands were no longer beautiful, but that didn't mean the rest of him couldn't be.

He reached into the small carved box that contained what few coins and trinkets he owned, and pulled out a shell bracelet. Holding it up in the light from the doorway, he admired its swirls of pastel pink and iridescent gray. Only the finest shells had been selected for it, and he struggled for days trying to thread the tiny things together. He was clumsy in his first attempts at craftsmanship, but

Kerrik helped him, almost to the point of doing it himself. But Reiv was in charge of the project, watching over the boy's shoulder as he told him which order the shells should be strung in and which direction they should face. As Reiv admired the bracelet now draped over his fingers, he could not help but beam. It was the first thing he had ever made, well almost, and he hoped Alicine would like it.

He tucked the bracelet, along with a few coins, into his coin pouch, then rushed out of the hut to join the band now making its way up the road. He caught up with Jensa and Kerrik quickly, and glanced over at Torin who walked a cool distance away. Even he, Reiv noticed, looked particularly well-groomed today. But Torin was not one to socialize with girls, at least not that Reiv was aware of, even though the man possessed above-average looks. Reiv assumed it was because he always had a sour expression on his face and a personality to match.

Kerrik hopped alongside Reiv, babbling about something or another, but Reiv didn't pay much attention. He was too busy rehearsing in his mind what he would say when he saw Dayn and Alicine. He thought he might start with an apology, a thousand apologies if that was what it took. Hopefully his pride would not get in the way, although it likely would. But he had to convince Alicine and Dayn that he had changed, that he was a better person than he'd ever been. Surely he could make them understand that his departure had been for the best. Dayn would probably accept it, but Alicine? She had a stubborn streak in her, even worse than his own. He could only hope that she would realize he was more suited as a Shell Seeker. Maybe she would even agree to come back to Meirla with him. Now that he was employed, they could have a future together. He would build them a hut—the biggest one in the village —and he would hunt for shells to sell. Then they would have coin to buy things, and could start a family. Yes, he finally had something to offer her, his heart as well as a lifetime of security. His chest swelled with determination. He was somebody now, and there was nothing short of an act of the gods that could stop him.

Dayn held up the dirk, examining it in the dim light of the shop's back room. The glow from the forge danced along the blade, giving the illusion of flames trapped within the metal. He held it out, noting the straight line of the blade, then tightened his grip on the handle he had so meticulously crafted. During the past few weeks he had made dozens of weapons in this back room, illegal weapons for insurgents who meant to make things right for the Jecta. Most of the weapons were crudely fashioned, there was little time for fine craftsmanship, but this one wasn't for an insurgent. It was a gift for Reiv. And it had to be perfect.

"Dayn!" Alicine screeched at him from the doorway.

Dayn jumped, his heart pounding. "What are you doing here?" he demanded, trying to regain his composure.

"What am *I* doing here? God, Dayn, what are *you* doing here?"

"Lower your voice and close the door! Are you trying to get us both arrested?"

Alicine did as instructed, then stormed toward him from across the room. She tossed a bundle onto a nearby work bench and eyed the dirk. "Do you know what kind of trouble you could get in having a weapon like that? Where did you get it?"

"I made it," he said, grinning. "What do you think of it?"

"Made it? Is *that* what you've been doing here all these weeks?"

Dayn moved to a crate across the way. Inside, an assortment of knives and short swords lay barely concealed beneath a tumble of oily rags. He rearranged the rags, then closed the lid.

Alicine stared wide-eyed down at the crate. "It's a good thing I stopped by to bring you lunch, otherwise I wouldn't have known you'd gone completely mad. You'll stop this immediately, Dayn," she said.

Dayn marched over to put up his tools. "I don't have to take orders from you. They need my help and I'm going to give it."

Alicine followed him over, flustered by her brother's unusually defiant tone. "I'll not stand by and let you get involved in this," she said.

"I don't think there's much you can do about it."

"Oh, really? Well, I think there is something I can do about it."

"Like what?"

"I'll tell Nannaven."

"She already knows."

"Then I'll tell Jensa and Torin."

"They know, too."

"God, Dayn, who doesn't know?"

"Reiv. And I'm telling him today when he gets here." He wrapped the dirk in a ragged swath of cloth and placed it inside a leather satchel.

"Reiv. Humph! I doubt he'll even show up."

"Why do you say that?" Dayn said, "You heard him. He said he'd be back for Market." He swung the strap of the satchel over his shoulder.

"Since when does he ever tell the truth. He's been gone for almost a month now. I'm sure he's settled in just fine with Jensa and has no more need of us."

"He didn't go to be with Jensa. He went to make something of himself."

Alicine laughed. "Oh, sure. Like he didn't notice how beautiful she was."

Dayn's eyes flashed. "Enough, Alicine. I won't listen to any more of this." He made for the door. Alicine followed close behind.

"Well, you will listen!" she said as she hustled to his side. "There is no longer any reason for us to stay here, Dayn. Brina has not been to see us in weeks and neither has Reiv. You promised you would take me home and I expect you to live up to that promise. I'll not stay another minute in a place where my brother could be executed for sheer stupidity."

Gair looked up from his anvil as Dayn and Alicine marched past him through the main room of the shop. "Leaving so soon?" he asked.

"Reiv's coming today, remember?" Dayn said.

"Ah, yes, that he is," Gair replied.

"And you!" Alicine cried, stopping and pointing a shaky finger in Gair's direction.

"What did I do?" Gair asked.

"Why'd you let her in?" Dayn growled over his shoulder. "You should have known she'd bring me nothing but grief."

"Thought it was time she knew, that's all," Gair said to Dayn's retreating back. "Couldn't wait forever for you to tell her, now could I?"

"Fine," Dayn said as he stormed out the door.

Alicine caught up and rounded on him, bringing him to a halt. "I'm serious Dayn. You've carried this too far! We are leaving for home. Tomorrow at the latest."

"Don't be ridiculous," Dayn said. "And lower your voice. Do you need everyone hearing our business?"

"I don't care who hears it!"

Dayn yanked her by an elbow into a nearby alcove. "Listen, Alicine," he said in a hushed voice. "Reiv's coming today and then you'll feel differently about things."

"No, I won't. You've gotten in over your head and there's nothing that can make me stay now."

"Not even Reiv?"

"No, not even Reiv." She turned to walk away, but Dayn regained his hold on her arm.

"Where are you going?" he asked. "Aren't you coming home with me to wait for him?"

"No. Nannaven had to go run some errand and said it couldn't wait any longer. She left me to finish the rounds by myself. I don't have the luxury of going home and waiting for someone who has no loyalty to me and won't likely be back to see me anyway!" She shrugged her arm away, then spun on her heels and marched away.

24
The Quick and the Dead

The drapes were drawn in the king's bedchamber, leaving the room dimly lit and stifling with summer heat. Scented candles flickered, their sweet perfume unable to disguise the stench of sickness that lingered in the air.

Whyn sat by his father's bed, listening to the rattling breaths of a man soon to draw his last. "Is there nothing else you can do?" Whyn asked the healer.

The healer shook his head. "It is just a matter of time."

"But the potion the Priestess conjured; it should have worked." Whyn rose and reached for the glass decanter on the table next to the bed. "You are still giving him the same potion, are you not?" He lifted the decanter to his nose and sniffed. The familiar, but repugnant, odor made his stomach sick. "Gods, we have been forcing it down his throat for weeks now. Why has it not worked?"

The healer took the decanter from Whyn's shaking hand and set it back on the table. "His soul is in the hands of the gods now, Lord Prince."

"Well what about *her* god!" Whyn snapped.

Two male attendants spoke in hushed whispers, their eyes watching Whyn cautiously. The healer's face grew stern. "Blasphemous words about our Priestess will not save your father. You must accept that which is meant to be."

King Sedric moaned and stirred slightly. Whyn threw himself back onto the chair by the bed and grabbed his father's hand. "Where is Mother? Why is she not here?" he asked the healer.

"She has been by our lord's side day and night. Surely you would not deny her a moment's rest?"

"No, I would not deny her," Whyn conceded, realizing his mother might be a selfish woman, but she always did her duty by her husband.

For a moment Sedric's breathing slowed, then increased its rhythm to shallow, staccato breaths. His eyelids fluttered as a tremble moved along his body, vibrating the coverlets that were draped upon him.

Whyn felt the fear of the inevitable clench his chest. "Fetch Mother immediately!" he ordered the healer. "The rest of you—out!"

The healer nodded, and he, along with the attendants, hustled out.

Whyn stared into his father's skeletal face. "I am here, Father."

"Ruairi," Sedric rasped.

"No, Father. It is Whyn."

Sedric half-opened his eyes, the once vibrant color of them now clouded with pain. "Whyn," he croaked.

"Yes, Father. Whyn."

"Ruairi. Is he safe?"

"Of course he is safe."

Sedric's drawn features softened as a smile wavered on his lips. But then his lungs exploded into spasms and his eyes rolled back in his skull.

The coughing gradually eased. Whyn moistened a cloth and dabbed the blood left on his father's lips. "No more talk, Father. You must save your strength."

"Please, son, let my last words be those of redemption," Sedric whispered. He lifted a weak hand and Whyn took hold of it.

"You need no redemption, Father. The gods have prepared a special place for you. I only hope that I will be as great a king as you have been."

"I have been a good king, but a poor father," Sedric said.

"You have been a fine father," Whyn insisted.

Sedric turned his fading eyes up to him. "No. I could not save my son."

"I told you, Ruairi is safe."

"But you are not. The fire saved Ruairi . . . but it will not save you."

"What do you mean it will not save me?"

"She—she—" Sedric's lips remained parted as a long last breath rattled his lungs. His eyes grew wide and staring, but it was clear they could no longer see.

A sob escaped Whyn's throat. "No, Father! You cannot leave me. I need you."

He threw himself across his father's chest, crying like a child. "Please stay with me. I do not know what to do."

"Lord Prince," a voice boomed from the doorway.

Whyn turned his tear-streaked face toward it, but was too overwhelmed with grief to respond.

"The Priestess will see you now," the priest in the doorway said.

Whyn leapt up, his fists shaking. "How dare you summon me when my father has just passed!" he screamed. "Leave me!"

But the priest did not move.

"I said leave me!"

"You will come with me now," the priest said. Then he turned to the side and bowed his head to allow the Prince to exit before him.

Whyn wiped the tears from his face with the palm of his hand, then gazed down at his father one last time. "I will be back soon, Father," he said. "I promise." He lifted his head and stormed through the door, brushing past the priest without a word.

When Whyn reached the temple, the Priestess was not waiting for him in her usual receiving room, but in her private chambers. He had never been to that room before, it would not have been proper. His first instinct was to run in the other direction, but his body was too weak with anxiety to run, and his mind was too numb to invent a way out of it.

"My dear Prince," the Priestess' sultry voice crooned as she rose from her dressing bench. Whyn had not seen her when he first entered; she had been half-hidden by shadows in the corner of the room. Two young handmaidens could be seen at her side, their identical heads bowed. The Priestess dismissed them with a crisp command followed by a flick of her hand. They scampered out the room, leaving her alone with Whyn.

"Priestess," Whyn said. He bowed at the waist and remained.

She circled him slowly, her long white dressing gown sweeping the floor around him, but she did not motion him to rise. "So, your father is dead," she said.

"Yes, Priestess," he said to the floor.

"And now you will be King."

"Yes, Priestess." Whyn could feel the heat building in his cheeks, but he did not know if it was from humiliation or the blood rushing to his head.

The Priestess tilted his chin up with her finger. "You may rise," she said coolly.

He complied and pulled in a deep, but subtle, breath. He could not allow his body language to reveal his emotions. That would only serve to give her more power, and she had enough of that already.

"We have business to attend to, Whyn," she said.

"But Father died only moments ago!"

"Do you question my authority?" she asked.

"No, Priestess. I only thought—"

"You are not here to think. You are here to obey."

Whyn felt fury well within his breast. Maybe she was the supreme power of the Temple, but he was now King. What right did she have to talk to him in such a manner? He tightened his jaw, then said, "I am King of Tearia and as such I feel we are due mutual respect."

Her eyes flashed like lightening and she raised her arms upward, lifting him into the air. He lingered there for a moment, suspended, then she slammed him to the floor. His cheekbone cracked as it met the tile.

"You are due nothing!" she hissed.

Whyn raised himself onto all fours, then reached a hand to his throbbing face. He looked up at her with contempt; there was no way he could disguise it.

"Oh, dear," she said. "I fear that is going to bruise."

He staggered to his feet and watched as she strolled over to an ornately framed full-length mirror.

"Come," she ordered.

He did as he was told, his hand still on his cheek, and stood before the mirror watching her pale eyes stare at his reflection.

"Remove your hand."

Whyn slowly moved his hand away. His face was swollen and already bruising. Clearly the bone was fractured.

"Oh, my. And you had such a pretty face."

Whyn wanted to glare at the callousness of her remark, but he kept his expression in check. If she was capable of this, what else was she capable of?

The Priestess smiled, then swept her hand before his face. In an instant the injury disappeared, leaving his features as smooth they had been before. "How did you do that?" he gasped. He leaned in toward the mirror, running his fingers along his cheek. It didn't even hurt.

"I am capable of much more." She strolled over to a velvet cushioned chaise and draped herself across it. She gestured to a nearby stool and motioned him to sit.

Whyn walked over stiffly and lowered himself to the stool.

"Now that we have come to an understanding about the issue of respect," she said, "we have business to discuss. It seems your brother has not faded as was expected. He has, in fact, become the topic of increased discussion as of late."

"You mean the Prophecy," Whyn said.

The Priestess's distaste was immediately apparent. "Yes, the Prophecy. But the issue will be solved soon enough. And you will be the one to solve it."

"But what can I do? I do not even know where he is."

The Priestess plucked a grape from a nearby bowl of fruit and popped it into her mouth. "Then you must find him."

"And do what?"

"What do you think?"

"But he is my brother!"

The Priestess's eyes flared. "What is your point?"

"You would ask me to kill my own brother?"

"Not ask, Whyn—tell. Was it not you who pledged your full support? Was it not you that said no sacrifice was too great for Tearia."

"But the Goddess said he was only to fade."

"Do not forget there are other gods who work against Her."

"Then it is the Goddess's will that I do this thing?"

"Yes, and mine. You owe me much, Whyn. Do not forget the role I played in your brother's disinheritance. Your parents did not have the courage to do it until I gave you the information needed to persuade them. No doubt they thought disinheritance preferable to his death at my hand. Without me, he might be king-heir still. And what of Cinnia? You said you wanted her, did you not?"

"Yes, but—"

"That you feared your father would not allow a union between you because of your brother?"

Whyn swallowed deeply and nodded. "Yes, Priestess, I said those things. But Cinnia said she loved me and wanted me, too."

"Of course she did, after I was finished with her." The Priestess rose and moved to her dressing table, then lifted a brush and swept it through her long, white hair. "Cinnia is such a beautiful child. She did not like it when I showed her what it felt like to have hands like your brother's. It was illusion only. But it could have just as easily been real."

Whyn rose from the stool and felt his blood drain to his feet. "You mean she does not love me?"

"Of course she loves you. Never fear. You have her heart as well as her body." She curled her lips into a smile. "But I have the rest of her."

Whyn's mind raced as he replayed their agreement and all the events that had happened since. "Why did you have me attempt reconciliation with Reiv? And why have me give him the sword?"

The Priestess threw the brush onto the dressing table, sending bottled potions skittering across it and crashing to the floor. "Because I expected him to attack you with it, fool!" she snapped. "Then the guards could have taken care of him right then and there. But the cursed boy did not even touch it." She ground her teeth. "I always knew he was more trouble than he was worth. I should have taken care of him sooner. That was my original plan. His injuries gave me pause, but even as a Jecta he continues to plague me. If only I'd arranged for him to die from the fever that took him after the accident." She spun to face him. "Enough of what could have been. We need to discuss what will be. I have received word that a band of Jecta insurgents has been meeting. Our interrogations of suspects have turned up nothing, and the cells are filling. They are plotting against us, Whyn, and must be stopped. If they gather enough sympathy to their cause, and if talk continues about the Unnamed One, we will have more on our hands than we bargained for. I have received a document that may give us the information we need to defeat them. It may take time to interpret, so we must gather our forces and make a show of power immediately. Your family may grieve in private tonight. The announcement of the king's death and public condolences will begin tomorrow. But the formalities cannot be allowed to drag on. I have arranged for your coronation to take place in six days."

"But burial is always delayed eight days in order for the soul to—"

"I said six! Then the Purge must begin."

"Purge?" Whyn felt as though his legs were about to go out from under him. "Surely you do not mean—"

"That is exactly what I mean. The time has come for Tearia to be rid of the boils on her backside. It is time for Tearia to be purified once and for all."

"Priestess, I do not think I can be a part of such a plan." Whyn tensed, prepared for whatever was to come. Instead she floated toward him and ran her finger slowly down his neck, stopping at his breastbone. She planted her palm upon his chest. "You have left me no doubt as to what must be done now, Whyn. I do not have time for subtleties. The Purge must begin. And it must begin with you."

The hand upon Whyn's chest suddenly felt like fire burning through him. He cried out and struggled to retreat, but it was as though her flesh had melted into his, connecting them as one. He could not move, his arms, feet, and lips unable to offer a single defense. She pulled his startled gaze into hers, and her icy blue eyes turned black as coal. He could feel her hand within his breast, reaching for his quivering heart. But then he realized it wasn't his heart she was reaching for, it was his soul.

25

The Fire
and the Light

Nannaven struggled up the rocky hillside, slipping and sliding over the gravel that littered the overgrown path. Once she could have run up that trail without a moment's hesitation, but that was when she was but a girl, and many rotations around the sun had passed since then. She paused and wiped the sweat from her brow, leaning a hand on her knee to calm her labored breaths. The cave wasn't much further now. At least she didn't think it was.

She gazed up the path, squinting her eyes at the blurry landscape before her. Her vision was poor these days and her destination would appear as only a dark dimple in the rocks. She could not afford to pass it by; time was growing short and her arthritic body couldn't take much more abuse.

Her gaze fell upon a tall cedar just a short distance away. Its ancient branches clawed the sky as if in the throes of death. A painful memory grabbed at her insides, urging her to turn around and never look back. She closed her eyes, willing the image of two dark-haired girls high up in the branches to go away.

But she knew all the willing in the world would never erase that image, nor that which had lain beneath the tree.

She navigated the terrain and stopped before the tree, running her fingers over its gnarled bark. She gazed up with mixed emotions at the towering branches, a living monument to her childhood memories. "We are not so different from one another," she said. "Both of us old, both of us a witness to evil. But we once had fun together, didn't we?" She smiled. Yes, there had been some happy times in that cedar-scented world. It had been a retreat for her and her older sister, a pretend palace where they invented kingdoms and dreamed of handsome young men. But then one day they learned what men could be like, and the harsh reality of the world came crashing down around them.

Their mother died a cruel death beneath that tree, and Nannaven and her sister were witness to it. They had scurried up the branches at their mother's command, swearing that no matter what happened they would make no sound. They barely made it to the topmost branch when their mother was dragged beneath by the King's guards. There the men did despicable things to her, and there was nothing her daughters could do about it.

Nannaven felt a lump swell in her throat. After all these years the pain still felt fresh. But she was not there to give into pain; she was there for a much more important reason. She surveyed her surroundings. If memory served her right, the cave would be to the left, just a short distance away. It would be covered with brush and rock; she and her sister carefully concealed it before they left all those long years ago. But she was certain of its location now, and prayed it still held what she was looking for.

The entrance to the cave was indeed sheltered by overgrowth, but the rocks she and her sister had piled in front of it were now tumbled away. She pushed between a wide break in the shrubs and clambered in, an avalanche of pebbles trailing behind her. She straightened her back and worked to focus her eyes in the dim light. The cave was not deep, although she and her sister had discovered many tunnels worming into the hillside behind it. But what she was looking for was not in the tunnels; it was here in the main chamber. She stepped further in, her footsteps echoing against the high arched walls, the damp, musty smell filling her senses with more memories. There was no more obvious evidence of the life she had shared with her sister and mother in this place. She and her sister had taken what few possessions they owned when they left all those long years ago. But there were some things they could not risk taking. And that was why she was here now.

She hobbled over to a boulder resting alongside the wall and pulled in a breath. The last time that boulder moved was by the will of a woman and two adolescent girls. She prayed she could find the same strength within her now. Pushing her weight against it, she heaved with all her might. The boulder moved but an inch, so she tried again and again, but with little success. She sank to the ground, leaning her tired back against it, and turned her gaze to the recesses of the cave's dark throat. If she could not move this obstacle, perhaps the other would be easier.

She worked her way to the back of the cave, treading lightly on the slippery earth that bordered a bottomless pool. Footprints not her own could be seen outlined in the clay, and deep grooves made by digging fingers. Her eyes shot toward a dark space in the rocks up ahead. Her heart nearly stopped. There had clearly been a rock slide; the secret hiding place was now revealed. She cried out and struggled over, then fell upon the debris. Her fingers bled as they clawed their way through, but she felt no pain. Determination had a way of giving a person unrealized strength, even to one so old as herself. But the treasure was nowhere to be found; someone had been there before her. Her eyes darted back to the boulder she had abandoned earlier. Had the secret behind it been discovered, too? She rushed back and renewed her efforts, this time moving the stone easily, thanks to the power of her desperation.

She reached into a crevice in the wall and pulled out a tome with shaking hands. The book's twin was mysteriously missing, but at least the copy remained. Her mother saw to it that there was more than one, and the woman and her daughters had worked hard to keep them both safe.

Nannaven ran her fingers over the cover, recalling some of the history contained within the pages. Her mother told them that their people once took pride in their heritage, reading, and writing, and singing of it freely. But during the Purge it was discovered that knowledge gave "the impure ones" power, and so a campaign was started against it. Jecta parchments were burned, their writing tools confiscated, and songs silenced. Over time, all that was left was that which remained in people's memories. A few secretly retained the skills of documentation, and they were called the Memory Keepers. But they were also called the Enemy.

Nannaven's mother had been a Memory Keeper, as was her mother, and her mother before that. For generations they gathered bits and pieces of information, saving it within the pages of the tome. Scraps of parchments scribbled with symbols were tucked between well-written fables, random stanzas of songs, and snippets of poetry. It had been her mother's lifelong goal to duplicate the information, securing its survival. She and her daughters spent their candlelit days rewriting the words onto fresh parchment, ensuring the continued tradition of the Memory Keepers. But their mother's death changed everything, and Nannaven had turned her back on her heritage, choosing to be healer instead. Her sister chose a different path and disappeared from her life altogether. Only recently had Nannaven learned where she was. Her insides twisted at the recollection, but she could not think of such things now. She pushed her sister from her mind.

She carried the book near the entrance, selecting a spot where the light beamed in through the opening she had clambered through. Sitting cross-legged on the ground, Nannaven rested the heavy book in her lap and lifted back its cover. She recognized her mother's handwriting immediately, then that of her sister. She ran her eyes over the ancient symbols, symbols of a language believed to be lost forever. Strange how after all these years she still knew what they meant.

She turned back brittle page after brittle page, searching for the words that would hopefully leap off the parchment: *fire and light*. She was certain they were in a song, but she could not recall which one. It had been many years since she'd thought of songs. But something about those words, and the memory of her mother's voice singing them in the sanctuary of the cave, compelled her to keep on looking.

As she flipped toward the back of the book, she wondered if her memory had somehow failed her. Perhaps the words were not there after all. She found tales of great heroes, and poems about love, prayers for good health, and songs to the gods. There were writings of kings and priestesses, and lies told as truths, but she had yet to find the words she was looking for.

She scanned another page and her eyes suddenly stopped. "The Song of Hope," she whispered. "Yes. I remember."

She read the first stanza, smiling at its message. *The Maker said that it would be; the Spirit lifted life within; the earth, the wind, the flame, the sea; and so it did at once begin.* The familiar melody drifted into her mind, and she recalled how her mother's voice would lilt then deepen as she sang. *Then came one day when lies did part from evil hearts that lived within, and turned the eyes raised to the star . . .*

Nannaven paused. Star? She had seen a great star in the sky not so long ago, a celestial light blazing a trail across an indigo night. When was it? A few months ago? A year? Then she remembered. It had been the night of the fire, the fire that— "Reiv," she whispered.

Her eyes skimmed the page until another set of words caught her attention. *But in the face of night that came, a courage shown bright in the breast, of he who came as One Unnamed . . .* The Unnamed One! Could the whispers be true? She read another stanza, then another, her eyes moving faster and faster across the page. *The king did breathe her will once more . . . fields were bathed in crimson night . . . til memories brought by He*

Unnamed . . . Tears welled in her eyes. She wiped her face with the back of her hand and moved to the last stanza. *Then came the day when Earth and Sea, did part before their many eyes, but just as Fire had met Light, their spirits did as one survive.* And there it was—the message she had been looking for.

She lifted her head and stared at nothing, barely able to fathom what she had just read. How could she not have known? All this time everyone thought it destroyed, yet here it was, a song in her mother's book. But this was no ordinary song. This was the Prophecy.

She rose quickly, pulled the shawl from her shoulders, and laid it on the ground. She centered the book upon it, then pulled the corners of the shawl together and tied them into a pouch. Something else would have to be stuffed in, the book's shape was at risk of being recognized, but she could not leave it behind. The people thought they knew the words to the Prophecy, but they did not know them all. Nor did Dayn and Reiv, and they were the key to it all.

The sky looked bluer when she exited the cave, the sun a little brighter. For too long she had seen the world through milky eyes. Now everything seemed clear. She hurried down the path, but paused to gaze at the cedar one last time. She patted the tree's ancient trunk. "Time to say goodbye, my bittersweet friend," she said.

Nannaven turned her eyes to the distant horizon and all her hopes came into focus. The book would give the people back their history; the song would restore the future they had long been denied. Even now its verses were being sung. The Fire had met the Light; the Unnamed One was amongst them. Could crimson fields be far behind? A difficult path lay ahead, this she knew, but the people of Aredyrah had no choice but to walk it. The Prophecy would lead them there, but the Unnamed One would show them the way.

END

OF

BOOK

ONE

For a preview of Book Two . . .

Preview of
The Search for the Unnamed One
Book Two
The Souls of Aredyrah Series

1
Phantom

The air in the catacombs was thick and damp and permeated with the odor of human waste and lingering decay. Whyn pulled the stench through his nostrils and into his lungs, his belly tightening with a desire that tingled to his toes. It was not the same desire as that he felt for Cinnia, his wife. Nor was it like for any female who had ever pleased him. This was different, and yet the power it had over him was like that of an aphrodisiac.

Whyn stared at the slender back of the Priestess who walked but steps in front of him. She possessed a beauty unlike any woman he had ever seen, and an ugliness he found equally attractive. She seemed to him to be floating on air, her long white hair swaying at her back, the hem of her pastel gown drifting behind her. As Whyn gazed at her, he realized the longing in his belly was for her, but it was not like that of a man craving love. It was like a soul craving sustenance. Until recently, he had only thought of the Priestess as an authority figure; even now he feared her more than longed for her. But for some reason the need to drink her in was overwhelming. It was as though she was a separate part of him, and he had only to fill himself with her to find completion.

Whyn turned his eyes beyond her to the light in the corridor ahead. A grizzled old man shuffled several paces in front of them, leading the way through the twisting darkness. The lantern in the man's hand swayed back and forth, its golden orb casting distorted shadows upon the walls. One by one grimy doors came into view. Wide eyes watched through tiny, barred windows, only to melt into blackness as the lantern passed.

A hand clawed toward the light, the pale face behind it momentarily alit.

"Mercy, good prince," a woman's voice rasped.

Whyn kept his eyes forward, daring not a glance toward the woman, nor even an acknowledgement. She was only a Jecta, after all, and no doubt an insurgent bent on the destruction of Tearia.

"Does this place pain your heart, my young prince?" the Priestess asked, pausing to face him.

"No, Priestess," Whyn replied. "It lifts my spirits."

The Priestess smiled, her porcelain skin and gold painted features illuminating her satisfaction through the darkness. Her eyes glowed as she flashed them toward the old man. "Guide," she said. "You may leave us."

The man turned and nodded, then bowed his way back down the corridor from which they had come, taking the lantern with him.

Whyn and the Priestess stood in the dimness. The only light to guide them now was the occasional torch light reaching out from the walls. Wynn worked to focus his eyes, listening to his own steady breathing and the melancholy drip of water in the distance. The Priestess brushed past him and ducked into a passageway that branched from the main one, clutching a shoulder bag close to her body. She motioned Whyn to follow and led him in the direction of an orifice in the distance, its circular glow like that of a red eclipse on a starless night. As Whyn followed, it seemed to him that the Priestess was a phantom alit from within, leading him toward a glorious world to which few were privy.

More doors were revealed in the Priestess's aura as she passed, more moans and hushed whispers were heard on the other side of them. How many people were imprisoned in this place? It seemed like hundreds, but Whyn knew there would soon be thousands . . . or perhaps there would be none. After the Purge, there would no longer be any need to keep prisoners, no longer any need to waste the food and manpower on them. Now with his father, the king, dead, there was nothing to stop the Priestess from her magnificent plan.

The air became steamy, the stench more pungent. The orifice ahead loomed larger now, but it still seemed very distant. No longer did it look like the glow of a moon, but more like the mouth of a great furnace, its door rimmed by the flames that burned behind it. Sweat dripped down Whyn's neck and slid over his chest, leaving the thin, gold colored material of his tunic plastered against his skin. A chill raced through him. Strange how he could feel both hot and cold at the same time. It was as though his flesh had been set afire while at the same time his insides had been turned to ice.

"Here is where we will find answers to the Prophecy," the Priestess said, stopping before a door much like any other.

Whyn halted, but kept his gaze on the red circle at the far end of the corridor. He felt an overwhelming urge to continue toward it, as though it was beckoning him somehow.

"You will not be going to that place today," the Priestess said, recognizing the longing in his eyes.

Whyn nodded and turned his attention to the door before them. A flicker of candlelight could be seen beyond the barred window, a luxury none of the other prisoners were allowed. "Who is kept in this place?" he asked.

"The last of the Memory Keepers," the Priestess replied.

* * *

The Saga Continues
Don't miss the next book in
The Souls of Aredyrah Series!

Coming in 2007
Book Two
The Search for the Unnamed One

The Prophecy has come to life in Tearia, and the Temple wants nothing more than to see it dead. Whispers say the Unnamed One walks amongst them, and there is little doubt as to who that person is. Reiv is oblivious to the hopes that are turning in his direction, just as he is ignorant of a sinister plot against him. Praying for reconciliation with Alicine, he returns to the Jecta city of Pobu, hoping to find some happiness at last. But Tearia is unstable in more ways than one, and Reiv's hopes will have to wait. A quiet rebel movement is gaining momentum, and Reiv's cousin Dayn has joined them in their cause. Angered by the events unfolding with Dayn, and shattered by his reunion with Alicine, Reiv reverts to his old self-serving behaviors. He wants nothing to do with prophecies or rebellions, and isn't sure he wants anything to do with Dayn and Alicine either. But when tragedy throws Reiv into new turmoil, he finds himself facing a dangerous choice. Someone he loves is dying, and there is only one chance to save him. If Reiv chooses to be savior, he will be accepting a role in yet another prophecy, a prophecy that requires the ultimate sacrifice. Is Reiv the Transcendor, fated to give his life for another? Or is he the Unnamed One, a hero destined for glory? One will save the life of an individual, the other that of an entire kingdom.

Book Three coming 2008
Book Four coming 2009
Book Five coming 2010